The Importance of Being Aisling

Emer McLysaght & Sarah Breen

Gill Books
Hume Avenue
Park West
Dublin 12
www.gillbooks.ie

Gill Books is an imprint of M.H. Gill & Co.
© Emer McLysaght and Sarah Breen 2018

978 07171 8159 9

Copy-edited by Emma Dunne
Proofread by Susan McKeever
Print origination by Carole Lynch
Printed by CPI Group (UK) Ltd, Croydon, CRO 4YY

This book is typeset in Stone Sans 12/18pt.

The paper used in this book comes from the wood pulp of managed forests. For every tree felled, at least one tree is planted, thereby renewing natural resources.

A CIP catalogue record for this book is available from the British Library.

5 4 3 2

Praise for *Oh My God, What a Complete Aisling*

'Oh lads! This book! There aren't enough words for how much I love it. It's feckin' HILAIRE and very touching.' **MARIAN KEYES**

'Everyone in Ireland was reading *Oh My God, What A Complete Aisling* this Christmas and I got thoroughly swept up in the hype, devouring it in a couple of sittings. It's been called 'An Irish Bridget Jones' – and that should give you an idea of what you're dealing with. It's sweet and it's funny and it's moving.' **LYNN ENRIGHT,** *THE POOL*

'If I had a book of the year award for 2017 it would go to *Oh My God, What a Complete Aisling* by Emer McLysaght and Sarah Breen. I was expecting comedy and social satire but what I hadn't bargained for was the sheer humanity of the book that left me giggling at some pages and sobbing at others. Aisling will be back and I'll be waiting to hear more.' **SINEAD CROWLEY**

'A loving ode to a certain type of Irish woman that's hilarious, comforting and warm. A hot water bottle of a book, if you will.' *THE DAILY EDGE*

'A hilarious and heart-warming journey with our favourite country girl.' *THE IRISH TIMES*

'An utter ray of sunshine. Now that I've finished the book, I miss Aisling so much that it hurts. There's a beautiful rhythm to the way that Sarah Breen and Emer McLysaght have written *OMGWACA*; I've rarely read a book that has such a strong, distinctive voice but more than that, it's funny. Proper funny. Actual, literal, LOL funny. I laughed. Out loud. On the tube.' *RED MAGAZINE*

'I've spent the last 48 hours laughing my head off at this novel. It's not just comic, there's a real heart to it and it's often very moving. I'm hoping it becomes an annual event, like a new Ross O'Carroll Kelly.' **JOHN BOYNE**

'Sweet, charming, funny and poignant.' *THE JOURNAL*

'There's a little bit of Aisling in all of us.' *THE SUNDAY TIMES*

'One of the funniest books I've read in twenty years.' **PAUL HOWARD**

'One of my fave novels of 2017. It really does remind me of Marian Keyes.'
LOUISE O'NEILL

'Funny, charming, reminiscent of *Eleanor Oliphant is Completely Fine*.'
THE INDEPENDENT

'Sweet, funny, moving … perfect.' **THE POOL**

'A great big thumping heart.' **SUNDAY TIMES**

'You'll shed a tear as well as laugh your socks off.' **FABULOUS**

'This hilarious Irish bestseller, which came to life via a viral Facebook page, follows country girl Aisling as she moves from her hometown to big city living in Dublin. She's sweet, a little clueless but a force to be reckoned with.'
BUZZFEED

'You'll laugh, you'll cry, you'll want to invest in a shumper (though not for going OUT OUT) and as soon as you've finished it, you'll want to re-read this hilarious novel, which will also get you in the right feels.' **RED ONLINE**

'Hilarious … A well-crafted tale with warmth and emotion.' **WOMAN MAGAZINE**

'Funny and touching … we fell in love with the heroine of *Oh My God, What a Complete Aisling*, about a small-town girl in Dublin.' **GOOD HOUSEKEEPING**

'My unofficial autobiography.' **AISLING BEA**

'This quick-fire tragi-comedy is bursting with clever one-liners and acute observations.' **SUNDAY EXPRESS**

'Her voice leaps off the page … it's this depth of character and eye for detail that makes comparisons with Helen Fielding's *Bridget Jones* series spot-on.'
INDEPENDENT

'This hilarious and heart-warming book had us alternately laughing and crying. The year's funniest book to date.' **HELLO MAGAZINE**

'A runaway success … it's an uplifting romcom that combines elements of *Bridget Jones* and *Four Weddings* with *Father Ted*.' **KIRSTY LANG, BBC RADIO 4 FRONT ROW**

'Aisling is an absolute gem of a character and this book is a breath of fresh air.'
THE SUN

ACKNOWLEDGEMENTS

Thank you to everyone who bought *Oh My God, What a Complete Aisling*, who talked about it, posted about it on Facebook, recommended it to a friend. We continue to be overwhelmed by the love.

Thank you to our families and friends for the unwavering support and for not asking too many questions when it was clear we didn't have the answers.

Special thanks to Conor Nagle for persuading us to put Aisling's story on paper, and to the whole team at Gill Books, especially Catherine Gough, Teresa Daly, Ellen Monnelly, Avril Cannon, Paul Neilan and Nicki Howard, who have worked tirelessly to make Aisling a household name. Thanks, too, to Maxine Hitchcock and Clare Bowran at Michael Joseph for their invaluable input.

To our agents Sheila Crowley and Abbie Grieves at Curtis Brown, you are the best Bad Cops in the business.

Thanks to our longtime hero Marian Keyes, who will probably never know the immense thrill we feel every single time we talk about how she's helped and encouraged us.

Much love to Gavan and Ciara Reilly, experts in all things GAA, ICA and everything in between.

To our early readers: John Boyne, Louise McSharry, Fiona Hyde, Eoin Matthews, Áine Bambrick, Breda Gittons, Deirdre Ball, Sarah Kisch, Richard Toner. Your enthusiasm and encouragement have been extremely comforting. Thanks also to Marianne Gunn O'Connor, Donal Ryan, Louise O'Neill and Paul Howard for the words of wisdom.

And, finally, to Louise Keegan, who's only a tiny bit of an Aisling after all.

To mná na hÉireann, especially India and Esme.
The future is safe.

ABOUT THE AUTHORS

With more than ten years' experience in broadcasting and journalism, Co. Kildare native **Emer McLysaght** wasn't sure if she'd ever get around to writing that book. However, 2018 finds her with bestselling novel *Oh My God, What a Complete Aisling* under her belt, co-authored with longtime friend and collaborator **Sarah Breen**. Emer lives in Dublin and has somehow ended up with three cats.

Born and raised in the village of Borris, Co. Carlow, Sarah Breen started her career in journalism at KISS magazine. Since then her writing has appeared in many Irish print publications, as well as online. She and Emer co-wrote *OMGWACA* mainly in her children's playroom, and never dreamed it would be an *Irish Times* No. 1 bestseller. Sarah lives in Dublin 7 with her husband and two daughters, and dreams of the day Oasis will reunite.

Emer and Sarah are working with Element Pictures to bring their first novel to the silver screen, and have already started plotting about what might happen in book number three.

PROLOGUE

'Does it have any scaffolding around the bust?'

The dress is gorgeous but I'm looking at the €450 price tag wondering how it could possibly cost so much. It's an awful lot to pay for something you only wear once, although I suppose the pictures will last forever.

'Excuse me, madam?'

Happily Ever After is the poshest bridal shop in Dublin and the sales assistant – Grace, according to her name badge, but I'm sceptical – has been looking down her nose at me since I pushed the doorbell. I think it's because I'm wearing tracksuit bottoms and my Ballygobbard Gaels hoody, but it's important to be able to whip your clothes on and off at speed in these places. A good tip I picked up in an online wedding forum.

The shop is very swanky altogether – everything is pink: they know their audience – and we have the whole place to ourselves. I was delighted to get a last-minute cancellation – normally you have to book an appointment six months in advance.

'She's wondering if there's any corsetry,' Sadhbh calls out from behind the pink curtain of the fitting room. Thank God she's here to translate. I'm not the best in these situations, but Sadhbh's no stranger to the luxury boutique circuit and knows all the lingo.

'Ah, I see,' 'Grace' says tightly, as we enter our second and final hour of shopping. 'Not in this one, but if Aisling is looking for corsetry I can certainly show her some exquisite gowns.'

'Thanks,' I say, beaming and taking a sneaky photograph of the tag of the dress. You can get them for half the price online once you know the style number. Another tip I recently picked up – those forums alone are worth the price of broadband. 'A bit of corsetry would do me the world of good since the wedding is a week after Christmas.'

Majella ambles over with a glass of prosecco in each hand and a black dress draped over her arm. 'Now hear me out ...' she says, spraying crumbs – she's been at the free pink macarons – all over the pink carpet.

'You're grand, Maj,' I say with a grimace, putting the black dress back on the rail and wondering if she knows me at all. I'm not a goth!

The curtain of the fitting room flies open and Sadhbh steps out onto the raised platform wearing a floor-length, slate-grey dress. She looks like something out of a magazine – the figure on her. I don't know why she insists on draping it in those shapeless sacks and kimonos. I can't help it, I start crying – she's just stunning.

'Ah, Ais, not again,' she says, lifting up the dress and teetering over to where me and Maj are sitting on the pink velvet couch. In the corner of the room I catch 'Grace' rolling her eyes.

'I'm sorry, I'm sorry,' I say, patting my cheeks. 'It's just you're going to be the most gorgeous bridesmaid. Just faboo, Sadhbh. I think that's the one. Do you like it?'

'I like the colour – I'm just not sure about this,' she says, pawing at the cowl neck which I thought was very classy and sophisticated. She twirls again in front of the mirror.

'Can I make a suggestion?' 'Grace' calls out from where she's pouring out more Prosecco. Majella is keeping her busy. 'Would you consider the two bridesmaids wearing dresses in the exact same colour, but different styles?'

It's like a lightbulb goes off over my head. Why didn't I think of it? Just the right amount of cool and edgy.

'Absolutely!' I shriek. 'That sounds very … funky. But also classy. Doesn't it, Sadhbh? Would you be on for it?'

'You know me, Ais, I'm easy,' Sadhbh says, retreating into the fitting room. 'It's up to you.'

'Grace' smiles a tight little smile and heads off, nodding, to another rail of grey dresses. 'We get a lot of girls like yourself in here, Aisling. Lots of Aislings. In my experience, the idea of the bridesmaids wearing different styles in the same colour always goes down well.'

'I can see why,' I call over. 'It's a brilliant idea. Just brilliant.'

My phone buzzes in my Michael Kors and when I dig it out John's picture is flashing up on the screen. I immediately cover it with my hand – I know he can't see out of the phone or anything but the very idea of a man being in a bridal shop puts me on edge. It's a sacred space.

'Hi,' I whisper, standing up and heading for a corner. I don't want the dresses to even hear a male voice.

'Ais,' he replies. 'I know you're busy shopping but I was just wondering if you got Mammy a present. From me, like.'

John and I have been together eight years – well, a bit less if you include the little unexpected break we had recently –

and for the past eight Christmases I've bought a pair of slippers, wrapped them and put 'To Mammy, love John' on the label. Why would this year be any different?

'Under the tree,' I sigh patiently. 'With the baby Jesus wrapping paper.'

There was a time when I thought John's helplessness was adorable and his reliance on my knowledge of his mammy's slipper preferences was romantic, but I have to admit, it's getting a bit old.

'Now I have to go,' I say and hang up. Then I take a deep breath, plaster on a smile and turn around. 'Right, Grace, what do you have for me in grey with a nice bit of scaffolding? Nothing too glam, mind – we don't want to upstage the brides.'

'Elaine and Ruby don't actually care what we wear, remember?' Sadhbh laughs from behind the curtain.

She's right, of course. If our housemate and her fiancée had their way we wouldn't be here at all, but I couldn't let them get married without having bridesmaids. Lesbians or not, weddings have rules – and I know every single one of them.

CHAPTER 1

A bead of sweat drops down the back of my neck as I get down on my hands and knees one more time to check. Maybe I was wrong the first three times.

'Forty-eight, forty-nine, fifty, fifty-one.' I'm sucking the numbers in through my teeth like a teacher doing a headcount on a bus, praying to God she hasn't left anyone behind at Clara Lara. Maybe I'll just stay under the tree and never come out. Or at least until this afternoon is over.

Fifty-one presents. Fifty-three people for Secret Santa and fifty-one presents. Two useless articles haven't bothered their holes coming in today to put something under the tree. Probably decided they were going to treat themselves to a day at home seeing as it's the Christmas party tonight and generally seen as a bit of a doss around the office. It's not a doss if you're head of the Christmas Party Social Committee and took it upon yourself to organise Secret Santa. Donna used to do it, and even though I don't miss her scraping the porridge off her spoon with her teeth beside me every morning, I do miss her at this very moment. She used to swing wildly between calling it 'Kris Kindle,' 'Kris Kingle' and 'Kris Kringle' instead of simply 'Secret Santa,' which nearly drove me to distraction, but she was militant about making sure everyone who signed up had their presents under the tree in time for the big swap. Losing her and her uncanny festive organising during the recent scandal at PensionsPlus was probably the biggest casualty of the whole debacle. Well, that and the millions of euro that went missing in a fecked-up transaction, but it's not millions of euro I'm missing right now: it's two presents. And every eye will be on me after lunch when the big exchange is due to happen. What will I do?

Standing up nonchalantly beside the tree I cast a furtive eye around the office to see if there's anything lying around I can wrap up as stand-in presents. I had planned on getting a curly blow-dry at lunchtime for the party later. I have a lovely lace dress I got in Dorothy Perkins and I remembered to nab a pair of 'sandal toe' American tan tights in M&S yesterday (€8 for a pair of tights! Only it's Christmas I would have left them there) to go with my heels. Now I might have to forego the blow-dry to go and buy two presents so nobody is left empty-handed. Is there anything at all that might do?

My eyes fall on a promotional baseball cap on a desk over at IT. Could I pass that off as a gift? Could I Tippex over the gaudy lettering? What about the bottle of Ouzo somebody in Accounts brought back from a week in Mykonos? Although why you wouldn't just bring giant Milkas is beyond me. I have been known to buy my holiday Toblerones and Milkas in Tesco. I'm not paying airport prices! I would never bring back a sticky bottle of undrinkable poison though. At least make it a nice Pinot Greej or a West Coast Cooler duo gift set if you're going to arrive in with something that isn't chocolate. Anyway, I don't think I'll get away with passing the ouzo off as a Christmas present. I'll have to fly out now at lunch and panic buy some things for €10 or under. I don't even know who they're for! And I don't have time to go through the list and mark off the names that are missing from the assortment of wrapped bits under the tree. The stress!

****

If I'm not mistaken Declan Ryan is actually wearing his giant novelty Santa tie. You press a button on the back of it and Santa's beard falls away to reveal he's showing his arse while a tinny version of 'Jingle Bells' plays. Not my proudest moment, present-wise, but after sweating around the Dunnes food hall up the road and emerging with the most neutral things I could find (a bottle of wine, an abnormally large sleeve of After Eights and an eight pack of AAA batteries) I panicked and bought the tie from the Bits 'n' PCs phone and computer shop on the way back to the office to pair with the After Eights. Well, I say phone and computer shop but you can buy an assortment of things there while you're waiting to get your screen fixed. And you can send a fax, if the fancy takes you. I've never had to get my screen fixed, of course. My trusty flip cover means my phone is safe at all times. I wouldn't be getting it done anywhere dodgy anyway. Sure doesn't that void your insurance? And they'd probably be out the back stealing your contacts and sending nudes and what have you.

Anyway, Declan seems thrilled with his tie. He's swinging around there on the dancefloor flashing the arse to anyone who'll look. Siobhán from HR was equally thrilled with the wine but understandably baffled by the batteries. I think she suspects they're from me because I had to present them to her from under the tree in the absence of her actual Secret Santa. My 'oh ho, a little elf must have brought this in for you specially' didn't fool her. I'd be thrilled to get batteries if it was me. So handy for remotes.

Notably absent from the party, and the two people with presents back under the tree with their names on them, are Donal from IT and Marie from reception. I'll be presenting them with receipts for the wine, After Eights, batteries and arse-tie tomorrow.

'Will we dance, Ais?'

Sadhbh swings past me, swigging a glass of red and holding out her hand. She got a new colour put in her hair last week and even though she's my housemate I still get a fright every time I see her, although I think I hide it well. Grey. What twenty-nine-year-old dyes her hair grey? Sometimes I think she has a screw loose. But since she went from HR executive on the floor above me in PensionsPlus to my best Dublin friend, I've gotten used to her hipster ways. For the night that's in it she's put some purple through the ends of it and she looks gorgeous as usual. That's Sadhbh for you. She'd look good in a plastic bag, which I'm fairly sure I've seen her in. You'd never think we'd get on so well to look at us but opposites attract – isn't that what they say?

We had to do drinks tokens this year since the free bar last year landed three people in hospital after a particularly raucous rendition of 'Fairytale of New York'. People get too giddy with free drinks and go mad ordering double brandies and fancy gins, frantic the tab might run out. Besides, I was told by the powers that be that the budget was to be reined in after the money scandal. The hotel ballroom and dinner were already booked, so there was nothing we could do about that, but the four drinks tokens were received with not an inconsiderable amount of grumbling earlier this evening. It hasn't stopped the entire Escalations team dragging an unsafe-looking human train up and down the dancefloor to 'All I Want for Christmas Is You', poor old Des, the long-suffering team leader, clinging onto the back for dear life.

Sadhbh had wondered if I wouldn't pass the organising off to someone else, given all I had been through recently with Daddy's death, and minding Mammy, *and* with the organisation of Elaine's last-minute hen party on top of it. I was glad of the distraction and staying busy, and I'm always at my calmest in hen-planning mode, believe it or not. I've been dreading Christmas, though. Absolutely dreading it.

Elaine tried to get away without having a hen at all, but I was determined to squeeze one in before her New Year's Eve wedding. I still can't believe it took me so long to realise her and Ruby were a couple right under my nose. I was living in Elaine's swanky apartment for months and never really wondered why Ruby was there for breakfast five times a week. I just thought they were great pals who shared a Netflix account. In hindsight it was fairly obvious they were *together* together. Majella, my best friend from Down Home who lives over in Phibsboro, still slags me about it, although she didn't cop it either and she was a regular at our Friday Night Wine Downs. So much for her famous gaydar. Anyway, they were getting away without a hen over my dead body! Of course I wasn't a bit surprised when she insisted she didn't want one. Disappointed, yes, but not surprised. In the year I've known her I don't think she's been to a single one even though I have reason to believe she was invited to three. Imagine turning down an invitation to someone's hen? One of them was her first cousin too. I wouldn't be able to live with the guilt. I was born and raised on hens – as far as I'm concerned a proper send-off for the bride is just as important as the Big Day.

It took a while, not that we had that long anyway, but I eventually talked her into it. Even Sadhbh, who'll do anything to get out of 'organised fun' (her words), did some cajoling because she could see I was up to ninety over it. We've been officially designated bridesmaids. Elaine was all 'I'm not having bridesmaids' but I told her that was unacceptable and dragged Sadhbh around every bridal shop this side of the Shannon until we found our dream dresses. Well, my dream dresses. Then when we left the shop I ordered them straightaway from China. They arrived perfect – I think it was my proudest achievement to date, even though Elaine said we could just wear jeans for all she cared. Imagine! We're lucky, though – we could have had a scenario similar to Eleanor Bolger's wedding last year when she insisted on teal multiway dresses for her four bridesmaids and her busty cousin nearly took the priest's eye out. They looked good in the pictures, which I suppose is all that matters, but the cousin spent the day tucking herself in and shooting daggers at Eleanor. Anyway, as Elaine's housemates and friends we'll naturally take on the duties, and I was born to bridesmaid. Bring on the table plan, to be quite honest.

Sadhbh interrupts my train of thought and drags me onto the dancefloor like her life depends on it, and to be fair I do love a bit of a 'Single Ladies' boogie. I feel just like Beyoncé, flipping my hand around the way she does. Six years of Irish dancing lessons and I always felt like I had spot-on natural rhythm. Oh-oh-oh-oh-oh-oh-oh-oh-OOOHHHH! Suddenly, Des crashes into us sending me flying and Sadhbh's red wine all over her cream – I suppose you'd call it a dress. Something from Cos, no doubt. Or one of those shops with no names and just a few dots or a picture of a fox where their sign should be and rail after rail of deconstructed 'garments'. If you wanted something with the threads hanging out of it would you not just go back to fourth-year Home Ec. and whip something up from a pattern? I don't know how Sadhbh pays good money for some of the yokes she wears but she always looks lovely and stylish, and her mad jewellery helps I suppose. She even looks elegant now with the red wine dripping off the sleeve of her cream flour sack and Des nowhere to be seen.

'Come on and we'll give it a rinse,' I roar, dragging her in the direction of the bathroom.

The 'Single Ladies' effect means that almost every woman in the place is on the dancefloor, so we get to a sink with relative ease. 'It's grand, Ais,' Sadhbh insists. 'It'll wash out I'm sure.' She's so cool about it. I'd be at home already, elbow deep in a vat of Persil, cursing the tag on the dress which no doubt gives little information about washing instructions but tells you about the yurt in Mongolia where they sourced the fabric. She's probably right, though – dabbing at it with two-ply bright-blue toilet roll isn't going to improve it much.

And anyway, the red wine splash looks like it could almost be part of the dress. 'Maybe I'll sling a blue WKD at you too, Sadhbh, make the whole thing a bit more colourful!' She laughs, turning to the mirror to apply a slick of deep red lipstick. I'd put a bit of Rimmel Heather Shimmer on earlier but it's all gone now, lost to the turkey dinner and the multiple glasses of wine.

I always feel like a bit of a heifer beside Sadhbh, although I'd take my light-brown hair over the grey any day, even if the natural kink does get out of hand in the drizzle. She was in fits laughing when I first told her I've never dyed it. Why would I, when the sun gives it lovely blonde streaks in the summer? You'd be mad to jeopardise that with chemicals. I smooth my dress down over my hips in the mirror. It's very flattering, I must say. I've been semi-successfully doing Weight Watchers for the past six years but these last seven pounds are being very stubborn. According to my leader, Maura, I've 'plateaued' and she's insisting I swap the Kerrygold for one of those spreads. Jesus, Daddy would turn in his grave.

I've been doing my best to alternate the glasses of water and wine but after the stress of the Secret Santa and with the party successfully underway I'm letting my hair down. Work tomorrow should be interesting. There's been no mention of being allowed to come in late. In fact, there's been very little communication on anything from the powers that be in the past few weeks. Not a sniff of an email about Christmas bonuses. Maybe it will come tomorrow. I need four new tyres and I have the bonus earmarked for the third-dearest ones. 'Never scrimp on tyres or towels and your journey will be safe and your arse will be dry.' One of Daddy's pearls of wisdom.

I smooth my hair in the mirror too. I never got the curly blow-dry so I've had to let the natural kink speak for itself this evening. 'You've loads of hair,' hairdressers are always telling me as they battle through it. 'I know,' says I, proud as punch. No higher praise from a hairdresser than having loads of hair.

'Will we go?' Sadhbh turns on her heel ready to head back to the ballroom, where the unmistakable strains of 'Livin' on a Prayer' are sure to send Escalations into new heights of frenzy. Hopefully Des is having a sit down somewhere. Just as we exit, Maureen, one of the executive PAs, pushes past us, calling, 'Did you hear?'

'Hear what?' says Sadhbh. Her HR hat is never too far off and she's all ears. 'There's something big happening tomorrow,' breathes Maureen to the half-dozen women she's dragged into the bathroom with her. 'Shermer is making some kind of announcement. I had to patch through the call and then pass the memo on to the other partners.'

Sadhbh turns and runs from the bathroom, no doubt in search of her team to find out what the hell is going on. One of the other girls speaks up. 'What do you think it is?'

Maureen shrugs. 'I don't know, but whatever it is, it's not good.'

CHAPTER 2

I'm practically vibrating with nerves by the time I arrive at the office the next morning. I was awake half the night worrying about what this announcement might be. My greatest fear is that PensionsPlus is after being bought out by one of those big conglomerates and we're going to have to start standing at our desks like they do at Google. There's another few varicose veins for me.

The other half of the night I spent dreaming I was in the queue to drive out of the Dundrum Town Centre car park but I couldn't for the life of me find my ticket. This is one of my worst fears. I was tearing apart my good handbag and all the yummy mummies in their Beemers and Range Rovers were honking at me. My flannel pyjamas were soaked with sweat when I eventually woke up, clawing for my alarm clock, full sure I'd slept in. I hadn't, of course. I can count on one hand the number of times I've slept in. I was actually awake early; a mixture of The Fear and the Red Bull I ingested at the end of the night. Usually I'd avoid Jägerbombs like the plague, but I complimented Declan Ryan one too many times on his Christmas tie and he twigged that it was from me and insisted on buying me a drink. At that stage everyone had thrown all caution to the wind and were throwing shots down their necks like they were Rennies on St Stephenses Day. I walked to work in the end. I considered treating myself and driving in, but between the Jägerbomb and losing track of the wine with the dinner, I could easily have miscalculated the number of units I'd drunk and not given myself enough hours to get over them. I've seen the ads. I definitely couldn't live with the shame.

The bang of drink hits me like a sledgehammer when I arrive on the second floor, even though only a handful of people are in. Sadhbh was gone before I'd even left my bedroom. Not a good sign, but I'd say she might have her work cut out for her today if what Maureen said was true. I must remember to drop her up a slice of toast and two paracetamol from the stash in my drawer later. She's the type that forgets to eat, if you can imagine that.

I'm not feeling too fresh myself, truth be told, but I know something beige at elevenses will sort me right out. A croissant would be my personal preference, but they're considered a holy sin in Weight Watchers. Elaine has almost convinced me that I'm wasting my life counting Points and says she can't watch me doling out 'ten sad little almonds' into my hand in the kitchen any more. 'You're not fat, Aisling!' she yelps at me regularly, demonstrating that I fit into at least half of her mad tops. That's easy for her to say, though. She's another one who floats around like she might wobble off course if someone blows her a kiss, wilfully eating egg whites and whatever grass and weeds she whizzes up in the fancy blender – when she's not horsing into her hangover pizza (vegan, of course). My physique is more … sturdy. I'm sure my weight plateau has something to do with my lapses in judgement in the chipper after Thursday nights in Coppers, but the less I tell Weight Watchers Maura the less she'll look at me with her big disappointed eyes. I hate letting her down.

Elaine, meanwhile, is pure mad about that Nutribullet. A blender is only good for two things in my book: making breadcrumbs and the odd bit of soup. I'm getting soup for my lunch today, I've decided. Dempsey's around the corner from the office does a decent miscellaneous vegetable that's just the right shade of orange and salty enough that you need two pints of MiWadi with it. Just what the doctor ordered.

I check my watch – 8.58 a.m. – and crane my head around the side of my cubicle. The office is still more than half-empty. Turning on my PC, I scan the room and note that nobody is making eye contact with anyone else, but I'm not sure who knows what. In the good old days we used to have desk-decorating competitions at Christmas, but last year decorations were deemed a fire hazard and outlawed entirely. As the health and safety officer, I had to publicly enforce the rule but inside I was bulling. The place used to look grand spruced up with a bit of tinsel but this morning it just looks pathetic. I can actually feel the fear oozing out of the cubicles around me. You wouldn't wish the day after the work Christmas party on your worst enemy, and now we have this announcement hanging over our heads.

I refresh my email. Nothing – yet, anyway. Sadhbh swore she'd be on to me as soon as she heard anything upstairs. Desperate for a cuppa to settle my nerves, I tip into the kitchen only to find Des retching into the bin. And not even the normal bin: the recycling bin. Honest to God, you'd think he'd know better at his age. He goes running out the door with his hand over his mouth before I can give him the old 'ho, how's the head?' nudge-nudge treatment.

I'm drumming my fingers on the Formica counter – I always do it when I'm nervous – when my new desk neighbour, Suzanne, bursts in carrying her breast pump in a black backpack. I know it's her breast pump because she talks about it constantly and will tell anyone who'll listen that according to EU law she's entitled to a room with a lockable door to do her pumping once a day. She has poor Sadhbh's heart broken reeling off her rights, so every day, for half an hour, she marches off to the conference room swinging her backpack and daring anyone to so much as look twice at her.

She's very nice but has three children, and in the few weeks I've known her I have learned more about them than I know about my own family. I love kids and am very good for firing up the 'suits yous' under a picture on Facebook as soon as any coupled-up friend of child-bearing age appears holding a baby – people love that – but even I have to draw the line somewhere. Suzanne often careens in at ten past nine with tales of temperatures and puke and not being able to find shoes.

Of course, she wasn't out last night because one of them – Chloe? – has chicken pox or foot and mouth disease, and I suddenly realise she won't have a notion about the announcement.

'Oh *God*, you're a sight for sore eyes, Aisling. You're not going to ask me to bring you to the toilet or to wipe your arse, are you?'

'No! Hahahaha.' Should I tell her her top is on inside out, I wonder? She opens the dishwasher and takes out a freshly washed mug. Just the one. For herself. I don't say anything, though, because I know she sees the office as a bit of a holiday camp.

'I saw every hour of the clock last night. Is there no decaf Nescafé?' Suzanne is convinced Chloe will go mad hopping herself off the cot and what have you if there's even a trace of caffeine in her breast milk. I could write a book about Chloe now, to be quite honest with you.

'They know I can't drink the regular stuff,' she groans, grabbing a tea-bag and helping herself to the water in the kettle I'd just boiled as I empty the dishwasher. 'I'm going to have to get on to HR, it's just –'

'I wouldn't bother them today – they have enough going on upstairs,' I blurt out, desperate to cut her off and fighting the feeling of rising panic in my throat. I'm not able for all the breast milk chat on top of everything.

She puts down the kettle and swings around, nearly taking out her own eye with her ponytail.

'Why? What's happening?'

I immediately regret saying anything. Loose lips sink ships – isn't that what Mammy says? But she also says a problem shared is a problem halved, and if I don't talk to someone I'll do something mad like kick a door. I'll never forget when Miss Weightman kicked a door in third-year English after Helen Donohoe said Shakespeare talked a load of shite. Afterwards, Sister Anne sat us all down and explained that she was going through 'the change,' which explained a lot about Miss Weightman's general demeanour that year.

'I don't really know, to tell you the truth,' I whisper, doing my best to sort out the cutlery drawer while I'm restocking it. Low on teaspoons again – I'll have to make another sign pleading for them to be returned. 'Last night Maureen said there's going to be an announcement. I hardly slept a wink thinking about it.' I decide not to mention the Jägerbombs. I don't want to set her off on how much she craves a glass of wine but she says she might as well pour poison directly into Chloe's veins if she has even one drink.

Suzanne doesn't seem too concerned, though, and sighs with relief and waves a hand dismissively. 'Oh, I'd take anything Maureen says with a pinch of salt,' she says, heading for the door. 'She can't hold her drink for the life of her. She was probably just looking for attention.'

'Do you really think so?' I pick up 'my' mug – I won it along with tickets to see Brian McFadden on Today FM and am very protective of it – and follow her back to our adjoining cubicles, feeling hopeful. Maybe she's right. Maybe Maureen just wanted to have some toilet chats and was trying to drum up, I don't know, *something* to start the conversation. Suzanne used to work on reception herself, so she knows her well.

My relief is short lived when I see an email notification from Sadhbh. The subject reads: 'check your phone!!!' so I do. Jesus, the Chez SEA WhatsApp group, named after the apartment the three of us share, is hopping. Twelve notifications! Chez SEA stands for Sadhbh, Elaine, Aisling, and the group picture is a snap of us all piled into the bath. Don't ask. I came up with the name and Sadhbh ordered dressing gowns with it printed on the back for us. Majella was a bit sniffy when she saw them but got over it fairly lively when Sadhbh produced a 'Mad Jella' one for her too, even though she's only a regular guest rather than a Chez SEA resident.

I scan the messages from Sadhbh: 'It's major', 'meeting soon', 'redundancies'. *Redundancies?* It's worse than I thought! Elaine is desperate for information too. She works in sales for a tech start-up and spends a lot of her time hot-desking at home in our kitchen and putting on tops over her pyjamas to sit in Skype meetings – hence her vested interested in the comings and goings at PensionsPlus. She gets very lonely at home by herself all day when she's not catching up on the soaps.

I look over at Suzanne typing away, oblivious to it all. What if she's one of the unlucky ones? She cracked and had a Harp shandy in Dempsey's with her lunch one day and confided in me that she would go demented if she was stuck at home with the terrible three 24/7, so my heart really goes out to her.

Clap. Clap. Clap.

I nearly jump out of my seat with the fright. Standing at the top of the room is Martin Shermer, the elusive MD of PensionsPlus Ireland, looking white as a ghost, tie loose around his neck, shirt sleeves rolled up and no jacket anywhere to be found. Behind him are two of the partners – Bill Cullen with a Beard (I'm not sure of his name) and The Woman. They don't look great, despite none of them showing up at the party last night after RSVPing that they'd be there.

'Sorry for the short notice, but we'll need to see everyone in the big boardroom. Now.' Oh, this is definitely it. 'Seats are first come first served so expect …' I turn to look at Suzanne but she's gone, elbows flying.

****

We all pile into the boardroom, which smells like a brewery even with all the windows open. There must be eighty of us in there, leaning against the walls, arms folded like sullen schoolchildren, ready to hear our fate. The rest are probably asleep at home in pools of their own vomit or still wandering the streets clutching kebabs. Despite the number of bodies, the room is completely silent save for Eilish, one of the older receptionists, sniffling. There are fancy pastries on the table, untouched, practically waving at me. I don't think Weight Watchers Maura would begrudge me one on a day like this. Isn't sugar supposed to be good for shock?

'Look, you're probably wondering what's happening, and I'm sorry to do this so abruptly,' Shermer begins. 'I would wait until everyone is in but … I wanted to get this out to you before it hits the headlines.' Someone at the back mutters 'You bollix' and the atmosphere grows even more tense. Eilish emits a little sob. 'Long story short, PPH, our parent company, is closing down Irish operations and we're all being made redundant as of right now, myself and the partners included. Everyone.'

We're *all* being made redundant? Even *me*? The room erupts. Suddenly everyone is shouting. 'Are we still getting paid before Christmas? What about the bonus?' Natalie, one of the fund managers, calls. My tyres!

'How much will we be entitled to?' Des stammers, looking green about the face.

'What about the holidays I've been saving up to carry over to next year?' I say to nobody in particular.

'Please! *Please!* Settle down, everyone,' Shermer bellows above the din, flapping his arms and looking like he wishes the ground would swallow him up. The two behind him just stare at the floor. 'PPH is holding a public forum on 3 January in the Airport Travelodge. I've told you everything I know – they will have all the details for us then.'

Out of the corner of my eye, through the glass partition, I notice a group of big burly types in uniform standing in the foyer. When did they arrive? Alan from IT has obviously copped them too and shouts, 'Who are the heavies?'

Everyone turns to look and one of them, his neck about the size of one of my thighs, and that's saying something, gives us a little wave and they all start creasing themselves laughing.

'That's security,' Shermer says with a grimace. 'Now, I'm under orders to tell you to clear out your desks, and under no circumstances is anyone to take any company property. There's CCTV and you *will* be prosecuted. I'll see you on 3 January. Oh, and Happy Christmas.'

The room erupts again with talk of lawsuits and calling Joe Duffy and does anyone know how much you could get for a filing cabinet and an eight-year-old PC on DoneDeal. I see Sadhbh leading Eilish towards the lift, her arm around her shoulder, and I feel the tears begin to prickle in my eyes. Six years I've given this company. Six years of emptying the dishwasher, six years of being the health and safety officer, six years of assisting the Christmas Party Social Committee and running out to buy emergency Secret Santa presents. And for what? To see my glittering career as a pensions administrator and my team-leader potential go down the toilet?

The room empties and I'm just about to swing out the door when I turn on my heel and stride across to the table, buoyed up by the injustice of it all. 'Well, it would be a shame to see these go to waste,' I say, my voice high and indignant as I grab the platter of pastries. Martin Shermer looks up from his phone and just stares back at me blankly.

Walking back to my desk, I can see everyone totting up in their heads how many years they've done and how much they could potentially get. Some of them even have calculators on the go. I catch Suzanne looking up massive trampolines online the second she sits down. Very unsafe if you ask me.

The lift doors open and Sadhbh brazenly rolls out of it on an office chair with a few others from upstairs, shouting that they're all heading over to Dempsey's for a few pints and a debrief. She knows none of those thicko security guards will say anything to her. And if they do, she'll somehow manage to charm them into letting her keep the chair. She's always getting refunds for clothes in shops despite losing her receipts immediately. And then she slags me for having a special Receipts Box in my bedside locker.

Yes, I think I need something to steady my nerves and a pint would probably do the trick. Of course, I'm only going Out, not Out Out, as in I won't be in Coppers for the national anthem, so I mouth 'I'll follow you over' at the closing doors.

I manage to hold in the tears until I can find a corner of the building not occupied by someone crying into their mobile. My fingers shaking, I hit dial.

'Ais?'

'I've lost my job, John,' I bawl down the phone. 'What am I going to do?'

CHAPTER 3

The door swings open and his big strong arms are around me in a split second. I threw all caution to the wind and got a taxi out to his house in Drumcondra, even though I could easily have gotten the last bus. I was driven to flinging money away by the traumatic job news and four pints I had in Dempsey's. As I left, Sadhbh was sitting on Des's knee and calling after me not to forget to pick up the balloons tomorrow. Tomorrow. Elaine's hen party. We'll have to make sure to be in good form despite everything that's happened. She immediately WhatsApped us to cancel it in the wake of the PensionsPlus news, but I've organised thirty buns (I refuse to call them cupcakes. Since when were we too good for buns?) decorated with frilly bras, and after the shame I went through ordering them I'm not backing out now.

John's hugs have always been like stepping into some kind of isolation pod. So broad and familiar. Walking into those outstretched arms and burrowing my head under his chin is what kept me going when we found our way back to each other after Daddy died. Auntie Sheila calls John my 'rock of strength', and she's right. He's helped out on the farm at weekends and has been so understanding about my midweek trips Down Home to stay with Mammy. He's also been extremely patient at the things that have made me suddenly break down in tears – an ad for Bisto, Daddy-style slippers on sale in Dunnes, Phil Collins on the radio, anything at all to do with the impending Christmas. Here in John's arms now, I relish the familiarity. The safety. And I wonder how much longer I can get away with standing in the middle of the supermarket with hot tears falling helplessly down my cheeks as he dutifully turns me away from the honeydew melons. Daddy's Christmas specialty was digging out the melon baller and producing what he considered a very elegant starter, complete with a slice of ham on the side. He'd added the ham a few years back after seeing it on a menu in a fancy restaurant. Now, I never put the two into my mouth together, but he was very proud of it.

I look past John's shoulder and see my cousin Cillian in the sitting room, catching up on the latest Scandi-noir whodunit. I'm not able for the subtitles, to be honest, on top of trying to keep track of the characters, who all seem to be wearing the same jumper. It's always raining too. If I wanted a dose of misery I could just look out the window. No, give me *Strictly Come Dancing* any day. Nice bit of glam. Cillian is bet into it, though. He's the man responsible for me and John being together. John was my seventeenth kiss at my twenty-first Down Home, and Cillian brought him to the party, a big strapping lad in a Knocknamanagh Rangers jersey. Even the fierce rivalry between my hometown, Ballygobbard, and Knock – six kilometres away from each other but light years apart when it comes to the hurling – didn't stop my eyes following him around the room. That was eight years ago. Eight years of kisses and matches and holidays and rows and me always checking to make sure there's something not too spicy on the menu if we're going for dinner and him always inspecting the drinks to make sure the barman has given him Diet Coke for my vodka, not real fat Coke. Eight years minus the few months we were apart this year – our one and only break-up. I was so wild to get engaged and it seemed to be all that mattered. It drove us apart. Funny how things change. Then we got back together and, Jesus, my head was spinning between the grief and the love and the months that I'd missed him. Poor Cillian found my pants on the kitchen floor one Sunday morning a while back. Luckily I was able to scoop them up and pass them off as a tea towel before he got too close. The kitchen! It was like we were twenty-one again. Not that we ever did it in the kitchen when we were twenty-one, but the stairs in John's old house saw a bit of action when we were certain, *certain* everyone was at least two counties away. Now, me and John are getting back to some sort of normality – apart from all my crying.

John pushes back from me and looks down into my eyes, as if he can sense me thinking away. 'Are you alright?'

I'm not really alright, not at all. The panic of no job washes back over me, but as I open my mouth to respond, Cillian saunters out into the hall, giant burrito in his paw. He's graduated from a diet of Goodfellas and Supermilk to burritos, Goodfellas and Supermilk. I heard him telling John that he never imagined himself eating ethnic food, and here he is practically a Mexican. I'm not sure if burritos qualify as ethnic but putting rice in what is essentially a sandwich seems very exotic to me.

'What's up, Ais?'

John motions at Cillian to retreat, gently saying over my head, 'Loads of jobs gone at her place.'

'Oh, right. Shite. That's … shite. Sorry, Ais.' Cillian paws awkwardly at my shoulder and backs into the sitting room. He might not know one end of the hoover from another, but he is a dote.

It is shite. Everything is falling apart.

My phone goes in my coat pocket and I reach for it. It's Majella. Of course I texted her earlier to break the news, but she was out with her teacher pals, celebrating surviving the term and comparing war stories, (Majella probably won with her tale of one of her students piddling in her handbag in a fit of extreme boldness and the mother having to be called. It didn't help when she saw the same child and parent in Tesco that Sunday afternoon. Maj had nine bottles of wine in the trolley and nothing else. She described the look the mother gave her as 'caustic'.) I show John her name flashing up on my phone screen and he nods and squeezes my hand before following Cillian into the front room. I check the stairs for discarded jocks and sink onto the third step.

'Hiya, Maj.'

'Ais. Are you alright? I'm sorry I didn't get to ring earlier but my hands are in ribbons carrying bags of "best teacher ever" mugs and snowglobes. Just once I'd like a nice bottle of Baileys or someth–'

'You're grand, bird,' I say, hugging my knees to my chest. 'I'm over in John's, so I can't really talk. I'll catch you up on it all tomorrow.'

'Ah, no problem, Ais, but listen, don't be worrying, you'll be grand. Left here, please!' she roars suddenly, and I swear I hear her taxi driver swerve and curse, mugs clinking away on the seat beside her.

'Bye, Majella.'

'Bye, Ais!' There's the sound of a tussle as she hangs up and a faint 'Will you give me a hand with this poinsettia? Good man!'

John and Cillian are deep into a repeat of *Great British Bake Off* when I poke my head into the sitting room. 'That rise is poxy,' Cillian says confidently as a contestant pushes a loaf into an oven. 'That's an ambitious bake alright,' John agrees. Two lads whose only real knowledge of bread is down to their life-long kinship with Mr Brennan and Pat the Baker. I was always suspicious of the likes of sourdough myself. It sounds manky, but Elaine convinced me to give it a go and, do you know what, it's actually lovely.

John shifts over on the couch and pats the cushion beside him. I squeeze in between him and Cillian and try to focus on the telly, Majella's words about being grand ringing in my ears. John nudges me and mouths 'Alright?' as Cillian leans forward, unconsciously muttering, 'Come on, good lad' as a contestant slides a focaccia out of the oven. I smile tightly at John and try to concentrate on Bread Week, but my thoughts wander to tomorrow. The hen. Do we have everything ready? Do I have my good Oasis dress …?

'Oh, for God's sake!' I exclaim, thumping my head back onto the couch.

'You're dead right, Ais – he's mad to put thyme in that,' Cillian replies without turning away from the telly.

'What? No, I'm not on about the bread, you gom. I … I just forgot to get my dress cleaned for Elaine and Ruby's hen tomorrow.'

It's been hanging in my wardrobe since my cousin Doireann's twenty-first a few weeks back, and while I'm sure it's grand, I like a fresh dress for a hen. It's respectful.

'Jesus, you never stop going to weddings. When is that one?'

'New Year's Eve,' John pipes up. 'Dublin on New Year's Eve, if you can credit it.'

John's found it tricky to hide his disbelief at having to be in Dublin so soon after Christmas. There've been a few tense words about it. Our first hint at a real row since we got back together. But instead of letting it spill into a fight and bring reality crashing down, I've promised him that we can just drive up on New Year's Eve and that Elaine and Ruby will definitely have normal beers at the afters, not just alcoholic wheat shots or whatever they were planning in the apartment the other week.

'And are yourself and Sadhbh house hunting already or what? It's fairly competitive out there, or so I hear. Jesus, that needs to prove for at least another twenty minutes!' Cillian exclaims.

Elaine hasn't said it in so many words, but I know that me and Sadhbh are going to have to look for somewhere else to live. She and Ruby are going to be a married couple. They're not going to want to look at someone else's pants and tights drying on the clothes horse while they're firing strawberries at each other in their nighties or what have you. I know she won't turf us out on our ears, but we'll have to go sooner or later. I'll miss Chez SEA something fierce. It's been some craic and a real escape from the sadness Down Home. I hate the thought of having to gather up my good cushions and take down the Live Love Laugh decal above my bed when it feels like I just moved in yesterday. I'll even miss arguing with Elaine about her frankly reckless use of bags for life – the key is in the name, Elaine. You're not supposed to buy six every time you go to the supermarket. But most of all I'll miss the girls. It's hard to believe that only a year ago I barely knew them.

'Yeah, we'll have to move alright. I'm trying not to think about it this side of Christmas.' Cillian is already busying himself bringing burrito wrappers and pint glasses into the kitchen, though, making the most out of a lull in *Bake Off*. John squeezes my knee and gives me a supportive smile, but the elephant in the room is practically sitting on the arm of the couch.

Cillian sticks his head back around the kitchen door. He's obviously been deep in thought in there. 'Here's an idea, Ais. You could move in here? Piotr's room is empty – you could have a walk-in wardrobe.'

****

'You can stay here as long as you like, you know?'

John's voice is muffled as he pulls his Knock Triathlon T-shirt over his head. It's been washed so many times that it's as soft as any pyjama top, and that's what he uses it as.

I pretend not to hear him as I slide into his bed. I wonder did he feel me stiffen when Cillian mentioned Piotr's name. I don't let myself think about Piotr. Well, not if I can help it at all.

'Ais? You can stay here as long as you like,' he repeats.

'Oh, thanks, I know. Thanks, love.'

Neither of us mentions Cillian's suggestion that I actually move in. We could have talked about it many times, ever since Elaine and Ruby set the wedding date, but we've danced around it. A year ago I would have jumped at the chance – it was all I wanted. A month ago I might have jumped at the chance too, when we were still in the grip of getting back together and knickers in the kitchen. But now I feel like not mentioning it at all.

John climbs into bed beside me, first lying on his back and then curling his body around mine in that familiar way of his, moving his hand up and down my thigh. I think about responding, but I'm just so tired. It's been a while, though. I start to turn to face him but as I do he rolls onto his back and sighs.

'Will we watch something? *West Wing*?'

I watch his face as he watches the telly, the flashing images lighting up his furrowed brow. My lovely John. I close the half a foot between us in the bed and rest my head on his chest, but no amount of Jed Bartlet can make me feel better.

CHAPTER 4

Twenty past five and we don't even have the Micra packed yet. I didn't get home to Chez SEA until this afternoon, after a fitful night of troubling dreams and sweating in John's bed. Piotr featured heavily after Cillian mentioning him, with his strong arms and eastern European turn of phrase. I could hardly look at John when I woke up. He doesn't know about me and Piotr and that kiss we had not long after Daddy died. It was a moment of pure madness, but I know it would kill him.

Sadhbh was out late herself. She said it was close to three when she finally rolled – literally, she was still on the office chair – out of Dempsey's. She opened her handbag earlier and out poured Sharpies, Post-its and all the best stuff from the third-floor stationery press onto the kitchen island countertop. I hope I'm not somehow considered an accessory to her crime. The last thing I need now is never being able to get a visa to go to America.

We ordered a much-needed pizza for a late lunch (ham and pineapple on one side for me, blue cheese and a type of sausage I've never heard of for Sadhbh) and multiple cans of Diet Coke and analysed how much redundancy money we might get. Sadhbh's HR head means she's in the know about all this and she thinks the deal could actually be worth loads. I've estimated €20,000 but that could actually be conservative by her reckoning. A few people took voluntary redundancy last year, and if the holiday Siobhán from Client Services went on with Michael from Sales is anything to go by, the company was very generous and went way beyond statutory payouts. Michael's wife was less generous about it, by all accounts. So surely we'll get the same? I can feel my hopes rising and decide to nip that in the bud. I always like to keep my expectations low to reduce my chances of being disappointed. I honestly don't know how Americans go through life with their 'positive mental attitude' craic. What a nightmare. I also asked Sadhbh if she'd given any thought to what's going to happen to Chez SEA once Ruby and Elaine are married, and she admitted she knows disbandment is on the cards, although we're both hoping beyond hope that maybe the fact that Elaine and Ruby haven't mentioned it means they want us all to live together as one big happy family. Maybe they'd want one of our eggs for their babies. Although, as Sadhbh reminded me, they have enough eggs between them. But I've been thinking of trying to do a bit more charity work, so I'll make sure they know the option is there. It's more likely that Elaine and Ruby just haven't had time to think about it. The engagement and wedding planning has been so fast. Who knows, though? Ronan Keating was dead right about life being a rollercoaster. You just gotta ride it.

'Would you not just move in with John?' Sadhbh enquires as she picks up the first load of hen-party paraphernalia to head down to the underground car park – the feather boas, pink cowboy hats and the three-foot E and R balloons. We were going to spell out their full names until I found out they were €14 each. Feck that.

Sadhbh balances the box on her knee as she looks at me quizzically.

'Ah, I don't know. We're not that long back together. It might be a bit … soon.'

'Soon? Ais, you've been together practically since you were in nappies …' but she sees my doubtful face and changes the subject, marvelling at the vibrancy of the L-plate necklaces. She's good like that. She heads out the door with the box and I retreat into my room to get the rest of the stuff. I still have to bring down the bunting and the sashes and the inflatable ball and chain. I bought willy straws too – it was almost like a reflex – although, in hindsight, they probably won't go down well at a lesbian hen. Or maybe they will – you never know with this gang.

Sadhbh clatters back into the apartment and sticks her head around my bedroom door. 'It's getting tight in the boot, Ais,' she says, before I see her eyes falling on the packet of willy straws lying open on the bed, and she trails off. They're very detailed, to be fair. You can see every vein. She looks up and raises an eyebrow.

'I know,' I admit with a sigh, stuffing them into my handbag. 'But you can't have a hen without a willy straw. It wouldn't be right. They'll understand.'

'Did you ring your mum yet?' Sadhbh asks, leaning against the doorframe. Mammy doesn't know anything about my job. She doesn't need anything else to worry about at the moment. Paddy Reilly, Daddy's oldest friend, has been helping out with the outdoor work on the farm and with the accounts, but I have an awful feeling things are falling by the wayside.

'Not yet.' I sigh. 'Sure I'll be going Down Home tomorrow. I'll tell her face to face.'

Between the pair of us we drag the rest of the stuff, as well as two cases of Prosecco, down to the basement and cram it all in, Tetris-style. I had been thinking of trading in the Micra for something with a roomier boot, but I couldn't bring myself to. Daddy helped me pick it out years ago, kicking the tyres and sealing the deal with a handshake. One careful lady owner, or so we were told. It just passed the NCT too. Just as well, since I won't be changing it any time soon now.

The hen is in the Wilde Building, a new creative space and co-working hub in town overlooking the Liffey. It's a miracle we snagged it so close to Christmas but Ruby knows the owner so we're getting the room for free, as well as access to the roof garden with glorious views across the city and on out to the Dublin Mountains. On the drive in from Portobello I'm forced to ask Sadhbh what the blazes a creative space and co-working hub is, but in the time it takes us to get there I'm still not a hundred per cent sure. It sounds fab, though.

The brides are off getting glammed up but, thanks to the heavy traffic getting into town, we don't actually have much time to get the place decorated. I feel my stress levels rising. We're only having this do because I insisted on it, and if the girls don't have a good time I'll never forgive myself. Personally, I don't think it's a real hen party unless there's a compulsory activity or two – pole dancing, a make-up class, even making flower crowns, for the love of God – but Elaine said she had to draw the line somewhere. So it's drinks, canapés, some dancing and that's it. The good news is her dad, who clearly has money to burn, is forking out for caterers so the food and cocktails are all free. I've never seen the like of it. I'll have to be extra vigilant tonight with my glasses of water. It's easy to get carried away at a free bar, as anyone who works at PensionsPlus knows. I can't jeopardise the little surprise Sadhbh and I have planned for later.

****

'Jesus, Aisling, you've outdone yourself!'

Majella was supposed to help us decorate but she went Down Home this morning for a funeral and the Timoney's bus was late getting back into town. It always is on Saturdays because Tony Timoney insists on stopping to do the Lotto on the Naas Road. He swears he'll split his winnings with whoever is on the bus but I wouldn't trust that man as far as I could throw him. He doesn't even do the Euromillions. Majella's looking well – all glowy and happy – and I know it has nothing to do with the egg salad sandwiches and small talk she probably filled up on earlier.

'Thanks, Maj. How's the head after last night? Did the mugs make it home safely?'

'Don't talk to me about mugs! I never told you the best part on the phone. Wait until you hear this. A bouquet of red roses arrived into the staff room yesterday morning with a little teddy in the middle of them.'

'No!' I gasp, unable to help myself.

'Yes!' she squeals. 'And, Ais, the teddy was holding a little pillow ...'

'Go on!'

'And the pillow had the words "I Love You" embroidered on it.'

She squeals and I can't help but be taken up in her excitement. It's awful cheesy but, to be honest, it's long been my dream for someone to burst into the office with a bouquet the size of a fridge and a stuffed animal that needs its own passport. The pure romance of it. John is grand with the flowers but this classroom gesture has nearly brought a tear to my eye. The extravagance of it.

I've been best friends with Majella since junior infants and in that time I've seen her blaze through pretty much all the lads we know Down Home, leaving a trail of broken hearts behind her. Her first boyfriend was Phillip McCarthy, but he was forced to dump her after she followed him behind the sweet shop at indoor soccer and kissed him. They were eight years old at the time and he got an awful fright. That's Majella for you – she's pure Samantha, always has been – she gets what she wants. She gets things she doesn't want too, like chlamydia during her first year in college in Limerick, but it barely slowed her down (although she did have to send a few awkward texts). Mary I nearly lost its 'Mary Dry' nickname during Majella's four years there.

'The kids were nearly hopping out the windows asking me questions about my boyfriend and asking me if I'm getting married. I think he's The One. Can you believe it?'

I can't, to be quite honest. I really thought Maj would end up with one of John's friends – since I'm a Knocknamanagh Rangers WAG we pal around a lot with that crowd – or maybe even one of the Ballygobbard Rovers, although it would make the wedding a bit awkward for me. Team politics are tricky – it's a miracle me and John ever got together in the first place.

But no, she's in love with Pablo, the baby-faced taxi driver John befriended when we were in Tenerife for some winter sun earlier this year. Months later Pablo arrived in Ballygobbard, rucksack on his back, ready to embrace all Ireland has to offer – John is some man to talk the place up, to be fair – and when himself and Majella clapped eyes on each other it became apparent that he wasn't going back any time soon. But he's been going through a huge bout of homesickness recently and has taken to wearing shorts in December despite the Baltic temperatures. No doubt he'll have a kidney infection come Christmas Day. He's a great man for the lifts because he misses being a taxi driver, which is handy for Maj seeing as she can't drive, and the closest thing BGB has to a Luas is Constance Swinford's horse box. Pablo's also proven himself to be dynamite with a hurl, and John has his eye on him for a full-back position. He even had him convinced for a while that BGB stands for BallyGoBackwards, a Knocknamanagh joke that never seems to get old.

'That is *so* romantic, Majella. You must be delighted. I'm delighted for you, so I am.' I *am* delighted for her. Those early days in a relationship when you're shifting non-stop and dying to spend every minute together – you can't beat it. It reminds me of when John and I started going out and he'd send me a good-morning message first thing and God knows how many more throughout the day. Nothing exciting, just this and that, letting me know he was thinking of me. It was nice. When we got back together we were back at it like teenagers, with the miss yous and the love yous coming out our ears. Then last week he texted me making sure I was bringing toilet roll over to his house because Cillian was making an attempt at refried beans. Still, though, it's nice to be wanted, I suppose.

'I finally get what the fuss is about. I'm in love, Aisling.' She's beaming now and I think it's fair to say I've never seen her happier.

'Here, make yourself useful,' I say, throwing a bag of penis-shaped confetti in her direction. It was left over from Martina Cloghessy's hen last month. Waste not want not. 'Scatter a bit of that on the tables, will you? The brides will be here any minute.'

Half an hour later the place is looking stunning, if I do say so myself. The room has filled up nicely and Sadhbh has done a lovely job with what she tells me are minimalist Scandinavian Christmas decorations. The balloons are saving it, to be quite honest. There are waiters weaving around with trays of mad little vegan things, per Ruby's request. I really can't believe this is my life, out in Dublin at a lesbian hen party on a Saturday night. It's all very cosmopolitan. I'm in full Aisling-at-a-hen mode and commence chatting to the mothers of the brides and all the various aunties, sisters and cousins – and, Jesus, there are loads of them. Double the usual amount of relations, I suppose. Ruby and Elaine arrived a while ago in a cacophony of shrieks and hugs and I'm delighted that it all came together in the end. Sadhbh is doling out the props and I can see the tag-rugby girls making the most of the willy straws. I should never have doubted them. Nothing as gas as a willy straw, even if it's not your cup of tea, sexually speaking.

One person I don't see, though, is Maj, and it's unusual. She'd normally be going hell for leather on the dancefloor, swinging furry handcuffs over her head, at this point in the night. I check the bar: no sign; the toilet: no sign; then head up onto the roof. It's freezing – even for December – and the icy wind bites at the one bare shoulder my dress reveals (it was grand without a wash in the end). I spot her at a corner table, her good winter coat wrapped tightly around her. She's looking down at her phone, beaming away like a mad thing, and I know she's texting him. She's always texting him these days. I leave her to it and head back inside.

Taking a deep gulp of my cosmopolitan – I've never felt more like Carrie Bradshaw, although I suppose I'm more of a Charlotte – I tap the microphone. Immediately, everyone in the room turns to stare at me, and I can see Elaine nudge Ruby like, oh no, what's going on?

'Er, one two? Hello, everyone,' I say in a slightly shaky voice. I was never one for public speaking but this really has to be done. 'Now, I know the girls said that they didn't want a big fuss and I tried, I really did.' There's tittering and Ruby puts her head in her hands but I can see she's smiling. 'But I think everyone would agree that a hen isn't a hen without a slideshow. Roll it there, Róisín!'

A screen lowers behind me and Sadhbh hits Play on her phone as the first picture – side by side baby photos of Ruby and Elaine – bursts into view while 'Isn't She Lovely' booms out of the fancy speakers that seem to be everywhere.

The brides are in tears by the fourth slide, which is a new personal best for me. The trick is to include video messages from friends and family abroad who couldn't make it.

Nothing like a sister in Melbourne with a poem or a best friend in Toronto to really get the waterworks going. Of course, I was bawling away myself. How could you not?

By midnight the party is in full swing and the dancefloor is absolutely heaving, even though I'm not mad on the music myself. One of Ruby's pals is DJing and I haven't recognised a single song yet; when I requested anything by Ed Sheeran she looked at me like I had two heads. Still, me and Maj are giving it serious welly and I make a mental note to add a few Activity Points into my Weight Watchers tracker. Maura will be delighted. After my fifth or sixth cosmopolitan I'm feeling a bit worse for wear so I stagger out to the roof for a bit of fresh air. Sadhbh is there with some of her and Elaine's college pals, but as soon as she cops me she breaks away from the group.

'Okay, Ais?' she says, gesturing at my bare feet. Well, bare save for my black 100 denier tights. It's December after all. I go down to forty denier in the summer months.

'I forgot about drinking the water, again.' I shrug, and she steers me over to a quiet corner under a patio heater.

'Why don't you go home? It's been a crazy couple of days. You must be wrecked.'

Well, she's not wrong there. To think, forty-eight hours ago I thought my biggest problem was two miserable fecks not handing in their Secret Santa presents. Now I'm … unemployed. I've always had a job. When I was in college I worked in a deli for two years and a restaurant for another two. The unlimited supplies of coleslaw did nothing for my waistline.

'Maybe I will call it a night,' I concede. 'It's all over now bar the shouting. You're looking a bit chirpier?'

'I'm feeling better about the whole thing,' Sadhbh replies, lighting one of her complicated rollies. You'd think there would be an easier way to increase your chances of getting cancer. 'Worst case scenario, I'll just look for a new job. Best case is a nice juicy payout.'

'I hadn't thought about it like that.'

'Ah, fuck it, it was a shithole anyway,' she goes, and I realise she's three sheets to the wind too. 'And I was thinking, Ais, it could be a good chance for you to spend more time with your mum. I know you've been worrying about her. It might be serendipity.'

Serendipity. Now there's a classic film I haven't thought about in a while. Kate Beckinsale has a lovely head of hair – you can tell she minds it properly with leave-in conditioner and probably a weekly masque. Very shiny altogether. And maybe Sadhbh is right: being out of work will give me a chance to spend more time with Mammy. Silver linings and all that. Sadhbh catches me in a swaying embrace. 'But I'll miss living *and* working with you something rotten.'

Before I have a chance to tell her I feel exactly the same, Elaine totters over, arms out wide, her blonde bob looking a little dishevelled. 'There's my girls,' she sings, clearly more worse for wear than any of us. Job done. It's not a proper hen if the bride isn't slaughtered. 'What's going on?' Elaine has us both in an affectionate headlock.

'We're just being saps about work and everything. We'll miss each other.' Sadhbh gives Elaine's shoulder a squeeze. 'And … we'll miss you too,' she says hesitantly.

Elaine clamps her lips together and looks from Sadhbh's face to mine and back to Sadhbh, who continues, 'We know Chez SEA will soon be no more.' I didn't know she was going to bring it up but I suppose someone has to.

Elaine looks genuinely gutted. 'I didn't know how to say it. I know this has all been so quick, with the speedy wedding, but we just really wanted to get a move on, you know? We've waited long enough to be allowed to get bloody married.'

'It's grand, it's grand,' Sadhbh cries into Elaine's face. 'You deserve it, my love.'

'*Please* don't feel like you have to move anytime soon.' Elaine pulls the three of us down onto the nearby wicker outdoor couch. Damp as anything. My kidneys! 'We're going on honeymoon for three weeks after the wedding – Uganda and then on to some other cool locations in Sudan and Kenya.'

Sudan? Uganda? Mother of God, what did the Maldives ever do to them? Is it not the law that you have to go on the all-inclusive honeymoon?

'Please don't worry,' I reassure Elaine.

'Yeah, don't worry,' echoes Sadhbh. 'We'll find something.' She pulls the two of us into a vice-like hug and then says, 'Will we go? Let's go home and get on the couch and watch *Mean Girls*. While we still can.'

It seems like a crime to leave a free bar, but pyjamas sounds lovely and we have limited couch nights left, me, Elaine and Sadhbh. 'I'll get our coats,' I announce. The cloakroom was free too. A lovely touch.

CHAPTER 5

The next day, after leaving some presents under the Chez SEA Christmas tree (we have Twink on top in lieu of an angel – not my idea) and hugging Sadhbh and Elaine goodbye, I head off to collect Majella for our annual drive Down Home for Christmas. John is already on his way to Knocknamanagh after ringing me this morning to complain about Pablo's new habit of texting gushing declarations of his feelings for Maj to him, making him deeply uncomfortable. Pablo has an island passion that has never quite travelled to Knock or BGB.

It's handiest to pick Majella up at the Park and Ride at the Red Cow, but it's so manic I have to bip an old man while trying to pull in. God knows I don't dole out bips unless I'm pushed to my limit, but he was taking up three spaces and even I have a breaking point. I mentally promise to put a euro in the next poor box to cancel it out.

Maj is perched on a stack of suitcases and wearing her 'Santa, Define Good?' jumper with the flashing lights. I told her there wasn't much room in the car but she's taken to wearing something new every time she goes out with Pablo so it looks like her days of travelling light are over. If it wasn't for Penneys she'd be bankrupt.

'Howiya, Ais,' she roars, opening the boot and firing her small wheelie case on top of the foot spa, aka Mammy's big present. 'Will I just throw the rest on the back seat?'

'Go on so,' I say, as she commences jamming everything in around my carefully wrapped presents. I can hear my brother Paul's Lynx Africa gift set giving way under the weight of her make-up bag. Majella has gone mad into make-up the past few months. It's her obsession with Colette Green, Ireland's premier fashion and beauty blogger. First it was the palette, then the brushes, then the deo-scents. But now Colette has her own lip glosses, fake eyelashes, even fake tan, and Maj can't buy them fast enough. I saw on *Xposé* the other day that she has scented phone covers now too, so I suppose I can guess what I'll be getting for Christmas.

Beeep. Beep. Beep. Dublin drivers just don't give you a minute, do they? Honestly, you'd think people would have more patience considering it's Christmas.

'Are you in?' I say, as Majella slides dramatically into the passenger seat brandishing a plastic bag full of taytos and sweets as is our tradition.

'I'm in,' she goes, fastening her seatbelt. 'On Dasher, on Dancer, on Aisling!'

And off we go, inching our way down the N7, a bit giddy, despite the fact that my life is quite literally falling apart. Majella had her official work party weeks ago (teachers are always a step ahead of the game), but there was a whole heap of drama after two of the staff were caught shifting in the disabled toilet in Supermac's on O'Connell Street, and the latest is that the deputy principal has handed in her notice. Not that she'll be missed – she was a tyrant by all accounts.

'You could cut the tension in the place with a knife,' Maj says, tearing open a bag of wine gums and rooting around for a black one to press into my hand. A true friend. Everyone knows they try and do you out of black ones because they're the nicest. 'I've had to stop going into the staff room to watch *Home and Away*. I just sit in the junior infants toilets and watch it on my phone instead. My calves are in shite from it.'

'So is she – what's her name again? – going to be there after Christmas?'

'Imelda? No, she finished up on Friday. I wouldn't be surprised if she stuffed a trout behind a whiteboard or something. She'd be that type. No great loss anyway.'

'And who's taking her job?'

Majella has been teaching second class at St Anthony's in Santry for five years now. Being the Communion year, she's flat out, but she likes the variety. It's mostly based around learning off 'Zacchaeus was a Greedy Little Man' with some maths and phonics and a nature table thrown in for good measure. I nearly did teaching myself – got more than enough points for St Pat's or Mary I – and sometimes I'm sorry I didn't. Majella and her flatmates, Mairead and Fionnuala, are always getting their hair cut at 4 p.m. on a Wednesday and jetting off to the Canaries for mid-term breaks. Maybe I'll look into doing a HDip. I'm very patient and I like a bit of discipline.

'No idea. There's a constant stream of CVs coming in. Everyone wants a permanent teaching job, so they'll have no problem filling it.'

'Have you thought about going for it yourself?'

Maj looks over at me, her brow furrowed. 'It hadn't even entered my head,' she goes. 'Do you think I'd be able for it?

The deputy principal has fifth class as well as all the admin and the rest of it. I think I'd miss dossing in the church and all the glamour of the Communion.'

The parents at St Anthony's don't mess around. Last year one family arrived to the church in a limo. Another eight-year-old had her hair done in Toni & Guy and a very suspicious all-over tan to make the white dress pop. It can be very competitive, but Majella loves getting done up because she's in high demand for pictures on the day. She says it makes her feel like a celebrity, which is fair enough.

'Of course you'd be well able for it, Maj,' I say encouragingly. 'I'm sure you'd get a nice pay rise too. Maybe you and the girls could find a place with another bathroom? And it would cut down on fights over the Lenor.'

Mairead is notoriously tight when it comes to the household kitty, and Maj and Fionnuala suspect she hasn't bought a drop of fabric softener since she moved in three years ago. Mairead and Fionnuala are good craic but they run a tight ship. I've always stopped short of writing my name on my shampoo and conditioner, but Majella's housemates have their own special waterproof markers.

'Actually, I had kind of a mad idea last weekend when I was Down Home,' Majella says sheepishly.

'Well?' I say, moving up to fourth gear for the first time. The traffic is as bad as I've ever seen it. It's like the days before my beloved Newlands Cross flyover opened. 'Spill it.'

'I was thinking of moving back Down Home. Like, permanently. Letting my room in Phibsboro go and going up and down to work on the Timoney's bus. I'd save money and see more of Pablo to boot. We could have a deposit in a few years.'

I'm gobsmacked. Majella? Moving Down Home? Majella loves Ballygobbard as much as me – loves the coleslaw in Filan's, loves the craic in Maguire's, loves the matches – but I always thought she loved Coppers on a Thursday more than all those things combined. I'm shook, to be honest.

'Sure half the country is at it, Ais. Rent is crippling. Our shower is broken, but we're too afraid to remind the landlord we exist in case the miserable fecker charges us more. So we're just coping with it. You have to kind of hold it over you, trying to wash yourself with the other hand. It's extremely undignified. I nearly landed out onto the floor the other day. Promise me, if I die falling out of the shower you'll put nice knickers on me before any ridey guards come? And make sure they use one of my last three Facebook profile pictures on the news.'

'I promise,' I say solemnly.

'Would I be mad to do it, Ais? Give it all up for a boy?' she asks in a small voice.

I know you're not supposed to do it under any circumstances but we're only going about 40km an hour, so for a split second I take my eyes off the road and look straight at her.

'Not at all, girl,' I beam. 'You're in love.'

She smiles back at me. 'I am. Seeing him at the weekends just isn't enough, and he can't afford to live in Dublin in a million years with the price of it.' She takes a breath. 'Are you sure I'm not a big gom?'

'Well, that goes without saying …' I duck as she fires a green wine gum – the worst one – in my direction.

'How are you feeling about the redundancy?'

'I still can't really believe it, Maj. Can you? Let go, right before Christmas. Dire.'

'You'll get a great reference,' she says confidently. 'You'll find something in no time. You're very employable with all the health and safety certificates you've racked up.'

I have to hand it to Majella. Even though she's an absolute hames ninety-nine per cent of the time, she can be very pragmatic when the mood takes her. It must be the teacher training. 'It's just a job – plenty more where that came from. It's Christmas week – you've had your shopping done and wrapped since October, I'm guessing?'

She's right there. 'You're right, of course.' I actually started back in the January sales but no point in bringing it up now. It's not the time to gloat.

'It's actually great timing. Everyone is off for the next couple of weeks so we'll have loads of time to figure it out. And don't forget, you'll probably be getting a load of dosh.'

She's right again.

'If you're worried about paying your rent, you could always move Down Home too. Sure, you can stay with John when you need a break from your mother. You and him will be living together in no time.'

It just rolls off her tongue, and I haven't the heart to tell her that we haven't even discussed it. How do I explain that I'm worried John and I would have nothing to talk about after all this time? I barely even understand it myself.

Instead I pick up on her other point. 'Yeah, Sadhbh already suggested that. We're going to have to move out of Chez SEA anyway after the wedding. Mammy *is* lonely. Wouldn't it be nice to mind each other for a while? And all the better if you're around too. It might even be a bit of craic.'

'Will you move back down with her for good? Not in with John?' Majella sounds surprised and grimaces as she shoves a green one into her mouth.

'I don't know, Maj. I don't know.'

My brother Paul has been home from Australia since Daddy died but I know he's itching to go back. The rest of the lads went on fruit picking without him and now they're moving on to Melbourne, and there's talk of getting real jobs and a proper flat with rooms and beds and not the pile of coats or whatever they were all sleeping on in County Coogee. It's a chance to make some real money. I've told him it's up to him – I won't hold him back. But at the same time I'm a bit worried about having to do all the looking-after Mammy myself. It would be easier if I was at home, I suppose. Auntie Sheila is around, of course, and the neighbours have been incredible, but I'm feeling a bit, I don't know, responsible. It's a lot, even for me.

'God, Ais, could you imagine, both of us living at home again!'

She has a point there. We can survive anything, me and Maj, once we're together. The first year we went to the Gaeltacht is proof of that. She hadn't a word of Irish and would have been sent home if it wasn't for me hissing verbs and declarations about the weather to her. We used to have a secret Club Béarla in a locked bathroom every evening, where we'd whisper frantically in English about what we'd just had for dinner. How she's now teaching Irish to children is beyond me.

'Me and Mammy might kill each other, though.'

I'm worried that we might without Daddy there to mediate. Although, I've become a full grown-up in the last few months. Like, I was already grown up, but now it's gone beyond not being afraid of driving on the M50 and having health insurance. You never know when you might find yourself with kidney stones up the side of an African mountain or whatever other scenarios those ads scare you with.) Fighting with Mammy isn't really on any more. We have to mind each other. Our relationship has definitely changed for the better – we talk more, hug more – but I'm worried it won't last if she starts demanding my whites for washing and timing my morning showers – all very likely to happen. She's extremely frugal when it comes to hot water. Majella and I are quiet and deep in thought as we clear the worst of the traffic and fly down the motorway, bound for BGB.

After mulling over the pros (clean sheets every Friday; unlimited apple tart) and cons (Mammy's long-standing love of *Mrs Brown's Boys*), Majella eventually says thoughtfully, 'I think you and Marian will be grand.' Then she opens the Pringles and passes me a little stack. 'And at least there's loads of room in your place. It'll be a tight squeeze in Mammy and Daddy's, although I'd pay them a bit of rent, of course, and they'd be glad of that with Daddy not working much at the moment.' Shem Moran, Majella's father, has been in and out of work for as long as I can remember. A bit of boiler maintenance here and a bit of painting and decorating there. Mrs Moran is a teacher, like Majella, and keeps the house going as well as doing a few scones for Filan's. Majella pipes up again. 'At least Daddy will have something to say to Pablo now that he's started training with the Rangers.'

'Come again, girl?' I say, cocking my head towards her as I finally turn on to Main Street BGB, where the massive town Christmas tree is twinkling in the distance. I've been dreading this moment and sure enough I feel a hard lump form in my throat. Christmas. Without Daddy. Our first Christmas without Daddy.

I blink back tears as we wait patiently behind a car unloading wreaths for sale at a little street stall, and I notice there are more people than usual around. Some are dipping into Geraldine's boutique for some last-minute present ideas – she does a good line in floaty scarves, which is always a rock-solid Mammy gift. A few are heading into the charity shop too, no doubt picking up the Christmas tags designed by the children from the primary school. They're a BGB tradition, even though a monkey with a paintbrush could probably do a better job. On the corner I can see a small queue forming outside Boland's butchers: people collecting the turkeys they ordered back in October and picking up some of Marty Boland's famous sausages. There are more signs and declarations about the sausages around the red-and-white-tiled exterior than I thought possible – 'Best Sausages in the "County"!' 'You've Tried the "Rest" Now Try the "Best"!' He's very proud of them, but could go easy on the quotation marks. There's a 'Leased' sign plastered over the Scissor Sisters façade beside Boland's. Róisín will be badly missed. I've been a loyal Scissor Sisters fan since my debs, but she had to let the premises go when she got pregnant with her third baby and it turned out to be twins. Four under five – she has her work cut out for her. A few more locals are coming and going from Filan's, and I'm glad. The Aldi out near Knock hasn't done the local shop any favours, although they've been doing their best to diversify with the Linda McCartney fake chicken nuggets and the introduction of a third till.

Majella's still talking and shakes me out of my reverie. 'I was just saying Daddy and Pablo have something to talk about now,' she says. 'It'll make things easier when he moves in.'

Without thinking I hit the brakes and the car comes screeching to an abrupt stop outside the butcher's. Marty Boland looks up suddenly from where he's shoulder deep in a festive ham display. I'm in such a state of shock I don't even think to mouth an apology.

I swing back around to face Majella.

'You're going to ask *Pablo*? To *move in*? To your *parents' house*?'

I've heard it all now.

CHAPTER 6

'Hiya, Mammy.'

She's home more often than not now when I arrive at the house. 'Sure where would I be going?' she always says with a sad sigh in her voice that breaks my heart. I'm not able for letting things get too sad, though, because I'm worried I might start crying and never stop. The C-word hasn't been uttered once in the house or between us, even though it's only a few days away now. Our first Christmas without Daddy. I feel sick at the thought of it. Who's going to go out and buy the tree, making best friends with the man selling them outside Knocknamanagh Garden Centre, if they even have any left? Who's going to put the lights on the big ash tree out the front? Mammy loves that tree at Christmas, partly because Una Hatton called it 'gaudy' two years ago. Well, she said it was 'lovely and gaudy,' but Mammy knew what she was getting at. The Hattons are Protestants and only have very tasteful matching wreaths on their gate and front door and only the one colour of light on their tree, twinkling through the bay window. Mammy went and bought an extra multicoloured string last year and, to be honest, I don't even think she knew she was muttering the word 'gaudy' to herself as Daddy dutifully leaned the ladder against the tree to put them up. Maybe Paul could make a last-ditch attempt at it this year? Although, do we even want to put them up? I'd love to cancel the whole thing to be quite honest.

'Any news, pet?' Mammy smiles weakly. She looks tired and older than her sixty-three years these days. I hadn't planned on mentioning anything about the redundancy until later, but as soon as I see her, I can't fight the urge to pour my heart out. I lower myself into the cat's armchair in the corner of the kitchen with a sigh. I'll be rotten with hairs but feck it.

'I got a bit of bad news on Friday, actually. Our parent company in work is closing the Dublin office and ...' I pause, 'we're all being made redundant.' My voice wobbles a bit.

Mammy stops in her tracks and puts her hand to her mouth. 'What? Ah no, Aisling. The absolute lousers! And all the work you've done for them. What are you going to do?'

I knew she'd take it badly so I'm well prepared.

'I'll be okay, Mammy. I'll get a good payout, I'm sure. It could be a good lump in my case, seeing as I'm there a few years.'

She still looks like she's been shot so I hurriedly add, 'I've already set up email alerts from all the websites for possible new jobs.' I logged on first thing this morning and scoured the listings. If there are worms to be caught, I'm going to be the punctual bird that pecks them up.

'What about your NCT?'

Mammy has become obsessed with keeping the cars running since Daddy died. She's convinced that now he's not here to check the oil and kick the tyres we're all going to go hurtling off the side of a cliff due to neglected brakes.

'I just passed it – one less thing to worry about anyway.' I'm eager to get out of this conversation.

Mammy steps forward and puts her arm around my shoulders. 'You poor craythur. I'll put on the kettle.'

****

On the spur of the moment I decide to take the Christmas decorations out of the garage. I don't want to go the whole hog with the inflatable reindeer for the lawn – Daddy loved an Aldi special buy – but a few stuffed Santas might make the house look less sad. There's a stack of unopened post, obviously Christmas cards, on the kitchen dresser, and I feel a fresh wave of grief rising inside of me. No Christmas cards from us this year. It's not the done thing.

I invited Majella over for an emergency glass of Pinot Greej to discuss the Pablo bombshell, and by the time she arrives at the back door, a bottle in each hand, I've hung up a few sprigs of holly and put the crib on the hall table, making a mental note to go out to the back shed for some straw tomorrow. Mammy insists on an authentic crib, although an unfortunate incident in the late nineties has meant one of the wise men is now made of Lego, but it wouldn't be the same without him at this stage. We've no tree yet but maybe we just won't bother.

'Well, did you tell them?'

'Not yet, no. I need some Dutch courage first.'

Majella's parents are very open-minded – for example, they know all about her brother Shane smoking hash while waxing his Subaru in the garage every night and say nothing

– but I think even the Morans would draw the line at her shacking up under their roof. I know Mammy wouldn't really like it if it was me and John and no ring involved. And don't get me started on John's mammy. His parents scare the shite out of me and always have. They're mad Catholics the pair of them. Fran is a nurse, but she'd be in mass twenty-four hours a day if she could, and they always sit right in the front row to prove they're never late. She's hosted Padre Pio's glove twice and is a competitive blackcurrant jam maker as well as being secretary of the local ICA guild. And his daddy is not much better, although at least he lets his hair down in Maguire's every once in a while. Oh, they're both very nice to me, of course – I'm from good people – but I wouldn't want to cross either of them. I can tell she's been torn for years about wanting me and John to get married to absolve any sin at all we might have built up between us, and trying to hold on to her precious little altar boy for as long as possible.

Maj pops in to the sitting room to say hello to Mammy while I pour the wine and try to locate some nibbles. Nothing to be found. She doesn't even have the Christmas *RTÉ Guide*. How will I know when the good films are on? I'll have to bring her in to do the Big Shop in the next day or two. People will be calling and we'll need to have something to offer them, especially the Hattons. They'll probably be expecting jam with their cheese or some other Protestant nonsense.

'She's very quiet, isn't she?' Majella notes, closing the kitchen door behind her and taking a seat at Mammy's fancy Considered by Helen James kitchen table, bought specially to impress Sadhbh and Elaine on their maiden voyage to BGB last year. Not that she'll ever admit it, of course.

'It's hard.' I sigh, pushing a glass towards Majella. 'But we'll be grand. We just need to get through it. Auntie Sheila is having us over for the dinner so it'll be good to get out of the house. She puts on a lovely spread – sausage meat in the stuffing and all.'

'You're some woman, Ais,' Maj says and I just shrug. I'm barely holding it together, truth be told. But I have to.

'So …' I say, keen to change the subject. 'Pablo and you and your folks and Shane all living together. Are you mental or what? Willy won't like it.'

The Moran family Jack Russell is notoriously territorial; he gnawed a hole in the kitchen door when Derek Hayes came to collect Majella to go to a GAA dinner dance. Maj just laughs and takes a big sup of wine.

'I know, it's mad,' she says. 'But I think it's our only option. Pab is working two days a week in Filan's Garage and three nights in the Ard Rí. He's renting the flat above the charity shop with three Brazilians – they're like sardines in it. Two of them in each room. He hasn't a bob to his name and anything he does have he's spending on presents for me. He's talking about going back to Tenerife if he can't get more work.'

Jesus, when she puts it like that, I suppose there's no other option. 'Will they let you … share a room, though?' I have to ask.

'Ais, I'm thirty next year!' she squeaks back at me, topping up our glasses. 'But yeah, no, I don't know. I'm hoping that they'll just be so delighted to have me at home they'll overlook Pab entirely. Sure he's only small. We could try converting the garage into a fourth bedroom, but Shane has his PlayStation and virtual-reality shite and car stuff in it so we'll have no choice. Jesus, I'm dreading asking them, though. I'll do it now. What do you think?'

'It's as good a time as any, I suppose,' I concede, topping her up again. If they say no at least it might numb the pain.

I actually can't believe she's managed to tear herself away from Pablo tonight but he's working at a wedding beyond in the Ard Rí, slinging drinks and 'Olé you big mucker' at anyone who'll listen. He's really starting to fit in.

'Who's getting married in the Ard Rí?' Usually I'd be all over it but I've been fierce preoccupied. I know Majella will have all the info. She thrives on local gossip – telephone, telegram, tell Majella.

'Triona Kinsella and Donie McDonnell, wouldn't you know.'

Wouldn't you know is right. Even though four of the eight weddings I was at in the past year were on Fridays, anything but a Saturday is still seen as a bit on the cheap side in BGB. Donie McDonnell would peel an orange in his pocket so it's no surprise he's taken the Ard Rí up on a Sunday deal and the Sunday before Christmas into the bargain. Although, I was at a wedding on a Tuesday last year and it nearly killed me to put the money in the card. A Tuesday! I don't think even Donie would be so brazen.

'I haven't seen Triona Kinsella in years. What's she up to?'

'She's still cutting hair in Crops and Bobbers in Knock, but Donie was telling me there's a new beauty place opening where Scissor Sisters used to be in BGB and she's sent in her CV. She'll be saving about €2 a month on petrol – he'll be delighted.' So that's what's happening to Róisín's old salon.

'Jesus, that's very exciting. Although we'll miss Róisín something fierce. Nobody could do a French plait tighter than her.'

'I know! We'll be back level pegging with Knock again and about time too,' Maj squeals.

The rivalry between Ballygobbard and Knocknamanagh knows no bounds. They're both typical Irish villages separated by a warren of country roads. Combined, they'd actually have enough in them to make up a decent town: a bank (them), a Chinese (us), a chipper (them), the Scout den (us), the library (them) and a whole clatter of pubs, as well as the requisite schools. But unfortunately each only has a few of these amenities. In my opinion, Knock is a bit more glamorous due to the thriving Brazilian community that arrived a few years ago, but I would never admit it. The Rovers and Rangers inevitably end up in the county final every year and it can get very dramatic with punches being thrown both on and off the pitch in the past. Daddy used to be mad for the drama, being a former centre forward himself.

'I've heard they're going to be doing nail art and everything.'

'In Ballygobbard?' I say, slightly incredulous.

'Yeah, in BG-feckin-B, Ais! Shove it up your hole, Knock!' And we both clink glasses.

She stands up and drains the last of the wine. I relieve her of her glass and she's gone, out the back door into the night. I lock it behind her, leave a key under the bin for Paul and head upstairs to turn on Mammy's electric blanket.

CHAPTER 7

We've settled for a small tree Paul got in Filan's. It's more of a shrub but Eamon Filan had sprayed a bit of fake snow on it and added ten euro to the price so it's festive enough for us, and beggars can't be choosers the morning of Christmas Eve. I just couldn't bear the thought of no tree at all, and Mammy's suggestion of putting the presents around the spider plant on the hall table was never going to wash. It's a weird old morning, tinged with the excitement that always hangs in the air on Christmas Eve, no matter how hard to you try to ignore it, but overshadowed by the three of us wafting around the house, intermittently sniffing and sighing, avoiding each other in case it's too sad. I caught Paul in the front room rubbing his eyes, looking at pictures on the mantelpiece. The four of us on the ferry to Wales – our first holiday abroad and memorable for the fact that Daddy forgot the pegs for the tent and had to go around begging one each off loads of other families in the campsite. He made best friends with a man from Yorkshire who still sends a card every year with a joke about the pegs. This year's is probably sitting in the unopened pile.

'Will we go, Mammy?' We've agreed that we need to go and do the Big Shop, no matter what. We've done it together every Christmas Eve for as long as I can remember, firing cocktail sausages and stuffing mix and pâté for the Hattons into the trolley. This year neither of us broached the subject until Paul went into the Nice Things press last night and exclaimed that there wasn't even a Pringle to be had. 'We can't have Christmas without Pringles,' he said in a small voice. He was right. We're not complete animals. Ordinarily there'd be at least two boxes of Tayto under the (full-sized) tree by now, several pipes of green Pringles in the press, two packets of mince pies on top of the bread bin and three more in the freezer and enough minerals in the shed to put out a fire. Not to mention the few notiony bits I usually pick up from Marks and Sparks before I leave Dublin. It's the only time of the year I'd do anything even approaching a Big Shop in there. Sure you couldn't leave three-for-two chicken filo cranberry parcels behind you. And if you can't have a Prosecco-flavoured kettle chip at Christmas, when can you? I've been known to fill an M&S basket with my Christmas bits. I've never gone for a trolley, though – I'm not completely mad. Do they even have trolleys at M&S? What would people be putting in them besides cookies the size of your head and turkey and gold leaf sandwiches?

Anyway, I didn't make the M&S pilgrimage this year. I didn't have the heart. But sitting down last night without even a Terry's Chocolate Orange to smash off the kitchen table (3 Points per segment) or a Curly Wurly to fight over (3 Points for a bar, but who's counting at Christmas, to be fair), I announced that we were off to Aldi in the morning. The 'new' Aldi, as everyone calls it. It's been there for two years but there was such excitement when it opened just outside Knock that nobody's really gotten over it yet. It's still the talk of the town when the new catalogue comes out every week. There are families in BGB who are lucky to get pancakes once a year in February and whose only exposure to Asian food is the chicken curry in BGB's Chinese takeaway but are now the proud owners of a waffle maker and a dumpling steamer, thanks to the new Aldi.

'Have you the trolley token, Mammy?' She may be beside herself with grief but there's no way Mammy would ever go to the supermarket without a trolley token. And she's dead right – you could be caught without a euro, and some of the trolleys now only take a €2 coin. It's like Russian roulette. I've gifted more trolley tokens to Sadhbh and Elaine than I'd like to admit, and I still catch them coming out of Tescos with bags of quinoa and freekah falling out of their arms. I'll miss the pair of them all the same.

Aldi isn't as heaving as I feared, and we get a space after circling the car park only three times. Constance Swinford was in front of us in the queue, and as we pull in I spot her climbing out of her Range Rover like she's abseiling down the Cliffs of Moher. Daddy had a jeep for the farm, all right, but what would you be at bringing a horse of a car like that to Aldi? The spaces are notoriously narrow. Tessie Daly, who volunteers in the charity shop with Mammy, wrote to the council about them after getting stuck between her Ford Focus and a Renault Megane trying to exit the driver's side. They had to call the driver of the Megane over the speaker in the shop.

'Showing off,' Mammy says, as if reading my mind as I stare at Constance. Are all her clothes just different shades of brown, I wonder? Rich people are mad about brown clothes.

She's fierce posh and doesn't really seem to do much except ride horses and host the odd charity dinner above at Garbally Stud. She's also heavily involved in Tidy Towns, probably so her swanky friends aren't traumatised by the state of the hanging baskets and the 1996 Memorial Community Games flower bed when they come through the town. BGB and Knock jointly hosted the Community Games regional finals in 1996 and the pride is still strong. Mammy and Tessie Daly have a debrief on the phone about Constance after every Tidy Towns meeting. There's a lot of talk about the way she pronounces the 'mulch' for the flowerbeds. Mammy's impression of her is good. 'Mmmaaalch.'

It's not too bad inside Aldi either, thank God. We have a list and can always stop off at Filan's for any extra bits on the way home. Green Pringles, for example – the Aldi ones just won't do for Christmas. Paul is at home hoovering the whole house. I warned him to do it as we were leaving. The house is always spotless for Christmas and I don't want Mammy getting down about the state of the floors. If we can get through the next few days with the least amount of upset possible, I'll be bloody delighted to see the back of the whole thing. For now, though, we need sprouts and at least three packets of 'just in case' crackers and everything else in between. I don't think we'll have many visitors given the circumstances but you never know, and Una Hatton's beak is not going to be put out of joint by a half-arsed cracker plate, not on my watch. Paul emitted a strangled gasp when I suggested not getting a turkey. Mammy didn't order one from Boland's and, even though they have mounds of them in Aldi, we really don't need one. We're going to Auntie Sheila's for Christmas dinner and it will be just the four … the three of us on St Stephenses Day, we've decided. So a chicken will do. Or one of those boned and rolled yokes at the very least.

We're just rounding into the bakery aisle for some trifle sponges – Mammy has no heed on making a trifle this year, but it's not Christmas if you don't buy some to sit in the press – when we run smack into Constance Swinford.

'Marian,' she exhales, grasping at Mammy's sleeve. 'How. Are. You?' Each word comes out like a separate honk on a tuba, her Camilla Parker Bowles hair shaking under her frankly ridiculous Crocodile Dundee hat. Why is she even wearing a hat? We're inside!

'Ah, sure. It's … hard enough.' Tidy Towns is on winter hiatus so this might be the first time Mammy's seen Constance properly since the funeral. Mammy's voice shakes as she places her hand in a firm grip over Constance's, in the way women of a certain age tend to hold onto each other. I shift from one foot to the other, biting my lip and frantically blinking to get rid of the prickling tears. 'I'm sure, I'm sure.' Constance is looking straight into Mammy's face and nodding. Her own husband died about fifteen years ago, so I suppose she knows what it's like. My eyes flick over to her trolley. About twenty packets of smoked salmon and a box of Weetybrix. Even Constance Swinford isn't too posh for imitation cereal, I see.

'Marian,' she says again, 'you have my number, don't you? Do give me a call. I'd love to have you over for tea. We widows have to stick together.'

Mammy does a tiny little gasp. It's probably the first time someone's said the W word out loud to her, and it's quite shocking to hear. But she gathers herself and gives Constance's hand another squeeze.

'I will. That would be lovely. Really lovely.'

'Now, did you hear?' Constance changes the subject swiftly. 'They're finally doing something with that building out near me.'

Some Dublin construction company started a mini apartment block just outside BGB at the height of the boom, but it was never properly finished. I think they were hoping to lure poor tourists down to 'luxury rentals' near the bit of a lake over by Garbally and 'authentic Irish pints' back in Maguire's. Authentic Irish Guinness farts more like it. The building has been lying idle for years, though, and regularly features in the rundown from the local council meetings posted on the back of the church newsletter.

'Oh?'

'Well, something's going on with it anyway.' Constance's voice booms over the mixed peel. 'There's been some activity over the past few days, and there's talk of them finishing the flower beds out the front too. They contacted me to see if I could provide them with any mmmaaalch.'

Somehow, me and Mammy managed to wait until Constance had moved far enough away towards the tills before completely collapsing with laughter. 'Mmmaaalch,' I whispered to her as we bade our goodbyes and Happy Christmases and headed for the roulades. '*Mmmaaalch.*'

'Shhh,' Mammy responded furiously, but her shoulders were helplessly shaking.

****

'Do we have enough, do you think?' Mammy asks as we unload everything onto the kitchen table, Paul rooting in the bags, emitting sounds of satisfaction as he pulls out a tin of Roses or a frozen pavlova. 'We're grand, Mammy,' I reassure her. Besides, you can run down to Filan's on Christmas morning and knock on the door if you're stuck and they'll give you whatever batteries or rashers you're looking for, if they have any left. Mammy even got a ham out of them the year That Bloody Cat ate a quarter of the one she'd cooked on Christmas Eve. Daddy had gone a bit soft after three festive brandies in Maguire's and let her into the kitchen (the cat, not Mammy) and forgot to put her out again. She was discovered the following morning, belly like an enormous turnip and the ham looking like something out of *Saving Private Ryan*.

'Mammy?' I ask cautiously as I load rashers into the fridge. 'Are we … going to mass this year?' Paul's head snaps up to look at me and then at Mammy.

Traditionally, Christmas Eve involved a trip to midnight mass at eight and then a few drinks in Maguire's before they'd hoosh everyone out at half eleven, Mikey Maguire bellowing at everyone that he still had a *My Little Pony* Dream Castle to put together. Last year Mad Tom tried to make off with the giant plastic donkey from Maguire's legendary life-size crib. He was sneaking past Mikey Maguire, only concealing about half of one of the donkey's ears under his coat, the rest of it dragging behind him, the hooves taking the ankles off people. Mikey has the patience of an absolute saint.

The thought of mass brings a feeling of dread over me. I'd definitely cry when the BGB Singers broke into 'The Little Drummer Boy'. Daddy's favourite.

'I don't think I will, no, Aisling. You go if you like, pet.'

The relief is almost unbelievable, and I can feel it wash over Paul too. We couldn't have let Mammy go to mass on her own.

'We'll light Daddy's candle for him and put it in the window, and then we can watch Santy on the news,' she continues.

Daddy always lit a candle in the window on Christmas Eve, 'to guide the lost souls home'. The mention of it is too much for me and I hurry from the kitchen, muttering something about having presents to wrap.

****

'Knock, knock?'

I didn't even hear John coming in the back door. Or Mammy calling me to let me know he was there. I must have fallen asleep on my bed, phone in my hand, combing through the job sites.

'Come in,' I call, sitting up and raking my hands through my hair.

His dark head pokes around the door and he waggles a small wrapped box at me. 'Ho, ho, ho,' he says gently, and I move over on the bed and nod at him to sit down. We always give each other our presents on Christmas Eve. John spends the evening and Christmas Day beyond in Knock, and then everyone's back together in the pub on Stephenses Day. I ordered John's present online a month ago and broke my own rule about getting stuff delivered to work to make sure it arrived safely. Some people have packages arriving every second day and the time theft doesn't bear thinking about. Imagine how much of it they've ordered when they're supposed to be processing calls and what have you. Not that it makes much difference now, I suppose.

Over the past few years John and I have slipped into a routine of getting each other the same old things: jewellery or perfume for me and watches or aftershave for him. You run out of ideas, don't you? But after getting back together I wanted to make more of an effort and get him something special. Something meaningful. Digging around in the bag of presents at the foot of the bed, I retrieve a rectangular box and wave it at him shyly. 'You go first.'

He grins and dutifully reads the card before tearing the paper away from the plain brown box.

'Oooh, what's this now?' he teases. Lifting the lid, he gasps. 'Ah, Ais. Isn't that just great?'

He lifts it out. A lovely steel and leather hipflask with the number seventeen engraved on the front. He turns it over in his big soft hand. 'Love, A' is engraved in smaller writing on the back.

'For seventeen kisses,' I offer, although he already knows that. We're always nudging each other when we see the number seventeen anywhere. Our own special little thing.

'I love it!' he exclaims, lashing his arm around my waist and planting a kiss on my lips.

His smile wanes a bit as he thrusts the small box at me, and I weigh it in my hands for a second, trying to guess what it could be. Nothing like the anticipation of a present. Ripping off the paper I see the familiar branding pop out at me.

'Oooh, Pandora!' I can't help but feel a nudge of disappointment, though. This won't be the first Pandora he's gotten me. Still, though, I'm sure it's lovely.

Sliding open the box and moving the layer of tissue paper aside, my heart drops a little. 'Ah, it's lovely.'

He bites his lip. 'Do you not like it?'

'No, no, it's lovely. But ...'

I hold out my arm and pull up the sleeve of my Christmas jumper. John looks from my wrist to the box and back again.

'They're not ... they're not the exact same, are they?' he stammers.

They are. They're the exact same. Two Christmases in a row.

'I have the receipt,' he babbles. 'I'll get you something else. I'll bring it back.'

'It's grand, love. It's grand. I'll do it.' I laugh to ease the awkwardness but he's raging with himself, I can tell. 'Honestly, John, it's grand. It's the thought that counts. I love it. Again.'

'Ah, Ais, I'm sorry. I should have tried harder. You went to so much trouble and I ...'

Like me buying his mammy's slippers, I have a feeling John's mammy has been buying me the Pandora bracelets. He suddenly looks sad and I grab him in a hug and whisper, 'Happy Christmas.' He hugs me back even tighter, and we sit like that for minutes.

Eventually he releases me and stretches out his arms. 'I better hit the road. Fran is making soup before mass and I'll be killed if I'm late.'

He stands up and holds his arms out again, and I fold myself into them.

'Happy Christmas, love.'

I don't say anything, I just rest my head on his shoulder, turn my face in to his chest and breathe deeply. It's only a bracelet, isn't it?

****

It's an odd Christmas Eve. We skip the traditional sausages and mash for dinner and just have sandwiches instead. We watch Santy take off from the North Pole on the six o'clock news as usual – he always sounds like he's from Roscommon or Wexford; a very local Santy, it must be said – but instead of the rush then to get ready for mass and the pub, we settle down in the front room, a tin of sweets within everyone's reach and *Scrooged* on the telly. Nobody has spoken for at least fifteen minutes, alone in their thoughts, when Mammy suddenly gets up out of her chair and walks quickly out of the room. 'What's that about?' Paul is going for a Strawberry Dream, the animal. I'm a fan of the nutty ones. Partial to a purple, if it's going.

'Dunno, maybe she's getting her phone?' Mammy's deep distrust of her smartphone still hasn't left her, and she often hides it in her bedroom in case it tries to get her to do something she doesn't understand. She heard about scam phone calls on *Liveline* and now everybody is a suspect, even Auntie Sheila. But when she comes back into the room it's not a phone. She has two envelopes in her hand.

'These are for you, for Christmas.' She hands us one each. The scrawly handwriting on the front makes my stomach leap into my throat.

'They're from Daddy.'

CHAPTER 8

I have it in my pocket when the doorbell goes. I run my fingers along the edge of the envelope as Una Hatton holds out her glass for a Baileys top up. We weren't expecting the usual throng of post-mass Christmas-morning visitors, but we knew Majella and the Hattons at least would call in. And Tessie Daly from the charity shop. It's very much a case of too many cooks in there. Mammy has already started going back a couple of mornings a week, and Tessie has been very good to her, letting her sort clothes out the back when dealing with well-meaning customers got a bit too much.

Niamh Hatton is over talking to Paul, twirling the wooden beads around her neck between her fingers as I trace the outline of the card beneath the thin material of my skirt (Dorothy Perkins in the pre-Christmas sale – a lovely red check and a jumper to match). I bet you anything even the wood of Niamh's necklace is recycled. If wood can be recycled, that is. I'm sure it can. If they can recycle toilet paper they can recycle anything. Niamh is sipping from a glass of water, having rejected a Baileys offered by Paul and a cube of Wensleydale stuck under her nose by Majella, mouthing, 'Vegan, sorry' and 'Oh no, lovey, I can't, I'm vegan.'

'Did you know she's a vegan?' Maj whispers sarcastically as she passes me on her way back to the kitchen. There's no love lost between Majella and Niamh – Niamh protested dissecting a hare's heart in sixth year and Majella has always blamed her for the C3 she got in Leaving Cert Biology. After three vodkas she'll tell you the whole year failed, but I got a B1, although I usually just leave her off to have her rant. And Niamh has always claimed Maj is the reason Neil Ferrissy dumped her, but nobody has ever been able to prove the affair and Maj is not one to kiss and tell so who knows.

'Niamh from Across the Road is looking well.' Paul whistles as he pushes past me to sit on the couch. Niamh Hatton has lived across the road from me my whole life. She graduated from hosting an annual Amnesty International table quiz when we were in school to living in New York doing something with recycled Converse and yoga and posting pictures on Facebook of tiny cups of coffee and elaborate plates of leaves titled 'This vegan life' or simply 'Brunch!' How many times a week can one person eat brunch? I must admit I've developed a fondness for it myself since moving to Dublin, thanks to Elaine and Sadhbh and their insistance that only animals eat breakfast or lunch at the weekend, but I think even they'd say Niamh needs to calm down with the acai bowls. Her clothes are all various hues of wheat too, and I doubt she's ever suffered the indignity of a pair of fally-down tights from Penneys.

I take the opportunity of nobody talking to me to escape to the bathroom. Locking the door behind me and sinking down onto the edge of the bath, I pull the envelope out of my pocket. It's already curling at the edges. I'll have to put it inside a heavy book to keep it good. My Maeve Binchy anthology, maybe, or that Colette Green beauty manual Majella got me for my last birthday. Who knew you could get sixteen pages out of colouring in your eyebrows? 'Aisling' is scrawled across the small envelope in his unmistakable hand. I slide out the card, a Christmas penguin in a scarf on the front. One from a charity set Mammy brought home from the shop last year, each one worth one-fiftieth of a well in Africa or something. I open the card for at least the tenth time in the last twelve hours.

'Happy Christmas, pet. Buy yourself something nice. Love, Daddy.'

·Just the sight of his handwriting makes me catch my breath. The curl of the *y*, the swooping *l* – so familiar it winds me and I have to grip the edge of the bath to steady myself. A crisp €50 note is folded across in half, pinned to the inside cover of the card with a paperclip. There wouldn't have been a paper clip if the card was being posted, mind. Scammers would feel it and know there was money inside. We know all the tricks.

He gave the cards to Mammy months ago. When he was almost all there but not quite. Worrying already about Christmas presents he might not be around to give. I run my finger over the 'Love, Daddy' and give a big shuddering sigh. I slide the card back into its little envelope, taking care not to catch the paper clip. Back into my pocket it goes. Back out to the Baileys and the low hum of Mammy telling Tessie about what Constance Swinford said about the building site over on the Garbally Road, and Paul telling Don Hatton what the Kerrygold situation in Bondi is like.

'I'm actually going to be moving home,' Majella is saying matter-of-factly to Niamh as I rejoin them in the front room. 'And Ais might too,' she says, turning to welcome me, mouthing a 'thank fuck' as she does.

'Oh, you're moving home too, Aisling?' Niamh tilts her head.

'Well, no. I haven't decided what I'm doing. I … I'm about to be offered redundancy and I'm taking it. So …' Offered redundancy doesn't sound quite as bad as 'made redundant.'

'I'd say your mum is delighted.' Niamh smiles. She's not that bad, to be fair to her. I turn back to Majella to change the subject, though. I haven't even mentioned the idea to Mammy and now is not the time to be getting into it.

'BGB won't know what hit it with Maj back in town.' I nudge Majella and smile, while Niamh's face takes on a look of concern.

'Did the primary teaching turn out to be a bit much after all or …?'

Majella grits her teeth. 'I'm actually moving home to save some money. To save for a house with my …' she pauses for unmistakable dramatic effect, 'boyfriend.'

I don't think I've ever seen Niamh look put out, but that's how she looked leaving to go home for her nut roast. Majella cheerfully told her about Pablo and how he's from Tenerife and how brown he goes in the sun, and I realise I never even asked about how the chat with Shem and Liz went. The second Niamh is out the door I pounce on her.

'Well? What did they say about Pablo moving in?'

'Oh, Ais, you should have seen Shem's face.' Shem Moran contemplating a Spaniard moving into his house is something I would pay good money to see. I'd say he was puce.

'Mammy seemed to kind of like the idea. She likes Pablo. He's always complimenting her and saying he's never seen potatoes cooked so many ways before. He says he likes her "hanging waskets" too and, sure, she's delighted. Shem's not so convinced. So I says to him, "Shem."' Majella calls her father Shem when she's needling him for something. It only serves to drive him even madder. 'I says, "Shem, it's either he moves in here or you spend the next year driving me out to the Ard Rí or wherever to see him." That shut him up.'

'So he's moving in?'

'He's moving in,' she confirms with a beam and a satisfied nod of her head. 'In fact, he's at home now trying to convince them to put mojo sauce on the turkey instead of gravy.' Shem and Pablo sharing a bathroom and a remote. This should be interesting.

****

The rest of Christmas Day passes in a bit of a blur. It's strange going to Auntie Sheila's for dinner, but she insisted. It's the first time ever we haven't been in our own house for the turkey, and the thought of the table sitting there empty makes me sad. Also, my cousin Doireann had just folded the serviettes in half and put them beside the placemats. The table was definitely missing the flourish of my traditional and signature 'shaken out napkin in a glass' decoration. Very elegant.

John rings as we're on the way home to see if I want him to call down, but going to someone else's house on Christmas Night is practically against the law. You're not supposed to see anyone but your family. Besides, I'll see him tomorrow.

Elaine texts and Sadhbh rings too, sneaking out of a family row over Monopoly and whether or not her brother has been abusing his position as the banker. She's giddy on Prosecco, having started drinking at midday. How is she not in a heap? Maj was going home earlier to get stuck into the Bucks Fizz. I have images of Shem with Pablo in a headlock at this stage. Sadhbh thanks me for being a good friend and an even better housemate and drunkenly says she's going to miss me lecturing her on the difference between a hand towel and tea towel. I feel like she could start crying so I gently remind her that I'll be seeing her in a few days for the wedding. The call ends abruptly then when she stands on a hotel and signs off, swearing, and I stick my head into the front room and announce that I'm heading up to bed. It's only half nine but I'm glad to see the back of the day. Paul is glued to James Bond surfing a speedboat in his knickers and Mammy is dozing on the couch. I put on my new pyjamas (thanks, Mammy), wrap my hair up in my new Colette Green turban to clean my face (thanks, Majella) and slide the little envelope out of my skirt, lying on the chair in the corner. I gently pull the carefully folded fifty euro note and the paper clip off the card and lean over to pluck my wallet out of my bag, sliding the fifty into the compartment at the back along with Daddy's laminated mass card. You never know when I might need it.

CHAPTER 9

As much as I'd been dreading Christmas these last few months, I could never say a bad word about Stephenses Day. It's no exaggeration to say it's one of the highlights of my social calendar – every pub in BGB and Knock will be hopping from early afternoon, with people dying to show off their Christmas presents and get away from their families. And then it's always on to the Vortex 'till late', aka 2 a.m.

You'd think my gang would be sick of going to the Vortex, considering we've been at it since we were seventeen, but it's tradition, plus John always gets us in for free because being the Rangers centre forward gives him a certain gravitas around here. At least it's not too far, slap bang between BGB and Knock and attached to the side of the Mountrath Hotel. The décor hasn't changed since well before we first started going there, I should add – peeling yellow ceilings, 1970s wallpaper and sticky carpets all the way into the toilet cubicles and halfway up the walls. No problem bringing your drink onto the dancefloor in the Vortex either. The place has one bouncer – Jamesie Kelly – who's supposed to mind the entire Mountrath, so pints being sloshed around to 'I Gotta Feeling' and 'Sex on Fire' are the least of his problems, especially since it's become so popular with stags looking for a cheap place to go outside Dublin. He spends most of his time trying to control roaming gangs of Father Teds and Where's Wallys, God love him. And him on a crutch.

'I'd say you'd want to book Terry Crowley early, pet,' Mammy says, coming in to the bathroom where I'm putting on my make-up. While Majella has taken to doing a full face with her Colette Green products, I'm still loyal to my bit of tinted moisturiser, brown mascara and Heather Shimmer. She tried to contour me once and it was the closest both of us ever came to dying laughing; I was like a blended toffee apple. And anyway, aren't freckles a thing of beauty? You wouldn't want to cover them up. Sadhbh has persuaded me to do a flick of black liquid eyeliner the odd time but I have a shaky hand and I'd be afraid to start by myself in case I couldn't stop and I just had to keep making it thicker and longer, like when I used to cut my Barbie's hair: it was never just a trim.

Another day, another little reminder of Daddy's absence. 'Dad's Taxi' – he had the bumper stickers to prove it. He was always only a text away on Stephenses night, waiting up specially with one eye on the racing highlights and the other on his phone. But no, I'll have to book Terry Crowley to get us all home later. Oh, I could chance standing outside the Mountrath at half two and hoping for the best but that wouldn't exactly be my style, and I'm fairly sure none of the others would have the foresight to book him either.

Rain or shine, Terry has his window down and elbow out, all the better to roar a 'well, head' or 'hup' to anyone he passes when he's booting down either BGB's or Knock's respective main streets. He has a grand seven-seater and has been known to squeeze in eleven of us after a wedding or a twenty-first, whipping up and down the pitch-black back roads and pot-holed lanes, firing people out and collecting tenners. If I didn't know better, I'd say he had some kind of government interrogation training. His line of questioning can get *that* intrusive. Daddy applied for planning permission for a new calving shed once, and Terry was just short of shining a light in my face trying to extract the finer details of the plans. Although, if you're looking to know who just sold five acres or whether there's anyone in the funeral home, he's your man.

'Will do, Mammy.' I smile back at her weakly. Auntie Sheila will probably call down for a while but other than that she'll be in the house on her own, having rejected various invitations to cards nights and drops of sherry in houses around the village. Unless Paul is willing to sacrifice his Stephenses night and stay in with her, but that's highly unlikely when he's due to go back to Oz next week. I don't think he's noticed how down Mammy is. She's even stopped hiding the good biscuits. It's not like her, not like her at all.

I'm just checking the time on my phone – 3.30 p.m. – when Majella texts.

'Maguire's @ 4?'

I feel so guilty for even thinking it, but I'm looking forward to getting out of the house myself. It's been hard to put on the brave face, to mindlessly eat the Roses and drink the minerals while acting like we're not all just trying to survive this nightmare. I can't wait to go to the pub and talk and laugh and be a normal person for a few hours.

While magazines make a big deal about what you should wear on Christmas Day – a cosy yet sexy jumper – and New Year's Eve – something you'll freeze in – none of them mention Stephenses Day, which I've always found baffling. It's a hard one to nail because I'm going out early, but ultimately it's an Out Out night: there will definitely be shots and dancing to 'Country Roads' in my future. After much deliberation, I decide on jeans and a nice top, with my good Clarks boots. Sure you can't go wrong.

It's bang on four when Paul drops me into Maguire's, but Majella and Pablo are already sequestered at a corner table, wrapped around each other.

'Ais, I have the pints in,' Maj roars as soon as she sees me, and I'm barely out of my coat and scarf when Pablo is up kissing me on both cheeks. Of course I go red because, well, it's not normal.

'Well, what did you get?' Maj quizzes me, but before I can trot out the story I've prepared about how gas it is that John got me the same present two years in a row, she's pulling up her good glittery jumper to expose her chest, bringing me face to face with … Pablo. Pablo's big grinning face on a T-shirt, surrounded by superimposed hearts.

'Isn't he just gas?' Majella laughs, squeezing Pablo's knee. She leans in closer to me. 'There are knickers too. And a necklace. And a square of carpet from the Ard Rí in a frame – the location of our first kiss.'

'My God, he went all out!' I settle into my seat as John arrives in the door of the pub, and I wave and call over to him, grateful for the distraction. He's wearing a new check shirt I know his mammy bought him for Christmas and his good Levi's. Liam Kelly, one of the Rangers, and Denise, his new wife, are with him. John gives me a peck on the cheek (he's my boyfriend, to be fair to him, so that's allowed – not like Pablo's big smackers) while Liam makes a big deal of pulling out a chair for Denise and practically helping her into it. I notice she has a big new Michael Kors on her arm. Fair dues, the boy done good.

'Pints, lads?' John says, doing the international hand signal for 'pints, lads?'

'We're grand,' I reply with a smile, turning away from Maj and Pablo, who are staring at each other like a big pair of loved-up dopes.

'Just a soda water and lime for me, thanks, John,' Denise says quietly, and Majella and I both immediately whip around and lock eyes.

Another one bites the dust. That's the third WAG now to get pregnant in the last six months, and there's already been talk of a joint baby shower. Being the organiser of the group – well, *any* group – I'd usually be all over it, booking the venue and delegating jobs, but I'm finding it hard to get on board with these American trends that seem to be all the rage. What next, carrying little pink guns in our handbags? Suzanne in work did a gender reveal on Chloe and I nearly choked on my Light Babybel (1 Point) when she explained it to me. Apparently, whoever did the scan in the hospital wrote the sex of the baby on a piece of paper and sealed it in an envelope. Then Suzanne's sister brought it to a bakery and asked them to bake either a blue or pink cake, depending on what was written on the paper, and cover it all in white icing. That weekend they had a party and Suzanne cut the cake and everyone went spare because it was pink for a girl.

I don't know why, and I hate myself for it, but I'm suddenly very conscious of my bare ring finger. It's my competitive nature – I can't help it. I glance over at John and think back to all the other Stephenses nights we've had here together and now something seems ... off. Missing. This awkwardness between us just won't go away. I'm trying to remember when it started but I just can't. Everything was so perfect, so *easy*, when we got back together. But something has slipped away in the meantime.

'Not drinking tonight, Denise?' I ask casually. I can see she's dying for someone to comment on it and it's only fair. I'd be the same.

'I can't, Ais, I'm on antibiotics,' she replies with a little smile, not quite meeting my eye. It's a common dance among women my age and I'm well used to it at this stage.

'Is it the, eh, breast?' Pablo asks, making a vague hand gesture in the direction of her boobs, and Denise flushes and looks over at Liam.

'Jesus, Pablo,' Majella shrieks, extracting herself from his arms, 'what are you on about her breast for?'

'It's as I was saying earlier,' Pablo says, doing his mad hand gestures. 'Same as Eamon, with the breast infection.'

'*Chest*,' I say firmly, picking up my pint of Coors Light and taking a sip. 'It's a chest infection Eamon Filan has. Mother of God!'

Thankfully, John arrives back at the table with the drinks before Pablo can mention Denise's breasts again.

'Where's everyone else?' he asks, cracking open a can. 'It's nearly half four.'

'Maeve Hennessey, Sinéad McGrath and Deirdre Ruane are over in Dick's in Knock, but Dee just texted me and they're leaving shortly,' Majella replies. 'Apparently there's a bit of drama outside – a dog bit Mad Tom and he bit it back. The vet is on the way.'

Dick's is the Maguire's of Knock. As well as being pubs, they both sell a few grocery essentials and a bit of miscellaneous hardware. Light bulbs, fishing tackle, that kind of thing. The shop part of Maguire's was recently refurbished so we certainly have the upper hand there – they accept debit cards and all. Since the local garda station closed down neither pub observes the licensing laws too carefully, although Maguire's tends to stay open the longest and thus pulls in the late crowd. Dick Shea doesn't have the stamina for it anymore.

'My cousin is coming out tonight too,' Denise pipes up. 'She's actually moving to Ballygobbard in a couple of weeks so I told her tonight would be a good night to meet everyone. She won't be here till later, though, because she's driving up from Waterford.'

'No offence, but why the hell is she moving here?'

Majella doesn't mince her words. I mean, I'll defend BGB until the end of time, especially if someone from Knock is slagging it off, but I have to admit there's not a lot going on here compared to the buzzing metropolis of Waterford.

'She's opening the new beauty salon beside Boland's,' Denise explains, and I notice John and Liam drifting off towards the tellies showing the racing action from Leopardstown. Pablo remains glued to Majella, listening to Denise and holding one of Majella's hands between his two little brown paws. They're fierce cute. I can't help but feel a pang of longing for that fresh flush of a relationship. You can't beat it.

Denise continues. 'She'll be doing hair, massages, nails, everything. It'll be dead handy for weddings in the Ard Rí, and she's even talking about doing a mobile service down the line, once she has enough staff, where she'll come to your house and give you a blow-dry in your kitchen.'

The door opens and Maeve, Sinéad and Deirdre walk in, followed by a selection of the lads in their Out Out uniforms of Rangers zip-up jackets and bootcut jeans. A few of the BGB Rovers senior team are propping up the bar, but until training for the new season starts there's a temporary ceasefire, so cue lots of back slapping and beard rubbing and talk of turkey sandwiches, while Felipe doles out pints and cans and pre-emptive packets of taytos so we can all line our stomachs.

'Well, lads,' Sinéad says, sitting down opposite me, can of Budweiser in her hand. 'Did you all survive?' She glances around the table, her eyes lingering on me the longest.

'Ah, it was grand,' I reply, trying to sound cheerful. 'Different, but grand. Any craic in Knock?'

'Billy Foran was mouldy,' Deirdre says, squeezing in beside Sinéad. 'He was telling anyone who'd listen that some drug lord is after buying that eyesore of a half-finished building on the Garbally Road. He's sure the village is going to become a sort of hub for organised crime.'

Well, I've heard it all now. Good luck to anyone trying to smuggle arms or launder money around here. The Neighbourhood Watch would be all over it in ten seconds flat now that they have their text-alert group up and running. Every time a white HiAce drives through the village Mammy's phone starts hopping. According to Una Hatton, white HiAces are always a cause for suspicion.

'Actually, there is something going on out there,' I pipe up. 'Constance Swinford said something about it to Mammy in Aldi on Christmas Eve. And she'd know – it's out by her place.'

'Did she mention her mmmaaalch, Ais?' Majella asks, coming up for air, and two pints are knocked from the table with the laughing.

****

It's nearly eleven by the time Terry Crowley pulls up outside the Vortex, where the queue is snaking around the corner, almost reaching the main entrance of the Mountrath. I took one for the team and sat in the front passenger seat, ready to field the inevitable inquisition, but he went easy on me, apart from a few gentle enquiries about what we had for Christmas dinner and whether the early lambs have started coming yet and how is Mammy coping at all, at all?

'You know yourself, Terry,' is all I could muster, and he just nodded. He lost his sister to cancer a few years ago. Who hasn't been touched by it at this stage?

After everyone pours out of the car – John, Maj, Pablo and the three girls, all pretty fluthered and still clutching their glasses and cans from Maguire's – we troop to the top of the queue where Jamesie shakes John's hand and ushers us inside with his crutch to the opening strains of 'Mambo No. 5' – a Vortex classic if ever there was one.

Denise is still going, fair dues to her, and has our usual table behind the back bar secured after driving out to the

Mountrath ahead of us. It took years of deliberation, but in 2012 we all agreed that this spot has it all – equidistant between the bar and the toilets, ample space to take our coats and dark enough to cover you pouring out a naggin if you're nineteen and broke as a joke but determined to get a full night out of a tenner.

Sitting beside Denise is someone I don't recognise, someone who's definitely not from BGB – or Knock, for that matter. She's very brown and very tall (as tall as Baby Chief Gittons, although she's sitting down so it might be all torso – I've a very long back myself) with white blonde hair down past her shoulders. The lads – Baby Chief, Philip Johnsie, Titch Maguire, The Truck and Eoin Ó Súilleabháin, aka Cyclops – are at the next table nudging each other like they can't believe they're in the presence of such an out-and-out babe.

'Who's your wan?' Majella hisses in my ear from behind, before pushing a vodka and Diet Coke into my hand. 'Her eyebrows are amazing.'

Eyebrows are not something I think about from one end of the day to the next, but it feels like everyone around me is always going on about them. Of course I keep mine in check, plucking them fortnightly with a handy little tweezers I got from the JML stand in Tesco (it has a built-in light and a travel case) but Sadhbh and Elaine have professionals who look after theirs, and now Majella is at it too: 3D brows, microblading, embrowdery – they might as well be talking a different language for all I understand.

'Yeah, they're fierce … defined,' I chance, hoping it sounds like I know what I'm on about. I must go into the bathroom and smooth down my hair and see if I have any lipstick left on me at all.

Pablo suddenly appears behind Majella, and I realise that the three of us are just standing there in a row, staring this poor girl out of it.

'Girls, I have seats saved,' Denise calls over to us and we all snap out of it.

I'm the first to arrive at the table, hand outstretched. 'Hiya, I'm Aisling,' I say to the glamazon, who I realise is wearing a crop top. In the Vortex. Did we ever think we'd see the day? 'And this is Majella.' Maj waves a hello from a safe distance, as does Pablo, before dropping their drinks on the table and heading for the dancefloor. Pablo is not like the rest of the lads when it comes to dancing. It takes John at least eight pints to get going, and only if the DJ is playing The Killers, Kings of Leon or his beloved 'Mr Jones'. He doesn't have much rhythm but he makes up for it in enthusiasm, stomping his feet and swinging his arms, lost in the lyrics. Pablo, on the other hand, is very light on his feet and will dance at every opportunity. He was at it the other day in Filan's when I went in for a sneaky oil change – dancing around with the dipstick in his hand. I honestly didn't know where to look.

'This is my cousin Sharon, Aisling, the one I was telling you about,' Denise says pointedly, gesturing for me to sit down at the other side of her, opposite John and Liam. 'She's opening the new beauty salon. It's going to be way better than Scissor Sisters, isn't it, Sharon?'

Sharon nods emphatically. I always liked Scissor Sisters – Róisín used to do a lovely wedding up-do, nice and firm, just the way I like it – so I don't rise to Denise's bait. I'm loyal like that.

'Well, welcome to Ballygobbard, Sharon!' I say diplomatically. 'How are you finding it so far? It'd be fairly quiet now compared to Waterford, I'd say.'

'Thanks a million, Aisling,' she says, knocking back her drink as the opening strains of 'Mi Chico Latino' roar out of the ancient speakers. Majella's work, no doubt. I can only imagine the shapes Pablo is throwing. 'Yeah, it's fairly quiet alright but it's really cute, and the rent is much cheaper. Waterford is a nightmare now and it's only getting worse. I … I was mad to get out of there anyway.' She sneaks a quick look at Denise and then turns back to me, pasting on a smile. 'I can't wait to get settled in. You must come in for a manicure when I open.'

'Yeah, definitely,' I say, and I mean it too. I love a French manicure. Very sophisticated. Mammy put a DIY kit in my Christmas stocking last year but I never got the hang of the little moon-shaped stickers.

'What do you do yourself, Aisling?'

For a minute she has me. What do I do? 'It's a bit complicated at the moment,' I say, taking a gulp of my drink and explaining the whole redundancy situation.

'You'll be in the money so.' She smiles, clinking her glass against mine gently. 'Will you take some time off or are you going to go job hunting straight away?'

'I'm not sure, to be honest,' I admit. She's has a very gentle way about her and is a great listener, but I don't want to go into the whole story of Daddy and my responsibility to Mammy and the farm. I do find myself continuing, though.

'I've started doing up my CV but I'm low on hobbies and I can't bring myself to exaggerate. I'm really not sure what I want to do with the rest of my life. I'm sort of at a crossroads, I suppose.'

Sharon presses her glass against her lip for a minute and thinks. 'Well, what do you like doing? What are you good at?'

Jesus, I wasn't expecting these questions tonight. They're hard! I haven't even asked myself them yet. What do I like doing? What am I good at? All I really know is administration, and I do love it, as boring as that sounds.

'I like numbers,' I say eventually. 'And being organised. Planning. Anything to do with spreadsheets, I suppose.'

'You're a bit like me, hun!' she says, and I'm not sure if she's joking or not. We certainly *look* very, very different, although I notice a pair of ballet flats poking out of her handbag. Appearances can be deceiving.

'*Shots!* Shots, shots, shots!'

I'm just about to ask her what she did before she decided to open the salon when a couple of the girls stumble around the corner with what looks like a tray of thirty Baby Guinnesses. I know we're all a bit old for shots, but there's an unwritten rule that you can't leave the Vortex without doing at least three. I'm just glad we've moved on from tequila. The mid-2000s were rough on the lining of my stomach.

Like moths to a flame, Majella and Pablo arrive back at the table, sweaty and smiling, their hands interlocked. John is in a cluster with the lads and Deirdre is nowhere to be found. I suspect she's the first casualty of the night. The Ruanes are notorious lightweights. Looking around, I realise that the last time the gang was all together was probably Daddy's funeral.

'What'll we toast to?' The Truck shouts, helping himself as we all stand up. He got the nickname because he's built like one; no wonder he only let four goals into the Rangers' net last season.

'How about new beginnings?' Denise goes, holding up her glass of water. She cocks her head at Sharon who whoops and holds up her glass, a bit unsteady in her skyscraper heels. I'm not much better, to be fair.

'New beginnings,' John says, looking down at me. 'New beginnings,' I say back to him quietly. I raise a glass at Majella, who mouths the words back at me before throwing the shot into her. Down in one. No better woman.

Beside her, Pablo downs his too, but I notice his eyes are fixed firmly on Sharon.

CHAPTER 10

'**D**o you fancy going for a drive, Aisling? We could have cup of tea and a cream cake in the new café in Knock Garden Centre? Wait until you see the style.'

Mammy is puttering around the house, walking from room to room, feeling radiators. There's snow forecast and Paul and Paddy Reilly, who's always just a phone call away, have already brought in the sheep from the far field, just in case. Neither of us has stepped outside the house all day, but it'll be dark in a few hours and you'd have to be mad to drive in the dark with snow forecast, so we'd better make a move if we're going. Why do the days between Christmas and New Year's Eve feel so interminable? There's nothing to do and nowhere to go and, to be honest, none of it sits right with me. 'The taint' Majella calls it. John asked me if I wanted to go over and spend the day at his house today but my heart just isn't in it. I don't want to be at home but I don't want to leave either. I suppose I just want to stick close to Mammy. I have the house spotless and all the ironing done; I even briefly thought about starting to go through Daddy's stuff, but no, it's too soon. Far too soon. I could probably relax and enjoy the break if I knew where I stood for certain financially, but at the moment it feels like I'm stuck in limbo.

I've already decided I'm not counting another Point until the New Year so maybe a cream cake would be nice. I might even pick up a few bits in the sale – Knock Garden Centre has started selling designer wellies and Max Benjamin candles and hot tubs and calling itself a 'lifestyle destination'. Apparently they're going to be doing a pumpkin patch next Halloween. None of the locals are falling for it, bar Constance Swinford, who was spotted in there buying a new waxed jacket, but by all accounts customers are coming down from Dublin in their droves to check it out. The boom is back alright.

'Good idea, Mammy. Just let me change out of my slippers.'

It's freezing, and we're gone about ten minutes before the car finally warms up and our breath stops fogging up the windscreen. I'm crawling along the Knock Road, eyes on stalks, looking for the tiniest hint of black ice. You can never be too careful with black ice. Of course I have my hazard triangle and high-vis vest and all the rest of the gear in the boot as per the RSA's guidelines, but I'm not about to take any chances.

'Are you sure he definitely said widespread snow, Aisling? Not just on higher ground?'

'Definitely, Mammy.' I sigh. 'Do you think I'm making it up? He said snow everywhere, and also happy birthday to Raquel in Westmeath. Martin King knows what he's talking about.'

'But sure it's too cold to snow, pet.'

She's right, of course. Declaring it too cold to snow is one of my favourite pastimes. You can't have frost and snow at the same time, it's a well-known fact. I scan the sky for flakes – nothing. But the clouds *are* low and swollen. If I didn't know better …

****

It takes us nearly ten minutes to find a space in the Knock Garden Centre car park, such is the number of D-reg cars clogging up the place. But I'm relieved to see that the new café has a separate side entrance. I had visions of having to walk through the plant part with Mammy and being forced to stop and admire every geranium and hydrangea and peace lily along the way.

As soon as I get inside the café I realise what the fuss is all about. Mother of God, there are cakes as far as the eye can see! Buns, pastries, fresh cream cakes – it's heaven. I take my eyes off Mammy to grab a table and when I turn around I find her deep in conversation with none other than Una Hatton. Of course, I should have known she'd be here, being Protestant. She'd never let you forget it.

'There you are, Aisling,' she trills, rubbing Mammy's arm. 'Aren't you a dote bringing your mum out for tea and cake.'

Mum! I ask you. Niamh definitely didn't lick it off a stone.

'Hiya, Una, would you like to join us?' I enquire dutifully. 'We're just about to order.'

'Not at all, lovey. Don is just outside loading up the car. Now, how is everything going with you girls? Is there anything I can do for you, with the farm? Whatever you need, don't be afraid to ask. We're just across the road.'

Mammy looks very interested in the lino all of a sudden. 'Thanks, Una, but we're … managing fine.' Then she looks up. 'We're just finding our new routine, aren't we, Aisling?'

'We are,' I say, smiling over at her.

'Ah, you're both great. Just great,' Una says, giving us both a quick hug. 'Don't forget, a moment on the lips, a lifetime on the hips! Hahaha!'

Mammy and I throw our eyes up to heaven in unison and proceed to a corner table where Deirdre Ruane's little sister – the one on the county Under 16s camogie team – promptly takes our order for a pot of tea and two chocolate eclairs.

Mammy sighs. 'What am I going to get Cillian for his birthday at all, Aisling? Sheila says money will do, but I couldn't arrive with nothing for him to unwrap. I'm his godmother, after all.'

As cousins go, Cillian and I have always been fairly close, especially since himself and John started sharing the Drumcondra house. But the way Auntie Sheila treats him, you'd swear he was a child. It's not just the way she cut the corners off his Mr Freezes until he was thirteen so he wouldn't hurt his little mouth, or how she still insists he bring home his dirty clothes in a black sack every Friday to be washed – the latest is she's throwing him a big thirtieth birthday party in the Mountrath in January, finished off with a dance in the Vortex. Mexican themed to celebrate his new infatuation with burritos. Sadhbh is going to come down for it, though, so it should be a bit of craic. She hasn't been to BGB since the summer and I'm hoping this visit will be less dramatic. Mammy is under orders to nab all and any sombreros that come into the charity shop in the next week.

'Jesus, I haven't a clue, Mammy. Maybe a new check shirt? I can ask John to have a think if you like.'

'Thanks, love. That would be great. Aisling, have you heard anything more about the place out the Garbally Road? The building site?'

I've been meaning to drive out for a look at that, actually. Maybe it can be tomorrow's activity. The Garbally Road goes out past Filan's and Maguire's at the top of BGB, quickly turning into sparse bungalows and waving fields and the small lake in the distance. The site in question is about three-quarters of a mile out that road, just before the turn for the long driveway down to Constance Swinford's place, marked with a large brown gate and a horse engraved onto a beaten old plaque. The Swinfords have been raising horses there since I was a child. You could go for riding lessons on a Saturday morning if you wanted but Mammy wasn't able for the notions.

'Not a lot, Mammy. Like, there's definitely something happening but nobody seems to know what.'

'Tessie heard they're knocking it down to build a Lidl. And Paddy Reilly said he heard a celebrity is after buying it – Donny Osmond or Rod Stewart or someone looking to make an investment and cash in on some Irish fresh air.'

'I hardly think Rod Stewart is coming to BGB, Mammy.'

She shrugs. 'That's just what I heard. And we're very swish now that you can get gluten-free bread in Filan's.'

She's right, I suppose. BGB is definitely busier than I've ever seen it and Knock is the same.

'I was looking it up on Google Earth yesterday,' she continues nonchalantly, and I must say I'm taken aback. I didn't know she knew about Google Earth – although I have noticed she can get RIP.ie up on her phone these days with no assistance required. 'It's a grand size and has some nice outside space. Someone could do something lovely with it.' She pauses. 'Although new people bring new trouble.'

I don't know exactly what she means but I shush her as Deirdre Ruane's little sister approaches us with two cakes piled with cream the size of our heads.

'What do you mean, Mammy?' I quiz her as the waitress runs off to get us some cutlery.

'Well, I'm just saying that they opened those holiday homes outside Knock last month, and since then three bales of briquettes have been stolen from Tessie Daly's garage and Breege Gorman had her wallet taken from her car.'

'Mammy! Shush!' The young Ruane one is headed back to us again and I don't want it getting around that Mammy is some kind of intolerant crone, giving out about blow-ins.

We tuck into our eclairs and there's silence for a couple of minutes. 'I don't know, Mammy. Remember how suspicious everyone was when the Zhus opened Cantonese City, and Billy Foran swore blind he'd boycott it until the day he died? And now they're practically running the Neighbourhood Watch and Feilim Zhu is dynamite on the Under 12s team, or so I hear.'

Billy Foran didn't bank on the arrival of the spice bag along with the Zhus and had to eat his words fairly lively – now he's one of their best customers. Mammy pipes up again. 'I just don't want strangers coming up my driveway. That's all.' It hits me then. She's worried. She's worried about the house and herself. The few nights when she's been on her own in the house since Daddy died – when I was in Dublin and Paul was on a stag in Athlone – she said she didn't sleep a wink. I should be with her more. I decide to tell her.

'I think I'm going to move home for a while,' I declare, licking chocolate off my finger, barely pausing to gauge her reaction. 'The timing is right. And like you said yourself, BGB is becoming very fancy and cosmopolitan. I won't miss Dublin at all.'

'Oh, Aisling, that would be nice, wouldn't it?' Mammy says, looking up from the remains of her colossal eclair. 'Especially once Paul is gone back. It'll be just lovely.'

That's that then. There's no turning back now.

'Come on and we'll go before it gets too dark and cold,' I say, looking out the window.

As we turn on to the Knock Road back towards BGB and home, the first fat snowflakes are just starting to fall.

CHAPTER 11

'Will you come *on*! Paddy Reilly said it took them four hours to get five miles up the road yesterday. We have to get all the way to Dublin!' It wasn't too cold to snow, it turns out – it was just the right temperature, and the big, fat flakes fell for three days solid. And then the temperature dropped and the snow froze so that every road across the eastern part of the country is like an ice rink. There's an Orange Weather Warning, Doctor Maher is flat out in BGB with sprained wrists and turned ankles and Filan's have run out of salt. According to Paul, there was around €2 million worth of tractors parked outside Maguire's last night, with determined farmers unwilling to forsake their precious pints. Mad Tom had a field day filling the cabs with snow and by all accounts all hell broke loose at closing time. People have been slipping and sliding up to Filan's to get the essentials, but a panic went around the town yesterday evening that they were running out of bread. Mammy sent Paul out for some emergency rations and he came back two hours later with a gluten-free seeded loaf and four hot-dog rolls. Mammy is planning to give them to the birds. The roads are still in shite, which is making the preparations to get to Dublin even more stressful. We should be grand once we get out onto the main road, but we have to tackle the road from our house into BGB and back out onto the Dublin Road first.

It's New Year's Eve and Elaine and Ruby's wedding day. Well, I say 'day', but they're actually not getting married until 7 p.m. I checked twice to make sure it was the right time on the email but they're just having a quick ceremony, no sit-down dinner. I had to make sure we had a feed before we left. Then there's a party with vegan bits whirling around on plates, like the hen. Hardly a wedding at all but I'll bite my tongue and leave them to it. If I can sneak some flip-flops into the bathrooms I will. Mammy's been invited, but there were too many elements she couldn't get her head around and she's not really feeling up to it, so she's opted to stay at home with Auntie Sheila to ring in the New Year. A wedding starting at seven and with no beeforsalmon or trio of desserts or best-man (or woman in this case, I suppose) speech about waking up in a baby's cot in a hotel in Amsterdam on the stag? It's a brave new world, that's for sure. Mammy is wild about Elaine and has the wedding invite on the fridge, but saying goodbye to Paul will be enough upheaval for one day, I think.

His flight back to Australia isn't until tomorrow but he's going to come with me and John now, just in case he can't make it to Dublin in the morning in the snow. Tony Timoney has insisted he's running the bus from BGB as usual and that he'll drop Paul to the airport, but the last time it snowed he didn't even make it out of his own driveway and had to be hospitalised for palpitations, so it's safer for Paul to just come with us. It's only 11 a.m. but I'm so anxious about missing the 7 p.m. kick-off and me a bridesmaid that I'm trying to hoof him out the door. Elaine has insisted that she doesn't need me and Sadhbh to help her get ready. I was worried about who was going to pretend to put on Elaine's veil for the pictures, or who was going to slide her shoes onto her feet, also for the pictures. Everyone knows a bride can't do anything herself on her wedding day. She's practically helpless. But Elaine has assured me she's wearing a white trouser suit and she and Ruby are just going to take a few selfies, so I've dedicated myself to my limited bridesmaid duties of printing out the readings and making sure Elaine's granny has a brandy in her hand at all times.

'Will you *come on*, Paul!'

I've been dreading this goodbye. Paul has been home so long at this stage that we've fallen back into our routine of almost constant slagging and regular bouts of war. I've also reverted to putting his dirty dishes on his pillow when he refuses to put them in the dishwasher. This led to a particularly memorable incident on Stephenses night when he came in steaming at 3 a.m. and got straight into bed with two bowls of Crunchy Nut Cornflakes residue and an upended plate of cracker crumbs. He came down the next morning saying something had been biting him all night and his hair was sticky. 'Aisling! You *wagon*,' he roared as I shook helplessly by the sink, trying to get the words out about what he'd been rolling around in. Mammy had to break us up as he tried to rub That Bloody Cat's mitt into my hair. She's taken to brushing the cat, Mammy has. It will be wearing a tie next.

I'll miss Paul all the same. We've only had one conversation about what's going to happen when he's gone.

'Will she be okay, do you think?' he asked me as we peeled potatoes together for dinner one evening. Mammy nearly had to fetch some smelling salts when she saw us, but we shooed her into the front room to watch some Christmas special with Graham Norton flipping old ladies off the red chair. I hope he put a cushion down for them. Mammy loves Graham Norton on account of his Irishness and his carry-on with Tom Cruise and the likes.

'She'll be grand. I'll mind her,' I told him.

'I know you will. I feel a bit bad leaving you to do it, though.'

'I'm happy to move home for a while. Just to keep an eye on things.'

'Fair play, Aisling. I'd go mad, I think. I'm dying to get back.'

'Well, someone has to do it. And sure look at you here peeling spuds. That's earned you at least another two years in Australia.'

And then he flicked a foot-long piece of peel into my face and I went at him with a tea towel and that was the end of our heart to heart. It felt strange, our grown-up talk. Like Mammy was the child and we had to provide for her.

We've made Paul promise to keep up his weekly Skype calls. They'd become something of a highlight when he was away. He used to get an awful slagging from Daddy about his tan and his Aussie slang and whatever Sheila or Kylie had popped up in his recent Facebook posts. Daddy was well up on his lingo because of his decades of devotion to the lunchtime episode of *Home and Away* – perfectly timed for his dinnertime. Sadhbh and Elaine could never get their heads around me sometimes slipping up and calling lunchtime dinnertime. But Daddy always had a plate of chops and spuds in front of

Home and Away at half one. Sure, he'd have been up since all hours. I'm a bit worried about the farm with Paul going back, to be honest. Paddy Reilly has been working away and I've been doing as much as I can, but Mammy is going to need to take on more long-term help if we're to keep it going.

Paul is finally dragging the biggest of his BGB Rovers kit bags down the stairs and through the snow and into the boot. My bridesmaid's dress is hanging carefully off a hook in the back seat, and I've already instructed him to sit far away from it on the other side. John is already dressed in his wedding gear. He bought a new skinny-legged suit a few months ago and he's getting the wear out of it, although I think it might have shrunk on its last wash. I'm not sure if either of us is ready for the outline of his bits to be visible through the crotch. I know it's the fashion, but I feel like I could pick Conor McGregor's mickey out of a line-up at this stage.

Paul would be better off with a suitcase on wheels, of course, especially given the volume of sausages and black pudding Mammy has secreted in each of his shoes, but you can't go to Australia without a club kit bag slung across your back and a jersey on. They'd hardly let you back in through Sydney airport. Mammy is standing on the doorstep holding out the scarf she bought Paul for Christmas. He's been trying to leave it behind, given that he's heading straight into the Aussie summer and has been talking of little else for the past few days but the sweating and the fights over the one fan they have in the flat. I wouldn't be able for it at all. I start getting flustered in anything over twenty degrees and have to dash into bathrooms to run cold water on my wrists. I saw that trick on an episode of *Xposé*. They were in Marbella for a segment about sweating in fake tan. It was Glenda presenting, and I often switch off when she's on because I find her very cold, but even Glenda warmed up a bit in the July Spanish heat.

'Will you just take it?' I hiss at Paul, eager not to make this any more difficult than it needs to be. John is already in the car. He's not a man for scenes. Paul reaches out and takes the scarf from Mammy and she grabs his arm and pulls him in to her.

'Mind yourself out there now,' she gulps into his shoulder. 'Don't be letting anyone put drugs in your bag or baby snakes in your backpack.' Mammy has been watching a lot of *Border Force*.

'I won't.' Paul gives her a big squeeze and then pushes away, grinning. 'What about all the cocaine in my wallet?' She shrieks and shouts at him to get into the car, and when he does I notice him wiping his face with the back of his hand.

'Bye, Mammy.' I go in for a hug too. Hugging has become a big part of my life over the past few months. I was never much into it – it's very invasive – but the girls up in Dublin are mad for it and Mammy seems mad for it these days too. 'Go on,' she says to me, straightening up her face with a steely resolve. 'I'll be fine. Auntie Sheila's coming later with a bottle of Baileys.' Oh Jesus. They'll be swinging from the lampshades by midnight.

CHAPTER 12

The occasional smell of the clutch burning is the only thing breaking the atmosphere in the car. It's been a tense five hours and we're still nowhere near Dublin. I've been trying to limit my sharp intakes of breath as John skids every now and then or gets a little too close to the car in front as we crawl along the N7. It's half four, and with every second that passes I can feel the bridesmaid's dress in the backseat calling out to me, 'You're late, you're late, you're late.' I'm mentally cursing every other car on the road, and Paul's running commentary isn't helping. 'Yes, I know you wouldn't get this in Sydney,' I snap at him somewhere near the Kildare–Dublin border.

I haven't seen snow like this since that winter a few years ago when the whole country shut down and even PensionsPlus was on hiatus for a few days. The state of the fridge when we eventually got back in – I had to put up extra signs in the kitchen to get things back on an even keel. So many unclaimed Tupperware containers. The thought of work makes my stomach sink, until I remember that I actually don't have work to go back to. Well, not actual work. We have that big meeting and then I suppose I'll find out my fate. I haven't finished my CV yet but I've been keeping an eye out online for jobs – I saw a good one in another pensions firm, one in an insurance company and one in Facebook. The last one is a bit of a long shot but I spend enough time religiously looking through wedding photo albums and dutifully Liking holiday snaps of cocktails. Wouldn't it be great to get paid for it? John has been telling me to relax and try to enjoy the break, but all he's doing is annoying me. He's mad if he thinks I'm throwing away my career in pensions – I got 475 points in the Leaving!

It's heading for five o'clock and we still have to drop Paul off at John's and I have to get changed and put on my make-up and add another few layers of hairspray. A cold sweat rises up the back of my scalp. It's unthinkable that I might not be there on time. A bridesmaid! I'd never live it down. I wish I had listened to Majella and gone with her and Pablo yesterday, but I wanted one more day at home.

'We're never going to make it on time,' I whine, panicking.

'Will you ever give it a rest, Aisling? I don't want us to end up in a ditch.' John speaks quietly but I can tell his teeth are gritted. Wish the same could be said for the roads.

'You're like the youngest old married couple I've ever heard,' Paul jokes from the backseat. I look at him in the rear-view mirror to give him a filthy glare and catch John's eye instead but he looks away. I really don't want to have a row today. I've enough to be worrying about.

'We'll have to drop you off in town, head,' John says, looking back at Paul. 'We won't have time to go to Drumcondra and then back over to the southside.'

So at half six we barely slow down the car to let Paul out in the city centre. He has to shout after us to get his bags out of the boot. 'See you in the morning before you go,' I roar at him as we screech away. 'Go, go, go!' I shout at John, whose shoulders are hunched up around his ears in concentration. The roads are mercifully much clearer in town – a godsend after hours of slush and ice. It's 6.51 by the time we pull into the car park of The Grainstore, a warehouse in Ringsend. People are already parking and milling around, heading into the main door of the venue.

'How am I going to do this?' I groan, leaping out of the passenger seat and opening the back door.

'Get in, and I'll cover you.' John opens his arms out wide, spreading the flaps of his jacket as far as they'll go. I clamber into the backseat and pull the zip down on the garment bag. I reach out for the dress, exposed to the world in my bra and sucky-in pants. Nearly there. I did my make-up in the car – the old favourites of a base of BB cream, a slick of brown mascara and a touch of Clinique blusher I got free with a set. Mammy got me a new eyeshadow trio for Christmas so I stuck some of that on too, going for that smoky-eye look people are so fond of. I've tried it before and I usually end up looking like I've been in a fight, but I think it looks okay, given the circumstances. Right. Dress, American tan tights, sandals, one last blast of hairspray and I'll be good to go. Kneeling on the backseat, I pull the dress over my head and manoeuvre it to minimise the up-do damage. I wrench up the zip and peer into the rear-view mirror – not a hair out of place. It really was worth splashing out on that industrial-sized tin of Elnett.

****

I suppose I didn't know what to expect from a lesbian wedding, apart from the fact that a priest would be definitely off the cards. No great loss, if you ask me. They can be very hit and miss. The ceremony was beautiful, and at one stage I caught John's eye. The number of weddings we've been to together over the years must be in double digits at this stage. And yet … here we are, the two of us, no different than when we were twenty-one. If we were ever going to get married, I'm starting to realise that we'd have done it by now, and I think he knows it too.

My so-called reading turned out to be the lyrics of a Tegan and Sara song but you'd never know – it's all in the delivery. I even said 'this is the word of the Lord' accidentally at the end, but one of the tag rugby girls roared 'thanks be to God' and everyone laughed so I think I styled it out. I've done more than my fair share of readings at weddings so I can usually tell if I've bombed.

The one thing I couldn't understand is why the girls insisted on this DIY look, especially since we all know full well that Elaine could probably have had Franc himself minding her bouquet or getting people to sign the guest book. There wasn't even a hint of a white tablecloth or chair cover to be found, and the flowers were all in jam jars. If you could call them flowers – they were quite obviously weeds. Candles as far as the eye could see too, but I had the fire exits figured out within minutes. Once a health and safety officer, always a health and safety officer. And I suppose none of it matters once the bride and bride are happy, and there was no denying that. They were glowing, the pair of them, despite the polar temperatures outside. And the speeches!

The parents didn't say a word and no pint glass to throw a fiver into either. But Elaine and Ruby said the loveliest things about each other and their hopes and plans for the future. I texted Mammy and told her she should have come and I meant it; she would have been dining out on this for months.

While Elaine and Ruby were having their first dance to 'Cheek to Cheek' – Lady Gaga singing it apparently – John asked me out of the blue if I'd given any more thought to where I was going to be living in the New Year.

'I'm going to move home,' I told him, looking into the bottom of my wine glass and not into his eyes.

'Right so. That's great that you've decided.' He sounded relieved. And when I looked at him he looked relieved. 'You and Majella will be thick as thieves up and down BGB Main Street.'

Him saying it out loud suddenly made it feel very real. I'd spent the bulk of my early twenties fairly obsessed with moving back home. I wanted the little job. The little car. The big wedding. The big house. It all hinged on John. I was desperate for him to propose – I got a French manicure every time we went on so much as a Groupon weekend away – but it never happened and I eventually realised none of that stuff really mattered to me, not when I actually thought about it. It seems mad now that I'll be moving home without him.

At ten to twelve we were all given our coats and glasses of bubbly and herded outside to the courtyard for the big countdown. It was magical in the snow, even though I nearly lost the big toe on my left foot to frostbite. When the clock struck twelve I looked up at John and he looked down at me and we kissed because, well, what else are you supposed to do at midnight on New Year's Eve when you've been together for eight years? There was nothing there, though – affection, yeah, of course, but no ... passion. And certainly nothing compared to what Pablo was doing to Majella across the courtyard. It was like kissing a friend and I was grateful when the fireworks started going off and Elaine's granny began belting out 'Auld Lang Syne'.

****

When the banging downstairs wakes me up it feels like I've only been asleep for ten minutes. I reach for my phone – 6.42 a.m. It was after four when we got in, John speaking in tongues about needing meat and me clutching the bouquet that I really wasn't trying to catch. It just sort of ... landed in my lap, despite Majella quite literally diving for it. I offered it to her afterwards but she just limped away, too proud. Pablo was Velcro-ed to her all night, and I don't know if I was just imagining it, but I caught him squinting over at Sadhbh once or twice. And not looking at her like a normal person, looking at her like she was wearing something belonging to him. Very odd.

Paul's flight is due to leave at twelve, but he'll naturally insist on being in the airport four hours beforehand, so I suppose it's finally time to say goodbye. I'll make him a few sandwiches too, I decide, wrapping my fleecy dressing gown – Penneys, €10 – around me tightly. No point paying inflated airport prices when we have a perfectly good sliced pan and a packet – actually, more likely half a packet – of crumbed ham downstairs.

'Could you keep it down to a dull roar?' I whisper in the half-dark, making him jump. He's jamming the last of his overnight stuff back into the massive holdall, and I notice Mammy has furnished him with several full-sized bottles of Head and Shoulders. He was always her pet. The panic about the weight of the bag rises inside me but I push it down. I won't always be there to mind him. He has to start figuring this stuff out for himself. 'Do you have your phone charger?'

'Yeah,' he says, patting the bag, which looks fit to burst. We both stand there for a few seconds, suspended in silent understanding. Paul going back to Australia is signalling the next phase of our grief: trying to move on. None of us is ready. Are you ever?

'I'm having second thoughts about going now.'

'Don't,' I say, after a pause. 'I'm here to keep an eye on her. Amn't I always here?'

He just nods.

'Tea?'

CHAPTER 13

I was able to sort of distance myself from the reality of it over Christmas, but on 3 January I'm feeling more unemployed than I ever thought possible. Everyone is back to work. Everyone! Even Sadhbh, who was offered a role in the HR department of a record company, sight unseen, thanks to a recommendation from one of her pals. Flatlay Records. I got excited briefly thinking it was Flatley Records and we were about to score big time with the free *Riverdance* tickets, but it turns out it's Flatlay. Something to do with indie and techno. I've been to Berlin. I've had enough techno to last me a lifetime. Sadhbh is dead excited, though, especially with the lack of dress code. She'll be able to wear as much of her mad jewellery as she wants, and no doubt they'll all be dressed head to toe in hay- and stone-coloured get-ups. I thought her outfits at PensionsPlus were 'directional', but they were nothing compared to what she headed off in this morning. Clear vinyl boots – I'll say no more. I don't know what I'd put on me if I didn't have 'business casual' as a guide. I have a hoodie from my camogie-playing days and a pair of baggy combats from that summer Majella decided we were going to be mad into Blink-182. They're actually very flattering. I must dig them out again.

Ruby and Elaine are tracking endangered gorillas or swinging from vines in Uganda so it's just me on my lonesome in Chez SEA, faced with the task of packing.

I've been reassuring Mammy that everything's going to be fine. I know nothing would strike fear into Mammy's – and Daddy's, if he was here – heart like having no job long-term. I've told her that I'm going to be grand and I'll get a big lump sum and have a new job in no time.

Still, it could be worse: at least I have somewhere to go. Last night Sadhbh confessed that she's been trawling the usual places online but any room in her price range is gone by the time she rings up about it. I feel awful for her, even though the girl spends about €100 a week on organic avocados and craft gin and hand-reared coffee beans. I've seen her hoover up 1 and 2 cent coins too rather than just bend over and pick them up. Still, I know there's decent money in HR so I'm outraged. It's a ridiculous state of affairs that a young professional like herself is priced out of the city, especially since she's been so good to the economy with all the clothes shopping. The newlyweds will be away for another few weeks so the good news is there's no immediate pressure on her to move out.

Beep! Beep! Blibbbbb! Beep!

Christ, my alarm. It's time to head to this bloody public forum PensionsPlus is hosting about the redundancies. I'd rather just be going to work. In a few hours I'll know my fate, and Sadhbh will know hers too. She won't make it now, but I've promised to keep her up to speed. Suzanne sent me some kind of garbled text earlier which I think meant she'd be there. One of the kids probably got their hands on her phone and fired off a load of nonsense.

The 747 towards the airport is heaving but I manage to wedge myself between two Aer Lingus cabin crew at the back of the lower deck. How glamorous it must be, jetting around the world for work, telling people to put their tray tables in an upright position and deciding who gets two little cans of Diet Coke instead of the miserable single one. They always smell lovely too, probably because they have all that access to Duty Free. No paying high-street prices when you're cabin crew. Maybe I need to forget about the pensions industry and try something completely different? I make a mental note to read my horoscope later.

I can see the Travelodge coming into view, and as the bus slows to a stop I fight my way up to the front, even though the driver opens the side door as soon as he spots me. I couldn't just sneak out that way without shouting thank you, especially with so many tourists on board. They'd think Irish people were dragged up. No, I always make it my business to put my best foot forward for our foreign visitors. I've even been known to lurk around O'Connell Bridge and Temple Bar in case I spot anyone with a map who looks like they might need directions. It's just good manners as far as I'm concerned.

A sign in the hotel lobby informs me that the PPH Public Forum is taking place in the Anna Livia Suite. Down the seemingly endless corridor I tip until I notice a sort of low rumble getting louder and louder. I check my phone – I'm five minutes late! It's not like me, but this hotel is about the size of Croke Park and I didn't factor in the two-kilometre walk. Good for getting my steps in, though, so I can't complain. Think of the Activity Points, Aisling.

My phone beeps: three question marks from Sadhbh, but I have nothing to report yet. When I round the next corner it becomes clear that the rumble isn't a stray Boeing 747 or even a helicopter touching down to drop off a sheik or a celebrity to pick up a few bits in the sales – it's three hundred angry individuals roaring at a panel of men – and one woman – sitting stony-faced on a stage. I've found the PPH Public Forum and it doesn't look good.

My eyes are on stalks looking for anyone I recognise in the room, which I suppose is par for the course when you realise PPH was the umbrella company for something like twelve other businesses. Still, I'm suddenly not so confident about getting much of a payout. It seems like I'm in quite a queue and nobody's happy.

I slink down the side of the room and slip into an empty chair. Kevin Shermer is standing centre stage at the podium trying to get everyone to calm down but people keep shouting at him and, I swear, the language is borderline obscene. And I say that as someone who was on the line in 2011 when Rangers beat BGB by a single point in the county final.

'Please, everyone, if you could just give me a minute,' Shermer hisses into the microphone, and the noise finally dies down just enough to hear someone shout 'You're nothing but a pox!' Des from Escalations! He's het up, but sure who could blame him. I spy Suzanne in the front row.

'As I was saying before you all kicked off, this will only take a few minutes. Can I please get some quiet so I can fill you all in? Come on, lads, I don't want to be here either.' He's sweating now, wiping his brow with a scrunched-up little hanky, and I feel sorry for him. The crowd of shitehawks behind him aren't offering anything by way of support and I'm not surprised. If you're the type to RSVP to a party and then not show up, well, you've lost my respect and that's the truth.

'The news is good,' Shermer continues. 'The news is great, actually. PPH is definitely closing its Irish operations but –' and there's a pause like he's about to tell us who won *Ireland's Got Talent*, 'everyone who is entitled to redundancy is getting it ...' He continues talking but the cheer from the crowd – myself included, to be fair – drowns him out. I feel a weight lifting off my shoulders. I was half-worried they might say we're getting nothing, but sure we're protected by law. Sadhbh is blue in the face repeating it.

I whip out my phone to text Sadhbh the good news as a few down the back start singing 'Olé Olé Olé'. There's a text from Suzanne.

'Well fuk it anyway. I told the kids we were going 2 Disney.'

What is she on about? We're getting the redundancy – Shermer just said it. My phone vibrates in my hand. It's her again.

'Mayb could stretch 2 a trampoline. A sml one.'

'Did you not hear right? We're getting payout!' I fire back.

Shermer is still talking from the stage, and I can barely hear what he's saying, but he's pointing to a bank of tables at the side of the room manned by a group of serious-looking types in suits. Accountants, by the looks of it. They have boxes of envelopes laid out in front of them and are beckoning people over.

I rise up and automatically join the closest queue. It's an instinct of mine – if you see a queue, join it. You might get a free yoghurt or something. Standing on my tippy-toes, I scan the room again and spot Suzanne in the distance, talking to Eilish, the receptionist, but there are about a hundred people between us and I can't risk moving in case I lose my place. The queue is bombing along and that doesn't happen very often.

'I'll be lucky to get a grand or two.'

I'm trying not to eavesdrop but the lad behind me is shouting into his phone. He's tall but looks young – maybe twenty-one or twenty-two.

'What an epic fucking waste of my time, Mum,' he's braying. 'I never even wanted to go into pensions and I fucking hated it but now it's all I have on my CV.'

I'd never get away with saying fuck in front of Mammy, even at my age. Bloody or feckin' would be my max, unless it was a life or death situation. Oh, it's a different story in the Morans', though. When Majella and Shane were younger they used to get into blazing fights and call each other every name under the sun. She even told Shem to go fuck himself one day when he complained that she was watching Wimbledon instead of earning her pocket money picking stones. He didn't even flinch. I wanted the ground to open up and swallow me. The things we did for Lleyton Hewitt.

'Name?'

I'm at the top of the queue and there's not so much as a by-your-leave from the woman in front of me. That's when I see it – the envelope with my name on it at the front of the pile. I just point to it mutely and she hands it over shouting, '*Next?*' to the fella behind me, who looks fit to kill someone.

What is everyone so annoyed about, I wonder to myself, sliding my finger under the flap of the envelope to open it. To my left, I catch sight of Suzanne walking towards me, waving, and as I go to wave back a single piece of paper slips out of the envelope and glides slowly to the floor.

'Ais! Ais! Hang on there!' she's shouting as I bend down to pick up what turns out to be a cheque. Flipping it over, the room starts to spin and I realise I'm struggling to focus – €9,499. €9,499? How could it be only €9,499? I've worked at PensionsPlus for six years. I have to be entitled to more than that? What about Sadhbh's conservative estimate of €20K?

Suddenly Suzanne is there beside me, black backpack flung over her shoulder. 'Statutory redundancy.' She sighs dramatically. 'Two weeks' pay for every shagging year I've given this place. What a crowd of bastards.'

CHAPTER 14

'Don't let them get in front of you,' I hiss at Sadhbh, my eyes firmly trained on a couple skulking suspiciously near the top of the queue. He looks smug, like he's already rented the place and done the big IKEA shop in his head. Not on my watch, mister. You can put those skrimtops and fluggelwaffles back. We are getting this place. Well, Sadhbh is getting it. Elaine and Ruby are back next week, and while I felt sorry for her initially, when I quizzed her on her methods it turns out she's been doing a frankly woeful job of finding somewhere new to live. She's arrived to viewings with not one reference printed out, she's failed to find out the name of the estate agent so she can go straight in with, 'Hello, Gary, I'm very interested and I have a bank statement here and all for you,' and claims that there just isn't much out there. I mean, I know the rental market in Dublin is tough, but is she trying at all? So I've offered to help her. I've been up and down from home like a yo-yo, between helping Mammy on the farm and personally dropping CVs into all of the top pensions companies in town. Of course, I've been applying for jobs online, but I read on KickstartYourCareer.com that some places like to see you face to face too. It shows enthusiasm, apparently. It's certainly helping me get my steps in. With the shite redundancy money, the reality of having to get a job sooner rather than later is hitting me, and I really don't think the opportunities are going to be a dime a dozen in BGB. I'm starting to wobble a bit about moving home too, although Mammy is delighted. It just seems like a bit of a step backwards. So I've had to give myself a few shakes and remind myself that I'm lucky to have a home to move back into – and sure isn't minding Mammy an important job in itself? Still, I never thought I'd say it about Dublin, but I'm going to miss going for brunch. It's mad what you can get used to if you've been exposed to it enough.

Sadhbh has the new job sorted, though, so she's alright there. She just needs the new place to live. Despite her effortlessly elegant appearance, rich, swingy hair and fondness for putting weekends in Oslo on her credit card, she doesn't come from money and there's not much support on the home front. Her mam rents a one-bed place in Rathfarnham, and there's no mention of her dad at all. For the first little while I knew her I was only dying to ask about him, but it became clear fairly quickly that he wasn't a talking point and the nosiness soon wore off me. Sadhbh and her mam are very close, and she's giving her a chunk of the disappointing redundancy to help her out with a few things. But it means she doesn't have the luxury of moving home, and she's keen not to have to stay with two newlyweds.

I haven't had to look for a place to live since college but, with the right email alerts set up and a solid picture of what all the Garys, Deirdres and Simons showing apartments across the city are looking for, surely I can crack this problem for Sadhbh. So here we are outside a Georgian building in

Ranelagh, ready to pump Gary/Deirdre/Simon's hand and say, 'We'll take it.' I must say, I'm surprised to see quite so many people here, and they all seem to have Important Envelopes with the deposit ready to go in their hands – not just me. There are two couples ahead of us in the queue and at least ten people behind us. It's ten past ten and the viewing was due to start at ten so we're all starting to shift around on our feet and make impatient huffing noises. At fourteen minutes past the door swings open and the estate agent barks out, 'First three lots in.' The six of us at the top of the queue shuffle forward into a dimly lit hall. Nothing too concerning about that. Sure, she's not planning on living in the hall and the pictures of the flat itself looked lovely and bright and spacious with a classic feature wall painted a different colour behind the fireplace. That always screams elegance. The estate agent – Steven is his name; I was close enough – leads us up a flight of stairs and immediately I'm on alert. 'Access to delightful garden' had me thinking it was on the ground floor. But then again, maybe there's an outside stairs. All good, all good.

Steven stops outside number four, where the door is already ajar, and pushes it open. 'In you go,' he calls down the stairs where we're all bunched up, trying not to viciously elbow each other. Couple number one file in and we all slowly follow. 'Bathroom in to the left,' says Steven as Sadhbh and I pass him. I'm barely in the door when the father–daughter pair in front of me stop dead and I accidentally graze the back of his heel with my runner. 'Sorry, sorry,' I bluster, but to be fair it's his own fault. We all have to get in. Looking around past him I see what the issue is. There isn't room for us all in the flat. And it really is the whole flat. What looked like a separate bedroom in the pictures is actually a bed shoved up against a wall with a bedside locker separating it from the couch and doubling up as an end table. The couple who were first in the queue are already in the kitchen, with the man's arse nearly in the sink. It had looked deceptively large in the pictures, although I did find it strange that the microwave was bolted to the wall at a height practically out of reach. Whoever took the photos must have climbed on top of the fridge to get the angles and maybe used one of those lenses they used to get the pictures of Kate Middleton in the nip in France. I'm not great on photography but there's definitely been some trickery here. At least the feature wall is there behind the fireplace, although it spans the length of the room and isn't so much the feature wall as the whole flat. Sadhbh shuffles behind me in to the left and peers into the bathroom, which mercifully is in a separate room. 'Oh,' she squeaks, 'a … hose.' I look around her and see what she means. It brings me back to one holiday Majella and I took to the Canaries and the only shower was beside the pool. Sure, how can you be expected to scrub your oxters in your swimsuit with seven Germans looking at you? I couldn't bring myself to do it and was making maggots with the filth the whole week. Luckily, this hose in the apartment isn't outside, but it is just a hose attached to a tap and then hung from a hook on the ceiling. No wonder there were only pictures of the toilet. I turn on my heel to quiz Steven.

'The ad said a one-bedroom apartment?'

'One bedroom and studio are kind of interchangeable these days,' he rattles off, shoving a loose wire under a bit of carpet with his ludicrously pointy shoe and completely ignoring my gesturing towards the hose. 'People love this kind of bijou living.'

'You can open the fridge from the couch,' Sadhbh retorts. 'And the kitchen is behind a curtain.'

'Yeah, it's great, isn't it?' Steven doesn't even have the decency to look ashamed.

'What about the garden?' I probe further. 'There's access to the garden?'

'Yeah, you need to go back downstairs and around the side of the house, and there's a creche on the bottom floor so there might be a few kids out there occasionally, but grass in this part of Dublin is at a premium so it's a really stunning feature.' His sales drawl nearly has me convinced. You can't beat a bit of space to dry sheets.

'You're grand,' Sadhbh snaps at him, grabbing my arm and pulling me out into the hall and back down the stairs. As we head out the front door we hear the first couple and the dad rustling their envelopes and clamouring about having three months' rent. Sadhbh shoots past the people waiting outside, growling 'Don't bother' at IKEA man through gritted teeth. I've never seen her so het up. She flies off down the road, and even in my Skechers I have trouble keeping up. When she finally slows to a manageable pace, I sling my arm through hers and give it a squeeze. 'We'll find something else. That place was a joke. And Elaine and Ruby aren't just going to kick you out.'

Elaine and Ruby may not be about to kick Sadhbh out until she finds something, but the time *has* come for me to make my move out of our lovely Portobello palace. I put off my final night until they got back from their honeymoon, so we could have one last evening of drinking wine and the playlist slowly evolving from their inexplicable seven-minute-long 'mixes' to my Corrs and Westlife *Best Of* collections. I'll never get tired of the image of Elaine and Sadhbh screaming 'go-oh-on, leave me breathless' into the necks of bottles of rosé. Beats their LSD Soundsystem and DeadmauFive any day, if you ask me. We had a little cry to 'So Young', with each of us taking on the persona of a Corrs sister. Sadhbh is always Andrea, of course. She has the hair. Elaine is usually Sharon and I'm Caroline. My tambourine playing in the school nativity plays was always highly commended by Mrs Irwin, and I've since felt that my calling as a percussionist was never realised. Ruby magnanimously agrees to be Jim, given that she's only an honorary Chez SEA member, even though she is now Elaine's actual wife.

But now, with a heavy hangover that no amount of cold cans of Diet Coke will sate (you need two minimum: one for drinking and one for pressing against your temples), I'm packing the last of my stuff into the Micra and getting ready for the final journey home to BGB for … God knows how long? Majella's already moved home properly and has been successfully getting Timoney's bus every day. At least it drops her within walking distance of her school on its way out to the airport. She's up to her eyes in planning her First Communion arts-and-crafts strategy, although she admits that making chalices out of CDs and holy doves out of doilies doesn't really change from year to year. She has a few problematic parents this time round, including one who wants to bring in a professional camera crew for the Big Day, so even though it's months away, she's bringing Communion chat home to Pablo every evening.

Pablo is happily installed under the Morans' roof. Shem's initial insistence that he sleep in the sitting room went out the window on the first night, with Majella announcing that it is the twenty-first century and dropping into the conversation that her own mother's wedding dress was suspiciously tight around the belly. Shem was never going to get away with keeping them apart. He's had his heart broken trying to control Majella since the day she was born. He always says if it wasn't for me she would have ended up running away to join *Riverdance*. Joining *Riverdance* is a bit of a dream scenario, if you ask me – a bit like winning an Oscar for playing Mary Robinson or something – but Shem seems to think it would be like Sodom and Gomorrah with them all lepping in and out of clothes and beds. At least with Majella and Pablo under his own roof he can keep an eye on them. I was convinced Willy the dog would run Pablo out of the house long before Shem, but he seems to have taken quite a shine to him instead. In fact, I would go so far as to say Willy is harassing Pablo, hammering away at his leg whenever he gets a chance. I was over the other evening and Pablo was frantically trying to shimmy behind the old armchair beside the Aga in the kitchen, exclaiming, '*Dios mío*,' and burning his arse on the hot plates of the range while Majella and her mother ignored him and bickered over the delegation of towels in the house. Pablo doesn't appear to grasp the difference between a hand towel and one he might dry his feet on and is blissfully ignorant of the shortage of good bath towels. Tensions are high already.

It's a quieter affair in our own house. With Paul gone back it feels emptier than ever, although Mammy still has a steady stream of visitors. Women are great for visiting, but I'm looking forward to seeing John at Cillian's thirtieth to even out all the oestrogen I've been exposed to. We've hardly set eyes on each other at all since New Year's. Busy, I suppose. Mammy's even had the new girl, Sharon, out to the house to do her hair while the salon is still under construction beside the butcher's. According to Tessie, Marty Boland is gearing up to lodge an objection to the extension for the sunbeds. Tessie thinks it's the idea of women being waxed within a 500-metre radius of him that's the issue, but, truth be told, Marty Boland is just a bully. Tessie has a mole in the planning department in the county council so she's always up to speed on planning wars. BGB could be set for a battle to rival the great bypass controversy of 2009, when plans to reroute the dual carriageway close to Michael Fennessey's land and what he claims is a fairy ring nearly brought the council down from the inside. I don't believe in fairies myself, but I'd rather walk across the M50 than walk across a fairy ring. I'm not stone mad.

CHAPTER 15

'Are you serious? Sombreros?'
Does Sadhbh know nothing about Mexico?
Sombreros are their signature hats. You couldn't have a Mexican-themed thirtieth without them. Likewise the ponchos and fake moustaches that Auntie Sheila and Mammy bought in bulk from the costume warehouse on the N7. There's even going to be piñatas filled with Babybels and bags of tayto because Cillian can't stomach sweet things.

We're in Mammy's kitchen getting ready for what is being billed locally as the party of the year. Everyone is going. Everyone!

'Aisling, have you ever heard of cultural appropriation?' she asks, taking a glass of the Merlot bought in especially for her. Mammy claims red wine causes migraines and actually believes Sadhbh is a bit of a medical marvel since she can drink it and not immediately have to lie down in a dark room with a wet facecloth over her eyes.

I'm on my second glass of Pinot Greej and, honestly, I haven't a bull's notion what cultural appropriation is, but it sounds too heavy to be getting into now.

'Listen, Sadhbh,' Majella goes, helping herself to a handful of Doritos from the party stash. 'Cillian loves everything

Mexican so I'm going to wear a sombrero and you're going to wear a sombrero and Aisling is going to wear a sombrero and we're going to look like The Three Amigos but who cares? We're only going to the Mountrath.'

'Alright, alright,' Sadhbh concedes, trying it on. She's wearing dungarees, of all things, and silver boots and has turquoise going through the ends of her grey hair this week. Honestly, the sombrero makes the outfit and I can't believe I'm even saying that. It's not doing much for my own Savida wrap dress but that's life. At least it was on sale. Can't be buying new things in Dunnes these days, not since it's gone so fancy with all the cracked colouredy designer things and *Peaky Blinders* bits for men, and anyway I'm unemployed. Still. I've barely made a dent in my redundancy. Who knows how long I'll have to eke it out for? But I'm determined to stick to my New Year's resolution to stay positive and paste on a smile and stay firm in the belief that something will crop up. And if not, I hear they're looking for people out in the Garden Centre.

'If I'd known there was a theme I'd have brought some of the turquoise jewellery I picked up in Tulum a few years ago,' Sadhbh says, topping up our glasses. 'I only unpacked yesterday and I have loads.'

'So you're properly moved in then?' Majella asks.

Just when Sadhbh was at her wits' end with the rental market, a perfect solution cropped up. Majella's old room! Sure, she had vacated the house in Phibsboro she'd shared with her teaching pals Mairead and Fionnuala, and they had their hearts broken trying to find someone new. They had entire families trying to get them to let the room to them and the email address they set up especially for the ad (FionnualaMaireadHouseNoCouples@gmail.com) was inundated, so they were dragging their heels waiting for someone perfect. Sadhbh ticks most of their boxes. Well, she lied about smoking, and enjoying late nights, and taking showers no longer than seven minutes, and rinsing out recyclables, and never leaving a pot to steep overnight unless it really, really needs it. But apart from that she fits the 'clean, tidy, craic-loving gal (*no couples*)' that was stipulated in the ad. Well, apart from the couples bit. I *thought* she was single when I suggested she move in, but she has since let slip that she's been casually 'seeing' a lad she met in work. I finally got it out of her when she dodged an opportunity to come to a free wine yoke Majella got us invited to. Some launch of a new mascara she overheard two girls talking about in Brown Thomases when she was in buying her biannual bottle of Alien, her signature scent. She gets it in TK Maxx the odd time if she's lucky. Anyway, they were talking about the new mascara and the free wine and the next thing you know she has three invites in her paw. Sadhbh is not one to turn down a free glass of something, and throw in the make-up angle and I was sure she'd be there. But she vaguely said she was busy. So I rang her.

'Are you sure you can't come? Free wine and mascara? Me and Maj will stay out til the last Timoney's bus. I feel like I haven't seen you in ages.'

'I know, I know. But I have plans. I have … a date.'

I felt an instantaneous pang of jealousy. Well, two pangs. One for this lad who gets to spend time with our Sadhbh, and another for me and John and our early dates, grinning at each other over pints or snuggling together against the cold wind at matches.

'Well, who is he? Do we know his father?' I joked. Although, if she was in BGB chances are we would.

'Just someone I'm seeing. Casually. A lad.'

'When you say "seeing", how long does that mean? Have you stopped waking up early to put on a bit of make-up before he sees you?' I've never done this but I've seen it in the romcoms.

'Aisling, you're wild. It's only been a couple of weeks. I'm just seeing him. He's someone I met in work. A musician. I'll tell you more if it becomes a thing. Promise.'

A musician. Who could it be? 'Is it a family band?'

'Is it a what?'

I couldn't take the suspense. 'Listen, Sadhbhy, you can tell me. Honestly. I'll take it to my grave.'

'Aisling, it's not serious! And he wants to keep it on the DL.'

'It's Jim Corr, isn't it?'

She howled. I took that as a no, so.

'Mickey Joe Harte?'

'Aisling!'

'Is it Niall Horan?'

More laughing.

'Hozier?'

'Aisling, if you don't stop asking me I'm going to burst a blood vessel.'

I felt a bit deflated after that call. I didn't feel like I could push any further than that, even if she is someone whose back I've fake tanned more times than you'd care to mention. I already feel like Sadhbh is slipping away from me, and I know less and less about her life. There was a time when I would have tried to keep a straight face as she pulled the dungarees out of a bag in the Chez SEA sitting room, but now I don't even know who she's shifting.

Meanwhile, on the style front, Majella had yet another hair-dye incident this week and is sporting a questionable shade of orange, but she's styling it out to be fair to her. The sombrero and the maracas earrings will distract from it anyway. She's looking well. Being in love really suits her. She's another one who feels a bit farther away from me, even though we're physically closer than ever. I suppose she has to make space for Pablo. Speaking of Pablo, he's already beyond in the bar in the Mountrath with John and some of the lads. He's beside himself with excitement about the Mexican theme, even though Majella has explained to him several times that his abilities as a Spanish translator won't be called upon and there won't actually be any Mexicans there, including himself, the Tenerife native. He's made rumblings about hosting a Tenerife-appreciation evening in Maguire's in an effort to bring some of his homeland to BGB. It would probably go down well. Sure, half the town has probably been there on holidays, myself included.

'Aisling! Girls! Terry Crowley's outside.'

Terry has the seven-seater and is bringing the whole lot of us, Mammy and all and the back-up bags of Doritos, out to the Mountrath for the party. Somehow I doubt Mammy will be staying late enough to head in to the Vortex for a dance, but she's coming to the function-room part of the evening alright. It's her first proper family do without Daddy by her side, and I'm a little bit nervous about her being sad, but she'll have us and Auntie Sheila. Mammy and Sadhbh are particularly good pals, even though they make an odd pair with Sadhbh's get-up and Mammy's beige trouser suit with matching accessories. I'm forever reassuring her that, yes, the blue in that scarf is the same blue as the flecks in those trousers. And, yes, those red earrings do pick up the red on her handbag. I have a good eye for matching and I didn't lick it off a stone. It's probably why I can pull an outfit together at the drop of a hat. Need to jazz up a black trousers and nice top combo? A pale-blue belt and baby-blue dangly earrings will sort you out.

Terry Crowley drops us off at the front door of the Mountrath, even getting out to help Mammy down out of the seven-seater. He'd better not get any ideas. He's a widower himself and I've seen him in action with the single older ladies of BGB. Mammy is struggling with the sombrero and her two Good Scarves – one for outerwear and the blue one to keep on for the evening to complement her outfit. She got the trouser suit in Geraldine's during the week. She only went in for elastic thread and a pair of thermal socks and next thing she knew she was trying on midi skirts and camisoles.

I was in the Mountrath earlier with Auntie Sheila and my cousin Doireann, hanging up the piñatas and the 'Olé Happy Birthday' signs, but walking into the function room now it looks even better than I remember, with the solitary disco ball spinning from the ceiling and the rotating coloured party lights bouncing off it. I immediately spot John, Pablo and co. at the bar. Cillian is at the bar too, looking shiny cheeked in a massive poncho and a stiff pair of bootcut jeans. He must be roasting. Enrique Iglesias is playing as we walk across to them, Majella dancing up to Pablo singing, 'You can run, you can hide, but you can't escape my love.' How are they going to keep it up with Spanish-y sounding songs all night? I suppose there's always the 'Macarena' and 'Feliz Navidad'. And Chris De Burgh's 'Spanish Train' if they get stuck.

'Aisling, do you know what this is supposed to be?' Sadhbh asks, approaching with two radioactive-looking pints of yellow liquid topped off with little umbrellas. These must be the margaritas Auntie Sheila had Jocksy Cullen mix up to welcome the party guests, but I must admit they don't look very appetising. Mammy is trailing behind her, clutching one, with a face that suggests tequila wouldn't be her thing. Sure, I could have told her that. I'll have to get her a little Baileys to take the taste out of her mouth.

'I think they're Mexican?' I venture, taking a sip. Jesus Christ, my legs nearly go from under me. There must be half a bottle of tequila in it. Sadhbh clocks my reaction and throws an eye to the bar.

'Yes, please,' I mouth, adjusting my sombrero, which is starting to make my head sweat. 'West Coast Cooler and a glass of ice. I'll grab us a table.'

Majella careens over as 'Whenever Wherever' comes on and pulls up a stool with Pablo hot on her heels. He has a carnation between his teeth and his hips are moving in what can only be described as a snake-like fashion. It's not even 10 p.m.!

I tell her to mind the table and head over to check on Mammy, who's sitting in a booth with Sumira Singh from the nursing home and Tessie Daly. The three of them are sharing a bag of Scampi Fries, obviously not keen on the Mexican fare doing the rounds. I'm just about to help myself to a handful when I cop Sadhbh at the bar in conversation with Niamh from Across the Road. My first thought is what the hell is Niamh doing here? She was only home at Christmas. For a minute I suspect Sheila must have sent an invite all the way over to New York for the party, but then I notice the girl standing beside her with the long, blonde hair. She looks vaguely familiar and then I realise who it is. No, it can't be? Can it?

I start walking towards them, my feet propelling me forward.

'Niamh?' I say, and the three of them turn around. Then I see the flash of recognition on the other girl's face and I realise it *is*: it's definitely her.

'Aisling!' she says, going in for a hug. 'It's been – how many? Fifteen years?'

Natasia was one of those kids Adi Roche had shipped over to Ireland from Chernobyl to get away from all the radiation. Even in primary school, Niamh was a humanitarian and she ended up getting the whole of BGB and Knock into it. We couldn't take any in because Granny was staying with us, God rest her soul, but loads of other families did. Going into Filan's was like walking down Main Street Chernobyl. Natasia arrived looking frail and pasty and left a stone heavier with a hurl in her suitcase wearing head to toe Levi's. Well, the Hattons wouldn't have had her in anything less. Although she was technically Niamh's Chernobyl child, the two of us became firm friends and spent many's a day that summer trying to catch pinkeens in a net and playing marbles.

'Jesus, Natasia, you haven't changed a bit,' I gasp as Niamh goes in for the hug too.

'Neither have you,' she goes. 'I'm so happy to be back in Ballygobbard. It's so different now. You have the ATM!'

'I know,' I say, accepting a West Coast Cooler from Sadhbh. 'It's all go here. And you look great! The country air must have suited you. What has you back?'

'I'm a pilot now, with KLM, based mostly in London, but I have been spending more time in Dublin. My boyfriend is based in Ireland a bit. I told Niamh I'd be around and she said she's in Ireland too for work so here we are!'

I'm just about to ask her what the craic is like in Chernobyl and whether there's much radiation around these days when John appears at my side, throwing an arm around my waist, the remains of a pint of margarita in his other hand. He's been flat out in work the past few weeks doing the final tweaks on some new microchip they're working on. He's lead engineer on a project at the plant. Those twelve-hour days just aren't right, and he always feels the need to leather it home when he has a few days off. I suppose I'll be on minding duty tonight, so.

'What have you guys heard about that site over by Garbally?' Niamh shouts over the music. Beside us, John is swaying slightly on his feet.

'Feck all!' I call back to her. She hardly knows any more than me, does she?

'I actually know the guy who's bought it to develop – it's James Matthews.'

Of course she knows more than me.

'He was in school with Ben,' Niamh continues. 'I actually just bumped into him out in the bar.'

Niamh's older brother, Ben, went to boarding school, which earned him the local moniker Boarding School Ben. He wasn't around much when we were younger, and when he started showing up in Maguire's he stuck out like a sore thumb in his chinos and deck shoes and funny accent. I believe he lives in Hong Kong these days and has a house with a sauna.

'James was just saying he got the site for a pittance. He's turning it into a lovely commercial unit with apartments upstairs. It sounds divine for the right occupant.'

Hmm. Maybe we'll finally get a Supermac's.

John hiccups and rubs his hand up and down my back, smiling lazily. A sure sign he's about four hundred sheets to the wind. I'm just about to drag him out to the smoking area for a bit of fresh air and a burrito when the unmistakable opening bars of 'Livin' la Vida Loca' come on. Suddenly there's a mad dash to the thronged dancefloor, where Mad Tom is hoisting Cillian up on his shoulders and tearing around the perimeter, his sombrero hanging off him, the cord in real danger of choking him. Loving it all the same, it has to be said.

'Upside, inside out! She's livin' la vida loca!'

Full of Guinness and lethal margaritas, John is absorbed into a sea of check shirts and Wrangler jeans as the local lads come together in one heaving mass of Ricky Martin fans. The gas thing is they don't have a drop of Latino blood between them, but you'd never think it the way they're gyrating around the place.

'She'll push and pull you down, livin' la vida loca!'

I realise I'm pissed now too, screaming the lyrics at Sadhbh, who's happily screaming them back at me, arms in the air.

The girls – Sharon, Deirdre and Maeve – appear around us and we all fire our bags on the floor and start shaking what our mammies gave us. I'm surprised to see Natasia twerking but it's great that she has the mobility all the same. She wouldn't have been able to do that a few years ago.

'Her lips are devil red and her skin is the colour mocha!'

I'm aware of Majella and Pablo off to my left, bodies wrapped around each other, swaying in time to the beat. No six inches left for Jesus there.

'She will wear you out, livin' la vida loca!'

Even Mammy, Auntie Sheila, Sumira and Tessie are up throwing shapes, Mammy snapping her fingers in time to the beat, which is a pure giveaway that she's on her third glass. Jesus, I'll be minding her too if I'm not careful.

As the song is about to end, the lads, led by Mad Tom, naturally, decide to give Cillian the bumps. You'd think they'd know better after Chief Gittons, father of Baby Chief Gittons, hit the ceiling in Dick's on the night of his sixtieth, but no. Up he goes and everyone cheers, while Auntie Sheila runs rings around them saying they'll break his back, begging them to stop. And again, higher this time to louder cheers. And again and again, higher and higher until his nose grazes the disco ball on the thirtieth go.

'Who wants a drink?' I shout into the crowd, but no one hears me. They're all too riled up, faces shiny and red. I bend down to retrieve my good Michael Kors, and when I stand up, the crowd in front of me sort of parts and there, standing nonchalant as you like with his back against the bar, looking straight at me, is Piotr.

CHAPTER 16

I haven't seen him in months. In fact, the last time I saw Piotr was the eve of Daddy's funeral. He was standing in the kitchen in the house he shared with John and Cillian, tall and cheekboned and ruffled blond and reaching out for me. We had kissed in the silence of my grief and his unmistakable horn. And then I had fled. I never told John – sure, weren't we on a break? A break-up, or so I had thought. Piotr never told him either, and he moved out shortly afterwards.

Seeing him standing there now against the bar, we might as well be back in that kitchen. All I can hear is a kind of silent roaring in my ears as I move my arm imperceptibly as if to wave at him. If it was a film I might mouth a 'hi' and glide in his direction, smiling gently. But it's not a film and I haven't moved an inch I'm that flabbergasted, and the silent roaring is because they've stopped the music to bring out the cake.

Majella slings her arm forcibly around my shoulders, shaking me out of the trance. People close in to the space between me and Piotr, crowding towards the bar and obscuring him momentarily.

'C'mon, Ais,' she bellows into my ear. 'Cake time.'

I allow her to lead me to the other side of the room, where the burrito cake is proudly displayed. Jennifer Ryan makes stunning cakes, it must be said. She has an Instagram page and is flat out attaching Kinder Buenos and Kit Kats to everything from christening cakes to birthday creations. There's talk of her giving up her full-time job and just doing the baking. Sure, people have gone stone mad for macarons.

'Maj.' I pull on her arm frantically. 'Maj, did you know Piotr was coming?' She doesn't cop on to what I'm saying at first, a confused look passing over her face. 'Peter? Who's Pet–? Oh, *Piotr.*'

'Shhhh,' I growl at her.

We're surrounded by people crowding around the massive chocolate burrito, which Jennifer still somehow managed to adorn with Ferrero Rocher and M&Ms, which are not the most Mexican of accompaniments. Cillian limps behind it, still recovering from his spill on the dance floor, and Auntie Sheila leads the crowd in a raucous 'Happy birthday to youuu, happy birthday to youuu!'

She's drowned out on the 'happy birthday, dear Cillian' bit by '*You look like a muckerrr … And you smell like one too,*' and if looks could kill, every young man in a ten-mile radius would be six feet under. But her ire is short lived, as Titch Maguire pushes Cillian's face down into the huge burrito cake, holding him there for a second before releasing him, and up comes Cillian, panting through chocolate buttercream and pockets of Ferrero. A gasp is followed immediately by a roar of approval. Jesus, things are really getting out of hand. Those margaritas have driven the whole place berserk. I pull Majella back out of the crowd, my eyes searching hers for some kind of guidance, as the music fires up again.

'It's grand,' she reassures me over the noise of Las Ketchup. 'Sure, you don't even have to talk to him and nobody knows. Me, you and Sadhbh, that's it. And him. He's not going to say anything. It's grand,' she insists again, suddenly mashing her legs together. 'I've to run to the jacks!' Once Maj has broken the seal there's no stopping her. She turns on her heel and calls over her shoulder, 'Find Sadhbh.'

Find Sadhbh, avoid Piotr. Should be both easy and impossible in this tiny, crowded function room. Maybe Sadhbh's already gone through to the Vortex with a few of the others, eager to escape the Shakira and the J-Lo? Maybe she's outside smoking one of her rollies? Maybe she … *Thwump*.

'Sorry.' I stumble back, dazed.

'Aisling.' His voice is warm and kind and a little bit confused. His hands are on my shoulders.

'Piotr. Hi. I didn't know– I didn't see– I didn't know you were coming.'

'How are you?' His forearms are so close to my face that I can see the golden hairs and smell that smell of his that's not aftershave or deodorant but just him.

'I'm grand.' I step back, looking down at my feet. 'Are you here long?' I'm desperate to get out of there.

'No, not long. Cillian asked me but I don't know many people here so I just wanted to call in and say happy birthday.'

Call in? We're hardly in Coppers. This is the middle of nowhere, miles from Dublin.

There's a tug on my hand and I turn. It's John, emerging through the throng looking glassy eyed and tousled. His face changes as his eyes focus on Piotr. My heart stops beating for what feels like hours, but he smiles and roars, 'Look who it is!' drawing Piotr into a bear hug. 'How are you, man?'

He's pumping Piotr's hand up and down energetically. 'We miss you in number fifty-seven.'

Piotr opens his mouth to answer and I jump in, 'I'm just going to the toilet.' I'm loath to leave them together, but I can't bear to stand there with the two of them any longer. John and I were broken up when me and Piotr kissed, and I wasn't in my right mind, but it's still a complete hames. They were housemates, like. Friends. I am the worst person in the world. And why does it still feel like there's nobody in the room except me and Piotr? Shouldn't I feel like that about John?

I rush towards the toilets and, in my haste, go flying on a discarded sombrero, straight into the path of some poor unfortunate who just about manages to keep hold of his pint.

'Christ, I'm sorry,' I stammer and my hands fly to my cheeks.

He's tall, with dark hair just long enough to hold a few messy curls. His eyes are deep brown and his dark stubble is on the verge of beard territory. He doesn't look familiar and he's not wearing any Mexican paraphernalia so he must be staying in the hotel. I'd say he didn't bargain for this carry-on in the bar when he booked in.

'Hey, no worries,' he says in a soft English accent. Not a *Coronation Street* accent or even an *Eastenders* one – more like Hugh Grant's, wherever he's from. 'Are you okay? Where's the fire?' He laughs, revealing a dimple in his left cheek. I crane my neck around him to see what John and Piotr are doing but Niamh from Across the Road catches my eye and makes a beeline for me.

'Ais! Ais, this is James – my brother Ben's friend.' she says. 'James, we were just talking about you. Aisling here is my neighbour – she still lives in Ballygobbard, for her sins.'

'Well, I just moved back actual–'

But Niamh already has me interrupted. 'I don't know how you stick it here full-time, Aisling. There isn't even a decent café for a spot of brunch. I'd go mad.'

'I find it nice enough,' James says kindly and sticks out his hand. 'Nice to meet you, Aisling.'

'Hiya, James,' I say distractedly, trying to get John and Piotr in my sights. 'I hear you're developing that site outside BGB? That's great news.'

'I am. I am. I'm the contractor on the job too so I'm staying here for a few months.'

Niamh interjects with a laugh. 'The budget didn't stretch to the Ard Rí then?'

'Trying to keep overheads low on this one,' James replies, smiling. Mad for the smiling, he is.

'Lads, I have to go,' I call behind me as I turn and head for the bathrooms and Majella. She's at the sinks, lavishly applying what I think is supposed to be one of those nude lipsticks but looks more like purple against our Irish skin. Pablo is wearing a fair whack of it across his face as well. Her sombrero is lying limply beside her. 'Dropped it in the jacks.' She gestures at it as I approach her.

'Piotr and John are out there. Talking. To each other.'

'Aisling.' She sighs, smiling sympathetically at me. 'You're getting het up about nothing. These things happen. John doesn't know. Piotr isn't about to tell him. Everything is going to be fine.' She folds her arms drunkenly around me. Usually it's me doling out the sensible advice but now here's Maj, still dropping things in the toilet but at least she's graduated from phones to hats, in a stable relationship, talking me down off a cliff.

'I just feel so bad,' I mumble into her shoulder. 'And ...' I think about telling her about the funny feelings Piotr gives me, but I trail off. I haven't felt that funny feeling with John for a while now, but I don't know if I can say it out loud.

Majella starts up again, moving towards the door as I follow her. 'Look, you and John were broken up. Sure, he was with that girl Ciara.' This was true. John did have kind of a thing with a camogie-playing vixen we met on holidays, but it was short lived, and sure *I* had dumped *him*. Maj continues, pulling the door towards her, 'And anyway, Piotr's a ride and he fancied you. Why wouldn't you shift him?'

She turns into the little hallway and stops dead. 'John.'

My heart drops to my feet. I push into Majella's back to move her further into the hallway and step out, looking up into John's eyes, which are already narrowing. Behind him, Sadhbh pushes into the hallway from the function room, exclaiming, 'Oh, hi, guys, here's where you all are ...' She trails off, Majella shaking her head furiously at her.

John goes to speak and then closes his mouth again. Majella has a go. 'John, I ...' but he interrupts.

'Who shifted Piotr, Majella?' His voice is shaky but cold. He turns his gaze back to me. Sadhbh looks down at the floor and mouths, 'Fuuuck.'

There's silence for ... how long? Ten seconds? Ten hours?

'Did you shift Piotr, Aisling?'

My breath catches in my throat. You can see him working things out. You can see him wondering how and when it happened. You can see him realising why Piotr moved out. I bite my lip. 'Yes but let me—'

'When was it, Ais?' His eyes are blazing. 'Was it recently? When was it?'

'No! No!' I cry. 'It was ages ago. We were broken up. It was ages ago. It was nothing!'

John gives me a look I've never seen before, his eyes blazing, before turning on his heel and pushing out past Sadhbh. We three look at each other for a moment before Sadhbh and Majella scarper after him, Majella gasping, 'Jesus, what's he going to do?' I'm hot on their tails.

John is shoving his way through to the bar, his head snapping left and right. Who's he looking for? Not Piotr, surely? He pushes past Titch Maguire, who's topless and leaning against a pillar swaying, barely holding on to his lethal margarita. John comes up behind a group of lads: Cillian, Baby Chief and – I strain my neck to see who else – Piotr. He stands there for a second, seething. Majella rears up behind him, pulling on his sleeve. 'John, John. Leave it.' He shakes her off and makes to step into the circle. I reach him just as he raises his hands to push Piotr. I grab his arm, pulling him as roughly as I can out of the circle towards me.

'John. What are you at?' I never thought I'd see him going for someone like that. On the field he's rough, of course, they all are. But he's not a fighter.

John is shaking his head in disbelief. In my peripheral vision I can see them staring at us, Cillian and Baby Chief and Piotr. Sadhbh steps up to me and says gently, 'Maybe you should go outside and talk?'

'*No!*' John hisses. OhJesusOhJesusOhJesusOhJesus. How is this happening?

'John,' I plead, grabbing onto his arm. 'It was nothing. I was just upset over Daddy and it was just for a second and nothing else happened–'

He pulls away and goes to walk off but turns back and looks me dead in the face. There are tears glistening in his eyes, but he curls his lip into a snarl and shouts, 'Doesn't make you any less of a *slu–*'

Majella gasps and lunges for John before he can finish, and at the same time Piotr makes the same move, leaping towards John with his arms outstretched. Both of them look like they might kill him. Majella and Piotr collide, though, knocking John out of the way in the process. He lands on the floor and Majella jumps half on top of him and immediately begins pummelling him, stone mad on the toxic drinks. Nobody knows what to do and I make feeble attempts to pull her off him. She's not landing a single blow, and of course John makes no move to hit her back.

Piotr, meanwhile, has landed awkwardly, banging his arm off the edge of a chair. He's rolling around and groaning, but the assembled crowd is far too suspicious of this blow-in to ask him if he's OK. I shout at Majella to *get up*, but it's not until Pablo sashays over to help her that John's face is revealed. He catches my eye with such a look of hatred as he clambers to his feet that the hot tears spill over onto my cheeks. There's no sign of Mammy and I can only hope that she and Auntie Sheila are already safely on the way home with Terry Crowley. I'd hate for her to have seen this display.

Liam Kelly wobbles over towards us, completely oblivious, with his tie around his head and singing along to J.Lo. 'Don't be fooled by the rocks that I got, I'm still, I'm still *Liam from Knock.*' He stops suddenly and looks from me to John to Piotr, who's still lying on the ground, grimacing, with Sadhbh now kneeling by his side. 'Jesus, lads, what am I after missing?'

CHAPTER 17

When I wake up the following morning I have a merciful few seconds before my brain fully engages. I lie there in my bedroom, sniffing the air, hoping for a hint of sausage, and then it hits me. The party. Piotr. John's face, scrunched up in disgust. I've never seen him look at anyone like that before, and definitely not me. He called me a slut – well, almost called me a slut – in front of everyone. Niamh from Across the Road was there. Even Natasia from bloody Chernobyl was there! The shame starts to seep up through my body from my toes, quickly replaced by panic about John. Is he okay? Did he get home alright? What will his parents say? I remember the tears glistening in his eyes and my heart breaks a little. What am I going to do?

Majella. Majella Mouth Almighty Moran. Can she ever keep her trap shut? I know it was an accident but I can't believe it. And what was Piotr doing there anyway? He and Cillian were never that pally. What a bloody mess.

After the ruckus, Liam and a few of the Rangers pulled John up off the floor and bundled him out into the night. The party was well over then and that was the last I saw of him. Someone – I'm not sure who – whisked Piotr away. I tried ringing John when Sadhbh went to gather up my coat and good pashmina but there was no answer. The second time it went straight to voicemail.

We sat in the bright lights of the Mountrath lobby for an hour before Terry Crowley was able to squeeze myself, Sadhbh, Majella and Pablo in on a run back from the Ard Rí. Terry already had four hens from Dublin on board dressed as the Spice Girls. Scary Spice had her sights firmly set on Pablo in the back seat, but Maj was having none of it, throwing her leg over him territorially even though she was half-asleep.

There's a soft knock on my door.

'Ais?' Sadhbh has managed to scramble free from the nest of cushions, pillows and throws Mammy erected for her in the spare room. She pads across and slips into the bed beside me, resting her head on my shoulder and whispering, 'Are you alright?' Of course I start bawling. What else is there to do?

'How can I make him understand it was nothing?' I wail. It *was* nothing, wasn't it? Although what I felt when I saw Piotr last night wasn't exactly nothing. It was something. It was something I've felt about him before. I push it down. No. I need to fix things with John, or talk to him at least.

'We'll sort it out, Ais, I promise,' Sadhbh says, rubbing my hair. 'Honestly, John was so pissed he probably doesn't even remember it.'

'He was drunk, not dead. I think he'll remember,' I say soberly, taking a tissue out of my pyjama sleeve and blowing my nose. 'What the feck was in those margaritas, though? Everyone was in bits.'

'I don't know, but it's nearly nine o'clock and there's no sign of your mam.'

That's highly unusual alright. She'd normally have the hoover going by now. My phone buzzes on the bedside locker.

'Ne word frm John? I'm so sorry crying emoji.' It's Majella, of course.

'Nothing,' I reply. I can't muster any more than that.

The phone goes again but this time it's a text from a number I don't recognise.

'Hi Aisling it's Piotr. Cillian gave me ur number.'

Speak of the devil.

Sadhbh, obviously copping the look on my face, grabs the phone. 'Oh my god, he has some cheek,' she shrieks, holding it just out of my reach. 'He ruined everyone's night and now he's texting you? And no apology? This guy's a troublemaker.' She pauses for thought. 'He's very hot, though,' she adds quietly, and then her face turns even more serious. 'Like, he's ridiculously ridey. How come you never said?'

'Because I have a boyfriend!' My face crumples.

Sadhbh comes closer, putting her arm around my shoulders. 'Don't fret too much about last night. You can explain everything to John. You'll work it out.'

'It's not even about last night. It's … it's me and John. It's just not the same.' I'm sobbing now.

'It happens, Ais,' Sadhbh says gently, after a pause. 'It's exciting and lovely to get back together and feel more in love than ever, but a lot of the time it doesn't last.'

She's so wise. She just knows.

'I think seeing Piotr just made me realise, maybe. That there are people besides John. That I should be feeling a certain way about John.' Mammy always says there's a lid for every pot, and I thought John was my lid. Maybe he just doesn't fit anymore.

My phone vibrates again beside Sadhbh's knee and she picks it up and hands it to me.

'It's him again, is it?'

It's another message from Piotr.

'In General Hospital for X-ray. Big queue. My turn soon. Any chance a lift?'

I gasp. 'He hasn't left yet. He's in the General getting an X-ray.' He did go over very hard on the elbow, to be fair. 'He's after a lift.'

'The chancer!' Sadhbh gasps, although I immediately feel guilty as sin. It's my fault he's in the General. And he spent the night there? They don't even have a canteen past seven o'clock.

'Oh Jesus, I feel awful, Sadhbh. How is he going to get back to the Mountrath? He knows nobody.'

'You're too nice for your own good, Aisling. Look, why don't you go and give him his lift and make it clear to him that he's to leave you alone?'

She's right – I need to take action and send Piotr firmly on his way. That will get me back in John's good books and make me feel useful and productive. Besides, he'll need a few sandwiches. He must be about to eat his own fist. I hop out of bed and start pulling my trusty O'Neill's up over my pyjamas and reaching for my fleece. I take up my phone and try John's number one more time. Straight to voicemail. I look at Sadhbh and shrug.

'Will I come with you?' She yawns.

I shake my head no.

'Okay. Good luck with Piotr. I'm going back to bed.'

****

I haven't been in a hospital since Daddy but as soon as the familiar smell hits my nostrils it's like I never left. All those days driving him in and out to appointments and then the waiting, the endless waiting and lukewarm cups of tea in Styrofoam cups, when he started going downhill. The place fills me with dread.

Still, I can't leave Piotr alone here. Being from Poland, he might not understand the waiting-room politics. Who knows what it's like over there – they might have one of those fancy systems where you take a number from a machine. It's not like that in the General, and we all know queuing can be stressful at the best of times.

I squeak my way along the shiny lino until I get to A & E. He wasn't lying – the place is jammers, even for a Sunday morning, and I see a few familiar faces from last night, although I'm delighted to see Cillian isn't among them with a broken spine. Mad Tom is snoring loudly in a corner with his head against a vending machine and his foot wedged into a traffic cone. I wouldn't be surprised if Auntie Sheila was somehow behind it. She can be quite vengeful and I know she'd have access to cones through Mammy's Tidy Towns connections.

I tip down the corridor until I get to the X-ray department, which is one room with six unoccupied chairs outside it. The door is open and there's no sign of anyone around. I'm about to turn on my heel when someone taps me on the shoulder. I'm expecting it to be one of the patients looking for some toast or new batteries for their remote – I can't step into a hospital without being mistaken for a nurse, and I usually just do my best to get what they need – but it's him. It's Piotr. His left arm is in a sling and he's topless.

'I didn't think you'd come,' he says, wincing as he leans forward to hug me with his remaining good arm.

'I wanted to make sure you were alright,' I stammer. 'And, and to see why you came to the party. To see why you came here. After what happened between …' I gesture in the air between the two of us. This isn't really how I'd rehearsed it in the car. Piotr's face softens and I quickly add, 'How's the arm? Here.' I brandish a sad, prepacked sandwich from Filan's Garage at him. Egg and onion. Definitely the worst sandwich – not even a hint of meat – but better than nothing all the same.

'So good, Aisling, like always,' he says with a grin, sitting down in the empty corridor and tearing off the cellophane as best he can. The poor fella is obviously starving and I must admit I'm vindicated by his hunger. I take the seat opposite him and do my best not to notice his biceps bulging and how his abs ripple slightly as he horses into the sandwich. He's built like a Happy Pear twin but without all the 6 a.m. headstands and jumping into the sea. Although maybe that *is* the kind of thing he's into? I don't know Piotr well at all.

'Is it broken?' I ask, gesturing at the arm.

'A hairline fracture.'

Well, that's something, I suppose. I had visions of John or Majella being done for grievous bodily harm, but sure a hairline fracture never hurt anyone. I got enough of them lepping off hay bales back in the day. I take a deep breath and swallow.

'Piotr, why are you here? Why did you come to Ballygobbard?'

'Cillian's party.' He shrugs lopsidedly. 'He sent the invitation weeks ago, you know. It had a Chihuahua wearing a sombrero on it. How could I say no?'

'Is that really it? You wanted to see Cillian?'

He pushes the end of the sandwich into his mouth and looks at me studiously while he chews and rolls the cellophane into a ball. After he swallows he says, 'And you. I wanted to see you.'

'But why?' I practically shriek. 'What happened between us that time shouldn't have happened. I'm … I'm with John.'

'John who called you names in front of all your friends last night? Yeah, real nice guy John.'

The memory hits me like a slap in the face. Majella trying to stop him and Piotr … going for him. Piotr defending my honour like a prince in all those fairy tales I was force-fed growing up. When I was younger it was my dream to have two lads fighting over me – you know, like Hugh Grant and Colin Firth in *Bridget Jones's Diary*. Well, the reality wasn't a bit romantic, and now John hates me and Piotr's elbow is in shite. It wasn't supposed to be like this.

'Everything was going fine until you–'

'Until I arrived? Was it really fine, though, or are you telling yourself that? He found out about our, what do you call it, shaft? And he went crazy!'

'Shift!' I hiss, looking around surreptitiously to see if anyone heard him, my voice bouncing off the bare walls and down the corridor. 'Not shaft! Jesus! It was just a kiss. I don't know why he reacted like that. He was pissed. The drinks were lethal.' But with each protest I make I realise more and more that John suspects the same thing I do. We're in trouble. And the Piotr revelation pushed him over the edge.

'Piotr, you're lovely. You have lovely …' my eyes wander over his chest and down his strong arms, '… eyes. And you've been kind to me. But I'll drop you back to your car and then we'll leave it at that, okay? You were supposed to stay at the Mountrath, were you?'

Ah God. He looks crestfallen.

'Yes,' he says sadly. 'Your friend Tom drove us here last night. He had a traffic cone on one foot. I had to help with the pedals.'

Mother of God, he's lucky to be alive. Mad Tom was full as a bingo bus. 'Right, I'll drop you back so, although,' I check my watch, 'the breakfast finishes at eleven so you'll definitely have missed that – sorry for your troubles. Do you have … everything?' I point at his bare chest, his sallow skin glowing under the fluorescent lights. I'm worried the other male patients will feel inadequate if he parades out through the waiting room like that.

'My T-shirt, the doctor, she had to tear it off for the X-ray,' he goes. I'll bet she did. 'I have another in the hotel so it's okay.'

He still looks sad and I wonder for a split second am I being completely mad. What if Piotr is–?

He interrupts me. 'I'm sorry, Aisling. I believed you and John were no more. I really did. I came to the party to see you, yes. But I never meant to make you angry. We are friends?'

Friends. Piotr and I were never friends. He was a distraction. A distraction I don't need right now. A complication.

'John and I are … together, Piotr. I'm sorry if that's – if that's not what you wanted to hear.' Am I in some kind of alternate reality? Breaking this big blond ride's heart? I've never broken a heart in my life.

'Okay, Aisling. You let me know if that ever changes, okay?'

'Okay.' I smile and sigh and start to usher him towards the side entrance, trying not to touch his bare skin as my hand hovers at his back. I go first and hold the door open, but just as Piotr is about to walk through it, who comes around the corner in her perfectly starched nurse's uniform but Fran. As in, John's mam Fran.

CHAPTER 18

'So you just dropped him at the hotel? And that's that?'

Sadhbh is incredulous. I'm pacing up and down Mammy's kitchen but there's still no sign of the woman herself. Poor Sadhbh is having to forage in the fruit bowl for breakfast, but she seems happy enough with her wrinkly kiwi and few easy-peelers. I'm mortified – I don't think she's ever gone a Sunday without having brunch – but I don't fancy her chances at finding any halloumi or avocados in Mammy's fridge. Plenty of leftover stew, though.

'I was just checking to see if he was okay and he is. He definitely is. I've sent him on his way. I'm more worried about John's mam seeing me at the hospital with him.'

I'm surprised Fran didn't turn me into a pillar of salt with the look she gave me when she saw me with Piotr. And him with no top on! I groan and sink into a chair. How am I going to come back from this?

Sadhbh laughs. 'I'm sorry, Ais, I don't mean to – I really don't. But how have you turned into the scarlet woman of BGB?'

'Sadhbh!' She has the decency to look ashamed of herself at least. She's right, though. I was terrified I'd see someone

I knew at the Mountrath. I barely slowed down the car before nudging Piotr out with a byebyebyebye, and I was thankful for the pair of mad sunglasses belonging to Elaine I found in the glove compartment. Imagine that got back to John: me, spotted at Piotr's hotel the morning after, and him practically in the nip. John is hurt enough as it is. I grab my phone and text him again, my third that morning.

'Will you just ring me? Please?'

I've picked up the car keys at least twenty times already to drive to his house in Knock, but after all these years I know John – confronting him like that would be the last thing he'd want. Plus, I don't particularly want to run into Fran.

I wish more than anything in the world that I could escape back to Chez SEA today with Sadhbh and hide under a blanket, but instead I have to stay here and live with my shame. Although, to be fair, Sadhbh says her new living situation is nowhere near as much craic as Chez SEA. Mairead and Fionnuala actually sound a bit much – one of them made a rota of household jobs and put Sadhbh down for cleaning the bathroom three Wednesdays in a row when she wasn't there to defend herself. And apparently they have the whole fridge taken up with their individual Slimline milks – even I see the logic in sharing cartons of milk. And they're both in bed by ten every night so there's no chats over rosé or takeaway pizzas.

The kitchen door opens suddenly and we both turn around with the fright as Mammy stumbles in, her face scrunched up against the midday sun.

'And what time do you call this?' I say automatically. 'We've been up for hours.'

'Sorry, pet,' she croaks. 'I don't know what happened.' She looks at the clock above the kitchen window and visibly balks – it's after twelve now. This is unprecedented. 'Those drinks last night were very strong – weren't they, love?'

'They were, Marian,' Sadhbh concedes. 'Here, sit down out of the sun.'

Sadhbh's always such a lickarse when she's down in BGB, but I resist the slagging because Mammy is mad about her. I busy myself looking for some painkillers to offer Mammy but pickings are slim. It's not like in the apartment in Portobello where Elaine would frequently appear with armfuls of Ponstan and Difene as soon as I so much as mentioned having cramps. Not that I ever accepted. I value the lining of my stomach, thanks, Elaine.

There's nothing but Milk of Magnesia and some Andrew's Liver Salts in the kitchen press, but if I recall correctly, there may be a Solpadeine or two in the Important Drawer in Daddy's old writing desk in the front hall, saved for genuine emergencies. Like if someone loses a leg in the combine harvester.

'Auntie Sheila was the one who organised the cocktails,' I say, heading for the door. 'What exactly did she order, Mammy?'

'She got a great deal on the tequila from Eamon Filan so she told Jocksy to make loads of double margaritas and just put them in a bigger glass,' Mammy explains holding her head, her voice weak. 'I think she overestimated how much we'd need. The six cases she bought were all drank by ten.'

Well, that explains that, I think to myself, heaving up the lid of the ancient desk. Some people just have no cop on.

I only have the Important Drawer half-open when I spot the unmistakable white and red wrapper of the Solps under a sheaf of papers. I'm just reaching in to retrieve them when an official-looking document under a pile of mismatched keys catches my eye. The heading says 'Whitford Chartered Surveyors' above a Dublin address. 'A chara,' it reads, 'Pertaining to our recent survey of your property at Knocknamanagh Road, Ballygobbard, please see below our detailed valuation …'

I'm just about to pull it out to finish reading it when the door swings open and Sadhbh appears in the hall with my phone in her hand: 'It just buzzed!'

I slam the drawer shut and grab it, hoping to see John's name flash up, but it's not John at all. It's not even a text – it's just my Fitbit app wondering if I'm dead or alive.

With the precious Solps in hand, I head back into the kitchen. 'Here's something for your head, Mammy,' I say, firing the two tablets into a glass of water with a satisfying plink-plink-fizz. I dither beside her, the words 'survey' and 'valuation' pinging around my head. Why is she getting the place valued? She groans a little and I back away. Now is not the time to be quizzing her about that document. 'Do you want to take that back to bed? Don't worry about us, we're fed and watered. You might as well rest yourself. A tequila hangover is no joke.'

'I do not have a hangover,' she retorts, standing up and shuffling out of the room, clutching the bubbling glass.

I'm still pacing up and down the kitchen, my skin practically itching with anxiety.

'Ais, you're going to be okay. It's going to be okay,' Sadhbh says gently.

'I don't think so, Sadhbhy. Not this time.' And I finally sit down, the nervous energy draining out of my legs.

****

After depositing Sadhbh at the bus stop in town – again grateful for the mad sunglasses – I arrive home to find Majella at the kitchen table eating a Chocolate Kimberly. She must have gone deep into Mammy's stash to find such a high-quality biscuit. And Mammy didn't even bother hiding any this past Christmas – she didn't have it in her. I suspect they're actually from a couple of years ago.

'In a sealed sandwich bag inside the downstairs toilet cistern,' she says firing one at me, clearly delighted with herself. Mammy still hasn't resurfaced but Maj would know well how to let herself into the house without making a peep. The Morans are only two fields away and we both spent as much time in each other's houses as our own growing up. No play dates or any of that craic in BGB. We just ... hung around.

'I'm sorry about letting the cat out of the bag, Ais,' she says tracing the pattern on Mammy's oilcloth absentmindedly, and I know in my heart of hearts I can't stay mad with her. It was an accident – she didn't put a gun to my head and force me to kiss Piotr that night. No one did.

'It wasn't your fault, Maj. I'm sorry for being short with you,' I say, accepting her chocolate-covered peace offering.

'Any word from him?' she says.

'From John? No.' I'm about to tell her about Piotr, topless in the hospital, but don't have the energy.

She reaches for another Kimberly. They *are* irresistible to be fair. 'So …' She hesitates. 'What *is* the story with you and John?' She already sounds resigned. I guess she's seen this coming.

'It's so, so broken, Maj. And I'm not even sure if I want to fix it.'

'Oh, Ais. I'm sorry.' She doesn't even try to talk me out of it. 'Do you know what you need?' Her tone has changed. She's up to something. 'You need to get out of here for a while.' She knows full well what it could be like around BGB with the gossip. Between Denise Kelly being stone-cold sober and witnessing everything last night, and my run-in with Fran at the hospital this morning, I'd say everyone within a 15-mile radius knows my business.

'What about going away for a few days?' Majella continues, clearly thinking out loud. 'It's mid-term break next week so I'm free to head off. Pablo is broke – he won't mind. Shem and Liz are already starting to do my head in, and maybe with me gone for a few days Willy might leave Pablo alone for two minutes. What do you think? We could get a handy little last-minute deal and you have your redundancy money.'

'I'm not supposed to be spending that on a holiday, though,' I say. Who knows how long I'll have to make that money last. I've already spent €92. Every cent is like a knife through my heart. But she's on to something – it would be nice to get away. Maybe Sadhbh would come too?

'We'd have to be careful, though,' Majella adds. 'Hard to avoid kids on a mid-term break, and I don't want to end up swimming around in a pool full of toddlers and piss. I get enough of it at school.'

Just then, the front doorbell trills loudly, and Majella and I look at each other. Nobody down the country uses the front door, let alone the doorbell. I wasn't even sure it worked. Even the odd time Mammy orders something online, the courier instinctively knows to come around the back. (Her latest way to outsmart the Nigerian princes and phishing scammers is a prepaid Visa card. Constance Swinford put her on to them, and she's as smug as anything, delighted her bank account remains impenetrable.) Does the front door even open? I've long suspected it's just there for show.

'Are you going to … answer it?' Majella eventually says, cocking her head in the direction of the hall. I suppose I'd better. Maybe I've won one of those RTÉ competitions for a car and there's going to be a camera crew standing on the front step? God knows I enter enough of them.

But when I drag open the door it's not Ray D'Arcy or even Derek Mooney staring back at me: it's Denise's cousin Sharon. And she has two massive black sacks with her.

'Hiya, hun,' she goes, turning around and zapping her car locked. It's one of those Volkswagen Beetles with the eyelashes on the headlights. Very glam. Although why she's locking it is beyond me. She's just wasting her zapper battery in BGB. 'Denise brought home all this Mexican stuff from the party and I told her I'd drop it back to your mam.'

'Ah right, of course,' I say. 'Come in now out of the cold, Sharon. Will you have a cup of tea? We have the good biscuits out.'

She follows me through to the kitchen and I relieve her of the plastic bags, sombreros and ponchos and bits of banners tumbling out on to the lino. Mammy will be delighted to get them back. Nothing makes her happier than reusing party bits – she has a great knack for unwrapping presents without tearing the paper. It's a gift I'm delighted she passed on to me because it's saved me a fortune over the years.

'Did you have a good night, hun?' Sharon goes to Majella, sitting down at the kitchen table, and I busy myself putting the kettle on. 'Your boyfriend is some man to dance!'

'It's the Spanish blood,' Majella says proudly. 'He's teaching me salsa at the moment. It's great craic. I've been telling him he should run classes in the hall.'

'Well, I had a deadly night,' Sharon says, 'even if it was the first time I met Cillian. It seemed like the whole village was out.'

I wince at that last bit. The whole village *was* out. They all saw the fight.

'You were looking fairly cosy with Cyclops there towards the end,' Majella says with a smile. 'He's a nice lad – and a world-class centre back, in case he didn't mention it'

Sharon looks a bit stony-faced and takes a sip of her tea. 'Yeah, he did actually. He seems sound but … I'm not interested in a man right now.' She changes the subject. 'Why does everyone call him Cyclops, though? I didn't want to ask in case, I don't know, it was because of a medical condition.'

'His name is Eoin Ó Súilleabháin,' Majella says by way of explanation, but Sharon just looks back at her blankly.

'Súilleabháin,' I repeat a bit louder, but still no flicker of recognition from Sharon. I would have thought it was obvious. '*Súil amháin*,' I say even louder.

'One eye!' Majella yelps. 'Cyclops.'

'Ahhh,' Sharon goes. 'I get it now! Okay, that makes sense. Sorry, my Gaeilge is a bit rusty.'

'It's actually gas because his sister is an optician,' I chime in. 'Susie Ó Súilleabháin. She has a little practice over in Knock.'

'How's the salon coming along?' Majella asks, helping herself to the last hot drop of tea. She wouldn't be Susie Ó Súilleabháin's biggest fan after a dispute over the cost of contact lenses. She accused Susie of being a gouger and, long story short, she buys them online now.

'Nearly there, thanks. Hoping to open in a couple of weeks.' Sharon's expression changes and she lifts the cup to her lips but doesn't drink from it. 'I'm getting a bit of grief from your man next door actually, the butcher? He's complaining that my builders are interfering with his business, even though I'm just having a few sunbeds put in. He's in nearly every day to give out about something.'

I say nothing but I'm not surprised, and sure Tessie had already predicted this. Marty Boland has a terrible reputation in the village – he's an out-and-out bully. His sausages won the grand prix award at the threshing three years in a row and, to be honest, it went to his head. He has that massive sign on the front door that says 'Best Sausages in the "County". Handmade by Marty Boland.' Jesus, they're good, though. Word on the street is the recipe was handed down from Marty's grandad and he keeps it locked in a safe behind a picture in one of the walls of his house.

'Keep your guard up there,' I advise. 'Tessie Daly, you know from the charity shop? She had a fierce row with him a few years ago over her shop window. She had a very tasteful slip display and he lost the head and said it was indecent. She put her foot down and the names he called her at a Neighbourhood Watch meeting … I couldn't repeat them myself. And his poor wife is like a mouse. He thinks he's such a big man.'

'He's a prick,' Majella says flatly, and I nod. He *is* a prick.

'Noted,' Sharon says, finishing off her tea and standing up. 'Right so, I better be off. Thanks for the cuppa, hun. See you ladies soon.'

I let her out the front door, and when I get back to the kitchen Majella is sporting a massive grin.

'I've got it,' she says, slapping the table, sending the Chocolate Kimberly wrappers flying. 'I've thought of someplace we can go where we definitely won't encounter any children and where we're guaranteed right craic.'

'Will I get a tan?' I venture. Of course my Irish skin only alternates between red and white, but you're obliged to try and go brown, aren't you? How else are you supposed to prove you've been abroad?

'Only if you want to,' Majella counters. 'You can probably stay indoors the whole time if you like.'

'Where is this magical place?' I'm intrigued. I have a love–hate relationship with the sun, but it's nice to have options.

'Las feckin' Vegas!'

CHAPTER 19

John paces back and forth in my room, picking things up and putting them back down again, pretending to examine them. He's just picked up a box of tampons and turned them around in his hand, though, studiously 'reading' the back, so I'm fairly sure his mind is elsewhere. He picks up a pair of socks and peers at them intently, so I jump off the bed and take them, gesturing to the chair at my desk, which is still laden with my colour-coordinated Leaving Cert folders I just can't bring myself to throw away. You never know when someone might come looking for my detailed karst landscape diagrams. To this day I know a clint or a grike when I see one. And I can spot a sea stack from half a mile away.

Neither of us has spoken since Mammy let him in the back door and called up the stairs that he was here. Usually he'd just head on up. But things are different now. I haven't seen him since the party. John talks first.

'So I hear you're going to Vegas?' he says dryly. And then sarcastically adds, 'Without me.'

We had always planned to go to Vegas someday. Back when I had engagement rings and bouquets on the brain, I thought it would be a great honeymoon destination if we decided against the customary two weeks in the Maldives or Mauritius. Vegas and the Grand Canyon and San Francisco and all that jazz. You can get great deals.

'Well, I didn't think you'd want to come!' I shoot back, equally sarcastic

'Of course I wouldn't want to come!' he almost shouts, giving me an awful fright. Mammy's ears must be on stalks downstairs. 'I can hardly look at you.'

We've had rows before, obviously. Loads of them. Sure, we've had a break-up before. But this one feels different. It feels so sad and final. He's so angry and hurt. It took him days to acknowledge any of my messages or calls. It was him who finally reached out to me, although his 'I think we should talk' message didn't inspire any confidence.

'Look, I'm sorry, John. It wasn't nice for you to find out that way. I didn't think –'

'You didn't think I'd find out at all, did you?'

He's got me there. I really didn't think he'd find out, and everything would be fine. But everything hasn't been fine. Not for a while. And it has nothing to do with Piotr, really.

'My housemate, Aisling? And then my mother has to tell me she saw you at the General with him! Do you have any idea how tormented I am imagining how long you fancied him for? Were you giving him the eye behind my back?'

'*No!*' I really wasn't. I mean, Piotr was always a ride, I suppose, but until John and I broke up I never saw anything in him. And besides, John basically had a girlfriend when we were broken up.

'What about you and Ciara?' I counter, before he has a chance to speak again. 'Do you not think I was hurt when you turned up with her? Had you fancied her since we met her in Tenerife? Were you just waiting for your chance to … to … stick it in her?'

'Aisling! Come on! Stop that!'

But I'm off. I want to hurt him. I want to hurt him like he hurt me when he got with Ciara. I thought that getting back together and grieving together over Daddy would heal us, would make us stronger. But I was wrong. It all comes pouring out of me.

'And you didn't see me calling *you* a slut, did you, when you were parading around with Ciara? Oh no! But it was okay for you to say it to me in front of everyone! My daddy had just died, John. Piotr was there. I needed someone. I am not a slut!' I would have expected to be crying at this point. Roaring. But my eyes are dry and my chest is heaving.

Sadhbh warned me about this. She warned me about meeting up and the horrible things that might be said and how hurtful it might be. 'People have a huge capacity to say awful things to each other, Ais,' she said gently on the phone last night. 'Don't make it so bad that you can never come back from it. It's John. You've spent your whole adult lives together.'

Her words are ringing in my ears now as we gaze at each other angrily across my small room. Me sitting on the bed where we've lain together so many times, my head on his strong chest, watching episode after episode of *The West Wing* on my tiny portable telly. He got me the boxset one Christmas, and we were never allowed watch an episode without the other person. It has helped me no end in table quizzes. Nothing like pulling an answer about filibustering out of the bag when you're in second place and there's a bottle of vodka and two bales of briquettes at stake. John's across from me, leaning forward, elbows on his knees, head down.

'I'm sorry,' he mumbles, and I see a tear drip from the end of his nose onto my Forever Friends rug.

My eyes begin to water. 'What's after happening to us, John?' The hot tears spill over onto my cheeks. 'We've gone all wrong.' Full-blown crying now. Shoulders shaking, the whole shebang. John doesn't look up but in a sad voice says, 'I don't know, Ais. I don't know.'

We've grown apart. It was so good for a while. For a short, lovely while after we got back together it was warm and safe and us against the world. Us against my grief about Daddy. Us against everything. But it didn't last. 'You've outgrown him, Ais.' Sadhbh's words from last night ring in my ears again. 'He's all you've ever known.' She's right. I have outgrown him. So much has happened in the past year. I can imagine a life without him. It makes me so sad, but I can.

'John, do you think maybe this isn't right for us anymore?' My voice sounds remarkably steady.

He looks up in horror, more tears streaming down his face now. But in the next instant his face softens. 'Yeah. Yeah, I think maybe you're right.' He smiles through the tears and continues, 'I can't believe it, Ais.'

He crosses the tiny space between us and sits down beside me, our shoulders touching and both of us looking at our hands. He stretches his big dry palm out on my lap, inviting me to hold it one last time.

'Remember the first time you held my hand walking into Maguire's and the place nearly came down with the jeering?' I sniff, placing my hot little paw, wet from tears, inside his.

'I do.' He squeezes. 'I didn't care … that much.' He smiles. 'Remember the time we went to Amsterdam and you were so paranoid about people thinking we were doing drugs?'

How could I forget that? We were only going to Amsterdam because we won the flights in a GAA raffle, not to go berserk on hash cakes or what have you. I made sure we went to every museum we could find so I'd have something to tell people – Mammy, especially – when we came home. There's nothing I don't know about Van Gogh. Suddenly John starts to laugh … and laugh and laugh. Really creasing himself.

'What?' I demand. 'What's so funny?'

'Remem– remember–' He can hardly get the words out. 'Remember you thought the hotel was spying on us? You – you put a plaster over the peephole and made me check the lamps for hidden cameras and microphones.'

He's right, I suppose. I was a nervous wreck the whole time. I was sure we were going to get done for something or get something planted on us. Drug mules, the pair of us!

'Well, aren't you glad I did and we didn't end up on *Banged up Abroad*?' His laughter is contagious, though, and soon I'm hooting too, still squeezing his hand. As our laughter subsides I ask him: 'Remember the last night in Amsterdam, though, when we found the lovely restaurant with the burgers and the waiter thought my name was Ash-knee and gave us the free bottle of wine?'

'Yeah,' John says. 'Yeah, I do'. Silence falls between us as we think about that night. Walking back to the (bugged,

I still swear it) hotel hand in hand, drunk as skunks on the free wine and laughing like drains through the streets of Amsterdam.

John shifts around on the bed, turning to face me, breaking the silence. 'Aisling.'

'Yeah?'

'You were never with Piotr before that, were you? You never … you never kissed him before that?'

'No! No, never! Never anyone, John.'

He sighs. 'Okay, okay, just checking.' He's teasing, but his bad attempt at a joke is poorly timed.

I mull over it for a minute and then, quietly seething and wracked with guilt, I turn to him. 'Jesus Christ, who do you think I am? I've told you. It was once. I was in bits. It never happened again. How many more times do you want to ask me about it?'

And like that, our hands are broken. There's a million miles between us again. John sets his jaw and retorts, 'Well, you're free to go out with him now anyway.'

I sigh, exhausted by it all. 'John, I don't want to go out with Piotr. I'm not going to be going out with Piotr, and I've told him that. It was all just a stupid mess. I'm sorry that I hurt you. I really am. But you hurt me too. We hurt each other. Let's not do it anymore. Please.'

We sit in silence on the bed, shoulder to shoulder, for what seems like an age. We both cry at different points. John first, more tears dropping off the end of his nose onto his hands. I put my arm around him and he clings to me suddenly, sobbing. I've never seen him cry like this. I grip him so tightly that I feel like my fingers might go through his shirt.

After minutes, or hours, he retreats. Then it's my turn to weep. I think about us dancing to Snow Patrol in the kitchen at a party. I think about the time he made me a 'Couch Kit' for my birthday: a *Legally Blonde* DVD, Toffypops, fluffy slippers, multiple face masks and a mini kettle I could plug in right beside the couch. That was years ago. Long before duplicate Pandora bracelets. I cry for all the times he drunkenly told me he loved me. 'I love me county,' he slurred to me one year when they got through to the quarter-finals of the All Ireland and he drank too many of those fruit cider yokes. 'I love me county, Aisling. But I love you more.' That one makes me cry the most. He hugs me then. Clinging to me, his fingers digging into my shoulders.

At some point I lie down, exhausted, shoes still on. John curls in behind me, recreating those oh-so-familiar spoons, his warm breath ghosting at my neck. Downstairs I hear Mammy in the kitchen, scraping a pot and opening and closing the oven. But we don't move. I hear Paddy Reilly come and go, checking something about lambs and something else about fodder. I listen to the faraway noises and I listen as John's breathing gets deeper. At some point I must drift off myself, spent from the crying and the laughing and the emotion of it all. I dream that we're at a funfair, flying around on one of those treacherous chair-o-plane yokes. They're faster than they look. In the dream, I'm swinging around and John's ahead of me, looking back and laughing and reaching for my hand, but I can't catch it. I wake in total darkness and sit up, willing my eyes to focus. I can sense that John is still there, sitting on the edge of the bed. How long has he been like that?

'John?'

'Yeah.' He leans over and switches on the bedside light.

'What time is it?'

'It's two. I'd better go.'

'You don't have to go. You can stay. We can watch *The West Wing*. Wouldn't it be so easy to just watch *The West Wing* and pretend none of it is happening, just for tonight?'

I know it's over but I still don't want him to go. Not just yet. I want one last night of sleeping with my head on his chest, his leg over mine and the duvet ending up on the ground, like usual. No funny business. Just … Aisling and John.

He considers it for a minute and then gives a shuddering sigh and shakes his head. 'No, I'll go. I'll let myself out.'

John stands up, stretching his long legs and his long arms, and just stands there for a moment, his back to me. He turns, gives a weak, sad smile and says, 'Bye, Aisling. I suppose I'll see you when I see you.'

I thought I'd cry all night, but I don't. I switch off the light and lie there in the darkness, picking through my brain for some more inspirational break-up quotes. Majella would be a big fan of firing them up on Facebook after a shift in Coppers didn't text her back. 'Don't stress the should-haves. If it could have, it would have.' And her personal favourite: 'Don't cry because it's over, smile because that gobshite is now somebody else's problem.' They don't really apply here, though. What's that one Auntie Sheila has on a magnet on her fridge? It was Marilyn Monroe or the Dalai Lama or someone who said it. 'What's for you won't pass you.'

That's it. What's for you won't pass you.

CHAPTER 20

Half of the people in this queue are honeymooners and the other half seem to be going on stags and hens. Well for some. What's wrong with a bit of Carrick-on-Shannon or Kilkenny? We're lucky we're going this week and not next week. There's a fight in Vegas next weekend between the 'next McGregor' and some Russian lad. There's great hype over it but I've never heard of your man, truth be told. I can only imagine the number of home-improvement credit-union loans that are funding the trip. Would you blame them, though? It's not often we get to show our sporting prowess on the world stage. Mammy still tells the story of Daddy threatening to remortgage the farm in 1990 when Ireland got through to the quarter-finals in Italy. She nipped it in the bud fairly fast, and he made do with painting half a herd of cattle green, white and gold and threatening to name any future children 'Packie' or give them the middle name 'Cascarino'.

Sadhbh arrived for the flight wearing something she described as 'airport pyjamas'. They look too posh to be actual pyjamas, but they do appear to be fierce comfy. I nearly wish I'd invested in a pair myself but my tracksuit bottoms and old BGB Gaels hoodie are nearly as good.

Sadhbh almost took the hand off me when I told her me and Maj were going to Vegas. The new job is fairly hectic, and I think living with Fionnuala and Mairead is taking its toll too.

She won't say much in front of Majella, of course, because they're her pals, but Fionnuala had her parents staying in the house last weekend and they all slept in the room together, Fionnuala on the floor and the parents in her queen bed. 'It was like something out of *The Hills Have Eyes*,' Sadhbh insisted to me, traumatised. Then when Sadhbh was trying to watch *Sunday Brunch* Fionnuala's father came in and told her to switch over to mass on RTÉ One.

'Will you move again?' I hiss at her as Majella heads up to the bar for three celebratory proseccos in Terminal 2.

'Sure where would I go?' She hisses back. 'I can't afford anything on my own, and better the devil you know for the moment, I suppose. I could end up in a house share in Santry with some fella who wants to put my knickers in his pillowcase at night. There's not much else going.'

'And what about … himself?' Sadhbh's still being fierce cagey about this new fella she's seeing. Not a hint of him on Facebook, still haven't met him and all I know about him now is that his name is Donal and he's 'on the music scene'. Sure, who isn't on the music scene in her gang?

'Oh, he's away a lot with work. But I stay with him a good bit – whenever I can, really.'

'Any photos? Any goss?' I've tried to play it cool on multiple occasions, but she surely owes me some detail at this stage. And me single and sad. She dismisses me with a wave of her hand and deftly changes the subject.

'How are you, anyway? About John and everything?'

I've been mostly alright. I feel calm about it. I'm not up the walls like I was worried I would be. I'm more worried about being unemployed, truth be told. Although, the more I've been at home the more I've been dragging my heels on trying to find a new job. I'm worried about leaving Mammy. She keeps telling me what a huge help I've been to her and how she could never run the show on her own. I worry about the farm all the time. I'm convinced a 'For Sale' sign is going to go up any day. I can't bring myself to ask her about it, though. I'm not ready for that kind of conversation, and I know she'll tell me in her own good time. The idea of handing over our home and all of Daddy's memories to someone else is too much to even think about. I'm worried about everything. I envy Paul, so far away in Australia.

'Well?' Sadhbh nudges me. But I don't want to get into it now.

'I'm grand. I'm grand. So back to this Donal. When are we going to meet him, or see him at least?' I'm starting to think that maybe she's made him up.

'Okay, but you have to promise to keep your cool. I wasn't sure if it was going to last and he's really weird about "going public", but … here.' Sadhbh swipes through the photos on her phone and lands on one of her lying back on a couch, laughing, and beside her is …

'*Mother of God herself on the Cliffs of Moher! You're going out with Don Shields!*'

'Shhh, Aisling. Be cool,' Sadhbh admonishes, but she's laughing.

Don Shields is huge news. Huge. He's the lead singer of The Peigs. They were just on one of those American talk shows – I can't remember which one. Presented by one of the Jimmys. And one of their songs was used in a Vodafone ad over in England. No wonder he's 'away a good bit with work'– I saw him in a pair of Calvin Klein jocks on the side of a bus last week! I'm nearly sure Majella tried to chance her way backstage to drink Buckfast with The Peigs at Electric Picnic last year. They were the only reason she went.

'Majella is going to lose her mind! Don Shields was her phone wallpaper for ages until Pablo came along. I can't believe this, Sadhbh! She and a few from Mary I followed them around the country in a minibus before they made it big in the States.' I grab the phone out of her hand, on the hunt for more snaps, but she reefs it back off me again.

'Aisling! Number-one rule of other people's phones. Never swipe without permission!' Did I just save myself from seeing Sadhbh in her pelt? Or Don Shields, for that matter? I've never taken a 'nude' in my life. I'd be too afraid that the hackers would get me.

'Anyway,' Sadhbh continues, 'he's really sound and down to earth and lovely but I knew ... *some people* would go mad when they knew it was him, so I just wanted to be sure. And ...' She stretches out her lower lip in a you-might -kill-me way.

'What?'

'He might be in Vegas. He might meet us there, I mean. It's a total coincidence.' The words fall out of her like cement out of a mixer. 'But I swear I didn't know when we booked it. I know this is a girls' weekend. It's just a coincidence that the band are playing a showcase in LA this weekend and he said he'd try to come for a night. Don't kill me.'

Majella arrives back at the table, clutching three flutes and swaying her hips, singing 'Vivaaa Las Vegas.' I struggle to sit up out of the deep chair in the airport bar, my legs impeded by my backpack and the inflated neck pillow attached to the side of it. I've been on long flights before, of course – I've been to New York twice for Christmas shopping – so I have the deep vein thrombosis socks and the earplugs and everything. This Vegas trip is epic altogether, though. Nine hours to Atlanta, an hour's wait and then another four and half hours to Las Vegas. I've set my Fitbit to remind me to get up and walk every hour (it does that with a little vibrate anyway, to be fair, but I've set it to beep as well, just to be sure). I've googled what films are going to be on the flight, and I have the latest Marian Keyes audiobook on my phone. I'm all set. I'm delighted to be fitting in a visit to another US city, to be honest, even if it does mean a day of travelling. It's a lot of flying for three days away, but, sure, going on a transatlantic flight is nearly like a holiday itself with all the free food and entertainment. I must pick up some Atlanta fridge magnets and see about getting a stamp in my passport.

The flights weren't too bad considering we booked them last minute. I've committed to spending a bit of my redundancy money, egged on by Mammy, and Sadhbh is the same. Feck it. The bit of sun will do us good, and when Majella went to Vegas three years ago with her Chicago cousins she won $300 and swears blind she saw Linda Martin trying to cross the road in an Elvis wig. We have a suite with adjoining rooms booked in the MGM Grand. I've heard of it, and Majella says there's a great gift shop, so it seemed like a good pick.

'What time is it now?' Majella gives me a nudge. I catch Sadhbh's eye, which is glinting away, and she can't keep the smirk off her face.

'Quarter past nine.' It's early for prosecco, but sure we're on international soil now. I made the girls promise to be here at seven because of what I've heard about the queues at US Preclearance in Dublin Airport. Deirdre Ruane went to Boston a few weeks ago and nearly missed the flight with the queues. She only gave herself three hours. Our flight is at eleven and I was taking no chances. We're all wrecked already but it's worth it for the peace of mind. We'll get to Vegas in the evening, just in time to go out on the town. I'm already torn between wanting to sleep on the plane and wanting to watch the films. Sure, the films are nearly the best part – they're always brand new.

'I can't wait to get there and hit the town,' I say, wiggling my eyebrows at Sadhbh. She shakes her head, going crimson.

'What are you two at?' Majella looks from one of us to the other.

'Oh, nothing,' I snigger, 'just wondering if Sadhbh's new boyfriend, Don, is going to meet us there tonight. He's in America. For work.'

'Ah, Sadhbh, you sleeveen, this is a girls' holiday. You're not serious? No mickeys!' Majella's not impressed.

'Not even ... Don Shields's mickey?' I raise my Prosecco triumphantly, delighted with myself.

It takes Majella a moment to register. 'You're joking.' She looks again from me to Sadhbh. 'You're. Fucking. Joking.'

Sadhbh shakes her head. 'She's not joking. Look.' She offers her phone to Majella and Majella squeals and grabs it.

'He's such a ride, Sadhbh! You dark pony – I can't believe you said nothing!' Majella jumps out of her chair and swings her glass of prosecco around, nearly taking the eye out of an Italian man behind her. 'I thought he was going out with Taylor Swift!' Then she visibly pales. 'Have you told Mairead and Fionnuala yet?'

'Eh, no,' Sadhbh says, sneaking a quick look in my direction. 'We haven't had too many chats, actually. They seem to go to bed quite early.'

'They're going to *die*,' Maj squeals. 'Mairead had three Long Island Iced Teas in Majorca last Easter and threatened to get his name tattooed on her shoulder. The only way Fionnuala could talk her out of it was telling her she'd regret it on her wedding day when she couldn't cover it up. She was mortified about it the next morning.'

Sadhbh's hand flies up to her mouth.

'God bless youuu, Pierce Brosnaaaan …' Majella warbles into her flute, mimicking Don Shields's distinctive vocals on The Peigs's most well-known song. It's mostly about being from Navan, but the yanks have gone stone mad for it. It's fierce catchy, to be fair.

Sadhbh drops her head into her hands, laughing and moaning. 'Can you guys just *be cool*?'

It turns out that arriving so early for a flight and hoofing so many little flutes of prosecco into you in the airport really relaxes you for all the boarding shenanigans. I barely cared that we weren't up and queuing the second we were called, and Majella found me trying to wedge my backpack into the overhead locker so amusing that she developed a case of the hiccups. She and I got two seats by the window, with

Sadhbh just across the aisle from us, although she promptly put her eye mask on and snuggled down into her expensive pyjamas, ready to sleep off the mid-morning booze fest.

As we take off, me nestled in beside the window and Majella nudging me to stay awake for the drinks trolley, Maj gestures across at Sadhbh. 'How can she just sleep like that?'

'Well, it's a long flight and we've had a feed of drink.'

'No! I mean how can she sleep knowing she's Don Shields's girlfriend? Would you not be awake and thinking about it all the time?' Majella has a mad look in her eyes. I hope if we do meet Don she doesn't go ape. 'I'm delighted for her, though,' she continues. 'As long as she doesn't think she's too cool for school now.'

'She was always too cool for school, to be fair. Did you see her pyjamas?'

Majella nods in agreement that the pyjamas are cracked altogether. Suddenly she grips my arm again. 'Ais, between Don and Pablo, you're the only single gal on the holiday. We'll have to find you a fella!'

'Ah God, Majella, that's the last thing on my mind. Me and John are barely cold. I'm looking forward to being on my own for a while. No Piotrs, no Vegas lads. Nobody. Just me.'

Majella goes to tease me with a smile on her face but changes her mind. 'Are you alright, though, bird? About John and everything?'

'Yeah. Yeah, I am.'

CHAPTER 21

'Jesus! Notions eleven or what?'

Majella swings open door after door leading off the sitting-room part of our MGM Grand hotel room.

There are three bedrooms, each bigger than the last, with massive floor-to-ceiling windows. I can feel the heat coming through, even with the triple glazing, and immediately panic that I haven't brought enough factor 50. Sadhbh rushes over to take in the view. To be fair, the view is of another wall of windows, but looking down she gasps, 'Check out that pool! We are living the life, ladies.'

Behind a bit of a fake wall at one end of the sitting room is a mini kitchen, so I set to work opening every drawer and press. It's the law when you check into a hotel. If there's a trouser press or a mini hairdryer hiding anywhere, I'll find it.

'Any booze in those presses?' Sadhbh calls from her spot by the window, where she's scanning the pool area like a hawk. On Don Shields watch, maybe.

'Not yet.' I'm delighted there's no mini-bar, to be honest. I've never touched one thing in a mini-bar. They know if your fingers even graze the tiny bottles of wine or the freezing peanuts, and they charge you. Better to pretend it's not even there. 'There mustn't be any–'

'Dear Diary, *jackpot*.' Majella emerges triumphant from one of the bedrooms, swinging a full-size bottle of white wine from each hand. 'There's a bar in this room. There's probably one in every room.'

Sadhbh squeals and rushes into the second bedroom, with Majella calling after her, 'Under the desk, looks like a chest of drawers.'

'We're in business,' calls Sadhbh and appears at the door waving a bottle of what looks like very expensive Champagne at us. My heart is going ninety.

'Will ye put them back? They'll know we touched them – there's probably an alarm going off downstairs somewhere. They're probably a hundred dollars each!'

'More, I'd say.' Sadhbh shrugs and goes to pull the foil off the top of the Champagne. I dive for her, eyes peeled for some kind of menu or list of prices. But before I make it to her she's doubled over laughing. 'Your face, Aisling!'

'We're not made of money, Ais. As if!' Majella's laughing too. This is probably what they were whispering and scheming about in the airport in Atlanta as I was doing my anti-blood-clot laps of the chairs. The witches. They both rush forward to envelop me in a hug, skitting about room service and ordering a load of strippers. I give in and laugh with them. I feel so free. A million miles away from everything and in Las Bloody Vegas!

'Sure, we'll have a *glass* of something. We're not animals.' I am on my holidays after all.

An hour and a half later we're strutting down the hotel corridor in our glad rags ready to paint the town red. Majella and me are in our Jeans and a Nice Tops while Sadhbh is wearing a jumpsuit yoke that I swear to God must have been a Hallowe'en costume for an adult baby. The crotch of it is down around her knees. But she looks great, of course, with massive gold triangle earrings poking through her grey hair. She convinced us to throw caution to the wind and go thirds on a bottle of Pinot Greej from the mini-bar, so we're all fairly giddy waiting for the lift. When the doors open we come face to face with a group of lads in Hawaiian shirts with sunburnt noses. They all look like they might be called Chad. Or Josh.

'Going down, ladies?' one of them shouts in an American accent as we step in and they all cheer. I'm puce, to be quite honest.

'On your holidays, lads?' Majella goes with a wink, and another one produces a bottle of tequila, unscrews the cap and shakes it at her. Christ, everything I've heard about Vegas is true. They're all mad here.

'No thanks,' I say, gently pushing the bottle away from her and jabbing at the first-floor button with my other hand. She's not getting a cold sore on my watch.

'Hey, you're Irish,' the first one shouts and the others start cheering again. They've obviously been getting stuck in to their own minibars upstairs. Well for some.

'We are,' I say, cursing the day they put us on the thirty-fifth floor. The lift is taking forever.

'Can we buy you ladies a round of Irish Car Bombs downstairs?' one of them says directly to Sadhbh, who has taken out her phone and is studiously ignoring them all.

'A round of what?' I say.

The tallest one, wearing a fedora, smiles at me dopily. 'Irish Car Bombs. They're shots. Do you guys not have them over there?'

Majella gasps. 'You can't be serious! There's a shot called an Irish Car Bomb? That's a disgrace.'

'An absolute disgrace!' I echo, throwing them daggers. The only other sound we hear for the rest of the journey is a stifled fart.

When the lift door opens, we all spill out into the lobby and the lads skulk off towards the shuttle bus up the Strip. In the distance I can see rows and rows of fruit machines beeping and blinking in the casino, and I must say they look tempting. Of course, I've done my due diligence and I know the house always wins, but I also know that you can drink for free in Las Vegas as long as you're gambling. I'm conflicted because I've seen enough films to know how quickly it can become an addiction.

'Lads, we have to have a flutter,' Majella goes, her eyes lighting up.

'We need to line our stomachs first,' I say. I was on TripAdvisor last night trying to figure out the best restaurants, and I stumbled across the MGM Grand's all-you-can-eat buffet. Well, once I started reading, I just couldn't stop. You wouldn't believe the value of this thing! As much food as you can handle for $30. And we're talking all different types of food.

'I could go for some sushi?' Sadhbh says hopefully, but I'm already leading them towards the sign for the buffet.

'I was thinking we could try the buffet, Sadhbhy?' I say casually. 'I think it has Japanese food. And Chinese, Italian, Lebanese, all sorts of craic.'

'I'm actually not really that hungry,' she says with a shrug. Only Sadhbh could survive on bag of airplane peanuts.

I noticed she didn't touch her meal on the flight, even though I rang up and ordered the vegetarian, gluten-free, dairy-free option especially. I love airplane food – all those little courses, everything so tidy in the little trays. I was afraid to blink in case they somehow got past me with the trolley.

'I know for a fact they have a salad bar,' I say, as a last-ditch attempt to sway her. 'All-you-can-eat … lettuce.'

She has the good grace to laugh. 'Okay, Ais, I'm sold. Let's do it.'

I swing around just fast enough to catch Majella inching over to a blackjack table, where a man in a cowboy hat is patting the seat next to him. Mother of God, I'm going to have my work cut out keeping this show on the road.

'*Majella!*' I roar, and she turns around. 'How are you fixed for an all-you-can-eat buffet?'

'Go on so,' she says, coming back. 'As long as there's booze too.'

When the waitress – Shirley, an absolute dote – shows us to our table I try to stay calm. But it's hard with everything that's on display. The room is sort of divided into different countries with décor to match – in one corner there's Italy with a rake of different pastas and pizzas, in another there's India with more curries than you could shake a stick at and plenty of naan bread. And the dessert section! Don't get me started. Little pastries and cakes to beat the band, as well as a self-service ice-cream machine. I'm actually shaking.

'Guys.' Sadhbh is back looking at her phone again. 'I just got a text from Don and he said he's going to meet us here in an hour.'

'Thanks, Aisling, that's sound.' Don Shields thinks I'm sound!

'Should we head on somewhere?' Sadhbh says, picking a bit of fluff off his threadbare T-shirt and running a hand up his arm.

Head on? Is she mad? I haven't even visited China yet and none of us have had dessert. The house is not going to win on my watch!

Don catches my eye. 'Maybe we should stick around for another while?'

'Shirley,' Maj roars. 'More Champagne, please!' And everyone cheers.

****

There's a buzzing. What is it? Oh Jesus, my head. And my mouth. It's like each one of my teeth is wrapped in sandpaper. My blood feels like it's fizzing. And *what* is that buzzing? I peel an eye open, and then another. It's pitch dark, save for a sliver of light coming in through the thick blackout curtains. Where the blazes am –? Oh, of course, I'm in Las Vegas. This is the hotel room. The buzzing is last night's music ringing in my ears.

Suddenly there's a movement in the bed beside me and a deep sigh. I freeze and go stiffer than I have ever gone before. Holding my breath, the whole shebang. Who the feck is it? It's not Sadhbh or Majella. That sigh was … foreign. And where are my knickers? All that's over me is a light sheet and it's touching every bit of me. I'm starkers. Oh Jesus. Is there a giraffe in the bathroom to top it all off? Or a tiger?

I try to swivel my eyes around in my head without moving an inch, to get a glimpse at who or what is in the bed with me. The swinging of my eyeballs sets off a chain reaction of pain through my head, down my jaw and into my teeth. Am I dying? Take me quickly, Lord. Or at least deliver me a can of Diet Coke and a straw. What was I drinking last night? My blood feels like syrup.

The mass moves again and an arm comes through the air, landing over my stomach. I squeeze my eyes shut and go stiffer still. I wonder can I kind of plank sideways out of the bed like a crab without him noticing? It's definitely a him. I peel an eye open again. The one farthest away from him, just in case. A smooth brown arm lies across the sheet, and a round, brown bare arse rises from the crumples of the bedclothes. And it all comes back to me.

Shirley pleading with us to leave, that we'd drank them dry. Eating all the garlic bread Italy had to offer. Don handing out 99s to a queue of fifty people. Majella standing on a chair screeching, 'God bless youuu, Pierce Brosnaaan, though you're so faaarr from Navaannn' at the top of her lungs. Fast forward to us being ushered through what looked like an emergency exit off a seemingly never-ending corridor of lights and restaurants and gamblers and bars and people. Were we still in the hotel? Who knew? Next there were handshakes and back slaps and hugs and welcomes and drinks were thrust into our hands and Maj was taking selfies with our very own velvet rope and the rest of The Peigs crew were there, totting up who we had in common between us back home and who had shifted who in the Gaeltacht, and then there was dancing and I was dancing with a tall, beautiful man with dark-brown arms and smooth brown cheeks and black eyes and a fresh clean-clothes smell and … holy Jesus. He's in my bed. He's in my bed and he's moving. He's sitting up. Oh Jesus.

'Hi.' He turns his head on the pillow and smiles at me.

'Hiya. How are you now?' I babble and squirm, still trying to lie perfectly still and looking straight ahead at the ceiling. Where the bloody blazes are my knickers? Is there a top within reaching distance, I wonder? Himself – Andrew? Alan? Something like that – leans in and gives me a quick squeeze with the arm that's still lying over me and then rolls onto his back, groaning. 'Wow, that was some … craic we had last night. My head kills.' He has a slow American drawl.

Crack?! No, craic. He means craic, surely.

I grab my chance and shuffle sideways out of the bed, swinging my legs onto the floor and trying but failing to cover most of myself with the sheet. In the films they'd nearly have a debs dress made out of it, hemmed and all, and glide gracefully out of the room. As I sit up my brain ricochets off the side of my skull. Is this how I'm going to die? Of a hangover in a Las Vegas hotel room with Andrew/Alan? How will Mammy explain it to the neighbours? I contemplate lying back down, but a combination of a desperate need for rehydration and a ferocious shame over what I now remember vividly as my first ever one-night stand propels me out of the bed. I give the sheet a wild hard tug and it dislodges itself from under Andrew/Alan's groin area. He seems to be sound asleep again, his arm thrown over his eyes.

Wrapping the sheet around me twice and hoofing a bit over my shoulders for added coverage, I pad towards the door, slipping and sliding on multiple bottles and tripping on what I can only assume is my Jeans and Nice Top, and my knickers, and whatever Andrew/Alan was wearing. A red T-shirt, I think. I try to ignore the rustling of condom wrappers as the sheet drags them along.

I open the door a crack and peer out, expecting silence and a clear path to the little kitchen. It's probably the crack of dawn.

'Oh, hello, sunshine!' calls Sadhbh immediately, turning around on the couch. Don is beside her and gives me a little wave, grinning. Majella is on an armchair, sunglasses on, pyjama top on backwards, water glass held to her temple. I dither at the doorway, and Sadhbh stage-whispers, 'Well, out you come, let Antony sleep.' Antony! I was close.

'Er, how is everyone?' I say shakily, sinking down onto the end of couch, tucking the sheet in around me. 'Any more of that water going, Majella?'

'I'll get it.' Don leaps up and heads for the kitchen, making a big show of clattering around with glasses and taps.

Sadhbh leans in. 'Well. How are you? Sore head? I'm not surprised!' She's smiling.

'Are ye not dying as well?' I say defensively. 'We were all out!'

'Yeah, but you're the one who was back here raiding both of our mini bars and laughing and screeching half the night. You were having the best time.'

Christ. The bottles on the floor. The mini-bar. The bill!

'I'm dying.' Majella raises her hand limply. 'But I'm always dying.' This is true – Majella's hangovers are legendary. I once saw her drink a carton of orange juice in one go and then immediately vomit it back up, like a fluorescent Wavin pipe.

Don emerges from the kitchen and hands me a glass of ice-cold water. I gulp it down like my life depends on it. It kind of does, to be quite honest. I'd kill for a million ice pops, or a lump of pineapple or something. I'm usually a beige carbs woman when it comes to hangover food, but this is next level. I suddenly understand why Elaine and Sadhbh reach for the grapefruit when they're dying. The whole time I thought they were just punishing themselves.

'What time is it?' I say suddenly.

'Half twelve,' groans Majella. 'Can I just sleep all day?'

Half twelve. The hotel breakfast. I've missed it. For the first time in my life I've missed it. Maybe there'll still be a bit of toast going or a glass of orange juice? No, not orange juice. No Wavin pipes for me. Apple juice, maybe. I gather up the sheet and bustle back towards the room, calling over my shoulder, 'If we rush we might get the last bit of breakfast.'

Majella laughs tentatively, rubbing her head, and reaches for a menu beside her. 'This is Vegas, Aisling, the breakfasts come to you.'

I've never ordered room service in my life. God only knows what you might be missing down at the buffet. But right there at the very top of the menu it says, 'Fruit Bowl: a selection of fresh, tropical delights served ice cold.' There's no price beside it, or beside anything really, but the thought of someone bringing me a cascade of strawberries and pineapple right now is too good to resist. 'I'll have the fruit bowl.' I toss the menu back to Majella, who throws it at Sadhbh, groaning, 'Toast. All the toast they have.'

Sadhbh grins and nods towards the bedroom door. 'Does Antony want anything? Ask him there, Aisling.'

He jerks awake as I gently close the bedroom door behind me, turning over to lie on his stomach. Mercifully, he's located another sheet.

'Heyyy, Ashlinn.' He turns his head on the pillow and raises his arm about half a foot. He's dying too, obviously.

'It's Ais–' Never mind. Doesn't matter. This must be what Saoirse Ronan feels like all the time, living with the scourge of an Irish name abroad. Maireads, Róisíns, Gráinnes, Eimears, Caoimhes. We're all one big put-upon gang. And what about the Pádraigs and Caoimhíns and Seosamhs?

I sit on the edge of the bed and look at Antony over my shoulder. He smiles. What a smile. I remember seeing it a lot last night as we danced and talked and – yes, it's coming back to me now – swigged from bottles dancing around this very room. He stretches out the arm closest to me.

'Morning snuggle?'

I hesitate, but he leans across and trails a finger up and down my back, inching the sheet down. Feck it.

CHAPTER 22

The screaming is mortifying. Antony and Don can definitely hear it as they close the door to suite 353 of the MGM Grand. I'd say the whole floor can hear it.

'Well? Are you a new woman?' Majella is about two inches from my face as I collapse back onto the couch. The fruit bowl has been delivered, thanks be to Jesus. Although you wouldn't want to be starving. There's about four grapes, a suggestion of pineapple and a suspiciously large helping of chopped up apple. And don't get me started on the melon. A filler fruit if ever there was one.

'Will you *stop*?' My cheeks are burning for about the sixtieth time in twenty-four hours. I feel fizzy inside. I feel a bit like cackling out the window or running a 10k or something. Although I've done the Mini Marathon several times and 10k is no laughing matter. One year I nearly had to give up out by UCD. It was fierce warm and people were dropping like flies. Majella had been out the night before and an old lady offered her a go in her wheelchair at one stage. She took it and all.

Anyway, I am a bit like a new woman. I've been with John so long and only one other fella before him. Antony's been throwing me around the bed – and the floor, I tried not to count the bottles while I was down there – for the past hour, and I didn't even care that the girls knew what we were up to. Although, emerging from the bedroom, this time clad in my Winnie the Pooh pyjamas rather than the sheet, all I could look at was the floor. And then he went in for the goodbye kiss. 'Goodbye, Irish. Don't be a stranger.' I thought Sadhbh and Majella were going to explode. I decide to just give in to their quizzing and get it over and done with.

'How many times?'

'Twice, I think'

'Was one of them in the shower? There was definitely something going on in the shower last night.'

'Oh. Three times then, maybe.'

Pause for screaming.

'Is he nice?'

'Sooo nice. We were talking about work and life and Daddy and everything.'

Pause for aaahing.

'What was he saying?'

'Ah, this and that. Did you know he set up his own business when he lost his job? He was telling me all about it. He was saying … he was saying would I not do something like that. I think he thinks I own a zoo, though. Something was lost in translation about the farm and that one summer we had llamas. Still, though, maybe he's right? If there was something I was good at or passionate about, like. Antony managed it.'

'And look at him now,' Sadhbh interjects. 'Don says he's one of the best people he's ever worked with. His small label was bought by the one taking on The Peigs. Antony is really high up.'

Majella nudges me. 'Fair play, girl. He had his eye on you all night. I think it was your Britney moves.'

Jesus. Champagne and gin and 'Slave 4 U'. Never again.

'It's a shame he's going back to LA today.' Sadhbh looks dejected. But it's not Antony she's most concerned about, I'd say.

'And it's a shame Don's going back too. But he'll be home soon, right?'

'Another month or so. Yeah, I'll miss him. Isn't he a dote?'

Majella and I both agree that Don is a dote. Who knew a man with a nose ring and a face like a scruffy angel would be so good at knowing all the words to 'Never Ever', the talking bit and all. He's like one of us. No hint of airs and graces about him, despite having Bono's number in his phone. (I know this because Majella checked.)

'So, are you and Antony going to stay in touch?' Majella asks slyly.

'I dunno. Maybe we'll be Facebook friends. I don't really care, to be honest.' I've never been breezier. Or felt breezier. The girls fall around the place squealing again, Majella screaming that I'm the 'one-night-stand queen'. I feel like Madonna when she wrote that book.

It's nearly six o'clock by the time we make it out of the hotel room. Usually by this time in a city break you'd have a loop of the open-top bus done, seven of the fifteen things with pictures beside them in the guidebook seen, a lunch eaten (after scrutinising several different window menus and doing the euro conversions in your head if necessary), the bits from the hotel breakfast buffet rationed out over the day, and you'd be starting to surf window menus for a bit of dinner. I've been in Las Vegas nearly twenty-four hours and I haven't even stepped outside. So much for my dream of visiting one of those outlet malls for a half-price Gap hoodie and some Ralph Lauren towels for Mammy. Majella told me that you can come to Vegas and never see the light of day. I thought she was having me on, but walking through the casino attached to the hotel now it's impossible to tell what time it is at all. It's just bars and restaurants and casino as far as the eye can see. I'd say I'd be glad of it in the height of summer – five minutes in that Vegas sun and I'd be like a boiled ham. Even today I've slathered on the factor 50. Eighteen degrees can be very deceptive, even this close to sunset.

Stepping out into the fading light we all reel a bit and fumble for our sunglasses. We have truly poisoned ourselves. Majella in particular is looking very green. 'We'll just go down and look at the Bellagio and then have a bit of dinner,' Sadhbh reassures me. I might be hungover but I'm still in tourist mode. A dancing fountain? Right up my street.

There's a bus that goes down the Strip so we all limp on, with Majella hovering her head as close to the tiny window as she can. Sadhbh's doing some mooning of her own. Her phone is buzzing away, and she's giving us the odd update on the boys' hangover and their progress in the airport. 'Antony says hi,' she directs at me coyly. I blush again at the thought of him emerging from under the sheet earlier to say 'hi' from between my thighs. The carry-on of him. With a jolt, I realise I haven't thought of John since arriving in Vegas and instantly feel guilty. I wasn't long hopping into bed with someone, was I? Maybe he's right about me being a–

'What's up with you, bird?' Majella gives me a half-hearted nudge as the bus crawls along the Strip. I was so lost in thought I wasn't even using the opportunity to sightsee. Hotels rise like skyscrapers on either side, and there's the Eiffel Tower, and a pyramid, and a man in his knickers. Americans are gas.

'Ah, I'm just feeling a bit guilty, about John and Antony and–'

Majella grabs my arm now. 'Don't you dare. You're free and single and entitled to your one-night stand. Lads wouldn't think twice about it. They'd be following their mickeys at the first hint of the glad eye. Now, here we are.' She stands up as the bus bulls to a stop and points through the window. Following her finger I see a giant pool of water. No dancing shower heads just yet. My barely touched guidebook tells me it goes every half hour and we're just in time. We stumble from the bus and Sadhbh spots a vantage spot on a step by a wall so we plant ourselves there, ready for the action.

I wasn't ready for the opening strains of 'Time to Say Goodbye'. Majella briefly thought it was Celine Dion herself singing from inside the fountain but soon caught a hold of herself. Daddy loved this song. He used to pretend to be the blind lad singing it around the kitchen, even the Italian bits. I'm caught off guard with tears in my eyes as the water flings itself this way and that, like fireworks. The hangover probably isn't helping, to be fair. Daddy would have loved this. Him and Mammy had great plans for travelling here and there, if they ever managed to get a long enough break from the farm. I reach into my bag and pull out my wallet, eager to see his face smiling up at me from his memorial card, tucked in with the Christmas fifty eur– Oh no. Oh no, no, no, no, no, no.

I must have said some of those nos out loud because Sadhbh grabs me by the arm. 'What? What, Aisling?'

'Daddy's €50. It's gone.'

Sadhbh looks confused but Majella catches on immediately. 'Oh no, Ais. Are you sure?' She mutters to Sadhbh. 'He gave it to her for Christmas, in the card.'

Sadhbh's face falls. 'Oh no, Ais. It must be there somewhere.'

But it's not. I must have spent it. Last night, probably. I search my brain for a memory of pulling it out. In that club, maybe? At the blackjack table? Were my suspicions correct and it turns out all of those 'free as long as you're gambling' drinks were not free at all? It did seem too good to be true. But there's nothing jogging my memory. God only knows where it's gone. Dejected, I turn away from the Bellagio as Celine's warbling comes to a close. Sadhbh plants an arm around my shoulders and gives me a squeeze. 'Let's get some dinner. We'll feel better then.'

****

'Is that mad hot, now?'

The waitress looks at Majella like she has ten heads. 'I'm not sure what you mean, ma'am.'

'Is it mad hot? Mad spicy, like?'

'*Ní thuigeann sí*,' I mumble at Majella, delighted to get the use of the *cúpla focail* wherever I can. It's a real feather in your cap when you're abroad, although when Majella did her J1 in Chicago years ago she was gossiping like mad about a fine thing at the table next to her, and next thing he turns around and says, 'Well, girls?' in the thickest Drogheda accent she'd ever heard. Her knees still go funny thinking about it to this day.

'*Ní thuigeann sí* "mad hot",' I explain again.

'Ah, sorry.' Majella finally cottons on and repeats herself slowly. 'This chilli, is it very spicy?'

We've settled for dinner in a restaurant in our own hotel. We all badly need our beds so we might as well be as close to them as possible. The thought of chilli turns my stomach, but the all-day brunch menu is calling to me. Never thought I'd be actively seeking out eggs, bacon and smashed avocado but it's the closest thing to a big dirty fry this place has.

'I'll have the brunch. Extra rashers … er, bacon,' I call to the waitress over Sadhbh recounting her memories of all the dancing from last night.

'She had the glass in each hand and her arse was nearly touching the floor each time.' She's talking about me. No wonder my thighs are in bits. I thought it was maybe from the shower. Majella is creasing herself laughing and I join in, and it does me good. It was only €50 and I still have Daddy's card. There's no point getting into a tizz about it. Majella's phone goes – Pablo again, no doubt – and she excuses herself to go off and make moony faces at him. The waitress brings our vats of Diet Coke and reminds us about the free refills. Sounds like another swizz but, Jesus, isn't America brilliant all the same?

'The €50 aside, are you having fun?' Sadhbh inquires.

'I am. I really am. The thought of going home, though.' We have another day and night in Vegas, but I'm already getting that Sunday-night feeling about returning home.

No job to go back to. Worries about Mammy and the farm. Life without John.

'Stop! Don't even think about it,' Sadhbh demands. 'Let's stay positive, positive, positive.'

'Did you know … An–' I struggle to get his name out without blushing, 'Antony just bought his mother a house? Just bought it for her, outright.'

'Well, isn't that lovely?' Sadhbh teases. 'And any excuse to bring up his name, what?'

'No!' Feck her anyway. I'll never hear the end of this. 'Maybe I *should* think about opening my own business. I've got the bit of redundancy money. I love nothing more than organising and planning. I've no clue where my career or whatever is going from here. Why couldn't I set something up and run it? Maybe I could help Mammy out too.'

'Alright, you have me convinced. So what would this business be, then?'

I pause. It's a cracked idea that I've only really just formulated in the past ten minutes, addled by the hangover.

'I was thinking a café. In BGB. I suppose there's never been much call for it when you can get coffee in Filan's, but there are more and more Dubs arriving down all the time. And the Garden Centre is heaving with people wanting scones the size of their heads. I feel like I could get in on some of that action if I got the right little spot.'

Sadhbh's face looks encouraging, so I keep going.

'If I'm going to be staying in BGB, why not make the most of it? And why not show the best it has to offer? All that lovely local produce. The finest of everything on our doorstep. Give people a reason to come and maybe a reason to stay.'

Sadhbh looks impressed with my speech. 'I'd visit your café, Ais. I'd say you'd have the place running like clockwork.'

'And I was thinking, what BGB is really missing …'

'Yeah?'

'Brunch. I've had a mad idea to bring brunch to the sticks.' I pause to gauge her reaction, but then, before she can even speak, my gumption leaves me and I bluster in with, 'Sure it's a completely mad idea, isn't it? Where would I even get the money? It's mad altogether.'

But Sadhbh has a glint in her eye. 'It's a *brilliant* idea, Ais. And, sure, there are grants and everything for people setting up their own businesses. It's a fab idea. Go you!'

By the time Majella arrives back at the table I've floor plans drawn on napkins and Sadhbh is excitedly suggesting menu options. 'Cloud eggs with salmon parcels! Avocado mousse with hollandaise crisps!' She needs to calm down. I was thinking more along the lines of an all-day breakfast and maybe a few mimosas on a Sunday.

'You'll never guess what.' Majella throws herself into the booth, all ready for chat, but then notices all of my drawings. 'What's that?'

'*You'll* never guess what,' Sadhbh says proudly. 'Ais is opening a café. A brunch place, actually. In Ballygobbard.'

'No way, Ais. That's a deadly idea! Filan's needs a bit of competition for the deli counter. They seem to think there are only four food groups: stuffing, hot chicken fillets, cheese and more stuffing.' I don't know where Majella gets off being a snob about Filan's legendary hot chicken fillet and stuffing rolls. She's the sole reason they were able to afford a new meat slicer last year. Still, though, her enthusiasm is infectious.

'I think it could really work. There's that new unit your man James Matthews is building near Garbally. It would be perfect. My redundancy definitely wouldn't cover it all, but Sadhbh is right about those grants.' Mammy and the farm niggles in the back of my mind, but I push it even further back for now. 'What were you going to tell us, Maj?'

'Oh, I don't want to bring the tone down. It's about John.'

My heart leaps a little, but not as much as I would have thought, hearing his name. It's more an under-14 Community Games 200m hurdles leap than an Olympics high jump leap.

'No, go on,' I urge her. 'It's grand.'

'He's been recruited to the county team. Got a spot as a selector on the coaching squad. Pablo says they turned up at training today and offered it to him.' Pablo's barely been in the country six months but his devotion to hurling knows no bounds. He's already done the Croke Park tour twice and both times had to be fed tissues because he was so overcome with emotion.

'That's … great. I'm delighted for him.' And I am delighted for him. He always dreamed of playing for the county, but he's a bit long in the tooth now, so this is the next best thing.

'Alright, enough about John. Back to Aisling's café.' Sadhbh really means business. I wonder can I pull it off at all.

An early night does us the world of good and the next morning, my mind jumbled with dreams about eggs and cutlery and dancing €50 notes and extremely odd flashes of James Matthews the contractor, of all people, dancing to Britney Spears around the unit back in BGB, Sadhbh convinces us that a helicopter ride to see the Grand Canyon is the only thing for us. I wish I could say I enjoyed it, but my heart was in my mouth the whole time. Helicopters are for Beyoncé and saving people up mountains. The Grand Canyon was lovely but I couldn't take a single photo because my hands were glued to the Oh Jesus handles on either side of my seat. I've never been happier to be back on solid ground. Plus, I have to stop spending money if I'm to become a rural brunch mogul. None of us could stomach much more drinking so some sedate gambling and another mammoth American dinner later – about 324 Points, but who's even counting at this stage? – and we've nearly reached the end of our mini Vegas adventure.

Sadhbh has provided running commentary on what Don and Antony are up to back in LA, but I'm happy to leave my one-night stand behind me in America. Sure, that's why they're called one-night stands. Our flight in the morning is an early one so I take on the dreaded task of clearing the mini-bar bill before going to bed. I squeeze my eyes shut as the receptionist prints out a ream of paper, complimenting me on my accent and asking if I know her cousins in Kerry. I skit that all Irish people know each other but, to be honest, her cousin Maureen from Tralee sounds very like a girl I met at a wedding last summer. I'm grilling her for details on Maureen's colouring when she interrupts me with an 'and $85 for the fruit supreme'. I have to cling onto the edges of the reception desk – $85 and not a strawberry to be seen? Between the three of us, the bill is in four figures. I nearly have to sit down. It's time to get a grip on my finances. Enough is enough – $85 fruit bowls do not a successful businesswoman make.

CHAPTER 23

'There's a lot of forms to fill out, hun, which is a pain in the arse.'

We're sitting on blocks in the middle of the building site that will be Sharon's salon, trying to come up with a name for it. She's already vetoed three: Hair Lingus, Braziliant and The Best Little Hair House. The last one was mostly to rile up Marty Boland, but she nearly committed to stationery for Hair Lingus before changing her mind at the last minute. I'm not much use to her, but she did write down my suggestions of The Two Ronnies and Hair Dot Comb, so maybe I'm in with a chance of naming the place. If she's not careful it'll just be called Sharon's, and where's the elegance in that? In return, she's filling me in on the Entrepreneur Ireland Women in Business grant that she's certain I'll qualify for. Little does she know, filling out forms is one of my favourite pastimes. I sat beside Majella once when she was renewing her passport, and she had to go back into the post office three times for new applications because she kept making a balls of it. It's hardly rocket science – if she read the instructions first she would have known full well it was supposed to be all done in block caps. And black pen.

'That part won't be a problem,' I say confidently. 'And you're happy to have a look at my business plan?'

I spent last night on my trusty Toshiba laptop writing out my plans and projections for BallyGoBrunch. That's what I'd call the café. The mention of brunch will lure in the hens and stags and Dubs. It won't be all avocados and halloumi and Sadhbh's cloud eggs, whatever they are – I'll be doing good, honest-to-God fodder too to keep the locals happy. It felt great to throw myself into it and, despite Mammy's internet running at a snail's pace, the more I read about café ownership online, the more enthusiastic I got – although, talk about counting your chickens. If I don't get this grant, my carefully curated folders of research will be going in the bin. Still, though, I spent a significant amount of time daydreaming about being my own boss – why didn't I think of it before? All the responsibility and no one to take orders from. I spent an hour struggling to think of what I'd actually miss about working in an open-plan office, and the best I could come up with was someone saying 'bless you' when I sneeze. The bless yous got borderline competitive at PensionsPlus, but I usually managed to be the first to shout it out. It's like poker – you learn people's tells.

I know it's hard to get a new business off the ground, but I have my head screwed on and I'm being realistic about the work I'll need to put into it. It took three hours to print it all out, and I owe Mammy a new ink cartridge, but I'm delighted my brain is up and running again after the recent hiatus. It's a relief that I didn't do any permanent damage that night in Las Vegas.

'I'm more than happy to take a look,' Sharon says, and I hand over a thick red folder with 'Business Plan' written across it in large letters. Her arms fold under the weight of it. 'It's very thorough,' I add with a nod. 'Everything is colour coded.'

I called Ruane's estate agency in Knock this morning to confirm that the lease on the unit was still available. Deirdre answered the phone, and even though her father Trevor usually handles the commercial lets, she said she'd show it to me tomorrow afternoon before trying to convince a couple from Dublin that having a detached house is more important than being able to walk to the IFSC. She said the rent on my unit is €350 a month but, after I heard a door in the background slam, whispered that her dad said the developer would take €300 for it. That's the figure I have in my business plan so bring on the negotiations.

The salon is starting to take shape, although the big glass vase of lilies inside the front door is looking a bit out of place. I say nothing, though, and pick up a few of the cards she has displayed around the makeshift office. 'Good luck, Sharon, we are so proud, love Mam and Dad.' 'Best of luck to all at Hair Lingus, from the Maguires.' They mustn't have heard it's been vetoed. There's also a corporate-looking one signed by James Matthews.

'How do you know James Matthews?' I ask.

Sharon looks up from where she's engrossed in my folder. 'He's my contractor,' she says. 'For the sunbed room and the refit. It's a small enough job so he's only here with the lads one day a week, but I must say they're doing a very tidy job.'

'And no card from himself next door?'

She sighs. 'Pfft. And I wouldn't expect it either. I swear, he's somehow pumping the smell of raw meat in through the vents. I don't know how, but I'll prove it. If not I'll be broke buying lilies to cover it up.'

She goes back to my business plan, and my eyes fall on a copy of *RSVP* magazine. There's a picture of four glamorous-looking women in bandage dresses on the cover. 'Meet the GAA WAGs' it screams in thick block capitals, and I pick it up and flick to the feature where they're talking about 'staying warm but looking cool' on the sidelines and what they're wearing to the GAA All Star Awards. I wonder is this all ahead of John.

'My ex John will probably be moving in these circles soon.' I gesture at *RSVP* and Sharon picks it up, looking from the girls on the cover to me in my leggings and navy fleece. In my defence, I am extremely comfortable and I haven't had to shave my legs or anything.

'Oh, right,' she says, 'and how do you feel about that? I can see the one on the left's chicken fillets poking out of her dress.'

Chicken fillets? I doubt she brought snacks to an *RSVP* photoshoot. And if she did, I assume it would be something like a salad or a Special K Bar.

'It's grand,' I say. 'Wouldn't be my scene now.'

'I hear it's already going to his head a bit,' Sharon offers.

'Oh, that doesn't sound like John.'

'Yeah,' she continues. 'One of the lads doing my tiles was saying he was over in Maguire's demanding a stool be held for him on an ongoing basis. Because he's so important.'

I can't imagine him carrying on like that, but I suppose we haven't been in touch since this whole GAA thing took off. Still, though, not my problem. I just hope he doesn't lose the head altogether. That's a one-way street to being a topic on *Liveline* for antisocial behaviour in your county jersey. It happened last year after the All Ireland, and one of the player's mammies rang in herself she was so ashamed.

'Actually, since I have you here,' Sharon says, heaving my business plan off her lap, 'I want to start planning Denise's baby shower and gender reveal party. Have you any ideas?'

Gender reveals have reached BGB. They're surely ready to embrace brunch.

'The Ard Rí does a lovely afternoon tea. Sandwiches aren't too small. It's very classy.'

'Oh, that sounds perfect! I'll look into it so.'

I better start thinking about a present. Denise and Liam's house is cavernous. They got the land off her daddy, so they could put in as many bathrooms as they wanted. The baby will probably have two ensuites. They'll regret those cream carpets, though, when it's rubbing its Frubes into them. I would traditionally wait until the baby is born before picking out a present, either a little pink or a little blue outfit, but this baby-shower shenanigans means I'm now having to buy two presents per baby. When will anyone buy me a present, I silently wonder, before giving myself a little shake. Sharon is asking me something.

'What are you up to this afternoon?'

'Oh, I'm calling over to Majella once she's home.'

I haven't seen Majella since the weekend. She called in looking to borrow my grey interview suit – a knee-length pencil skirt and matching jacket. I bought it full price – not like me – but it got me the job in PensionsPlus so I suppose it owes me nothing. I actually thought I'd get loads of wear out of it, but I stuck out like a sore thumb on my first day when everyone else was in trousers and blouses. After that I usually wore my black work slacks and something from my collection of shumpers (so handy to have your shirt collar stitched into your V-neck jumper, I find).

Maj decided to go for the Deputy Head position at her school, and I couldn't be more delighted. Pablo called in with her, desperately trying to avoid the dog. Apparently Willy has taken to following him into the bathroom and staring at him in the shower. 'It's the eye contact, I can no longer take it,' Pablo told me while Maj rubbed his thigh reassuringly. 'Willy, he never look away. I cover my *bolas* with the shower cap.' Poor Mammy nearly choked on her scone.

'Do you need any other help with planning or decorations or anything, Sharon? Bit of bunting? Some balloons? I have loads at home.'

'Not at all, but thanks a mill, hun!' she says, heaving the business plan over to the reception desk and putting it underneath. 'I'll look after all that. I might do one of those baby-picture games, though – where you have to guess which baby is which guest. Get rooting for a picture, will you? And tell Majella too?'

I haven't the heart to tell her there are only three baby pictures of me in existence: one taken at my christening, another on my first birthday, where I'm sitting in front of a sponge cake with a thick purple candle stuck in it, and another on Paddy's Day, when Daddy thought it would be gas to give me a pint bottle of Guinness to hold. Good luck to Sharon if she thinks Mammy will release any of them from her precious photo album. I suppose I could always cut a picture of a baby out of a magazine and pass it off as myself. I was a very plain child.

'Baby picture, no problem,' I chirp, heading for the door. I'm nearly there when I spot Eoin Ó Súilleabháin loitering outside pretending to examine the tray of lamb chops in Marty Boland's window. 'I think you have an admirer there,' I say, cocking my head in his general direction.

Sharon looks up from her laptop. She's obviously saving the business plan for later when she can dedicate a proper amount of time to it.

'Ah yes, he dropped me in a bottle of bubbly yesterday to say good luck with the opening. Very decent of him.'

'Any excuse to come in for a chat. Did he ask you out yet?' I venture.

She looks up. 'No. God, no.'

I look back out the window at Cyclops, who's still inspecting the chops like he doesn't eat them for his tea twice a week, obviously waiting for me to leave so he can come in.

'Well, I have a feeling it's on the cards,' I say with a smile.

'If he does he'll be disappointed,' Sharon replies quietly.

'Too busy with the salon, is it? Keeping the place clean and tidy alone must be a full-time job. I can only imagine what it'll be like after the opening.'

'Yeah, that's true,' she says. 'But I'm also off men for a while. That's actually sort of the reason I left Waterford and ended up here.' Her face goes dark and I say nothing and just let her keep talking. 'It was a bad break-up. You know yourself.'

I do, although judging by her expression, I have a feeling Sharon's must have been much worse than mine.

CHAPTER 24

I had told Mammy about me and John before I went to Vegas. I had to get it out of the way. I was absolutely dreading it. I even had a bottle of brandy on standby in case she went into shock. But she just gave me a long hug and sighed and said, 'It's probably for the best, pet. When it's done it's done.' She's taken to palling around with Constance Swinford these past few weeks, and they've been doing yoga in the morning using YouTube tutorials. All the downward dog and sun salutations have made her very zen. Although, I found her asleep on her mat yesterday morning while Adriene from *Yoga with Adriene* was wittering away about breathing from California.

She's less zen when I tell her about my plan for the café, though.

'Ah, Aisling, are you sure? You have no idea how hard it is being self-employed,' she says arranging a selection of good biscuits – Toffypops, no less – on a plate. 'I don't mean to sound negative but I'm just worried about you, pet. You'll never get a day off. Look at how me and Daddy were with the farm. And what do you know about running a café anyway? You burnt the arse out of my good small saucepan making porridge yesterday.'

I thought I'd gotten away with it. She really doesn't miss a trick. 'You don't need to be a chef to run a café – I'm going to hire someone else to do the cooking,' I explain, swiping a biscuit when she has her back turned. 'I'm only the brains of it. Nothing is finalised yet, but I'll be doing full Irish breakfasts and toasties and a few simple lunch things. Plenty of coleslaw. And mostly using stuff from local farmers and producers. Nothing too over the top, don't worry. I've thought it through.'

'But how are you going to afford to get it off the ground, love? I don't think I'll be able to help you much at the moment, and your redundancy won't stretch to it I'm sure.'

I sigh. 'I know that. But I've applied for a Women in Business grant. Sharon told me Entrepreneur Ireland are firing money at women this year. She was very impressed with my business plan – it took her six hours to get through it. They gave her €15,000 to open the salon, and she said I'd be eligible for the same. I'd be mad not to at least try. I'm getting nothing decent back on the CVs I've been sending out.'

She's still at the biscuits. I'm just waiting for her to take out the compass and protractor.

'Honestly, Mammy, you should see the profit margins on tea and coffee. It's basically a licence to print money.'

'Well, if you're doing sausages you'll want to get Marty Boland's in. You won't be short of customers then.'

I'll take that as her blessing so. 'Good idea,' I say, nudging That Bloody Cat out of the way and heading for the back door. 'See you in a few hours. Good look with your man.'

Myself and Paddy Reilly convinced her it was time to hire someone to help out with the farm on a more long-term basis.

Money is tight but Paddy recommended William Foley, a fella from Knock who'll do it on the cheap, and Mammy is determined to woo him with the biscuits and the promise of flexible hours. I never said anything to her about finding the valuation document, but I'm guessing things can't be that bad or I would have heard about it. I set a reminder in my phone to have a little worry about it in bed tonight.

My appointment with Deirdre Ruane is at 3 p.m. but I want to get there early so I boot out the Garbally Road. It only takes me five minutes, to be fair. There are a couple of builders knocking around, but the property looks as good as finished – from the outside anyway. The building is three storeys tall, and the commercial unit takes up the whole ground floor. It's massive, with loads of floor-to-ceiling windows. There are spaces for at least fifteen cars at the front. It's sitting on about an acre, and I can see the landscaping has already started. The flower bed at the front is looking well, too – there's no denying the quality of Constance Swinford's mmmaaalch.

I'm sitting in the car trying to imagine where the sign will go and how big it should be when there's a sharp rap on the window and I jump. It's James Matthews wearing a bright-yellow hard hat and a high-vis jacket. I'm nearly blinded.

'Jesus, you put the heart crossways in me,' I gasp, rolling down the window. The last time I saw him he was dancing to 'Oops I Did It Again'. Well, in my dreams anyway.

'Sorry about that,' he says, laughing, in his Prince Harry accent, taking off the hat and running his fingers through his hair. 'You were a million miles away. I was just wondering if you were lost or having car trouble or something.'

'Neither,' I say, opening the door and stepping out. 'I have an appointment with Deirdre Ruane to view the commercial unit. I'm interested in leasing it.'

'You mean *Trevor* Ruane?' James goes, furrowing his brow. His beard and Snickers work trousers make him look slightly dishevelled, but whatever aftershave he's wearing definitely smells like money.

'Dee is his daughter,' I explain. 'We were in school together so she said she'd show me around.'

'Ah, I see,' he says. 'Sorry, still getting used to life in the country. I keep forgetting you all know each other.'

I nod towards the building. 'Am I right in thinking you're almost done? I'd say you're fairly sick of the Mountrath by now.'

He smiles then does a mock grimace, pushing his hair out of his eyes. 'It's fine, but, yeah, I've probably had my fill of carvery dinners. I'll be here for at least another month, though. We've just about gotten it weather tight, plenty more to do. And I have another few jobs locally to finish up. Come on, I'll bring you in.'

'Are you sure? I can wait for Dee. It's ten to three.'

'Not at all, follow me. Just watch your step.'

On closer inspection, there's still a fair bit to be done, but as soon as I step inside I get a good feeling about the place. There's light pouring in from all three sides, and I'm imagining how bright and cheerful it will be when it's all finished. At the moment it's just bare concrete floors and raw, unplastered walls, but the potential is definitely there.

'What do you have in mind for the unit?' James asks, his hard hat dangling from his finger. 'A crèche or something?'

If I'm not being mistaken for a nurse, it's a childcare worker. Honestly, if you have a kind face and slightly matronly figure it's as if there are only two career options.

'Er, no, I was thinking more like a café,' I say, peering around the room. 'Casual but good, hearty food. No shortage of grass-fed beef or free-range eggs or fresh fruit and veg around here. It's what they all go mad for in cafés above in Dublin. But, now, I won't be having DJs or any of that craic.'

'That sounds very much like certain parts of London,' he says. 'Do you spend much time in Dublin? I thought you were local. My grandparents are from Ranelagh.'

'I was living up there until a few months ago and working in finance. I suppose I'm looking for a new challenge.' I don't mention the redundancy. I don't know why, but I'm still a bit mortified.

'You picked a good spot here anyway,' he says, going into business mode. 'The ceilings are 12 feet so it's nice and airy. All those vents and pipes will be covered once the suspended ceiling goes in, and the lighting will be recessed into it.'

I'm so busy looking up that I don't see the coil of cables snaking across the floor and trip straight over it. I'm just about to go face first on to the concrete when he puts out his arms and I fall straight into them.

'I'm so sorry!' I say into his armpit before I can extract myself. His tool belt is digging right into my hip.

'My fault entirely!' he says, hooshing me up easily. 'Are you okay? How's the foot? I completely forgot to give you a hard hat on the way in. I hope you won't sue.'

I burst out laughing just as the front door swings open.

'*Ahem.* Am I interrupting something?'

We both wheel around as Deirdre Ruane steps over the threshold. I blush automatically and I hate myself for it.

'Of course not, I just got here a bit early,' I stammer, smoothing my hair down.

'You must be Mr Matthews,' Deirdre says, walking in our direction beaming, her arm outstretched. 'Dee Ruane. Trevor couldn't make it so I'm showing Aisling around this afternoon. She has big plans for the unit!'

James shakes her hand firmly and then puts back on his hard hat. 'Yeah, she was just telling me. I'll leave you ladies to it so. Nice to see you again, Aisling.'

As soon as he's out of earshot she leans in to me and lets out a low whistle. 'Is he a sight for sore eyes or what? The arse on him. Daddy can have his shite if he thinks he's hogging this one.'

I didn't notice the first night I met him – probably because of all the John and Piotr drama – but she's right. He's a fine thing, no doubt about it. Very notable arse.

'Are you and Titch not back together?' Dee and Titch have been on-again off-again since they played Beauty and the Beast respectively in our joint transition-year school concert with the CBS. I was Mrs Potts, which was no skin off my nose, although I auditioned for the sexy feather duster. Majella accused Sister Bernadette of typecasting me, but she flat out denied it. I still have my suspicions till this day because my rendition of 'Tale as Old as Time' didn't exactly get rave reviews in the school paper.

'Yeah, I suppose we are,' Dee admits with a coy smile. 'I picked him up from the General after Cillian's thirtieth.

Jesus, he was in a bad way – I was worn out shaking the fizz out of bottles of 7Up. I'd still be hard pressed to say no to your man Matthews if he came asking. He sounds like Idris Elba.'

'He surely has a girlfriend,' I say in a whisper. 'A man like that. Possibly even a wife.'

'Well, he wasn't wearing a ring.' Dee shrugs. 'Anyway, what do you think of the place? Big enough for your café?'

'Definitely,' I say. 'And plenty bright.'

'Come on and I'll show you what's out the back.'

I follow her through swinging double doors to the back room, which would make a very decent kitchen.

'The electrics aren't in yet, so we can get it all done to spec for your equipment,' Dee says, pointing to a load of loose wires. 'And out here is a storeroom and the toilets. The finish is going to be really high-end. Matthews is adamant about that. I have a brochure out in the car for you.'

'It all looks faboo, Dee,' I say. 'When will it be finished? I'm mad to get going.'

'He's saying six weeks but Daddy says it could be eight. Does that suit you?'

'That's perfect. I'm still getting my ducks in a row.' I don't mention the nagging feeling in the back of my mind about the bloody grant. I try not to let myself think about what will happen if the money doesn't come.

'Oh, I'm sure you're well on top of things, Ais. No flies on you, and if they are they're paying rent. Majella was telling me you're going to be doing brunch. About time, I said. It's the twenty-first century, like. Mammy still insists on sitting down to a full roast at twelve on a Sunday. I'm rarely able for it after the night before. Going out for brunch with the girls would be a bit of craic – very Instagram.'

'Any idea what's going in up top?' I enquire, pointing up to the ceiling.

'I can't show you just yet because the actual stairs isn't in, but there'll be three luxury three-bed apartments. Completely separate entrance so don't worry about that. I'll be getting a nice little commission once they're rented.'

Well, I'm delighted to get all the facts straight from the horse's mouth (no offence to Dee). And I'll be able to put a stop to all these rumours of celebrities and Lidls and drug barons. Although part of me is sad Donny Osmond won't be knocking around. That'd surely be good for business.

As I drive back through BGB I spot something that makes me do a double take. Is that–? It *is* Pablo on Main Street, sitting on his own on a bench outside Maguire's. Maybe he's having a little drink for himself, given that the sun is out. And sure why not? As I drive away I catch sight of someone coming out of the pub and sitting beside him. Looks very like Susie Ó Súilleabháin, although I can't be sure. Do they even know each other? I must ask Majella.

CHAPTER 25

It's my fifth day in a row waiting for Pat Curran – yes, the BGB postman is called Pat – but, once again, nothing back from Entrepreneur Ireland. Apparently it can take a month or more. Mammy, on the other hand, is continuously getting reams of letters, which she immediately secretes away. I've an awful feeling they're bills – first, second and third notices on them. Although, I've been keeping my eyes peeled for red envelopes and nothing so far. Are red envelopes only in films, though? It's hard to know. I've been trying to get her to take a few bob off me for rent but she won't hear of it. 'You're opening a business, pet,' she says. 'You'll need every penny.'

Herself and Constance Swinford have become a right pair, gallivanting off on their ladies' days out in the Range Rover. Mammy has gotten so used to the higher altitude that when I was driving her in for a look around Geraldine's the other day she complained she wasn't able to see over any garden walls from my Micra. Apparently they have Auntie Sheila and Tessie Daly roped into doing the Camino with them in the summer.

'But what do you talk about?' I quizzed her. I'm imagining Constance honking away about supper and clay-pigeon shooting at every opportunity, or boasting about the quality of her horse's shite and the effect it has on her rose garden.

'Ah, this and that,' was all Mammy would say. 'Never you mind.'

Still, this new friendship has come in handy for me – some aristocrat family the Swinfords know are having money troubles and need to leave the country in a bit of a hurry. It sounds dodgy, but they used to cater weddings in their manor house and are going to be auctioning off a load of professional kitchen equipment for next to nothing. I might just have to turn a deaf ear to Mammy's suspicions that Lord Thingamebob is being done for insider trading. The auction is next Friday, so I lit three candles this morning in the hope that I hear back about the grant by then. Desperate times and all that.

Another upside to Mammy getting out more is Paul beyond in Oz is finally calming down. He's had me mithered with WhatsApps for the past few weeks: 'Are you filling her tablets box?' 'Do you know her blood type?' 'Should we get her one of them personal alarm yokes?' I think he's feeling the distance between Melbourne and home. He even confessed that he's been getting up at 2 a.m. every Sunday to tune in live to the *Farming Weather*. There was just no convincing him to watch it at a more reasonable hour on the RTÉ Player.

Majella said she'd be getting the early Timoney's bus down today, so I decide to tip over to pass on the baby-shower invitation and grill her about the interview. All she would tell me in a text was that it 'went grand', but I'm going to need more detail than that. I hope she used some of the prep questions I sent her last weekend. Where *do* you see yourself in ten years, Majella? I'd like to know myself.

Shem is climbing out the back of a jeep when I round the side of the house.

'Aisling,' he roars across the yard, 'you like a bit of water sports, don't you?'

Well, I don't know where he got that idea. Dearbhla Walsh insisted on going surfing for her hen and, honestly, it may have been the most traumatic day of my life. Would you be well asking your friends to get into the Irish Sea in January? I'm fairly uncoordinated at the best of times, and while I was decent enough at 'popping up' when we were on dry land, I wasn't popping anywhere when we got out on the water. I ended up paddling in early and laying across the radiator in the hostel to warm up.

'Who told you that now, Shem?' I shout back, wondering where this could possibly be going.

'I just got a delivery of a few wetsuits. Brand new, tags and all. I was thinking it's the kind of thing that always comes in handy. You're a woman who likes to be prepared.'

When he's not doing odd jobs, Shem's a great lad for trying to sell you all manner of bits. He has a brother over in Bristol who's in the importing business, or so he claims. It used to be great getting to watch films on DVD before they came out in the cinema, and I still have the genuine Ray Bans he sold me for a tenner when I was sixteen, but ever since Aldi came on the scene, well, people can just go to the centre aisle for their random shite. I think it hit Shem hard.

'Ah, I think I'll pass on the wetsuit, thanks,' I say.

'Are you sure? I'm selling them for €40 but I'll give you a good deal. Say, €35?'

'You're grand, Shem. Is Majella inside?'

He nods and goes back to his unloading while I open the back door. Pablo probably isn't home from work yet. I realise I haven't seen him since I spotted him outside Maguire's that day. I decided not to say anything to Maj. She's not fond of Susie Ó Súilleabháin, and it probably wasn't her anyway. I don't want to start a row over nothing.

The Morans live in one of those bungalows that spread like dandelions all over Ireland in the 1970s. I spent many an evening of my childhood playing Discover Ireland at the big pine kitchen table and plenty of weekends on the couch with the girls from school watching the Disney Channel via a homemade satellite dish Shem nailed to the chimney. The reception was never great, but we could just about make out what was happening on *Hannah Montana*. Majella thought she was the bee's knees until a stiff gust of wind blew it down and the Morans had to go back to watching the Irish channels like the rest of us.

Majella is in the kitchen filling the kettle when I walk in. 'Hiya, Ais,' she goes, flicking the switch, 'you timed that well. Here, make yourself useful and pass me the spray bottle on the counter there.'

I'm walking over to get it when I hear an unmerciful howl coming from the utility room, followed by an ear-splitting crash. It's that loud that it stops me in my tracks, but Majella doesn't even bat an eyelid and just continues on her crusade around the presses to find two matching mugs. I'm thinking I must have imagined it when it happens again: a howl so loud it nearly splits my eardrums.

'What the blazes are you hiding in there?' I demand, firing the spray bottle at her.

Maj rolls her eyes and fills the bottle from the tap. 'It's fucking Willy, Ais. He's gone demented – he knows it's almost four o'clock and Pablo's due home any minute. He just won't leave him alone!'

At the mention of Pablo's name there's a loud thump from the utility room, which sounds suspiciously like Willy throwing his body against the door.

'Mammy brought him to the vet yesterday, she was that worried about it. He said Willy is just trying to exert his dominance. It's a power thing – he's trying to remind everyone that he's top dog around here. But I swear to God, it's …' she pauses dramatically and hisses under her breath, 'sexual. He sticks his face in Pab's crotch and hammers away at his leg until he, you know, finishes. It's getting to the point where Pablo is dreading coming home in the evening. He's saying it's harassment.'

That does sound quite stressful. But if it comes down to it, I know Liz would choose Willy over Pablo any day. The Morans have had that dog since Shane found him in a plastic bag down beside Smyth's River six years ago. He's slept on Liz's bed from day one, and I've seen her kiss him on the mouth. She sees him as a sort of adopted son, which makes the mouth-kissing extra disgusting.

'I don't suppose you'll be able to move out any time soon?' I say hopefully as Maj plonks the two mugs of tea on the table in front of us. Her lips twitch and then her face breaks into a wide smile. 'Well, actually, I got a call on the bus home to say I got the Deputy Head job!'

'Majella, oh my *God*,' I roar, jumping up to hug her. 'I'm so delighted for you. The Deputy Head of St Anthony's and you're not even thirty! I bloody well knew that interview would be no bother to you.'

'I screamed so loud Tony Timoney swerved and nearly clipped a BMW on the N7!' She laughs. 'I can't believe I'm finally getting a pay rise. Thank *fuck*! There just might be light at the end of the tunnel.'

'I think it was the suit, Ais,' she says as we clink mugs. 'You were right, it *is* lucky.'

Just then the back door opens and Pablo pokes his head around. At the sound of the handle the racket from the utility room starts up again, except this time it's twice as loud. I have to cover my ears with my hands.

'Hola, Aisling,' he shouts, slinking over to the table with one eye on the utility-room door, which is rattling on its hinges but seems secure enough – I hope. 'Please, Majella, my bottle.'

Maj throws the spray bottle over to him, but he fumbles to catch it and it hits him square on the forehead. He curses in Spanish and bends down to retrieve it as I look at Majella and raise an eyebrow.

'It's just water,' she explains. 'The vet said that giving Willy a few sprays when he starts humping might deter him. It doesn't hurt or anything – it's just the negative connotations. Like when you ate so many Crunchies on our school tour to Cadbury's that you got sick and now you can't even be in the same room as one.' She looks over at Pablo, who is as pale as I've ever seen him. 'To be honest, it hasn't worked yet,' she adds with a sigh.

He just shrugs. 'My bottle, it makes me feel safe.'

I turn back to Majella and look at her expectantly. 'Well, are you going to tell him? About the job? I can't believe you haven't blurted it out yet!'

'Oh, I rang him from the bus,' she says, looking away quickly. 'He's taking me to the Ard Rí for dinner at the weekend to celebrate.'

Pablo stands up and sashays over to her before reefing her out of the chair and twirling her dramatically around the kitchen.

'I'm so proud, Aisling! *Mi amore*, the Deputy Head!' He's still twirling her while reeling off what I can only assume are sweet-nothings in Spanish. Majella is laughing and squealing while Willy howls away in the utility room.

'I'll head off so,' I say quietly, taking the invitation out of my bag and leaving it on the table. 'Don't worry about the suit – I'll get it off you again.'

'What's that, Ais?' Majella roars above the din, while Pablo nuzzles her neck. 'You didn't finish your tea,' she calls after me, but I'm already gone.

CHAPTER 26

J ust €6,122. That's all the redundancy money I have left. What in the name of Jesus was I at in Vegas clearing out the mini-bar? That's where the bulk of it went. Booze and $12 little boxes of Pringles. I've been watching my bank balance like a hawk since then. Even buying a stamp kills me. I call Ruane's and Deirdre answers on the first ring. She promised to text me if anyone else showed an interest in my unit but she can be very flaky. Titch Maguire will testify to that.

'Oh hi, Aisling,' she says, 'I had my hand on the phone. I'm actually waiting for someone from the GAA to call back.' The GAA! How glamorous.

'What do the GAA want?' I'm struggling to keep the excitement out of my voice. Maybe they're going to open a training academy or something in BGB. That would really put the town on the map – not to mention the potential for me to corner the lucrative all-day breakfast market.

'They want to buy two acres to the east of the Rangers pitch in Knock,' she says. 'Billy Foran is in for a windfall, by the looks of things. He might as well just name his price. If I broker it I'll be able to go to Marbella for a fortnight.' She lowers her voice. 'I'm talking all-inclusive, Aisling. Even drink.'

God forgive me, but I feel a real pang of jealousy. Why doesn't any of our land touch the Rangers pitch? If Mammy could sell a couple of acres to the GAA she wouldn't have to worry about money for a while. That would alleviate some of our combined stress.

'Actually, you'll think this is funny, Aisling, the GAA man was asking if I know John,' she goes on. 'As in your John. Or, I mean, your former John.'

'Why?' I'm truly baffled now.

'Apparently he's making a serious name for himself up at HQ with the work he's doing with the county team. There's talk of them being good enough to get into the semi-finals this year. Maybe even going all the way! Do you know that hasn't happened since 1984? They're saying he might be promoted to manager next year. He could be the next Brian Cody.'

I snigger. John wouldn't be too impressed with that comparison, although fair dues to him all the same. Maybe microchips weren't his calling after all.

'I was ringing about my unit, Dee,' I say, keen to get back to business. Entrepreneur Ais doesn't have time to waste gossiping, although I must remember to tell Mammy later. This kind of information would be major currency in her circles. Nothing like a sale of land to get tongues wagging. 'It's still available, isn't it? I think I'm ready to sign.'

There are some muffled sounds on the line, and then she tells me she has to go away and double check.

'Aisling, I'm sooo sorry,' she says when she comes back a couple of minutes later. 'Dad – I mean, Trevor looks after all the commercial stuff, as you know, and he took someone to see it this morning. It's in the system as let. I can't believe I dropped the ball, but this GAA commission – Ais, I could be flying Aer Lingus. I could be doing priority boarding!'

'Jesus, Dee!' I can't hide my annoyance. This is an absolute disaster. If I don't have the unit, I can't open BallyGoBrunch. If I can't open BallyGoBrunch, my life is over. What the hell am I going to do? I've spent the last month planning this. I shouldn't have waited to sign the lease – I should have just gone for it. What was that quote I posted on Facebook last night? Fear is temporary, regret is forever. Never a truer word spoken. No wonder it got seven Likes.

'No, sorry, it's not your fault,' I add quickly. 'I should have told you I'd take it at the first viewing. I was waiting for this grant to come in, and I suppose I just waited too bloody long. I don't suppose you have any other units going at the moment?' I know it's a long shot. It's not like we have anything fancy like an industrial estate, and there's feck all on the Main Street.

'Not this side of Knock, I'm afraid,' she goes. 'Unless you'd consider the little place to the side of the abattoir in Rathborris?'

'I can't imagine the health inspector would be too impressed.'

'No, I suppose not.'

'Can you at least tell me who's leasing it?'

'I'm not really supposed to give out that kind of information, Aisling. It's confidential – you know that.'

'You know me, Dee, I won't tell a soul.'

'Daddy would have my guts for garters!'

'How would he ever know?'

She sighs and I hear her hesitate. 'You wouldn't even tell Majella?'

'Not even Majella. I swear on …' I let my voice wobble, 'Daddy's grave.' And then I do a long, elaborate sniff. If Daddy is listening, I know he'll be proud.

'Oh, Aisling.'

'I'm sorry. It's still a bit … raw.'

'I miss seeing him around the village myself. He was always so cheery.'

'He was, wasn't he?'

There's another pause. 'Okay then. It says here it's Marty Boland.'

Of all the fucking fuckers in the village, it has to be him – the bully butcher of Ballygobbard!

****

I knew Sharon would understand. I asked her if she wanted to go for a pint in Maguire's, but I didn't expect her to get so dressed up. She's wearing leather leggings and the shoulders of her top have been strategically cut out. I feel a bit self-conscious in the jeans and jumper I helped Mammy feed some pet lambs in earlier, and the less said about my hair the better. It's very windy – let's leave it at that.

'I know, I'm bulling,' I admit, passing over her vodka, lime and soda before taking a gulp of my West Coast Cooler. 'What does he want a commercial unit for anyway? He's hardly moving the shop.'

'Jesus, that would actually be music to my ears,' Sharon admits. 'Although I can't see it happening. Main Street is a prime location for a butcher.'

'What am I going to do?' I wail. 'What would you do? You're a businesswoman.'

She thinks for a minute and then slams down her drink with enough force that Felipe the barman looks up from the *Racing Post*. 'Aisling, this is *your* unit,' she says evenly. 'Go talk to Boland. Butter him up. Find out what he's planning on doing with it, and then we can make a plan to either sabotage it or somehow convince him to give up the lease. I have no problem stooping low, hun. I hate that prick. Yesterday he hung a load of rabbit carcasses in his front window. Nobody wants to see that when they're going for a half-leg wax. He won't rest until he's driven all my potential customers away. Speaking of the salon, what do you think of Now Hair This?'

I look at her dubiously.

'Get Nailed?'

That's even worse.

'I'm just going to end up calling it Sharon's, aren't I?' she wails.

I take another gulp of my drink and mull over what she's said. I've known Marty Boland all my life. Maybe he's not that bad? Mammy used to send me in to get bones off him for Trixie, God rest her soul, and she still goes to him for her chops and mince and the occasional leg of lamb. Maybe he'd understand if I explained to him how much I need to open this café? The bloody farm might depend on BallyGoBrunch being a success, although I try not to think about that.

'Do you think it will work?'

'You have to do something,' she says with a shrug.

I suppose she has a point. I can't just let it slip through my fingers. I've put in too much work as it is. I fire off a text asking Dee to cough up the numbers. It's the least she can do after making shite of my future.

'So, when did you hear from Entrepreneur Ireland? This morning?' Sharon says, getting up to go over to the bar. Her heels must be six inches and she's striding around like she's in FitFlops. She must have calves of steel.

'I actually haven't heard back yet,' I admit.

'Hang on,' she says, stopping in her tracks and wheeling around to look at me. 'So you don't know if you even have enough money to open the café?'

'I do, I do,' I say, nodding furiously. 'My redundancy will be enough to sign the lease and maybe buy a toaster and a kettle but that's it.' Just about, but I don't say that out loud. 'Did you not read the budget section in my business plan? It was all there in black and white. The headings were pink?'

'Eh, yeah, of course I did, hun,' she says, heading for the bar. 'Same again?'

I nod and check my phone. Dee's gotten back to me: 'He's paying €350 pm. Daddy says he hasn't actually signed any paperwork yet tho xxx.'

'Well, shite anyway,' I say as Sharon returns with my drink. 'He's paying €350 a month.'

'Is that bad? My rent is €550.'

€550 for the entire building seems like nothing compared to rent in Dublin, but it's high enough for Ballygobbard.

'You have the flat upstairs too,' I point out. 'And you have a prime location on Main Street with all that footfall.'

'Footfall?' She laughs. 'It's not exactly Grafton Street, hun.'

'Oh, I know, but you're near the church. That's prime real estate in BGB. Anyway, the thing is, Dee told me on the sly that the developer would take €300 for it if I negotiated. She obviously didn't let on to Marty Boland, though, which makes sense. She's fairly serious about her commission.'

'So you can't pay €350, with an extra tenner thrown in?'

'No. Well, I could, but it would interfere with my projected profit margins. Honestly, Sharon, I'm starting to think you didn't read the business plan at all.'

'What? Hun, no. I did, I definitely did. I just might have nodded off somewhere around page 437. We'll figure this out.'

Then I remember the other thing that Dee said.

'Oh, but there's good news too! Apparently Boland hasn't actually signed anything yet. Him and Trevor Ruane must have one of those gentleman's agreements.'

Sharon slaps her thigh and I jump.

'Aisling, this is deadly! It means you're still in with a chance. Now you just have to go and convince him to back off.'

'How the feck am I supposed to do that?'

CHAPTER 27

I was always jealous that Paul got the big bedroom at the front of the house. Definitive proof that he's Mammy's pet, if you ask me. The view from his window goes right out past Majella's house to the mountains, which are looking like a patchwork quilt this morning. Very picturesque. Except my eyes are trained on Postman Pat's little green van, which has been parked outside Morans' for the past twenty feckin' minutes. God only knows what Shem is trying to convince him to buy. Finally he emerges with a wetsuit slung over his shoulder and boots it down the driveway. I race down the stairs, fly out the back door and I'm standing in the yard in my slippers when he pulls in.

'Howiya, Aisling,' he says, 'come here and don't make me get out again. My back is in bits.'

Pat Curran has been complaining about his back for as long as I've known him. Daddy used to be adamant he made it up so he could sit in the van instead of delivering things into people's actual letterboxes like his namesake, a proper postman.

He reaches over to the pile of letters on the passenger seat and pulls a single envelope out from under the elastic band. Just the one. I watch it happening in slow motion because I know that if the grant approval doesn't arrive today, it's game over for me getting to that auction for the bargain dishwasher and fridge-freezer and what have you. My eyes are glued to it as he goes to pass it out to me through the window, and I can see the name on it as clear as day – but it's not mine: it's Daddy's. My stomach drops and my face must do the same because Pat pipes up, 'Ah, I'm sorry, Aisling – it's very hard to get his name off some of these mailing lists. I can give you a form to fill out.'

'Thanks, Pat, but it's not actually that,' I explain, taking the letter and shoving it deep into my hoodie pocket. He's rooting around behind him and I have to catch myself from telling him the whole story about the café and the lease and my worries about Mammy and the farm. If Pat knows, he won't be long about spreading it and I don't want word getting around.

'Here you go now,' he says, turning back to face me. 'Can you sign this for me?'

'There's no rush, Pat, I'll fill out the form another day.' I have to go and figure out a way to turn my five grand into fifteen. But how?

'No, this one's for you Aisling,' he says, pushing it towards me. 'It's a registered letter. You have to sign for it now or I can't give it to you. Your mammy will have to fill out the other form.'

And there it is right under my nose – a white A4 envelope with the Entrepreneur Ireland logo printed in the top left-hand corner. I can't believe it. I scrawl my name on Pat's little device yoke and high-tail it back into the kitchen, where Mammy is eating a boiled egg, a guidebook about Ireland's

Ancient East open beside her. Herself and Constance must be running out of gardens to go and admire. Running out of scones to eat, more like. I tear the envelope open – I would normally be a bit more careful, but I'm not made of stone – and the letter slides out onto the table: my application has been approved and there's a cheque for €15,000 attached to it with a shiny silver paperclip. It's a miracle it wasn't stolen.

'*Yes!*' I roar and punch the air. 'Finally something has gone right.'

'You got your grant!' Mammy says, gesturing for me to pass over the letter, and I do. 'Good woman yourself! I didn't doubt you for a second, love.'

'Thanks, Mammy,' I say, helping myself to her toast, my hand shaking a little. All the plans can go ahead now. What would I have done if that cheque hadn't arrived? Quietly tipped myself into the nearest slurry pit, maybe. No use thinking like that, though. I turn to Mammy. 'I'll definitely be going to the auction on Friday now if you want to come with me? I'd say it'll be good for a nose if they're selling the entire contents of the house. This could be your chance to get on *Antiques Roadshow*.'

'I'd love to, pet, but I can't on Friday. Myself and Constance are going up to Dublin for the day.'

God, maybe they're not going around gardens at all. Maybe Mammy is going up to see that land-surveyor crowd. She's been going on recently about cleaning out some of the back sheds. Is she gearing up to sell? I can't bring myself to ask her, and I suspect she's shielding me from worrying about it. I can't bear the thought of her selling off the house and the farm and moving to … where would she move?

If I was any use I'd have built a mansion by now with a granny flat attached. Some daughter I am.

'Do you … do you need me to come?' I venture, hoping that she might finally tell me what's going on. Isn't it she who's always saying a problem shared is a problem halved?

'Not at all. Sure don't you have your auction to go to anyway?' And she goes back to leafing through her guidebook like she doesn't have a care in the world.

****

Marty Boland closes the shop at 2 p.m. on Tuesdays, so I decide to swing out to his house and see if I can convince him to give up this lease with Sharon's words ringing in my ears: 'Aisling, this is *your* unit. You have to do something.' I can see now why most people prefer to toddle into work every morning and punch in and pay their PRSI and get a salary at the end of the month. It's certainly easier than setting up a business but I must admit I haven't felt this alive since I earned the Gaisce Gold Award in 2006. Truth be told, there was never this kind of buzz when I worked in pensions.

The Bolands live on the Rathborris Road, about three miles this side of Knock. You can't see much of the house from the road, and as I turn down the long, curvy driveway, I realise I've never been down here before. I don't even know if they have any kids and I'd only know the wife, Carol, to see her at mass. She's a tiny little thing, almost folded in on herself. According to Mammy she 'suffers with her nerves', which could really mean anything.

I drive around the back of the house and notice Marty's red 'Boland's Fine Victuallers' van isn't there. Balls anyway. Although, I still don't know what I'm going to say so maybe it's for the best. God forgive me, but the only ace I have up my sleeve is my dead father. Can I really use that to manipulate the situation? On one hand, I think I deserve to go straight to hell for even considering it, but on the other, I think Daddy might be up for it. If only he was here to tell me himself.

I take a deep breath and hop out of the Micra. The smell in the air hits me immediately – it's an intoxicating mix of garlic and basil and all the mad herbs Elaine used to have in little pots on the windowsill of our apartment kitchen. I didn't know what any of it was, but I said nothing and just gave them the occasional drop of water. She was atrocious at minding them, and I've got a good knack for keeping plants alive, whether they're legal or not.

The smell is heady, and a pleasant change from the aroma of slurry that usually hangs around BGB. But there's not a soul to be seen. I'm just about to rap on the back door when I hear a sound from one of the whitewashed outbuildings that frame the back yard. Unlike our home place, the whole setup is very orderly and neat, but I suppose it would be when you don't have cows and sheep wandering through the place every other day. There's the sound again – it's a low whirring, like machinery. Not farm machinery, smaller than that. Following it, I tip over to the largest of the buildings and notice that the delicious smell gets stronger too. My stomach growls in appreciation.

I follow my nose around the side of the building, where I discover a wide-open window – and the source of that smell.

I hate to be snooping but, at the same time, I can't help myself. With my back against the wall, and feeling like Nancy Drew or Jessica Fletcher or one of those, I sidle down the narrow gap between the wall and the hedge until I'm close enough to peep inside. That's where I see Carol Boland standing in the middle of an industrial-looking stainless-steel kitchen. She's wearing a hairnet and an apron and in front of her is a whirring food mixer and about twenty little bowls. I watch her for a minute, adding this and that to the mixing bowl and smelling whatever's inside. Behind her on the hob is a pan of sizzling sausages. I'm nearly weak with the smell of them.

Suddenly, my stomach rumbles loudly and she looks up. I duck, but I don't think I was quick enough. I'm sure she's seen me.

'Is there someone there?' she calls out, squinting towards the window.

'Eh, hiya, Mrs Boland,' I shout up from the ground below it. 'I'm looking for Marty if he's around?'

I hear her walk across the kitchen towards the door, so I head back around the front. You know, like a normal person.

She looks confused for a second and then places me. 'Aisling? Seamus and Marian's girl?' she says softly, and the door swings open. Even hearing Daddy's name hits me right in the stomach. I nod at her, though, and smile. 'What are you doing here?'

'I wanted a word with Marty. Just a quick one. Sorry, I didn't mean to frighten you. I just followed the smell ...'

'How are you, love? How is your mammy?' She steps outside the building and pulls the door firmly shut behind her before pulling off her hairnet and blue rubber gloves and stuffing them in her apron pocket. She looks different outside mass, without her good coat and handbag. Taller, somehow. 'Marty's not here, I'm afraid. He had to do down to Tipperary to pick up some rabbits.' More rabbits. Sharon will be thrilled. 'Can I help you with anything?'

'Actually, maybe you can, Mrs Boland.'

'You'll come in for a cup of tea, so. Come on.'

She leads me across the yard and into the kitchen, which is warm and cosy and smells like freshly baked brown bread. Displayed proudly on the wall across from the table is Marty's award for the sausages, blown up to epic proportions and sitting in a thick gold frame. I notice two spotlights trained on it from the ceiling, on the off-chance you could miss it.

'The smell of that bread is something else,' I say, inhaling deeply, leaning back against the kitchen counter. A cluster of pictures hang on the wall opposite me – Mrs Boland and Marty wearing seventies gear on their wedding day, an aerial shot of the house just like the one we have of ours at home, and a yellowing snap of a woman and a young girl standing under a banner that reads National Ploughing Championship 1964. The woman is holding a big plate of sausages with a huge first-prize rosette stuck to it. I squint – the little girl looks familiar.

'Is this … you, Mrs Boland?'

'It is,' she replies. 'I'm seven there. And that's my Granny Nellie. She raised and slaughtered her own prize Landrace pigs.' Then she moves so she's suddenly between me and the picture. In her hands is a steaming apple tart.

'The bread needs another half an hour in the oven but you'll surely have a slice of this?' She smiles, leading me to the table where she's put a bowl of freshly whipped cream. I take a bite of the piece of tart she's put in front of me. Jesus, it's heaven. She's put something fancy in it – maybe cinnamon? – and it's warm and sweet and maybe one of the nicest tarts I've ever tasted. No soggy bottom either.

'Marty is fairly proud of his sausages, isn't he?' I say, cocking my head up at the award and accepting a cup of tea. 'Are the rumours true? Is he the only one who knows this secret family recipe? He must be sitting on a goldmine.'

She just smiles and smooths the folds in her apron. 'So what has you looking for him?'

I'm just about to tell her when I hear the sound of a vehicle approaching and a red van flies past the kitchen window.

Mrs Boland immediately stiffens and looks at her watch. 'Is it three o'clock already? I'm sorry, Aisling, but I'm going to have to–'

She's interrupted by the kitchen door opening abruptly.

'I was wondering who owned the Micra.' Marty Boland fills the doorway and, across from me, Mrs Boland shrinks by about half. 'What can I do for you, Aisling?'

'Well, Marty,' I say brightly. 'How are you?' He says nothing, just stares back at me. 'Eh ... eh ... I just wanted a chat about that commercial unit on the Garbally Road.'

He smiles and leans against the door frame. 'Ah yes, my new sausage-making facility. What about it?'

Mrs Boland gets up and starts clearing away our cups and plates and forks silently. I'm momentarily thrown by the words 'sausage-making facility', but steel myself and respond.

'I actually viewed it a few weeks ago, and I was hoping to lease it myself. To open a café, you see. Bring people into the village …' I can't help babbling because he hasn't taken his eyes off me once. I swear he hasn't even blinked since he walked in.

He cuts me off. 'Bring people into the village? Sure, that building is two miles outside!'

'Oh yeah, I know, but I'd be bringing people closer to the village. They might come in to the shop and buy some of your … ham.'

'Ham?' He guffaws. 'Sausages are what people come to Marty Boland for, Aisling.'

'Oh yeah, I know, I was–'

'I see you're friendly with that young woman from the new beauty salon beside me,' he continues. 'Did you know she's been banging and hammering away in there for months? It's noise pollution. She's lucky I haven't called the guards.'

'I think she–'

He cuts me off again. 'Now, if you'll excuse me, these sausages aren't going to make themselves.' Then he takes a massive keyring out of his coat packet and rattles it at me. 'I'm working on a new recipe, you see. Handed down through the generations. All very top secret.' And with that he turns around and stalks out of the kitchen. Then I hear the back door bang shut.

I'm reeling. He's so confident that he has it. My lovely unit. Turned into a sausage factory. I have to get that lease. I just have to. I involuntarily let out a low whistle and smile over at Mrs Boland, who's wiping crumbs off the counter into her hand. 'He's some man for the sausages,' is all I can muster.

How does she put up with him? And how am I going to get him to give me that lease?

She smiles back at me weakly. 'Will you bring home some tart for your mother?'

****

I'm on my way home, half an apple tart wrapped in tinfoil on the passenger seat beside me, when it hits me. Instead of turning down Main Street, I take a sharp right and head out the Garbally Road. When I get to the unit, I immediately spot James Matthews up a ladder doing something with a downpipe on the side of the building. His arse … it really *is* nice. I suddenly wish I'd worn something other than leggings and a fleece. If Sadhbh could see me – all her good work has been undone since I moved home. But it's hard to stay on top of the latest trends when you live so far away from the shops. I can't even remember the last time Majella tagged me in one of Colette Green's #ootd posts, which are a masterclass in how to match a nude belt to nude shoes.

I stride across the car park until I get to the base of his ladder. 'Well, James,' I call up to him

'Hello,' he says with a smile. 'I wasn't expecting to see you today. Do you have an appointment with someone from Ruane's?'

'I was actually hoping to speak to you,' I explain. 'Just for a minute.'

'Oh, right,' he says warily, coming down the ladder. 'You'd better step into my office so.'

His office, it turns out, is the front of his jeep, and I'm surprised at how messy it is – there are empty San Pellegrino cans (he's a fan of aranciata – notions) and Snickers wrappers and scrunched-up crisp packets everywhere.

'Sorry about all the rubbish,' he says. 'Hotel living. So what can I do for you, Aisling?'

I take a deep breath. 'So I suppose you've heard that Marty Boland has beat me to the lease,' I begin. 'Well, I was going to ask–'

'Hold on, hold on,' he says, holding up his hands. 'The commercial unit has been leased? That's the first I've heard of it. I was under the impression that you were taking it.'

'Yeah, so was I,' I go. 'But I called about officially signing and Dee told me her dad has let it to someone else. It's Marty Boland, the butcher.'

'I'm so sorry about that, Aisling. They haven't said a word to me. Can I assume Trevor Ruane and Marty Boland are mates?'

'Oh, they would be, yes. Very pally. They probably did this deal on the golf course. Anyway, what I wanted to tell you is that Marty is planning on turning the unit into a sort of sausage factory. He told me himself not an hour ago. But when I was doing my business plan for the café I looked into zoning laws, and I was under the impression that this premises,' I gesture over at the building, 'is zoned for retail use.'

'That's right.' James Matthews nods emphatically, running a hand through his brown curls.

'And a factory would be considered industrial, wouldn't it?'

'It definitely would.'

'So, legally, Marty Boland can't expand his sausage empire here, can he?'

'No, he can't.' He's starting to smile now, and my heart is beating out of my chest.

'But I could open a café?'

'Yes, you would be legally permitted to open a café here.'

There's so much adrenaline coursing through my veins I can't actually stay still in the seat.

'Can we shake on it now before you change your mind?' I say, my arm outstretched. 'This *is* your office, isn't it?'

He bursts out laughing and I notice his eyes are very twinkly. 'Are you sure this is your first foray into business? You seem very well-versed in the art of negotiation.'

I just shrug. 'Speaking of which, if you accept €300 a month for the lease I'll pay you six months up front. Deal?'

He laughs again. 'Jesus, you drive a hard bargain. I'll have Ruane's call you when the paperwork is ready for your signature.' Then we shake on it, and even though I couldn't be happier, I can't help wondering who's going to break the news to Marty Boland.

CHAPTER 28

The auction ended up being so stressful I got a nosebleed all over my catalogue. Thank God I never leave the house without a tissue up my sleeve. You never know when your nose will let you down. There were about 150 of us jammed into the foyer of this country estate, and I swear I was the only one not wearing a silk cravat or a tweed hat with a pheasant feather stuck in it. The only stroke of luck was that all the kitchen equipment was lumped together in one lot. If I'd had to bid on each piece individually I think I would have been stretchered out of there.

Most of the excitement seemed to be around a picture of a man petting a springer spaniel. I'm no art expert, so I can't pretend to understand why this particular painting was so important. It's not like the dog was doing anything gas like playing poker. If I was going to be spending four figures on a painting I'd at least want it to have been done by one of the famous Renaissance lads. But each to their own, and I suppose it would look nice in a pub or something.

Once the dog painting was gone, the crowd thinned out a fair bit. Pablo had come through for me something powerful with intel from the chef at the Ard Rí, who said to pay no more than €5,000 for the kitchen equipment. Majella's cousin manages a restaurant in Galway, and I had plagued her for advice too over the course of three Skype calls. I must send her a thank-you card, now that I'm going to be in the business too. It's a very classy move, a thank-you card. And James double checked the measurements for me and assured me there was space for everything I've been told I need. He's installed a kitchen or two in his time.

There were only three of us interested when the kitchen lot came around, and the first lad dropped out when it went over €1,000. A chancer if ever I saw one. The other one hung in a bit longer, but I could see him going pale when it got to €4,200. I was sweating profusely myself at that stage, but I didn't let on. In the end I got the whole shebang for €4,800 and convinced them to throw in free delivery too. Delighted is not the word.

Majella texted me earlier to see if I'd meet her for an early pint in Maguire's and the timing couldn't be better – I'm mad to celebrate. But there's something I need to do first, so I hop in the Micra and point it for Rathborris. It only takes about forty minutes to get to Bolands', and again, when I get out of the car, I'm met with the most mouth-watering smell. It's 2 p.m. so I know the coast will be clear. I'm about to walk over to the house when I turn around and head for the big outbuilding instead. One gentle knock is all it takes – I can hear the key turning in the lock and it inches open.

'Aisling, hello,' Mrs Boland says gently through the crack. 'Marty's in the shop – he won't be home till after five.'

'It's actually you I was hoping to talk to, Mrs Boland.' I can hear the sausages sizzling away on the pan behind her. The smell today is different – there's less garlic and more … I think it's sage? That furry leaf that's in stuffing. Whatever it is, I'm practically drooling.

'Oh. Right,' she says. 'I'm actually just in the middle of something here, you see …'

'Honestly, it will only take a minute.'

She sighs gently. 'You go on over and let yourself into the house so. I won't be long.'

The kitchen is pristine, save for a tempting-looking carrot cake sitting out on the counter. I recognise it immediately by the cream-cheese icing. I remember the first time Elaine tried to introduce me to the concept of carrot cake – I thought it was an April Fool's joke. But then I tasted it. Let's just say I ended up eating enough for it to qualify as one of my five-a-day. Hard to believe she eventually had me eating courgette cake, which is not half as manky as it sounds.

'Would you like a slice?'

Mrs Boland suddenly appears behind me, pushing her glasses up her nose. She's very light on her feet considering how many cakes she must eat.

'Jesus, it looks gorgeous,' I blurt out. 'Did you make it yourself, Mrs Boland?'

'I did,' she says softly. 'And, please, it's Carol. The secret is a pinch of allspice in the batter.' Then she smiles. 'But don't tell anyone.'

She cuts two generous slices and we sit down at the shiny kitchen table. It's no exaggeration to say that my first mouthful is a religious experience. It's so moist, and don't get me started on the flaked almonds in the icing. I can't believe this woman isn't sweeping the boards at ICA baking competitions.

'It was your cooking I wanted to talk to you about, actually.' She furrows her brow, and I take a deep breath and decide to just motor on in case himself comes back early and we end up in a brawl about the lease. 'If I get my little café off the ground, would you be interested in looking after the food? I don't want anything fancy, just good home-cooking. I think you'd be faboo in the kitchen, Carol. I'll be focusing on the business side of things, but I need someone who can put together the men–'

She interrupts me. 'You got the lease so?' She looks a bit terrified as I nod, but she continues, 'Marty mustn't have heard yet. Otherwise I'd know all about it.' God he must be an awful trial to live with.

'I … I did get it. I did a deal with the developer. I hope it doesn't cause any hassle for you, but it's such a lovely space – I think the café will be the best thing for it. And I'd love to have you on board, if you fancied it?'

She looks a bit taken aback. 'What makes you think I can cook? I'm just a housewife,' she says. 'I wouldn't know anything about cooking for a café.'

I say nothing and just glance up at the massive gilt-framed Superior Sausages Award above my head. She follows my gaze and her hand flies to her mouth.

'I don't know what you mean,' she whispers.

I can feel the emotion rising inside me. Marty Boland is nothing but a bollix. All this time he's been waltzing around like he's God's gift to sausages when it's Carol who's obviously been making them. I'm convinced the original recipe was her Granny Nellie's and now she's working on a new one, but he's happy to let her slave away out in that kitchen while he takes all the credit. The neck!

'Carol,' I say, in what I hope is a reassuring voice, 'I know you're the one behind the sausages. I saw you with my own eyes mixing up the new recipe. The smell of them – I was weak. You'd give Rachel Allen a run for her money. It's your granny's recipe, isn't it?'

For a minute she's frozen, then she nods. It's a tiny nod, but it's there. 'Aisling, please. Can I ask you not to say anything? Marty … he wouldn't react well if people knew.'

I knew she was scared of him. And I can't say I blame her. I'd be scared of him too.

'I won't say a word, I promise. I know things can be delicate. And sure don't men love thinking they're the boss?' My attempt at a little joke falls flat, though, and Carol looks down at her hands, rending her fingers together. My heart leaps into my mouth and I look around the kitchen, wondering what kinds of things have happened here.

'He doesn't … he doesn't hit you, does he, Carol?' I can't believe I'm sitting here in Mrs Boland's kitchen asking her this, but I'm ready to bundle her out into the Micra right now if I need to. God love her. 'Don't worry, I'm not going to tell anyone,' I add, reaching out and putting my hand over hers.

'No,' she says quickly. 'God, no, Marty has never laid a hand on me. He wouldn't do that.'

'I'm sorry to ask,' I say. 'It's just that, you seem … frightened.'

'He can be … domineering,' she eventually says, looking out the window. 'I'll leave it at that. I think he has himself convinced he really did come up with the recipe for the sausages. But you're right, it was my Granny Nellie's. She was some woman.'

'You should be getting the credit for those sausages, not Marty. And I know that if they're on the menu of my café, it'll be a success.' I pause. 'Will you at least tell me you'll think about coming to work with me?'

'I'm just a housewife,' she says again, staring into the distance. It sounds like a phrase she's been told more than once.

'There's not a thing wrong with being a housewife,' I say, and she turns to face me. There are tears in her eyes and I can feel myself welling up too. 'I was dying to be a housewife myself for a long time,' I explain. 'But now I'm about to do this café and it's given me a new lease of life, if I'm being honest. And if you come and work for me, you'll have some money of your own. You could become more ...' it takes me a minute to think of the word, 'independent. Go on, will you at least think about it?'

'He won't hear of it. He doesn't really think women should be working outside the home.'

'Who cares what he thinks? Aren't you your own person?'

'I wish it was that easy.'

'Please, Carol. I'd be honoured to have you on the team. I think it would do us both the world of good. Go on.'

She flashes me a little smile, squeezes my hand and says, 'Okay, I'll think about it.'

****

My arse has barely hit the seat in Maguire's when my phone rings – it's Mammy. I've already texted her to say I got everything I needed at the auction, so before I answer it I make a mental bet with myself that she wants to talk about a) food or b) washing. I wonder does Sheryl Sandberg's mammy ring her about her whites? I doubt it.

'I'm making a curry – will I put you in the pot?' I knew it. When I lived in Dublin I discovered that there are a seemingly infinite number of curry types: korma, tikka, massaman, Thai green, Thai red, Thai yellow (a personal favourite due to the potato content). But I know that when Mammy says curry she means a packet of Knorr Medium powder with some bits of leftover roast chicken thrown in. And that's fine by me because it's actually the nicest of the lot. Some of the others are fierce spicy.

'Oh yes, please,' I say, 'but I won't be home for a while. I'm meeting Maj for a pint and – oh, hang on, she's just walked in. I'll let you go, Mammy. Byebye byebyebye byebyebyebye.'

I wave over at Majella and do some elaborate gesticulating at the two bottles of West Coast Cooler in front of me so she knows she doesn't have to go to the bar.

'Well, bird,' she says, plonking herself down in front of me and reaching for a bottle. She does it very slowly, though, and I'm wondering if she put out her neck again. Communion prep at St Anthony's is going full throttle, and since it's her last year she says she wants to out with a bang. She'll be in full Deputy Head mode come September so she's giving it all she's got. Her choir conducting can be very vigorous at the best of times.

'Drink up, Maj, we're celebrating!' I roar. 'You'd want to see what I bought for the café today. BallyGoBrunch is officially *go*! And that's not all – I have loads to tell you.'

And I raise my glass and shake it in her direction. But she doesn't cheers me. Instead, she slowly lifts her hand and starts running her fingers through her hair. I shake my glass at her again, the ice clinking away, but she just keeps doing it, a massive smile plastered on her face. Over and over again, running her fingers from her scalp down the length of her hair, which is a newer, more violent shade of red than it was the last time I saw her. I start to panic and wonder if she's had a stroke. Is her face gone wonky? Is she slurring? What's that acronym I'm supposed to remember? F.A.C.E.? Or is it F.A.S.T.? Jesus, what do the letters even stand for? I'm about to stand up and shriek at Felipe to call an ambulance when it catches my eye ...

'What the *fuck* is that, Majella?' I scream.

She stands up and pushes her left hand right into my face until it's mere millimetres from my eyeballs. Ohmygod. Ohmygod. Ohmygod. It is. It is what I think it is.

'It's a *ring*, Aisling,' she screams back. '*I'm engaged!*'

CHAPTER 29

'Tell me *everything*.'

I'm barely sitting down and Sadhbh is nearly in my lap, looking for news. I suppose there's loads to catch her up on: Majella, the café, Carol Boland and the sausages, what I bought in IKEA. Most people whinge about going to IKEA, but I think it's like going on holidays. The little pencils. The ordered arrow system pointing customers to follow the flow of traffic. The absurdly affordable food. They're practically giving it away! Now, I know it's hard to come away without at least seven things you don't need, but you can never have too many laptop cushions, bins and dish sponges, if you ask me. I headed this morning for some essentials for BallyGoBrunch. I had a list and was determined not to stray from it. Place settings, napkins, vases and aprons. I'll order a load of the other stuff wholesale, but for the time being I need to get going and get the place looking like a café, and I have a very particular look in mind. Shabby chic is what I'm going for. I saw it in a magazine and, besides, half the cafés in Dublin look like you accidentally stumbled into someone's granny's house. You'd nearly expect to find a set of teeth in your water glass. I'll have my eyes peeled for anything with flowers, bees or old wellies on it. Sadhbh has begged me to add a few 'modern twists' too. Something to do with irony. Maybe a few silver butter dishes and plugs for people to charge their phones will keep her happy. People go berserk for places to charge their phones. And if they can charge their phones, they can put pictures of their grub on Instagram and put BallyGoBrunch on the map.

Sadhbh had me convinced to drive into town afterwards to meet her for lunch. I've barely seen her since we came back from Vegas, and it's about time we had a catch up, to be fair. She knows the bare bones of Majella's news, of course, but she wants all the details.

The car park earlier was gloriously empty. The absolute luxury of coming on a weekday morning. I could get used to this self-employed lark. I left BGB late enough to skip the morning commuter traffic but still gave myself enough time to sail around the whole place before I had to leave to meet Sadhbh. In I went, arming myself with a pencil, an order sheet and a little paper measuring tape. I'd hardly need it but you never know – they are just so handy. I must have at least five of them in various handbags and coat pockets. John used to love a trip to IKEA as much as me, but you'd hardly be as far as the shower curtains and you'd be rowing. It's around the shower curtains that most of the rows start, and if you stop and observe for a few minutes you can see people left, right and centre storming off with trolleys or firing a bathmat back to the wrong spot with a *'Fine'* or a *'Get what you like so.'* And if bathrooms didn't finish off your relationship, pictures frames surely would. John and I sometimes wouldn't get past kitchenware. I'd be trying to fire dishcloths and self-sudsing scrubbing brushes into his trolley in the hope he might tackle the kip of a house he lives in, and he'd be going hammer and tongs for the shelves and screws, with no intention of ever putting a thing up. We'd be lucky to be speaking when the time came for the traditional tiny ice-cream cone after the checkouts. I don't miss that, that's for sure.

This morning, though, there were no rows. Just me and a handful of others gliding around serenely, with nobody hacking the backs of anyone else's ankles with a trolley or pushing past them at the Billy bookshelves with an 'excuse me' through gritted teeth. Pure bliss. I loaded up on four cases of slate-coloured plates, bowls and mugs, treated myself to a selection of flowery milk jugs, and fell upon a pile of napkins with old suitcases on them. No aprons but maybe I'll get some online. A quick pit stop for a ludicrously reasonably priced bit of fish and chips and Daim cake (12 Points – worth it) and I made it out with only two extra bins and four rogue photo frames. Not a bad morning's shopping.

Parking in town during the day is a luxury I would usually only allow myself at Christmas, but I make an exception for Sadhbh. She's very good to me and sent me a text just before I set off for IKEA reminding me, 'No wavy mirrors.' I would argue that nothing modernises a space like a wavy mirror and a print of the New York skyline, but Sadhbh knows her fashion. She only buys beige cushions and streamlined storage solutions in IKEA. No coat hangers that look like dogs' arses for her.

I arranged to meet Sadhbh at a café on South William Street near her office. My eyes were on stalks looking for hints and tips and décor tricks. I wore silver bangles and my skinniest jeans in case any of the other Flatlay Records crowd were going to be there. I haven't gone full skinny, of course. I just can't bring myself to and my calves would never forgive me. Every jean needs a little kick to it, in my opinion. To my relief, it's just Sadhbh sitting there hunched over her phone. I'm a few minutes late, but it was the difference between €3.40 an hour and €2.80 an hour in the car park so I left the car further away and hoofed it over here on foot. My Fitbit will thank me for it.

'Ais,' she squeals, and jumps up for a hug. I was never much of a hugger before I moved in with Sadhbh and Elaine, but they'd have the stuffing squeezed out of you by midday.

'Hiya, Sadhbhy. Any craic?'

'Never mind me. Tell me *everything*.' She shoves a menu in my direction. She's already warned me that she only has an hour for lunch. Busy times in the music biz.

'Well, you know he got the kids in her class to kind of flash mob her with flowers?'

'I know, I know. I still can't believe it. It's so deliciously cringy but so adorable at the same time.' Sadhbh has long-held feelings about public proposals, i.e. don't do them. I mean, if you're going to be tasteful and get someone to hide in the bushes to get pictures for Facebook I suppose it's okay, but she has a point. Some people go way over the top. Last year at a Knock wedding the best man proposed to his girlfriend after the first dance and there was war. You never know when it might all go wrong. Luckily for Pablo, though, it went right.

'So the kids went up to her desk, one by one, and put a flower on it.'

Sadhbh squeals again, holding her menu up to her face.

'Majella thought they were going to kill her for a second. Some kind of ritual they were conned into on the internet. But then the door opens and there's Pablo holding a full bunch of flowers and the children all chant "Missus Moran, will you marry him?" The shrieks brought people in from four classrooms away.'

I pause to order and let Sadhbh soak in all of the details.

'Can you believe it?'

'I know! Isn't it mad?' I'm as breezy as can be but Sadhbh still senses my hesitation.

'Are you not sure about it?'

'Ah no, I am.' I look at my hands. 'But at the same time they're only together a wet weekend. I'd worry she's rushing into it – I love Pablo but does she even know him, really?'

'Ah, she does. Hasn't he been living with her and the fam for a while now?'

Sadhbh is right, I suppose. 'How are Elaine and Ruby? I haven't seen them since the wedding, if you can believe that. I'll have to get them down to the … café.' I blush at my own words. It still doesn't seem real.

'Oh, I know! Tell me all. Did you say something about sausages on the phone or was I hallucinating?'

Sadhbh's open salmon sandwich arrives, and I gaze at it with pity as my chicken burger is placed in front of me. I'm sorry, but a sandwich is not a sandwich without two slices of bread. What's the point? They definitely saw her coming.

'Well,' I start, 'you know Marty Boland, the butcher?'

'Yeah. The prick that's been giving the new beauty girl all the hassle.'

'Yeah, well, his wife is a dynamite cook, and it turns out that she's behind the amazing sausages he's been making a name for himself with. They serve them for breakfast at the Ard Rí and people go crazy for them.'

'Sure, I know them well. You used to bring them up to Dublin all the time. I swear Elaine thought about giving up the veganism once or twice for them. But did they not have his name and face plastered all over them?'

'That's the thing. He's taken her granny's recipe that she's perfected and put his mark all over it. It seems like she's powerless to stop him. He's such a bully.'

'But you told me she's coming to work for you, right?'

'Oh, Sadhbh, it's not just the sausages she's got under her belt. The bread and cakes and potato farls are out of this world.'

'Go on, Aisling! Look at you, little miss entrepreneur.'

'And she hummed and hawed over it, afraid of him more than anything, I'd say. But we sealed the deal by telling him about the exposure the sausages will get if the café does well. He's mad to get them into supermarkets. Carol said he actually went purple when he found out I'd told James Matthews that he was planning on putting his sausage factory in the unit. Serves him right for thinking he's above zoning laws. Things between them are fairly tense because of it, but we're hoping he'll get over it soon enough.'

'And so his wife *is* coming to work at BallyGoBrunch?'

'Yeah. He decided to *let her*. Said they need the money for another van for distribution.'

'Big of him,' Sadhbh scoffs.

'So she's been working on some recipes and menus and, do you know, Sadhbh, I can't believe I got her. It seems too good to be true.'

'Well, I'm delighted for you. Cheers to that.' She lifts her sparkling water and we clink glasses. 'Here, tell me more about this James Matthews person. This isn't the first time you've mentioned his name.'

I've tried to keep the mentions of Mr Matthews to a minimum, to be honest. Truth be told, the thought of him makes me blush to high heaven. Of course she picks up on my discomfort right away.

'Oh? Is he a looker?'

'If you like horsey, *Made in Chelsea* types, I suppose. He's very Constance Swinford.' Sadhbh knows all about Constance. She's entranced by her and Mammy's friendship. 'They're like us, kind of,' she jokes. 'Chalk and cheese.'

I'm being a bit unfair to James, I suppose, but I don't want any more romance chat after the last while. After going out with the same lad for years, I'm wrecked out with all the drama and the fighting and the sheet wrangling of the past few months. Speaking of which …

'How's Don?'

'I was just texting him.'

I wait for her to slag me about Antony, but she stays mercifully silent on that front, thank God. What happens in Vegas and all that.

'Is he still over in the States a good bit?'

'Yeah, they're touring the east coast at the moment. About twelve of them sleeping in a bus. Just thinking about the smell makes me queasy.'

'Have Fionnuala and Mairead found out about you two yet?'

She puts down the phone. 'Yes, and it's not good. Fionnuala saw him on some local New York chat show that she recorded and the interviewer asked him about having a girlfriend ...' She spears a cherry tomato with her fork.

'Well, *go on*,' I almost shout. Has Don professed his love for her publically? Is Fionnuala now on hunger strike? Is Sadhbh's life in danger?

'Sorry,' she says, swallowing. 'I'm starving – totally forgot to eat breakfast. Anyway, he said he was seeing someone blah blah blah and pointed to the S he'd just had tattooed on his finger.'

I nearly choke on my burger. He got her initial *tattooed* on his body permanently. Then she holds up her own hand – where there's a D etched just above the knuckle on her middle finger. They're like something out of a sexy perfume ad.

'Sadhbh, you didn't,' I squeal, and she smiles back at me.

'I did. And so did he.'

'You're mad about him, aren't you?'

She shrugs. 'He's a keeper. At least, I think he is.'

He's some catch, I'll give her that. I can't believe I'm only finding out about this now, though. I fight back the feelings, but I'm a bit sad.

'And has Fionnuala scratched you off her Christmas card list?' I know for a fact she has one – she asked me to update my address when I moved back Down Home.

'Quite the opposite, in fact,' Sadhbh says. 'She's now trying to be my best friend. Like, she normally reefs my clothes out of the washing machine the minute they're done, even when she's not putting on a wash herself, but she let them sit in there for two days last week.'

I do have to remind myself that living with Sadhbh and Elaine wasn't all plain sailing. I'm just about to quiz her on the latest celebs they've had through the office – I have my Kodaline CDs ready for signing whenever she gives the nod – when Sadhbh exclaims and gestures out the window. 'Speak of the devil – isn't that Pablo right there?'

I follow the direction of her gaze and, sure enough, there he is, standing on the street opposite the café and hugging Susie Ó Súilleabháin!

'Oh my God! What's he at?'

Sadhbh looks confused. 'What do you mean, what's he at? Who's your one?'

'Susie Ó Súilleabháin. She's from BGB – Cyclops's sister.'

One of Majella's mortal enemies.

'What are the pair of them doing together up in Dublin?'

Your guess is as good as mine, Sadhbh.

'D'you know, I wasn't going to say anything, but something about Pablo's been bugging me for a while. I keep catching him eyeing people – women – up. Staring at them, like. And that's the second time now I've seen him on his own with Susie.'

'Yikes, that's a bit suspicious!' Sadhbh looks shocked, and rightly so. Everyone who meets Pablo finds him to be so dotey. But what if everyone is wrong?

'Will you tell Majella?'

Will I tell Majella? It would break her heart if Pablo hurt her. She's been through so many positive changes over the last few months with the new job and the engagement. Okay, so living on top of her family and Willy the insatiable hound isn't ideal, but she seems so happy.

'I don't know, Sadhbh. I really don't know.'

CHAPTER 30

I don't have to wait too long to decide what to say about Pablo because Majella drops into the café, which is still looking rough and not-very-ready, the very next day, dying for a nose around and a gossip. She's mad for all the latest on Don and Sadhbh and nearly comes off the crate she's sitting on when I tell her about the tattoos. I seize the opportunity to mention Pablo.

'Did I see Pab up in Dublin yesterday too?' I say casually. 'He should have told me he was going, I could have given him a lift.'

Majella looks confused. 'No, can't have been him. He was away on some kind of bar training course for the hotel, but it was in Kilkenny, I think, he said. He must have a doppelganger. Two fine young things walking the streets of Ireland.'

Doppelganger, my hole. I know what I saw. Why on earth would he lie to her? I decide not to push it there and then and store it away in my brain to maybe ask Pablo himself.

The next fortnight is so hectic I barely get a chance to even think about it, though. I comfort myself by deciding that Pablo's probably planning something nice for Maj, and there's no harm in it at all. It keeps the guilt at bay for the time being anyway. She's so wrapped up in her engagement joy too – I couldn't do anything to ruin it for her. She's ordered one of those jewellery-cleaning kits she saw on QVC, and she nearly has the ring polished away already. I'd say poor Pablo is sweating that some of the colour might come off it.

Me and Carol are up late every evening in her workshop, coming up with menus and recipe ideas. Well, she's coming up with the recipes, and I'm not sure if my suggestion of sprinkling a few seeds on everything is much use. They're all at it up in Dublin. I wouldn't be a bit surprised to get a cup of tea with a few seeds sprinkled on it one of these days. It's bad enough when they put half a flower bed on something and expect you to say it's delicious. Pansies taste like grass – and That Bloody Cat uses Mammy's pansy bed as her own personal ensuite, so I'll leave them on the side, thank you very much. Marty Boland has left us alone for the most part, but I can only call over when Carol's made him his dinner and he's settled in front of the telly for the night. I'm a bit worried about how she's going to get out to BallyGoBrunch every day for work – I can't keep giving her lifts – but she says there's an old bike in the shed that she's going to fix up. I told her it's a shame she can't drive, but it turns out she can. She just has no access to a car. 'You'll be able to save up for one when you're working,' I told her, but she looked dubious. That mean old bastard Boland. Sitting on all the cash. If I could magic him away I would.

Carol is totally on board with using local producers. We both agree that if we're going to put BGB on the brunch map then we should showcase the very best it has to offer. There's only so far a top-notch Chinese takeaway and a decorative water pump can take a town. There are so many stories about rural villages dying a death, so if I'm going to be staying in BGB then I might as well give it my all.

We're taking all our veg from three farmers in the area and another two local farms are supplying the eggs. They're as free range as they come. I know because I've nearly ended up in the ditch several times avoiding a loose hen on the road. Sweeney's strawberries are only delighted with the massive order we've put in. Carol has a strawberry compote yoke to go with pancakes that's to die for. It'll take me a while yet to come to terms with the idea that you can have pancakes on more than one day of the year, but I'm not one to stand in the way of progress.

Mammy can't get her head around the different types of coffees we're going to be doing, but Sadhbh sent me an article from the *Irish Times* about coffee culture and how it's showing no signs of waning, so I am a hundred per cent getting on that train. There's people who never looked beyond an instant cappuccino sachet until a few years ago who are now practically flying to Guatemala to pick their own beans every morning. I'm still partial to an instant cappuccino myself. I'm not mad on coffee, but I'm a divil for the little packet of chocolate shavings. Felipe in Maguire's knows a lad out beyond Knock who roasts his own beans, so we've been in touch and he's going to come in and teach us a few things. Sharon is thinking of getting coffee in to the salon too, so he's got new customers coming out of his ears. She finally opened last week, and I took a night off to toast the occasion with two glasses too many of prosecco. I had some head on me the next morning and me having to meet a man about sanitary bins for the café toilets. The glamour never stops. The salon is still unofficially called 'Sharon's'. She has a makeshift sign above the door while she agonises over the latest possibilities: Hair 2 E-Tanity or She Bangs.

I'm blue in the face telling her that nobody will concede to calling fringes 'bangs', so she's still working it out.

'Coffee machine is here, Aisling.'

'Ah, thanks, James.'

Four days to go until the soft opening and James is still finishing off bits and pieces, while Carol is finally in the kitchen, getting used to how everything works. I've made noises about paying James for all the extra bits he's done for me, but he's having none of it. I really do feel like it's outside his remit, though. He's done solar panels on the roof, which I think is cracked. You'd be lucky to get two sunny days in a row in BGB, but he claims it makes a huge difference. More progress. I'll be driving to work in a car with no steering wheel yet. Mad Tom actually did have a car with no steering wheel for a while, but that was more down to gross negligence than technological advances.

James and the delivery man are just huffing and puffing the machine into place on the counter when Mammy pokes her head around the door.

'Anyone for scones?'

I think she's a bit put out that Carol is going to be doing the scones for BallyGoBrunch, so Mammy has taken to pushing hers on us any chance she gets. She's also got it into her head that James needs feeding up with all the work he's doing. He looks sturdy enough to me, but I think maybe he reminds Mammy of Paul a little bit with the brown curly hair.

'Lovely, Mammy!' I call to her. 'Carol, any compote going?'

Carol brings out a tray of bits, and we have a makeshift scone picnic at one of the tables me and Maj put together at the weekend. There were two screws left over, and Majella just opened the door and fired them into the nearest bush.

I didn't sleep a wink that night thinking about them, but the table is still standing so we'll hope for the best.

James waves Mammy away when she offers him a scone but gestures at her to follow him outside. 'I've something to show you, Marian,' and she's off out after him like a hare out of a trap. I'd say he's charmed some number of mammies in his time.

'What are that pair at?' I muse at Carol as James helps Mammy over some rubble and points at God knows what around the perimeter of the building.

Carol shrugs and says gently, 'They're good pals, your mam and James.'

Between James and Constance, Mammy is one step away from a pair of Hunter wellies and doing her Big Shop in Avoca.

Carol and I clean up, and I set about reading the manual that came with the coffee machine. Felipe's pal will show us the ropes, but I want to have my homework done. I look up as I see James give a shout and wave and hop into the jeep. Off for yet more supplies, no doubt. Mammy comes back in, her cheeks flushed from the fresh air.

'What were you doing out there?' I ask innocently.

'Ah, he was just showing me this and that. I'm interested. Your father was very handy, and I miss watching him and helping him.'

Daddy was very handy alright, although his DIY skills were self-taught – you still need to turn on the light in the press in the hall to get the lamp in the front room to work.

'And James is a lovely young man. Very ... handsome.'

Mother of God, does Mammy have a crush on James Matthews? She pipes up again before I have a chance to tease her.

'I hear John let the school down the other day.'

Talk about jarring. I haven't heard or thought about John in weeks. Mammy's tone implies she's less than impressed.

'He was asked to do a medal ceremony for the sports day, and he was too busy to be there. The children were very disappointed by all accounts.'

The louser! Talk about getting above his station. And him only a selector. Imagine if he was actually on the team. I'm disgusted.

'Mrs Timoney says they had posters made for him and everything.' Mrs Timoney has been known to use local primary-school child labour to weed her garden. She's fond of the odd 'nature walk' to her herbaceous borders, so I don't know if she's the right one to be acting the role of the morality police, but it does sound very lax of John.

'I suppose if he's busy, he's busy.'

Mammy hasn't said much about me and John since we broke up, so I don't know how she really feels about him. But I still feel like I have to defend him a tiny bit. Even if it does sound like he's well and truly up himself.

'Ah, here's James back again. Isn't he great?' I think there's a new number one in Mammy's eyes. I watch him as he heaves three terracotta pots out of the back of the jeep. He gets good deals in the Garden Centre, and I want the outside looking as nice as the inside.

'Are you all set anyway, pet?' Mammy's eyes travel around the café, and I follow them, imagining what it will be like in a just a few short days.

She turns to me, with tears glistening in her eyes. 'I'm so proud of you Aisling. And Daddy would be beside himself.'

CHAPTER 31

My heart is in my mouth as I turn the key in the BallyGoBrunch door. I'm opening for customers for the very first time. Tessie Daly is ready and waiting, and so is Constance Swinford. Majella and Pablo are just pulling into the car park, and Deirdre Ruane and Titch Maguire are right behind them. Pulling the door open, I welcome Tessie and Constance inside. They're in like hot snots at a table with Mammy, oohing and aahing over the menu. We have a limited selection on offer for the day that's in it. A 'soft opening' it's called – no big fanfare. It's fierce common with restaurants, and it takes a bit of the heat off. It's a good thing, really, because my nerves are nearly gone already. I'm putting a lot of faith in the sausages and Carol Boland's homemade ketchup to go along with them. The tomatoes come from Mossy Folan's farm next door to Bolands'. For a while there was a suspicion they might have been growing hash plants in the polytunnels along with the tomatoes, but only because Mossy is away with the fairies half the time. We have eggs cooked various ways too and as much freshly baked bread as people can shovel into them. I consulted with Carol and ordered a heap of avocados as well. I don't know if BGB is ready for them just yet, but you never know what people will be after. I am promising brunch, after all, and if it's smashed avocado they're after then I'll put them in a bag and drive over them in a Massey Ferguson if I have to.

'Ais! Hiya, Ais!'

Majella and Pablo have already seated themselves at a table by the window, and Majella is waving over at me like a madwoman, giving me the thumbs-up. Beside her, Pablo is giving me the oddest look. A dirty look, if we're calling a spade a spade. Eyes narrowed, brow furrowed. It sends a bit of a chill through me. I wonder did Majella mention to him that I thought I'd seen him in Dublin. Images of him waving his lad at Susie Ó Súilleabháin dance around my head. When he realises I'm looking straight at him his face relaxes and he starts waving like a lunatic too. I ignore him as Deirdre and Titch join them, and I wince as Titch lowers his mud-stained training shorts onto my gingham cushions. He must have been out on the pitch early this morning. It's amazing how many pints those lads can sink on a Friday night but still manage to drag themselves to training first thing on Saturday morning. That's dedication. Majella beckons me over but I'm relieved to be able to wave her off with an 'I'm busy' and an apologetic smile. She looks at me funny but turns to Maeve Hennessey's 16-year-old sister, Paula, who's trying to take Pablo's order. There seems to be some confusion about his desire for 'huevos rancheros' and her insistence that we don't actually sell crisps yet.

I'm just about to tip into the kitchen to see if Carol and the lad we have interning from the Mountrath are coping okay when another car pulls into the car park, and another behind that. And here's Melanie Rice and her husband, Turlough, with the tiny hands, coming in on foot pushing a buggy. Word spreads fast, it seems, even if your opening is as soft as a baby's arse. Sharon's just behind them. She said she'd call in if she could get away from the salon.

'More customers, Paula,' I call to her, as she delivers open sausage sandwiches to Mammy, Tessie and Constance. I took some convincing not to put the sausages between two slices of bread, but Carol swears that one big doorstep of batch is enough to sit them on and it will look more attractive. Anyway, they can always ask for more on the side if they want. Unlimited bread is a dream concept, to be fair. Maybe she's onto something.

Sharon, Melanie, the husband and *their toddler* squeeze in beside Majella and their gang. Thank God I took James Matthews's advice and ordered a few high chairs. I didn't have it as a priority but he said I'd regret it. I've read more books and websites about running a café over the past few weeks than I thought could be in existence, but there's still a never-ending snag list of things to sort out.

Four more people have come through the door out of the two cars, and it's time to put my student waitressing days to good use. I don't recognise any of them – they're not locals. I don't know if that's better or worse for my nerves.

They sit down together, shedding their jackets, and look around the place. As I approach with my special soft-opening menus – another ink cartridge gone – one of them, a blonde with one of Sadhbh's mad Cos dresses on, nods approvingly, 'Very shabby chic. Love it.' I nearly fall over my own feet with delight. I have to stop myself from pointing out the plug in the floor by her feet, in case she wants to put a picture of my huge lampshades on Instagram. People put all sorts up on Instagram. Half-eaten breakfasts, them laughing at their own feet, whatever Majella and Sharon are doing across the room right at this minute. Now, when Sadhbh pointed out the lampshades sitting skew-ways on top of some standard lamps in a charity shop in town on another reconnaissance trip, I nearly got sick laughing, but she was right: they do 'fit in with the aesthetic'.

More sausage sandwiches, one portion of poached eggs with avocado (thank you, gentleman inexplicably wearing sunglasses inside) and a pot of strong tea ordered for this gang. I suspect there are hangovers all round. They probably missed the hotel breakfast over at the Ard Rí after a wedding.

'Can I ask how you heard about us?' I enquire as I place the scalding pot down in the centre of the table, lowering a cosy over it.

'Oh, the barman at the hotel last night was raving about it. Don't know where he was from but he's definitely not local. He kept saying "The sausages, *hup.*" We were in stitches.' She adopts a vaguely Spanish accent to mimic the barman.

I look over to where Pablo is mostly obscured from view by the crowd at his table but is gesticulating wildly with a heel of bread. What a dotey thing for him to do, bigging up the café like that. Maybe I have him all wrong.

I barely have time to turn around when the door goes again. I didn't even see Mad Tom careen into the car park on his bike. He careens everywhere on it now, after finally losing his licence. One too many penalty points. He had to go to court and the local paper said it must have been a record for the number of times the word 'menace' has been uttered in one sitting. He's a divil for Boland's sausages, though it was only a matter of time before he was in for ours like a homing pigeon.

I dip into the kitchen to collect the food for the table of blow-ins – Carol's face is the colour of a poinsettia, but everything seems to be in hand. The young fella, Noel, is having something of a baptism of fire after his days of lobbing on vats of chips over at the Mountrath. We managed to convince him to jump ship for half the pay with the promise of Carol giving him a bit of training.

'All going okay in here, troops?'

'Aye-aye,' shouts Carol, never once moving her eyes from the poaching eggs in front of her.

'Table one!' roars Noel over my head. He's caught up in the adrenaline of it all, pushing a plate into my hand. 'Extra sausages,' he bellows. 'Service, please.' He'll be throwing overdone black pudding against the wall next, à la Gordon Ramsey.

The frenzied pace of everyone arriving at once calms down a bit, and I survey my little kingdom, keeping a firm eye on their bread supplies and ready to swoop in with more tea should anyone need it. I start to wander over towards Majella and Pablo's table to see how they're getting on. Melissa's baby is tucking into a bowl of Carol's Very Special Porridge, with all manner of berries and jams heaped on top of it. Paula beats me to the table, inquiring if they're alright for everything.

Melissa mouths silently over the baby's head, 'I'd love a can of Coke. A. Can. Of. Coke.' She forms the words exaggeratedly with her lips. 'She goes absolutely ape if she hears the word,' she explains, pointing at the baby. She doesn't even like the taste of it that much. It's just the mention of it.'

Sadhbh had said not to bother with cans of drink and just get in artisan lemonades and hay-and-lavender cordials and what have you, but I know a hungover head when I see one, and I know what it wants too. Paula nods conspiratorially at Melissa and is about to head back to the kitchen when Pablo pipes up.

'I too will have a … eh … eh … a … a … C-O-C-K.'

Turlough explodes. The scrambled egg he's just put in his mouth goes all over the baby, and he snorts some down his throat while he's at it. I fly in with a tea towel as the toddler screams in displeasure and Paula stares at Pablo in horror.

'The C-O-C-K, you know? C-O-C-K.' He desperately tries to mime the shape of a can with his hands, while Majella shakes helplessly with laughter on the chair. Deirdre and Titch aren't much better and Sharon leaps up to look for a mop.

'*Coke!*' I grimace at Paula, helping Melissa to wipe down the child's face, while she twists like a cat at the vet at the mention of the illicit beverage.

Paula has at least finally caught Pablo's drift and gone to get him his C-O-C-K, and Pablo is beseeching the table to tell him what he did wrong, as Sharon plucks a stray bit of scrambled egg out of her hair and gives me a reassuring smile. Mild chaos, you might call it. There's a tap on my shoulder.

'All going well?'

It's James Matthews, grinning at me and holding out something in one of those wine gift bags. I'll be reusing that – very handy. I'd put the tea towel on my head in an effort to amuse the baby, but at the sound of his voice I snatch it off and swing around to him.

'It's going great, as you can see.' I gesture ruefully in the direction of the egg-covered table where Turlough had just managed to catch his breath.

'Don't mind her,' Majella pipes up. 'It's going just brilliantly. You're never happy, Aisling,' she adds, rolling her eyes and smiling.

James presses the bottle into my hands. 'Something to celebrate with, when you get a chance. Just wanted to pop in and see how it was all going.'

'Ah, you're too good.' Can I put the tea towel back on my head to hide the blushing, I wonder?

'Not at all. Look, I'll see you around during the week. Lots still to do upstairs.' He strides back out to his jeep, cramming his brown curls under a baseball cap.

'Do you see much of John these days, Aisling?' Turlough interrupts my mini daydream, seemingly recovered from his mishap.

'Eh, no. Not really.' I haven't seen him in ages.

'He's hardly ever in training with Rangers now that he's the big county man.' Turlough's tiny hands mean he's never made much of an impact on the pitch, but the lads do go training religiously, rain or shine. 'There was no sign of him this morning. He's around visiting clubs when he can – scouting for talent, I hear,' Turlough continues. 'Sure, we'll be lucky if he talks to us at all anymore. Baby Chief Gittons says he hasn't seen him in weeks.'

'Any sign of that VIP area in the Vortex he was after?' Melissa chimes in with a roll of her eyes. 'It was the talk of the new salon yesterday. Apparently John was demanding his own private area. Imagine – a velvet rope in the Vortex. I know sportsmen are heroes, but you'd look a right sight nipping out from behind it to go to the bar for your pints and Jägerbombs. It's a shame you're not still with him to rein him in, Aisling.'

Jesus, none of this sounds like John at all. He'd sooner die than put himself in the limelight. Unless it's karaoke, they're playing Garth Brooks and he's had eleven pints. He's become quite a different person by the sounds of things. Oh well, it's not my problem, I suppose. I have a café to run.

'Now, anyone for more tea?' I swing around with the pot, eyes peeled for a cup that looks wanting. The door goes again. More customers! But the big, hulking presence who lands in doesn't look like he's after poached eggs. Marty Boland.

'Well, Marty.' My voice has the tiniest shake in it, but I steel myself immediately. 'Will you have a seat and we'll get you a menu?' I move back towards the counter.

He follows me, nearly pushing me back into it with a stare. In a low voice, he growls, 'I don't want a menu and I don't want a seat, missy.'

Carol emerges from the kitchen, wiping her hands on a tea towel. 'Marty, what are you–?'

'The pair of you think you're clever with your little café, don't you?' The people sitting nearest us have turned to look now.

Carol pleads, 'Marty, don't make a scene.'

He straightens up and takes a menu from my hand, but leans in closer still. 'I know what you're up to. Taking my business. Taking this lease out from under me.

And that one.' He gestures at Carol. 'Where has my dinner been the past two nights?' he asks her. She just stands there. He's talking low enough so only we can hear him. My heart is pounding in my ears. He throws the menu back on the table. 'Be home on time tonight.' He turns on his heel and walks out, throwing a nod here and there like nothing has happened.

Carol retreats into the kitchen. 'Are you okay?' I ask, following her in. 'Let me make you some tea.'

'Not at all, I'm fine,' she says matter-of-factly. 'He's just in a mood. It's grand. Don't worry.' How can I not worry? But the door goes again and Paula calls, 'More hungry customers.' I hope it *is* grand.

CHAPTER 32

Sharon is picking me up for Denise's baby shower in ten minutes, and I'm still in my apron and Crocs. Yes, Crocs. It was actually Constance Swinford who put me on to them – her house is so big she gets blisters walking from one end of it to the other, even in her 'investment slippers'. Talk about first-world problems, although I can only imagine her bills. A big house is hard to heat.

The Crocs are so soft and cushiony – a godsend when you're on your feet sixteen hours a day. And between sorting the stockroom and shining cutlery and taking orders and cleaning tables and filling sugar bowls, I rarely get so much as five minutes to sit down with a cup of tea and a purple Snack. My Fitbit is giving me no end of praise for it, and I'm exhausted but happy. So, so happy. The happiest I've felt in a long time.

After a few teething problems in the first couple of weeks (I under-ordered on the tea bags: lesson learned) BallyGoBrunch has really come together and, honestly, we're busier than I ever imagined. There was a queue around the corner at twelve o'clock last Sunday! I took a picture and sent it to Sadhbh and she sent back a record number of emojis. I managed to get one of my Crocs in the shot, and I don't think I'll ever hear the end of it. I rang her and tried to explain that sometimes you just have to go for comfort over style, but I don't think she heard me with the screams of laughter.

Carol has to physically push me out through the swinging doors of the café kitchen as I fire questions and problems at her.

'What if a vegan comes in?'

'I just took a loaf of sourdough out of the oven, and we have plenty of Jim Doran's mushrooms. They'd be lovely on toast with a bit of thyme.'

'Do you know where the fire extinguisher is?'

'Under the sink.'

'What do you do if someone starts choking?'

'Aisling! Would you just go!'

Carol's menu has been a real hit, but neither of us could have anticipated the demand for the sausages. She can't churn them out fast enough, and with production at an all-time high and money flowing into Marty Boland's pocket, he seems to have calmed down a bit. Carol assures me there have been no more incidents at home. I've had all sorts of mad ideas, like doing a BallyGoBrunch cookbook or trying to get *Nationwide* to come down and do a piece on her recipe. Anything for a bit of publicity.

I'm on my way into the toilets when Sharon walks in. I see her eyes fall on the Crocs, and she has to grab the back of a chair to steady herself. Honestly, if I could just get any of them to try on a pair they'd see the appeal. It's like walking on clouds. Ask any nurse.

'I'm just getting changed – I'll be back in second,' I say, holding up my I Heart Penneys tote bag. Inside the toilet, I throw on a purple wrap dress (from Savida but thirty per cent off), my trusty eighty deniers and a pair of black kitten heels that I've had since Majella's twenty-first and are still going strong. I smooth down my hair with a drop of water and put on a slick of brown mascara. It's not ideal, but I've been up since 6 a.m. Then I give the sinks a quick wipe down and restock the toilet roll. Like I said, you're never off.

'Love the dress, hun,' Sharon says when I eventually emerge.

'Oh, it's only a rag,' I say, shaking my head and mouthing 'bye' over to Paula, who's passing out extra sausages to a table of six. As well as putting them in the full Irish and the open sandwiches, we're now doing sausage rolls, sausage casserole, bangers and mash and toad in the hole. I'm reading a book about vertical integration and I think this is it.

It's my first time in Sharon's little Beetle, and I must say I'm very taken with it. She has one of the fancy Yankee Candle air fresheners and a little pink flower in the vase attached to the dashboard! I'd kill for that. I used to have a cat teddy in the back window of my Micra, but I had to get rid of it when me and John broke up. Too many memories. Now I have a fancy box of tissues, which I think is very sophisticated. Hard to reach, mind.

'Sharon, would you mind slowing down here for a second?' I say as she's pulling out the front gate. I'm thinking of asking James Matthews if he'd put in a cattle grid before he finishes up – there was a herd loose on the road last week, and I had to leave my post at the toast station in the kitchen to block the opening or they'd have made shite of the flower bed. Carol was not happy but, as I told her, at least we discovered that the fire alarm works. You can't be too careful with health and safety, and I haven't had time to train her properly yet.

I'm trying to gauge whether a cattle grid would actually fit between the two granite gate posts when out of the corner of my eye I spot what looks like a silver car parked tight against the ditch up the road a bit. Why would anyone do that? I think to myself. Everyone knows two cars can barely pass on this road, but it doesn't stop the lorries flying along, despite all the bumps and sharp bends. You'd have to have a death wish to park there. Sharon pulls out and turns left and, as much as I try and find the silver car in the wing mirror, there's nothing there. Maybe I imagined it. I'm half-mad with the tiredness, and I have to do a load of admin tonight too.

I actually get a fright when I see Denise in the foyer of the Ard Rí. You know those pregnant women who stay absolutely tiny all over except for the bump? The ones who look completely un-pregnant from behind and like they've just swallowed a basketball from the front? Well, she's not one of those. She's ballooned. Even her face looks pregnant.

'Denise, you're looking well,' I say, beaming, trying to get close enough to get my arms around her for a hug. And you know what, she is looking well, despite it all. She's glowing. And you can tell the bulk of it is water retention anyway. 'Not long to go now! You must be fierce excited.'

'Three more feckin' weeks.' She sighs, rolling her eyes. 'I don't know how much more I can take. I can't stop eating, Aisling. Even when I'm chewing I'm thinking about where my next meal is coming from. I don't understand the hunger. I was bulimic in fifth year!'

Sharon has the table looking faboo, I must say. She's done a three-tier nappy cake and there's a big balloon with a rabbit on it anchored to the top. There's a good turnout – a few faces I don't recognise, though. I pull up a chair beside Dee Ruane to prove we're all water under the bridge since the lease debacle. To be fair to her, she's been a BallyGoBrunch regular since she's started bringing people around to see the show apartment upstairs. Apparently the interest has been off the charts. The sale of land to the GAA went through last week, and she's regaling Maeve Hennessey with her preparations for the upcoming fortnight in Marbella.

'I'm trying to get Titch to go in to Sharon for a back wax, but he won't even entertain the idea,' she says, helping herself to a little cucumber sandwich. 'It's not that I find the hairy back that bad myself – I'm just worried it'll offend the other guests. It's a five-star hotel, like. There could be celebrities there.' Maeve is nodding along furiously. The chat gives me a flash of inspiration and I call out to Sharon: 'What about The Hairy Backers?' She shakes her head no. There's only so long I'm going to keep throwing out these gems of salon names.

'Pssst, Ais, will you make yourself a bit smaller there.' It wouldn't be any kind of organised event if Majella wasn't slinking in late.

'What took you?' I say out of the side of my mouth. I had tried to siphon off a few egg sandwiches for her, but Denise had them hoovered up as soon as the plate hit the table. I was able to hide a ham one under a napkin, but all that's left is smoked salmon, and good luck getting Maj to eat that.

'More feckin' drama with Willy,' she hisses back under her breath. 'I had to bring Pab with me for his own safety. He's out in the bar having a whiskey for his nerves. Did I miss the big reveal?'

'No, Denise is going to pop the balloon and the confetti is either going to be pink or blue,' I explain. 'The water spray isn't working then?'

'If anything it's making Willy more determined,' she says, reaching for a cucumber sandwich, sniffing it and then putting it back. This afternoon tea is €30 a head – she's getting a raw deal out of it if all she gets is one miserable ham sandwich and a few scones. I always make sure to get my full entitlement at these things. The price of them!

'Sorry, girls,' Sharon says, leaning down between us. 'Did you bring those baby pictures? We're going to start the games now.'

Ah, baby-shower games. I could do without them, to be honest. Well, most of them. Guessing who's who by baby pictures is a bit of craic, but some of them can be a bit disgusting. Like the one where you have to eat the melted chocolate bar out of a nappy and guess what it is. I'm fierce good at it, but that doesn't make it right.

I pass Sharon over the picture – it's actually one of Karen Koster's kids that I printed off myself, but she'll never know – and excuse myself to go to the bathroom. I want to be in situ when the next course comes out or Denise might do me out of my mini raspberry cheesecake. Not on my watch, Denise. On the way through the lobby of the Ard Rí I spot Pablo out the bay window, sitting at a garden table nursing his whiskey. I'm just about to go over and knock and say, '*Hola*, what's the craic,' when Susie Ó Súilleabháin leans foward in the chair opposite him. And then, as I watch, she keeps leaning in to him until their lips are practically touching and gently caresses his face. I feel my blood run cold and quickly jump behind a potted ficus. What the hell are they playing at, cosying up when Majella is not 30 feet away? How dare they! And why do I feel like I've done something wrong? We're here to celebrate Denise, and I don't want there to be some kind of scene before I can present her with the tiny Knock Rangers jersey I had made up especially. It wasn't cheap.

When I get back to the table everyone is shrieking, and I assume they must have popped open the balloon to reveal the baby's gender. It takes me a second to work out that it's not Denise who's at the centre of it all: it's Majella. Dee is cradling Maj's left hand, demanding a go of it, while Maeve is roaring, 'Prosecco! Quickly, we need prosecco!' at the waitress. Denise is looking a bit put out, and I can't say I blame her. Someone's baby shower is hardly the place to unveil your engagement ring. To be fair to Maj, though, she doesn't have much choice in the matter.

'Oh, it's *fab*. Looks much bigger than on Facebook,' Maeve coos over it. 'You're the cutest couple, the pair of ye.'

If only they knew. If only *Majella* knew.

'Ah yeah, isn't it … great,' I stutter. 'Great altogether.'

'Sorry, Denise,' Maj mouths at the party girl, who's balanced a plate of shortbread expertly on her bump. She was never going to get away without at least ten minutes of ring chat though.

When I was going out with John, Maeve used to forensically examine my hand every weekend. She's like one of those pigs who sniffs out truffles, except with diamonds. I tap Maj on the shoulder and whisper, 'Can I have a quick word?'

She reefs her hand back from Maeve and follows me through the double doors into the famous Ard Rí function room, BGB's number-one wedding venue. It doesn't look much now, all bare and empty, but this room has been the scene of some legendary sessions over the years.

'What's going on, Ais?' Majella goes, her words bouncing off the walls. 'Denise will have our tiny cakes gone if we don't get back out there.'

'I don't know if I should say anything,' I say, wringing my hands. I genuinely don't. But at the same time, I can't have Maj walking into the lobby and catching Pablo and Sinéad in flagrante. She'd surely keel over.

'You're going to have to tell me what's going on, bird,' she says sternly. 'I'm getting worried here.'

'It's about Pablo.'

'What about him?' She absentmindedly twists the engagement ring. Apparently it belonged to Pablo's grandmother, but I'm not convinced. He probably got it in a lucky bag, the sleeveen.

'I'm sorry, but I think he's up to something. With Susie Ó Súilleabháin.' As soon as the words are out of my mouth I regret it. The colour drains from her face and her bottom lip starts to tremble. Majella is not a crier. In fact, I don't think I've ever seen her shed a tear. She laughed at the really sad bit in *Titanic* because she said it was clear Rose had plenty of room for Jack on that door.

'Why?' she stammers. 'Why do you think that, Ais?'

'It's actually a few different things,' I start, 'and it's been going on for a while.' I'm about to launch into my evidence:

his weird leching at women, and then the sighting of himself and Susie outside Maguire's and then again in Dublin when he said he was at training, and now the two of them cosying up in the garden, but I don't get a chance.

'Oh my *God*,' she roars, eyes wide, and I nearly jump out of my skin. 'I can't believe you're doing this.' She spins around and flings the swingy doors open. I follow her, nearly taking a door to the face, and make a grab for her shoulder but she's absolutely motoring. I can't reach her.

'Majella, come back,' I cry. 'I have to tell you–'

We're back in the restaurant now and the baby-shower gang are nearly within earshot, but she continues marching towards the table oblivious. Then she turns around, hand on hip, and, I swear, she looks me up and down. I see Maeve and the girls swinging around in their seats. Denise has perked up a bit, and sure why wouldn't she with four mini cheesecakes in front of her.

'I knew this would happen,' Majella spits at the top of her voice, shaking her head. 'You can't just let me be happy, can you, Aisling? You're *jealous*. You're fucking *jealous* of me.'

Honestly, I can't believe Majella said fucking in the hallowed halls of the Ard Rí. They had one of Princess Diana's outfits on show here in the late nineties as part of a touring royal dress exhibit. Say *fucking* in the Mountrath all you like, but you have to draw the line somewhere.

'What?' I stammer, completely taken aback. I'm confused. Why would she think I'm jealous? Her bloody fiancé is doing the dirt on her, and he's not even trying to hide it. I'm only telling her because I don't want her to get hurt.

'Oh, don't play dumb, Aisling,' she screams, spit flying, face puce. 'We all know you're anything but dumb.' Denise and the others are openly staring at us now, as are the people at the other tables. Well, I say people. It's women, really. I don't think I've ever seen a man having afternoon tea, and God knows I've been to enough of them.

'You can't handle the fact that I'm engaged before you, can you, Aisling?' she rages while I stand there like a pillock. '*Can* you, Aisling? I got the big promotion in work, and I'm engaged, and now I'm going to be married before you. You didn't think that would happen in a million years, did you? *Did you?*'

By now people are nudging each other and taking out their phones, and I can see Denise's mam's mouth is open so wide her false teeth are in danger of falling out into her tiny lemon meringue pie. If I had one wish it would be for the ground to swallow me whole. This scene is up there with stealing a bride's thunder on her wedding day.

'Majella, please,' I stage-whisper. 'Just follow me outside and I can tell you what I mean.'

'No thanks, Aisling,' she roars back with a sneer. 'I'm sick of following you.'

'I'm not jealous,' I hiss. 'And I'm not making this up.'

But she's mad with the rage and doesn't seem to even hear what I'm saying.

'I'm sorry if it's driven you berserk, but I'm going to have a big wedding here,' she points towards the function room, 'with a sweet cart and free deodorant in the toilet and a band *and* a DJ. I thought you'd be happy for me, but it looks like I was wrong.'

'I *am* happy for you,' I plead. 'All I want is for you to be happy. I'm trying to protect you! If you would just listen to me for five min–'

'And to think,' she screams, 'I was going to ask you to be my chief bridesmaid.'

Then she snaps up her bag and flies out the front door, bawling.

Needless to say, the rest of the baby shower was a bit subdued, even when Denise popped the rabbit balloon and we all got a faceful of blue confetti. She was able to muster up a sad little cheer, but she cried on and off until Maeve placated her with a plate of multicoloured macarons while the rest of them took turns throwing daggers at me.

'What the hell did you say to make Majella go berserk?' Dee hissed from behind a napkin when I sat back down.

'Something I shouldn't have,' was all I could reply.

CHAPTER 33

I was going to go back to the café to give Carol and Paula a hand with the clean-up and re-stack the dishwasher properly, but I couldn't face it in the end. It was gone seven o'clock when Maeve dropped me home, and I found Mammy and Constance Swinford huddled in front of Mammy's ancient laptop in the kitchen.

'Hiya, lads,' I say, walking in and flicking on the kettle. If ever there was a time for a cuppa it's now. I keep thinking back to the row and the force of Majella's words nearly cuts me in two. Why did I open my big mouth in the first place? I'm not jealous. I just don't want Maj to get hurt. I should have marched her out to the garden and let her see Pablo and Susie with her own eyes.

'Hullo, Aisling,' Constance brays, standing up to retrieve her waxed jacket. 'Marian, I'd better be off. Let's regroup tomorrow and discuss …' she glances over at me surreptitiously, 'everything.'

Mammy busies herself gathering up sheets of paper, and I notice a Ruane's Estate Agents brochure sticking out of one of her notebooks. I only catch the first line – 'Woodlawn Park, Rathborris' – before she shoves it down briskly. Why is she looking at new houses? A feeling of unease creeps over me.

'Do you know how much energy it takes to boil the kettle?' Mammy asks out of the blue as Constance pulls the back door closed. 'Around 18 cents' worth. I hope you only have enough water in there for a cup.'

I stare back at her, not knowing quite what to say. Money must be even tighter than I thought if she's panicking about the cost of making a cup of tea. Surely tea is a human right. By my estimations, we boil the kettle around twenty times a day between the two of us. Probably more now that William Foley is in for his few daily cups. Do I need to cut back? Maybe make tea in the café and bring it home in a flask? Are the two of us going to be huddled around a two-bar heater for warmth this winter? I've pumped every penny I have to my name into BallyGoBrunch, but even if business continues to boom, I won't see an actual profit for another two years. I'm just barely breaking even at the moment.

'Sorry, Mammy,' I say solemnly, taking the steaming mug into the sitting room, not willing to get into another fight today. Although, on my way past the kitchen table I notice the unmistakable silver foil of a Tunnock's Tea Cake wrapper. Maybe if she wasn't trying to impress Constance with fancy biscuits we could afford more cups of tea. As soon as I get comfortable on the couch I google Woodlawn Park, Rathborris, on my phone. 'A new development of elegant two- and three-bedroom townhouses with every possible amenity, from Matthews Developments,' the website tells me, with a few sketches of what the houses will look like. They're bright and modern, and each has a cute little rectangular garden out the back. They look grand, to be fair to them.

Later in bed, sleep escapes me, and I start to imagine what life would be like for me and Mammy in Woodlawn Park. And Paul too, I suppose. Although I suspect he's got himself a girlfriend down in Oz. He's not on Skype half as much as he used to be. Sure don't I always look after everything? I just can't picture it, us without the farm, without the constant wellies beside the door and the spring lambs needing to be fed round the clock and the smell of silage on a warm day. It would be easier in winter, that's for sure, and only a few miles further away from BallyGoBrunch.

Then I let my mind go to Majella. We hardly ever fight. Not like this. Unless you count the month we didn't speak to each other in sixth class because we both wanted to take the same confirmation name: Emma – I still think it's cool. In the end Miss Maloney insisted there was no Saint Emma, so I took the classic Brigid to keep the peace, and Maj went for the slightly more obscure Lidwina, the patron saint of ice skaters. Ironic, really, since there isn't an ice rink within 60 miles of BGB. Jesus, I thought that confirmation mass would never end. It was drummed into us that we couldn't so much as make a peep since the bishop was there, but Majella got a terrible Mass Laugh, and there's nothing more contagious than a Mass Laugh. The mirth and fear of being caught create a kind of perfect storm of hysteria, and in the end both of us were sitting there staring straight ahead, shaking silently, with tears streaming down our faces. I had to dig my nails into my palm and think about poor Granny Reilly's coffin being lowered into the grave to try and get back to a state of equilibrium. The bishop knew well what was happening – I'm surprised he let the Holy Spirit near us.

I decide I'm going to head over to the café early the next morning to catch up on a bit of admin I should have done tonight. I've discovered that we're spending a fortune on cherry tomatoes – the one thing we can't get locally – and I'm half-thinking of putting a greenhouse out the back and growing my own. Now that I have unlimited access to Swinford manure, the world is my oyster in terms of things I could plant and fertilise. Maybe I'll look into hemp!

****

At 7 a.m., I measure out exactly one mug of water and flick on the kettle as quietly as I can when my phone buzzes on the table, giving me an awful fright. A picture of Sadhbh and one of the Blue Man Group flashes up on the screen – Jesus, Vegas seems like a lifetime ago now – and I dive for it. She often rings me on the walk from Phibsboro to Flatlay and I feel like it keeps us connected.

'Hey, Ais,' she says when I answer it. 'How was yesterday? Did they make you taste baby food?' Poor Sadhbh is on the baby-shower circuit herself these days, as much as she tries to get out of it.

'It was a feckin' disaster,' I say flatly, filling her in about my fight with Majella and all the rest.

There's some muffling on the line – it sounds like she's dropped the phone. I suppose the idea of me and Maj not speaking is a lot to take in before 8 a.m.

'Sorry, Ais, come again?' she says. 'I was just, *argh*.'

'Hello? What's going on – are you okay?'

She lets out a strangled moan. 'Sorry, sorry, I was just ... scratching.'

'Scratching what?'

'*Mmmng fhhh,*' she says. 'I think I've got *mmmfmf.*'

She must be on the Luas or something because she's whispering into the phone so quietly I can't hear a word she's saying.

'You'll have to speak up, bird,' I go.

'Head lice! I think I've got fucking head lice,' she hisses.

Oh my God. I can't imagine Sadhbh with nits, but this is the price you pay for fraternising with primary teachers. Her lovely grey – or whatever colour it is this week – hair. Now she'll have to put that manky shampoo on it and let it sit. I don't envy her – the smell of it would knock you out.

'Which one of them brought them home?' I ask, buttering my toast. My money is on Mairead. Her school is one of these hippie places with no religion. When they're not vaccinating their kids, some of the parents claim using nit shampoo is a kind of nit genocide. Cruel on the nits. Would you be well.

'Mairead,' she says. I knew it. 'Her whole class has them, little fuckers. There should be a law against white people having dreadlocks if they're also not going to treat their head lice.'

Poor Sadhbh. To think she went from living in our lovely Portobello penthouse to ... this.

'Oh, but it gets worse, Ais. Don had a couple of days off last week and he came to stay. I FaceTimed him last night, and I swear to God he was scratching. I can't bring myself to tell him why.'

'Back up, back up,' I say. 'Don stayed in your house in Phibsboro? How did the girls take it?'

'Well, Fionnuala went completely mute. Mairead wasn't much better, but at least she was able to mumble hello. When we got up the next morning there were six more teachers sitting in the kitchen. It was like they multiplied overnight.'

I stifle a laugh. 'How did Don take it?'

'Ah, you know him,' Sadhbh goes. 'Never any bother. They had him posing for selfies for an hour.'

'Sounds like you're all one big happy family now,' I say, reloading the toaster.

'Not a bit,' she scoffs. 'In a moment of weakness I used some of Mairead's Kerrygold last night – only a scrape – and she found out. She must have noticed the indentation of a different knife.'

There's more muffling on the line and I can hear her scratching again. I don't envy her with the nits. They're a right pain in the arse and a constant threat to teachers – and their housemates.

'So did I hear you right? You told Majella about Pablo and now she's not talking to you?'

'I don't think she's ever going to talk to me again, Sadhbh.'

'Ah no. You just need to explain the situation to her. Make her listen. You two will be fine then.'

I sigh. If only it were that easy. 'I'll let you go, Sadhbh. I have to go over and open up. Those avocados are not going to smash themselves, and more's the pity.'

'Talk soon, Ais. I'm coming down as soon as I get rid of the lice.'

'Tell Don,' I call down the phone. 'He'll only feckin' pass them on if he doesn't know!'

There's a gasp behind her as the word 'lice' passes through the carriage, and I instantly imagine every person within a three-foot radius of her taking a step back. There's the *ding-ding-ding* of the Luas and then Sadhbh faintly snapping, 'Nits actually only like clean hair so calm down,' is all I hear before the line goes dead.

I don't notice anything out of the ordinary when I pull into the BallyGoBrunch car park, but in hindsight that might have been because I was preoccupied with my future cattle grid. When I get out of the car I can't miss it – the back and side windows have been completely smashed in. There's broken glass everywhere. The back door is swinging open, and above it the blue light of the alarm is flashing uselessly.

CHAPTER 34

I walk around the café in a daze, my feet crunching on broken sugar bowls and slipping on spilled juices and drinks. My lovely cushions are all on the floor, sticky and stained. My carefully chosen bits and bobs on the wall seem to have been swiped off in one motion. They all lie in a heap; two of the three flying ducks Sadhbh spotted in Oxfam have their beaks broken. All of my lovely lampshades are slashed. I sink down into a chair, my knees going funny, barely able to think about going into the kitchen and the tiny side office where the safe is. Not that there'd be a fortune in it, but all of the day's takings. I take out my phone, my hand shaking. I would give anything to be able to ring Daddy. Anything at all. I'd sell my soul to see him pulling in the gateway in his jeep, cap on, meaning business. I scroll down through my contacts, down to the Js. John's name sits just below James Matthews's and my finger hovers over it. But he's not my go-to anymore. Sure, I hardly know him now. I go back up to James's number and press the little phone. He's still around, finishing up bits and pieces upstairs, and he's started working on the housing development beyond at Rathborris. I'm so shook I don't have the energy to hold the phone up to my ear, but I can hear it ring as I hold it in my hand, and ring and ring. It goes to voicemail. I scroll again and dial Mammy's number as I push myself up from the chair and step gingerly behind the counter and into the kitchen.

Carol's lovingly labelled pots and jars of herbs and spices have been pushed over and smashed. Tea towels and Paula's apron have been shoved in the sink. Pots and pans and plates and bowls are scattered and smashed on the ground, and wires going in and out of various devices and machines are slashed and jagged. Even the freezer and hob are bashed in. The damage must be in the thousands of euro, and that's before you take into consideration all the meat that's going to go off. I had gotten such a good deal on that whole pig too.

As I survey the damage, Mammy answers. 'Hello, pet. You're up and out early.'

'Mammy. The café. Something's happened. It's in bits.' I burst into tears, nearly upending myself on a smashed jar of homemade ketchup.

'Oh no. Oh, Aisling, love. Oh no. I'll be right there.'

The tiny office is a disaster too. My desk planner is ripped and on the floor, and the tiny cactus Majella got me has been flung against the wall. I know Maj won't answer the phone if I ring her. I try to gather the broken bits of tiny terracotta pot but it's beyond saving.

The safe looks miraculously untouched. Although, I would have nearly been more glad if it was gone or blown open or something. At least then this would feel like a robbery. But it feels like … hate. I spin the combination wheel – my birthdate, then Mammy's, then Daddy's and then Paul's, but all with the numbers backwards. I watched a bit on Sky News about how easy it is for people to steal your passwords and PINs, so I've about 101 tricks up my sleeve to put them off the scent. Nobody got into this safe anyways. All of the takings are still there.

'Aisling?'

It's Mammy. She must have driven like the clappers. I can hear her crunching over the debris and exclaiming, 'Oh no,' over and over again. I meet her behind the counter.

'What happened?' she gasps.

'I don't know.'

She grabs me by my elbows and pulls me in. 'The robbing, fecking, bastarding bastards,' she rages into my hair.

'I wasn't robbed, though, Mammy. The safe is still there. Someone just destroyed the place.'

'Did you ring the guards?'

'They're my next call. But we'll be waiting a while for someone to come, I'd say.' The closure of the Knock garda station last year gave BGB another string in its bow in terms of amenities. Now, that's not to say that BGB ever had a garda station of its own – far from it – but at least we had the good Chinese, the handball alley and one-and-a-half beer gardens. (Maguire's and out the back of Jocksy Cullen's house. Jocksy's isn't a licensed premises, but he'll throw the place open on a sunny day and sure there's no law enforcement for miles to shut it down.) Knock only has the one beer garden at Dick's, but it doubles as a storage area for barrels of liver-fluke dosing, so that's another check mark for BGB, thank you very much.

I call the guards while Mammy paces around outside. I've told her we probably shouldn't touch anything until they get here. They might want to put on their white overalls and check for fingerprints and semen and whatever else. I've seen enough episodes of *CSI* and *How Clean Is Your House?* to know the score. There's semen everywhere. I finish up my call with Garda Staunton – they'll be with us as soon as they can. They've to attend the scene of a 'suspicious character' looking in the window of a house out the other end of BGB. What is going on at all? Will we ever be safe to sleep in our beds again?

As I hang up, Carol cycles into the car park. She looks so confused to see me and Mammy standing outside the café.

'Is everything alright?'

She can already tell that it's not, though.

'We've had a break-in, I'm afraid.'

'Oh God. What did they get?' As she looks around me through the open door, her face changes though. 'Oh my Lord. What … what happened? It looks like a bomb hit it.'

'Some kind of vandalism or, or something.' I don't know what to call it. Who would do something like this? Who would hate the place so mu–

'Marty.' Carol interrupts me, her mouth tight. 'Could it have been Marty? He was in Belfast last night, or so he says.' I think back to that first day we opened. Would he be that much of a madman?

'Your Marty? Marty Boland the butcher? It was hardly him.' Mammy looks incredulous. 'I know he's a bit of a bully but he's not a criminal.'

Carol looks at her feet, her lip trembling now. She looks like she could sink into a hole in the ground if there was one available.

'I thought you said he'd been alright since then, Carol?'

'He's been awful. Worse than usual. I'm afraid of him. I'm afraid this could have been him.'

'What do you mean you're afraid of him, Carol?' Mammy can't believe her ears and I feel like getting sick. I've grown so fond of this woman I barely know and her shy ways. I feel murderous towards him, the big bullying brute. And I feel so guilty. I pushed her into this.

'He's just so angry about me and the job and the sausages doing so well here.'

'But doesn't he get all the money for supplying them?' Mammy demands. 'He should be delighted his creations are doing so well.'

Carol and I share the quickest of glances as Mammy continues.

'And forgive me for speaking out of turn, Carol, but he's as tight as a Cavan clam. Is he not delighted to have you working?'

'I wouldn't say he's delighted. No,' Carol says quietly. She looks terrified. Damn that man anyway. Damn him to hell. Carol speaks up again. 'Did you ring Paula, or Noel?' She looks delighted to be changing the subject.

'Oh no, I'll do it now.' God, I'll have to tell them there's no work for a while. I won't be able to pay them either. For the first time, I wish I was going back to Dublin in the morning. At least at PensionsPlus I was just a cog in a wheel, more or less. I didn't have all this responsibility weighing on my shoulders. There were no suspicious characters trying to do me harm and life was just easier, wasn't it? What am I going to do for money? How will I keep the place going? How will I replace everything?

Mammy puts an arm around Carol and says gently, 'Why don't you come home with me for a nice strong cuppa? No need to go back to him for the time being. Aisling, will you come too?'

'I need to get this broken glass boarded up, Mammy. Could William Foley come out and do it, do you think? I can't get a hold of James Matthews.'

'Oh, I meant to say, I saw James yesterday evening leaving the Mountrath.' My ears prick up as Mammy continues. 'I didn't stay late at Tessie Daly's sixty-fifth. The music was fierce loud and I was stuck beside Tessie's brother Phil. He's an awful gossip. Did you know Tessie's cousin the priest is after having an affair–?'

'Mammy! What were you saying about James Matthews?'

'Oh, of course, sorry. Well, when I was leaving I saw him leaving too, with Natasia. Isn't she looking well, I thought to myself? That summer here really did her the world of good.'

Even amid all of the awful mess and heartache behind me in the café, I'm surprised by the drop in my stomach at these words. Sure, why wouldn't he have a girlfriend?

'I didn't know he was doing a line with her,' Mammy continues. 'She's a lovely girl. What a pair they make.'

Of course! Natasia said her boyfriend was based in Ireland. I should have known. Lovely Natasia from Chernobyl and lovely James from England. What a pair indeed. I feel horribly and strangely disappointed but have to push it down to deal with matters at hand.

'I'll ring William Foley now and then follow you home. I'll put a sign up at the gate to say we're closed for the foreseeable.'

This will be all around town in no time. If the culprit is local, how will we know if they're in our midst? I don't think I've ever felt so unsafe in BGB.

****

Garda Staunton arrives with a detective and a lad to do the forensics – no white gear or semen light, though – and I go back out to the café to meet them. Did I see anything suspicious? Is there anyone who might have something to prove or a vendetta? Am I in conflict with anyone? The questions swirl around and around in my head. Am I in conflict with anyone? Majella? Marty Boland? I say nothing, though. And then just as the gardaí are preparing to leave and William Foley arrives to make the place sound, I stop Garda Staunton.

'Now, I'm not pointing a finger or anything.'

'Go on,' he says, taking out his notebook once more.

'But Marty Boland was angry that I got the lease on this place over him.'

'Mmm hmmm. That's the butcher beyond in the village – do I have the right man?'

'Yes. And his wife works at the café with me and I think … I think things aren't great between them. I think maybe he's not very nice to her.'

'Not very nice. Is that code for something? Is there any violence?'

'Well, no, not that I know of. But he's a bully. She's afraid of him.'

'Well, I can't arrest someone for being a bully, I'm afraid, Aisling. She knows where we are if she needs us.'

'I know. But I just thought I'd say something.' Daddy used to always say to try to give a voice to people who don't have one. I think it stemmed from a row back in the eighties with the county council over Travellers pitching on the roadside between BGB and Knock. Daddy found himself speaking up for the Travellers' rights and leading a small gang of BGB locals in a protest to let them stay for as long as they needed. Daddy never liked Marty Boland either. He had a good nose for these things.

Just before Garda Staunton sits back into his car to head away, something else springs to mind. 'Garda, can you tell me anything about this suspicious character looking in the window of a house? The call you were at before this?' BGB is a hotbed of crime at the moment it seems. I'm glad we have the strong arm of the law putting their resources to the best use.

'Oh, that was a cardboard cut-out of Daniel O'Donnell that Marie Fleming won in charity bingo last night. She left it in the car and her neighbour thought it was a peeping Tom staring in at her for hours. She accused him of touching himself, but it was just poor Daniel holding his microphone.'

'Oh. Right.'

****

Back in Mammy's kitchen, the burning Aga has never been so comforting or the hum of the kettle so soothing. Carol and Mammy have been talking for hours, Carol coming more and more out of her shell as that lovely warm woman I know she can be.

'I'm afraid to go home to him sometimes. I've thought about not going home more and more this past while. I just need the courage to do it,' Carol confides in Mammy, as the warmth of the kitchen soothes some of the shock of the day.

Mammy has persuaded her to stay for dinner, saying she hopes her pork chops and spuds can live up to Carol's high standards. Carol responds with a sigh and 'Anything tastes wonderful if you don't have to cook it yourself.' I wonder when was the last time someone made her dinner. My phone is hopping with messages all evening. Concerned locals and friends. Sadhbh and Elaine and Ruby with regular pictures of kittens and heart emojis. Nothing from Majella. I presume she's heard. I wonder if John knows, although I hear he's in London scouting for any local lads living over there who might be interested in coming back to play for the county. He's really taken to the new gig. Hopefully his head isn't as big as people say. He probably has a WAG by now, with hair extensions and a tan deal on Instagram. The glamour.

After dinner, and high praise indeed for Mammy's pork chops, Carol seems reluctant to tip off. I don't blame her. Mammy says she'll make up Paul's bed for her, electric blanket and all, but Carol insists on going home, saying there'll be war if she doesn't.

'There'll always be a bed for you here.' Mammy grips Carol's arm firmly. 'Just so you know.'

Carol looks surprised and then grateful. 'I've been thinking … I've been thinking of leaving hi–' but she doesn't finish and instead just says, 'Thank you, Marian.'

After Mammy heads off to bed, I turn on the telly and do a quick flick around to try and take my mind off today's events. No sooner have I spotted Graham Norton's gas head than my phone lights up in my lap – it's Paul on Skype from Melbourne. I hit mute on the remote.

'Well, Ais,' he goes when his picture appears on the screen. It's 11 p.m. here, which means it's 8 a.m. over there. He's wearing his Mr Tayto costume. Apparently cheese and onion Taytos have taken Australia by storm following the influx of Irish people in the past decade. They're the new Marmite. Paul and a few of the other lads are after signing up to a promotions agency – it's the dream, really. And he says it's handy enough work, once you don't mind sweating inside the costume for six hours at a time. They mostly hang around outside cricket matches and shopping centres handing out bags to delighted punters. 'Mammy texted me about the café. What a load of shite. Do they know who did it?'

'Not yet. The place is in bits, though, Paul. I don't know what I'm going to do.'

'Was it young lads messing?'

'I don't think so.'

'Is there anything I can do from this end?'

'I don't suppose you know anyone selling an industrial-sized freezer?' I chance. 'I've to replace everything. It's going to cost a bomb. And it was just getting going.' My voice starts to wobble.

'I don't,' he says, sitting down on a shady bench. He must be roasting. 'How's Mammy?'

'She's grand.'

'Still palling around with Constance?'

'She is.' I laugh. And then I remember the Ruane's brochure I saw in the kitchen the other day. 'I have an awful feeling she's downsizing, Paul.'

'What do you mean?' he says, leaning forward into his phone while a man and a toddler approach him from the left.

'I saw a brochure for a new housing estate. I think she went to see it.'

'In Ballygobbard?' he says. 'Where is there room for a housing estate?' The man taps him on the shoulder and Paul turns around. Then he shakes his head.

'What was that?' I go. 'Someone you know?'

'No, some father wanting me to keep an eye on his child when he goes into the bookie's. Happens every time I put on this feckin' costume. Like, I could be anyone! Now, what were you saying about the new housing estate?'

'It's not in BGB, it's in Rathborris,' I explain. 'I also … I saw a document from a property surveyor. It was a valuation for the house and farm.'

'Jesus,' he says.

'I know.'

He sighs. 'I suppose it makes sense in the long run. Her heart's not in the farm. That was Daddy's thing.'

'I know. But still. Our childhood home. All of Daddy's things. I don't know if I'm ready.'

'Has she said anything?'

'Not yet. I've been up the walls with setting up the café and now this. There hasn't really been a time. But I'm sure it's coming.'

'Keep me posted, will you, Ais? I won't say anything to her.'

'Jesus, don't,' I exclaim. 'She'll be on at me for snooping. You know how she is.'

'Do you need a lend or anything?' he says, standing up.

'Er, you still owe me 200 quid from Christmas, Paul. I haven't forgotten, you dope.'

'I know, I know,' he says. 'Look, I have to find a jacks. I'm bursting. Take her handy.'

And then he's gone. I'm about to flick off the telly when the camera pans away from where Graham is chatting to Benedict Cumberbatch, who has a head like a melted candle, and goes over to the stage. The lights come up and five familiar figures come into focus – it's The Peigs! Sadhbh never said. I suppose she knows I'd be on the first flight to London to meet Graham. I have to stay watching it on mute for fear of waking Mammy, but I must admit Don is looking well, holding the guitar and managing to pull off some questionable dance moves. From my limited lip reading I can tell they're playing 'Kick the Blarney Stone', their controversial new single, which Sadhbh was saying is banned in Cork. The drama! And then I see it – at the end of the song, just before the lights go down, Don scratches his head. Jesus, it's true – Sadhbh has obviously passed on the nits.

Heading upstairs, the house feels like a safe cocoon, keeping me and Mammy protected from whatever is out there in BGB. I let my mind go to the idea of saying goodbye to these walls soon. If Mammy has to sell, what will our lives look like then? I turn Daddy's card over and over again in my hands and let myself have a great big cry. I could use his €50 now. And one of his awkward hugs, patting my head the way he used to when I was a little girl in messy pigtails and half a field's worth of sticklebacks attached to my socks. Daddy used to call them sticky-mickeys and would spend an hour trying to get them out of the cat's fur. What would he think about the house, the farm being sold? It breaks my heart to think of it empty of us. Empty on Christmas morning. Empty on Daddy's birthday. Empty except for all of our memories.

As I pass the landing window on my way to the bathroom, I pause to pull the curtains, looking out over the fields towards the Moran house, wondering if Majella even cares about what happened to the café. I've almost pulled the curtains over all the way when something catches my eye, a flickering that seems to be reflecting off the windows of the Morans' bungalow. I squint and try to look closer. It's not reflecting off the windows at all. It's behind them. I nearly take the roof off with my screams.

'Fire! Fire! The Morans' house is on fire!'

CHAPTER 35

I don't remember coming down the stairs but, before I know it, I'm tearing out the driveway, screaming at Mammy to call the fire brigade. For luck my phone is in my back pocket, and I fumble through my recent calls until I find Majella's name and stab at it without breaking my stride in the darkness. It's ten o'clock. What if they're in the house? What if they're all having an early night and the thick, black smoke is pouring in through the doorways, engulfing them in their beds like something out of Pompeii? Knowing Shem he probably doesn't even have smoke alarms, and he almost certainly doesn't poke them once a week with the sweeping brush like I do to test the batteries.

I'm running full pelt down the lane now, towards the flames that are climbing about 20 feet into the night sky. I was never fast. Not a single community games medal to my name. The house is still a good 200 metres away, but I can hear the crackling and my eyes are already streaming from the acrid smoke. *Pick up, Majella! Pick up the fucking phone!* It goes to voicemail and I hang up and hit redial, my thighs already burning from the unexpected sprinting. I never had a chance to warm up! It rings out again and I scramble through my contacts, panting, until I find Pablo Tenerife Taxi and say a prayer to literally anyone who's listening that he picks up.

I can just about make out the Morans' front gate now and feel the heat from the fire on my face as I continue down the lane. The leylandii hedge is blocking my view, but the whole house must be gone up. It's massive and loud. Behind me I hear an engine in the distance – Mammy, no doubt. Come on, Pablo, pick up the phone. Then I hear his voice – '*Hola*, you mucker, it's Pablo.' Voicemail again. Fuck it anyway!

Suddenly a pair of headlights comes around the corner straight in front of me, and just as I reach the gate, Shane Moran's silver Subaru screeches to a stop. All four doors fly open and Shane, Shem, Liz and Majella clamber out. They just stand there for a few seconds, mouths open, looking at their family home going up in smoke. Then Liz lets out an almighty scream.

Shem bolts for the driveway with Liz hanging off his right arm.

'Shem, no,' she's shrieking into the night. 'You don't know how bad it is. You can't get too close, you'll hurt yourself.'

'The dog,' he roars. 'Willy! I don't think I let him out before we left!'

'Daddy, leave it,' Shane shouts after him, and Shem thankfully stops and turns back to Liz. They both silently touch foreheads, arms around each other, and I see their shoulders shuddering like the way mine and Majella's used to when we got a Mass Laugh. Except no one is laughing now.

Majella. She's standing beside Shane's beloved Subaru, her arms wrapped tightly around her body. Her face is expressionless, a blank mask, and I know from my health and safety training that she's probably going into shock, so I whip off my fleece and throw it over her shoulders.

'Aisling?' She's looking at me like she hasn't seen me in years. If only. 'Aisling, how did this happen? What's going on?'

'I don't know, I don't know,' I say, drawing her in for a hug, trying to keep her warm. I hear a car pulling in behind me and Mammy's footsteps flying across the gravel.

'Is everyone out, Shem?' Mammy shouts, looking at faces to see who's here and who isn't. 'Shem? *Shem?*' she shouts again, louder this time. 'Liz, where's Pablo?'

****

It took the fire brigade fifty-one minutes to reach the house after Mammy called 999. Not an atrocious length of time when you consider the state of the roads around BGB, but not quick enough to save the house either.

Mammy went back home for blankets and coats, and we all stood with our arms around each other in a guard of honour at the Morans' front gate while the eight strapping men got it under control. It turns out Shem did have smoke detectors, and the batteries were working fine, but unfortunately there was no one home to hear the alarm when it went off. And the working smoke alarms were somewhat negated by the full tank of green diesel he had in the shed. We're lucky the whole village didn't burn down.

Pablo was working a shift in the Ard Rí, as he apparently does every Sunday night. He saw me calling but decided against answering the phone, and I suppose I don't blame him after what happened at the baby shower. Majella was the same. She'd dragged the entire family up to the forty-eight-hour Ridey Bridey Wedding Showcase at the Exhibition

Centre in Dublin, and they were already on the way home, surrounded by brochures for Botox and teeth whitening, when she noticed my missed call. Again, no surprise that she didn't ring back. As soon as Mammy got off the phone with the fire brigade she called Liz, and Shane put his foot down and got them here in record time. God knows he's had plenty of practice speeding around the backroads of BGB in the Subaru. It's like he was working towards that call all his life.

It was close to 5 a.m. when I decided to call it a night and convinced Majella to come upstairs with me for a bit of rest. Shane was asleep in the cat's armchair with Pablo curled up at his feet. There was no talking to Shem and Liz – they were up and down to the house every half an hour, bringing pints of water and ham sandwiches to the firemen, trying to get closer and closer to the charred remains. Mammy was nearly falling asleep on her feet, butter knife in hand.

I give Majella my favourite flannel pyjamas, and we lie side by side in my single bed like we used to at slumber parties, except tonight the fight hangs between us like a brick wall. We've been wailing and crying and hugging for hours, but we haven't actually talked and I haven't apologised. Do I need to apologise, I wonder? I thought I was helping her. She's my best friend. I can feel the tears coming again.

'Majella,' I whisper. 'I'm sorry, I should never have said anything about Pablo and Susie. I thought I was doing the right thing. But I wasn't.'

'I should never have called you jealous,' she says quietly, turning to face me. 'But you really hurt me, Ais. I know Pablo would never cheat on me. I just know it.'

'Did you ask him?'

'He said he could explain. And I believe him. I *trust* him.'

Now isn't the time to get into this. I change the subject. 'What was the Ridey Bridey fair like?'

'Dire.' Then she smiles. 'You would have loved it.' She laughs softly. 'I can't stop watching *Don't Tell the Bride*. I have half a notion to go on it – you know they pay for everything? The price of weddings, Ais. I had no idea.'

Sometimes I wish I was more like Majella. Not a complete hames, of course, but just a bit more oblivious. She must be the only person on the planet who hasn't realised that weddings are mad expensive. She's never even priced a photo booth and, by God, she's been in enough of them – and walked off with her fair share of novelty sunglasses and blow-up guitars. And the lack of stress means she has hardly any wrinkles. It's definitely food for thought.

'Maj, did I tell you I'm worried that Mammy is selling the farm?' I know I didn't tell her but I feel like pouring my heart out. I need my best friend back. 'I don't think she has enough money to keep it going.'

'What?' she says, her eyelids slowly closing. She must be exhausted. 'Where is she going to go?'

'I don't know, Maj. But I'll have to go with her.'

'You could always live in the café.'

BallyGoBrunch. The break-in. I'd forgotten all about it. What a day. But before I can start panicking, Majella's gentle snores lull me into an exhausted sleep.

CHAPTER 36

I only get an hour's sleep in the end before I slip out of bed and into the bathroom to beat the rush. My hair stinks of smoke and my head feels heavy with the weight of my thoughts. Who smashed up the café? How did the Morans' house go on fire? And, the worst thought of all, are the two somehow connected?

Downstairs the sitting-room door is closed, and I suspect Shem and Liz are on the lumpy pull-out couch, God love them and their backs. I press my ear to the door and sure enough hear Shem crying Willy's name in his sleep. The poor craythur. There's no sign of life anywhere else, and the clock tells me it's ten past eleven. There's a list of things I need to do: get in touch with James Matthews, call the insurance company, tell my suppliers I won't need any deliveries until, well – who knows when I'll get BallyGoBrunch open again? And I have the Morans to think about too. Where are they going to go? They've got nothing. My problems pale in comparison. I can't bear to think about it.

'Aisling?' Pablo suddenly appears out of nowhere. Well, not out of nowhere. He must have still been at Shane's feet, only under the blanket. I think back to him and Susie Ó Súilleabháin face to face at the Ard Rí, and even though Maj is convinced he's innocent, I have to fight the urge to give him a clip around the ear.

'Hiya,' I say curtly instead. 'Tea?'

'Please, yes, that would be nice.'

I busy myself filling the kettle and getting the cups so I don't have to make eye contact with him, but he hovers around me anyway, getting under my feet. I don't know how Majella puts up with it.

'Will you ever just sit down?' I say, plonking the teapot in front of him on the table, and he immediately sinks into a chair.

'Can I please say something?' he says quietly after taking a sip. 'I need to do some, how do you say it, explanation.'

I glance at the clock and sigh. 'Go on. Majella will be up shortly. It's her you should be explaining yourself to, not me.'

'I need your help, Aisling,' he says, taking another gulp of tea. 'I don't want Majella to know … that's why I lie.'

So he *has* been lying! Jesus, he's not going to try and convince Maj to have an open marriage, is he? Or worse, is he one of those lads who insists on having a whole rake of wives? Well, he can feck off if he thinks I'm going to get into polygamy. Can you imagine the chat at the Tidy Towns meetings?

'What are you on about, Pablo?' I say, narrowing my eyes. He'd want to spit it out fairly lively.

'It's my eyes,' he whispers. 'My vision, is so, so bad. I can only see,' and he holds out his hand in front of him at arm's length, 'to here.' And then he looks over his shoulder and pulls a pair of glasses out of his jeans pocket and puts them on.

'Pablo. What are you on about?' I'm more confused than ever.

'I lie about my eyes. My terrible, demon eyes.'

'Hang on a second – has this all been about you getting glasses?' A few things start to fall into place: the staring, the squinting, the 'dirty looks'. But none of it makes much sense. 'Why are you keeping this a big secret from Majella, Pablo?' I say. 'It's hardly something to be ashamed of.'

He starts shaking his head furiously. 'Oh, you don't understand. *Mi amor*, she hates glasses. She told me she was, back in the school, with the bull?'

With the bull? What bull? There was that time that Billy Foran's herd broke into the football pitch but nobody got hurt – there was just a lot of shite around the goals. I can't even imagine it coming up in conversation between Pablo and Majella, although it did make the front page of the parish newsl–

'Bullying!' Pablo shouts, looking up from his phone triumphantly. 'Majella, she was bullying for wearing glasses. She hates them with some passion. She must never know about my eyesight. That's why I'm wearing the contacts.' He takes off the offending glasses and blinks at me furiously.

'But I saw you with Susie Ó Súilleabháin in the Ard Rí – she was going in for the shift.' As soon as the words are out of my mouth it dawns on me: Susie is an optician.

'No, you misunderstand.' He interrupts my thoughts, slapping his thigh. 'Susie is a nice lady. An eye doctor. She had just given me the lenses. She was making sure they fit. They make my eyes very, you know, dry. She says they won't work for me – I must wear glasses or accept no see.'

He's still blinking away, obviously in bits from the contacts. I'm trying to take all this in. But another thing is bothering me. 'What the hell were you doing in Dublin with Susie, though? I saw you with my own two eyes on South William Street. And not to rub it in, but I have 20/20 vision. And you lied to Majella about being there. She said you were training in Kilkenny!'

'Susie,' he says, smiling, 'she refer me to op– op– octopus surgeon.' He looks so hopeful that he might have got it right that I don't have the heart to correct him. 'And my English no very good – she go with me to, how do you say, translate.'

'Why are you making such a big deal out of this, Pablo? Would you rather Majella think you cheated on her than tell her you need glasses? You're carrying on like it's leprosy. She wears bloody contacts herself, you know.'

His face darkens. 'Majella must never know. She tells me, Pab, you are perfect specimen of man. You are flawless, much better than Irish muck savage. She cannot know my secret. I take it to my grave.'

'Pablo, you have to tell her! If you don't, how am I supposed to explain what I said?'

'Next week I find out if I can get the laser surgery, and until then Susie has given me enough contact lenses. They hurt bad. My fingers are crossed. Then no more secrets and lying. Please, Aisling, you must promise me it stays secret. I am forever indebted. I teach you salsa.' Then he gets up and starts salsaing over to me, his hips swinging like they're on hinges. Like I don't have enough on my plate.

'You're grand, thanks,' I say, draining my tea. 'How do I know you're telling the truth? About you and Susie? I didn't come down in the last shower, you know.'

'Aisling, you are smart. Majella always say it. I wouldn't lie to you. If you doubt me, please ask Susie. She will tell you all!'

I sigh. It's too early for this craic, but he does sound genuine. 'I have to go out for a while. Will you start making breakfast? There are sausages and eggs in the fridge. Good man.'

My phone rings as I'm tiptoeing out of the house.

'Hun, I heard what happened to the café. Are you okay? Can I do anything?'

'I'm grand thanks, Sharon,' I say, grabbing my keys. 'A bit shook, but there was no cash taken so I'm trying to stay positive. I don't know how long it'll take to get the place back together, though. They did a right job on it, the feckers.'

'They didn't get into the safe?'

'Nope. And I had the full weekend's takings in it too.'

'Are you there now, hun?'

'Just on my way,' I say, starting the car.

'I'll pop over so.'

James Matthews's jeep is already in the car park when I get there, but there's no sign of the man himself. The café looks worse than I remember, if that's even possible. I tip into my little office and call the insurance company, who explain they'll start processing my claim as soon as I get my crime number off the guards. And then it will take up to twelve weeks to get any money out of them. The lad on the phone must have asked me fifty times if the alarm was armed. I tried to explain that the light was flashing and I have no idea why the siren wasn't going. The bloody thing is only a few weeks old, and I said I have the receipt and warranty ready to produce at a minute's notice if he wants to see them. I threw in a mention of the Sale of Goods and Supply of Services Act

1980 for good measure. I know my rights and paid close attention in first year Business Studies. That shut him up.

'Knock, knock.' James Matthews pokes his head around the door frame. 'I didn't want to come in until you arrived. Wow, Aisling, I'm so sorry this happened.'

'Thanks,' I say, smoothing down my hair. 'I know it's a mess but I'll get it sorted. I need to get reopened, though, James. I'm haemorrhaging money here.'

'Right, well, I called in a favour and the replacement windows and door are arriving first thing in the morning. What else can I do to help?'

Finally some good news! I thought that would take weeks! I can't help myself – I jump out of my seat and throw my arms around his neck. His shoulders are good and wide and he smells like something citrusy. They must have upgraded the toiletries at the Mountrath, or maybe he uses his own posh stuff. Then I catch a hold of myself. God, Aisling, they're just windows.

'Sorry, it's just that I'll feel so much better once the place is secure again,' I stammer.

'Don't be,' he says, 'sorry, I mean. You've had a tough twenty-four hours. I heard there was a house fire last night over near your mum's too? I could smell smoke in the air this morning leaving the Mountrath.'

'It was awful,' I say. 'Majella's family home, completely burnt to the ground. Luckily no one was hurt.' I don't mention anything about poor Willy.

'Where do you want me to start?' he says, looking out into the café. 'There's plenty of room in the skip out the back – will I chuck some of the broken furniture?'

'That'd be mighty, thanks,' I say, turning back to my desk and consulting my list. 'I need to go through these figures here to see where I stand. Then it's hunting for more tables and chairs.'

'No problem at all,' he says, heading off.

I've only just picked up my calculator when I hear tyres on the gravel outside and then the unmistakable sound of heels skittering across the tiles.

'Hun?'

'In the office, Sharon,' I call out. Her arches must be fecked.

She's white as a ghost when she comes through the door. In fact, she looks like a completely different person. If it wasn't for the outfit – shiny leggings and a backless shirt – I wouldn't have recognised her at all. She doesn't even have eyebrows!

I spring from my seat. 'Jesus, Sharon, are you alright? Here, sit down, sit down,' and I sort of hoosh her in before she collapses.

'What? I'm fine,' she says, looking confused. 'Oh, I know what it is, I'm not wearing make-up. I left in such a rush I didn't get a chance.'

'You look so … different,' I say.

She's sort of fidgeting in the doorway, and I feel like there's something on the tip of her tongue.

'Are you OK, Sharon? Will you have some tea? The kettle actually survived, would you believe.'

'No thanks, hun,' she replies. 'Is it okay if I walk around? Have the guards already been?'

'They have,' I say.

'Did they have any ideas as to who might have done it?'

'None. They asked if I had any enemies. The only I person I could think of was Marty feckin' Boland? I have a whole pig in the freezer that's going to go to waste now. I don't think he'd be able to live with himself knowing that, but I really can't think of anyone else who'd do this.'

Her eyes dart around the room. 'What did they use to break the windows?'

'The guards said it was probably a steel bar.'

'And no money was taken?'

'Not a cent. It was pure vandalism,' I say with a shrug.

She taps her lower lip with her finger and stares into space for a minute, deep in thought. 'I have to go, Aisling,' she declares suddenly.

'Did you hear about the Morans' house?'

'I did, hun. How's Majella?'

'In bits.'

'Ask her if there's anything I can do, will you?'

'Of course.' And then after a quick hug she totters out again.

****

The longer I looked at the books, the more depressed I got. I might be able to pick up some new furniture in charity shops, and maybe do another trolley dash around IKEA, but replacing the big appliances – I just can't afford it. And I know I can't ask Mammy for a loan, not when she's clearly in dire financial straits herself. What the feck am I going to do? I can't stay closed for 12 weeks.

James Matthews did a fine job clearing out the dining room, and suddenly the café looks as bare and raw as it did before I moved in. Talk about coming full circle. The only good thing to come out of this entire episode is I've had an idea for a way we can help the Morans – in the short term, at least. It won't get them back on their feet entirely, but it will raise a few bob – enough to get them a lease on a new house and a few essentials to keep them going.

Mammy is up to her oxters in a stew when I land in to the kitchen. By the looks of the herbs scattered around on the table, Carol is not too far away. Mammy wouldn't be too up on using herbs. 'Not everyone likes flavour, you know, Aisling,' she told me once when she caught me bringing garlic into the house. She'll stretch to a bit of parsley for a white sauce to go with ham and cabbage, but that's it.

'Mammy, do you have a number for Geraldine?' I ask, inspecting the vat of mashed potatoes on the Aga. Nice and lumpy, her signature spud. Elaine once made me mashed potatoes using a potato ricer and, honestly, I couldn't stomach them. So smooth, not a bit of bite.

'Geraldine from Geraldine's?' she says, reaching for her phone. 'I do, but she won't be there this evening, pet. She does Zumba with Mags today.'

'It's grand, I can call her tomorrow.'

'Are you looking for a slip or something? I might have one upstairs.'

'No, it's something else. I'll tell you after I talk to her. Where are the Morans?'

'Over at the house,' she says softly. 'Or what's left of it. They're all coming back here in about an hour for a good feed.'

'Grand, I'll set the table so,' I say, heading for the drawer where she keeps the good tablecloths. I suppose it's a special occasion.

'Oh, there's a letter for you on Daddy's desk, Aisling,' she calls after me without turning from the pot. 'It was registered so I had to sign for it. Pat wouldn't even get out of the van, the lazy fecker. It has a Las Vegas postmark, if you don't mind.'

CHAPTER 37

'I'm sorry, how did you get my address?'

I usually know a scam when I hear one, but the letter from Vegas said I'd won a prize and to ring this number and it looked official enough. Better to be safe than sorry. I'm on high alert, though. They're probably somehow dialling into my phone to steal all my passwords every second I stay on the call.

'Ma'am. Ma'am, if you could just bear with me. Were you in Las Vegas in February of this year?'

By God they're good in this day and age. She'll probably be telling me the colour of my knickers next. 'Who is this?' I wonder if she's somehow watching me on the camera on my phone as I talk.

'You placed a bet in the lobby of the MGM Grand. A fifty dollar … Sorry, a fifty euros bet?'

Hold on a second.

'Ayes-ling … I'm sorry, I can't read the surname, but are you a Ms Ayes-ling?'

'Aisling. It's actually Irish and means vision or drea– eh, yes, that's me.'

She doesn't sound like she's going to scam me, to be fair. Although that's probably what she's been trained for. I must check my bank balance the second I get off the phone. The sophistication of these operations is off the charts.

'Congrats Ms Ayes-ling–'

'It's Ash-ling'

'You're the winner of our MGM Grand Prize Sweepstakes. You are the proud owner of a Ferrari 488. Can I just confirm a few details with you?'

'A what now?' Something is coming back to me. Ever so faintly.

'A Ferrari 488. Will you be collecting the vehicle in person or should I arrange delivery?'

Me and Antony in the hotel lobby, plastered. A big, red, shiny car. 'Daddy would have loved this.' Fifty euro pressed into the man's hand. 'Hey, big Irish spender. No skin off my nose. Money is money.' He was wearing some sort of clown outfit? Maybe a poker outfit, with the visor? I was very drunk, to be fair to me.

'Ms Ayes-ling? Are you still there?'

Scrawling my name and my number on an entry slip and guessing the number of … somethings packed into the car.

'How, how did I win this?'

'You guessed the number of poker chips inside the car with the greatest accuracy. Congratulations, ma'am. How may I help you to collect your prize?'

How in the name of blazes am I going to get in and out of a Ferrari? My knees are up around my ears when I sit on a bean bag, and it's not a dignified scene trying to get out of it. I'd have to be hoisted out of a Ferrari it's that close to the ground. I can't bring a thing like that home. You'd be plagued going to carwashes.

'Er, I'm Irish. I live in Ireland.'

'Okay, Ms Ayse-ling, that's no problem.'

Her voice is starting to get a little tight. I leave the correction of the pronunciation this time, although it nearly kills me.

'We can offer a cash alternative of two-thirds the value of the vehicle. It's all in the small print.'

Two-thirds. The lousers. Still, though, that's better than nothing. Every little helps at the moment. A few grand will certainly fix a few things here and there. I've already bought two Winning Streaks in the hope of getting on to spin the wheel.

'So I will be sending the cheque to – am I reading this right? Bally-Go-Berd? Can I ask for your house or apartment number and ZIP code, please, ma'am?'

'Oh, there's no house number. It's just the main road out of Ballygobbard, the Dublin side. Pat Curran knows me. And we all decided collectively as a country to ignore the postal codes so you needn't bother with th–'

'And the cheque for $200,000 will be made out to you, ma'am. Can you just spell your surname for me? Your entry really is like a chicken scratching, but we're used to that.'

Thud. I drop the phone.

Someone must be having me on. Someone is playing a cruel joke on me. I race to my ancient laptop and fling it open. I google 'MGM Grand Ferrari poker raffle'. I'm sure that's not what she said it was called, but surely it's close enough. There it is. There it is. A picture of the car and all in the lobby. It's from the MGM Grand's official Facebook page – 1.2 million Likes can't be wrong. They only give away two a year. Jesus, imagine how much money they're making off drunk eejits like me.

Two hundred thousand dollars. Mammy's farm. The café. Majella and Pablo and Shem and Liz and Shane. This could be the answer to all our prayers! I hear Mammy moving around downstairs and I race down to her, taking the narrow stairs two at a time and nearly coming a cropper in my stockinged feet. The Morans, Pablo and all are still at their house surveying what's left of it.

'Mammy!' I round the kitchen door and slide to a halt. She's sitting at the table, the place mercifully quiet for the first time in days. She's got the photo albums out. 'You'll never guess what! Just as well you're sitting down.'

'Ah, Aisling. I'm just being silly. Looking at photos of us all here over the years.'

She pushes the book towards me. I've seen the handful of photos of myself so many times – and all of our family photos, to be fair. I know them like the back of my hand.

'There you are on top of the hay bales. And Paul in the wheelbarrow. Haven't we had some great times here?'

'Mammy, I've got some news,' I say, gently closing the album.

She looks up at me in shock. Every mother's instant reaction to that sentence is 'she's pregnant'.

'I'm not pregnant.'

She looks relieved. 'It would be grand if you were, of course,' she says quickly.

'I know, I know. But listen to me. I've won some money. Loads of money.' I pause for dramatic effect. 'Two hundred grand.'

She looks immediately suspicious. 'What are you on about? Two hundred grand? Are you sure it's not a scam? Where did you win it? Hardly a scratch card? And the Lotto machine in Filan's was broken the other day. There was war over it. Tessie Daly's been playing the same numbers for fifteen years, and if they had come up this week and she not able to buy the ticket she would have put Matty Filan up against a wall.'

I have to interrupt her. 'I won it in Las Vegas. Well, I won a car but I'm taking the money instead. I googled it and everything. It's true. It's all true! Isn't it just great?'

My excitement is infectious and the scam scales start to fall from her eyes. 'Two hundred thousand. Did you really, Aisling? Well, isn't that just brilliant? And it couldn't have come at a better time.' She smacks a tea towel off the table with delight, and we both sort of shout at the same time.

'We can use it to save the house and the farm, Mammy.'

'You can use it to start the café back up again, Aisling.'

She looks at me, confused. 'Save the house and the farm? What are you talking about, pet?'

'Are you not going to sell it? I saw the document from that property-surveyor crowd in Dublin. And I know you were looking at a new little house in Rathborris. And, and … well, you just seem very stuck for money. And I haven't been much use. I'm not even paying you rent.'

'I don't want rent off you, Aisling. Don't you do enough to help me? What would I do without you? You keep me from going doolally rattling around in this house missing your fath–' Her voice catches.

'What's going on then? You were giving out about the price of boiling the kettle.'

Mammy stretches herself up proudly and fixes her lips in a prim manner. 'Boiling the kettle every ten minutes is one of the reasons the icebergs are melting, you know, Aisling. Constance and I are going into business. We're opening an eco-farm.' She looks pleased as punch. What in the blazes is an eco-farm?

'You're doing what? I don't think the Tidy Towns will go for wind turbines blowing away half of BGB. I can just imagine Mad Tom hanging off one of them.'

'No, Aisling. An eco-farm. Growing organic vegetables and opening a farm shop and installing solar panels and having a petting zoo for school tours. That kind of thing. We've been slaving over a business plan – inspired by you, actually. Constance's fondness for posh colouredy carrots means she's well up on the demand for organic vegetables, and BGB is closer to Dublin than ever with the good roads and Jamie Oliver chopping boards in Knock Garden Centre.'

She's right there. Nothing pulls people into the countryside quicker than a good road and a notions Garden Centre. And now maybe Mammy's eco-farm.

'What about the livestock?'

'We'll keep some sheep and cattle, but not too many. We've already ordered the piglets for the petting zoo, and William is flat out designing a hen house. He's going to build it from scratch.'

'Mammy, I really thought you were looking to sell up and buy a handy little two-bed?'

'Well, I'm not. I'm not dead yet, Aisling. Constance is downsizing, though. She's only rattling around that mansion by herself. She's putting the money from the sale into the eco-farm, and one of her friends is going to take her horses. I've been helping her find something smaller.'

So that's what the Woodlawn Park brochure was about. 'And where are you getting the money, Mammy?'

'Savings, pet. Me and Daddy were never short. We had great plans for when we retired. We were going to travel the world. And now, well, that's not going to happen, is it?'

I blink away tears. What a woman. You forget that mammies aren't just mammies. They have plans and ambitions and dreams. I've never felt prouder.

'Are you sure I can't give you money, Mammy?'

'No. I won't hear of it. And you know I would have given you the money for the café, pet, if it wasn't already tied up in the eco-farm? Now, if you want to invest some money, that's a different story. We're also looking at expanding into eco-tourism – yurts and the like. Hen parties go mad for them. Imagine BallyGoBrunch providing them with their sausage sandwiches after a night on the rosé by the campfire?'

I haven't seen Mammy this fired up since … well, ever! Yurts in BGB. Her and Constance running a business. She'll have Mammy in a wide-brimmed hat and a pair of riding boots in no time.

'Look at us, Aisling. Businesswomen!'

Well, my business is in tatters, but things are certainly looking up.

There's a clattering at the back door. The Morans are back. Shem and Liz are anyway. They look so defeated. I can tell Liz has been crying. I pull out a chair for her and usher her into it.

'Shem, Liz, I've to tell you something.'

'What is it, Aisling?' Shem is already down at the Aga checking it for fuel and giving it a stoke. He's like Daddy in that way. Not happy unless he's doing something useful.

Although, in Shem's case it's usually trying to sell sand to the population of Curracloe.

'I've come into some money. Unexpectedly.' No point in beating about the bush. 'And I'd love to give you some to help you get back on your feet.'

Shem stands up dead straight. 'No, thank you, Aisling. That's very generous of you, but no, thank you.'

'But–'

'No. Thank you.'

I look at Liz and she shakes her head. 'We couldn't, Aisling. We'll be okay. We'll have the insurance money and we'll get back on our feet.'

There's silence for a moment. Shem looks like he's trying very hard not to cry, gulping away like there's no tomorrow.

I pipe up again. 'Well, will you let me hold a fundraiser for you at least? Everyone in the village wants to help – Mammy's phone has been hopping for days. We'll raise a few bob.'

Shem is still struggling to compose himself. Liz speaks up, smiling gently. 'That would be lovely, Aisling.'

The back door goes again. Who could that be? It feels like half the town is already in the kitchen. Mammy crosses the kitchen to answer it as Liz and Shem settle at the kitchen table.

'Carol! Are you alright, love?'

Mammy swings the door open wider, and Carol is standing there, a small suitcase balanced on the handlebars of her bike and an old canvas rucksack on the carrier at the back.

'You said there might be a place for me here ... if I needed one.'

It takes Mammy a few seconds to compute, but almost immediately she steps back, swinging her arm into the kitchen. 'Come in. Come in. Shem, will you get Carol's bags there?'

Shem busies himself with the bike and the bags, and Liz makes noises about packing up their own stuff and slips out into the hall. The Morans are moving to the Mountrath for a short while. Majella and I always dreamed about living in a hotel, so while the circumstances aren't ideal, I'm delighted that someone is finally going to make her bed for her every morning.

Carol sinks down at the table. 'I've left him.'

'Oh, good woman,' Mammy yelps almost involuntarily.

Carol continues. 'He's away in Germany for a week at a butcher's conference, and as each day passes I'm dreading him coming back more and more. So I'm just not going to be there when he arrives back. I'll be on my feet a bit by then, please God.' She looks terrified, but her voice is steady.

Mammy swings into action. 'Aisling, get some sheets out of the hot press. The good ones. And lift up That Bloody Cat out of that armchair and let Carol sit somewhere comfortable.'

Mammy's in minding mode. Her default and best setting. Carol will be okay.

CHAPTER 38

I should have known Geraldine would completely take over. She's suddenly acting like the fashion show in the Mountrath to raise money for the Morans was her idea when in fact all I wanted was a few mother-of-the-bride ensembles to make up the second half. The first half is 'contemporary fashions', and Knock Garden Centre has those covered, although I'm not sure what's contemporary about pastel rugby shirts and colouredy wellies. Sadhbh is getting the 4 p.m. Timoney's bus down – God knows what she's going to make of it all. If she brings Don Shields there'll be a riot.

In typical Ballygobbard and Knock fashion, the entire parish has come out to help the Morans, and all 400 tickets were quickly snapped up. People can't resist the glamour of a fashion show, and it didn't hurt that Mad Tom stuck up signs advertising it right out as far as the motorway.

Father Fenlon offered to MC and, given his experience speaking in front of crowds, I couldn't turn him down. He'll keep things moving, too, and stop any small children invading the catwalk. He's good at that. I tried to cajole him into wearing a tuxedo, but he said he'll stick to the collar if I don't mind. Fair enough, I said.

The BGB Gaels camogie team are on modelling duty, and Sharon spent the whole afternoon spray tanning them until they turned a rich mahogany. There was a bit of a stand-off between her and Triona from Crops and Bobbers backstage about the hair, but they sorted it out between them, with Sharon saying she'd do make-up then since she's only a blow-in. I had to remind them that a charity event was no time for rivalry, but they assured me that it was all very good-natured. Like I don't have enough to be worrying about.

'If it tastes even half as good as it smells you'll be doing well, Aisling.' James Matthews is outside in the carpark on pig-on-a-spit duty, rotating it slowly per Carol's instructions. I was going to make use of that pig if it killed me. Filan's donated 300 baps and the local ICA guild has provided enough coleslaw to sink a very big ship. If I learned anything at BallyGoBrunch it's that you can never have enough coleslaw. They go mad for it around here.

'We were fierce lucky with the weather anyway,' I say, looking up at the cloudless sky. Someone is watching out for the Morans because the forecast was for twelve hours of rain.

'I'm going to go back to the house to get the rest of the salads, pet,' Mammy says, walking past on her way to the car. She has plates of hardboiled eggs and rolled up slices of ham all laid out under cling film ready to go. And a few lettuce leaves for a bit of token green. Carol has six buckets of potato salad chilling in the Mountrath's massive walk-in fridge. Her secret ingredient is chives – very swish.

Back in the function room, Maeve Hennessey and Dee Ruane are putting goodie bags on the chairs in the first two rows. That was another brainwave of mine – a VIP section, so we could charge twice the ticket price: €20 instead of €10. Sadhbh donated a load of CDs, T-shirts and miscellaneous shite from Flatlay, and Elaine got Colette Green to give us a case of her new scented pantyliners. Majella nearly died when I told her. What Maj doesn't know is that Colette felt so bad after Elaine told her about the fire that she's also donating two tickets to her Style Roadshow in Ballybunion for the raffle. What an absolute dote! We also have a €50 voucher for Cantonese City, compliments of the Zhus; an overnight stay plus dinner in the Ard Rí; a full pre-NCT service from Filan's Garage; ten bales of briquettes from Filan's Shop; and refreshments for up to 100 guests when you buy a wake from Filan's Funeral Home. I think the heifer, donated by Paddy Reilly, will steal the show, mind.

'Hiya, Ais, where will I set up the raffle table?'

'Denise!' I squeal. She only had the baby a week ago and she's back to looking like it never happened, albeit with a newborn now attached to her in a sling. Very Kate Middleton. 'And little ... how do I pronounce it? Coo? Coov?'

'Coo-al,' she says confidently. I'm obviously not the first person to ask. 'Cumhal was Fionn Mac Cumhaill's father. It suits him, doesn't it?'

'It does, he's dotey,' I say absentmindedly, looking across the room. James Matthews has left his post outside at the pig and is now carrying around stacks of chairs, lining them up. If I didn't know he was English I'd swear he was local the way he's bantering with Cyclops and Titch Maguire, who keeps bringing up the six counties. 'The table goes just inside the door,' I say over my shoulder, heading in his direction. 'Thanks a mill, Denise.'

'That pig is not going to turn itself, James,' I say with a hand on my hip. But I smile so he knows I'm only messing. Well, I'm partly messing. Someone better be turning it – if it's burning I'll have his guts for garters.

'Carol came back and relieved me,' he replies, setting down the chairs and wiping the sweat off his forehead with the back of his hand. 'Apparently I was doing it wrong?' He laughs. 'I suspect it's in better hands now. Everything going according to plan?'

'Right on schedule,' I say, tapping my clipboard with my biro. Then I pause, trying to choose my words carefully. 'I just wanted to say thanks a million for your help at the café the past few days. You went above and beyond and I appreciate it.'

As soon as I heard about my Vegas win I cranked up the laptop and replaced all the stuff that was smashed up in the break-in. I even upgraded a few things, truth be told, but I won't be too out of pocket once the insurance money comes in. My credit card was practically steaming, so when the cheque from the MGM arrived yesterday I flew straight in to Knock to lodge it. Joe Funge was in the bank twiddling his thumbs, but he still insisted I feed it into one of those big machines instead of just bloody well accepting it over the counter. I was livid. He was manning the place himself, just him and six machines and two phones. This is the future, apparently. Anyway, when I was off doing that, James Matthews was unpacking all the new delph and doing a final clean on the kitchen. I couldn't believe it when I called in on the way home – the place looked as good as new. Better, actually. I'm all set to reopen at the weekend.

'I felt very bad for you, Aisling,' he says, shaking his head. 'It was the least I could do. Have you heard anything from the police?'

'Garda Staunton rang yesterday,' I say. 'They questioned Marty Boland last week, but he really was at the Irish Butchers' Challenge Gala Dinner in Belfast.' James raises an eyebrow.

'I know, it sounds made up but they checked out his alibi and it's watertight. He was up on stage in front of 200 butchers accepting yet another award for the sausages. He couldn't have done it.'

There's a kerfuffle over at the door and I turn around, expecting to see Geraldine going for Tessie Daly. The two of them have been at each other's throats over the order of the models all afternoon. But it's not Geraldine who's drawing the crowd – it's John, who I haven't clapped eyes on in months. At the last minute, I decided to add a 'men's fashions' segment just before the interval. The audience is mostly women so I thought it would be a crowd pleaser – get them riled up right before Denise swoops in with her raffle. I roped a few of the Rangers into doing it, and James said to count him in too, but I wasn't expecting John to be around. He's big news now with his county team connections. I definitely wasn't banking on him showing up early.

'Sorry, James, I have to fly,' I say, rushing off. 'I need you backstage at half – okay? Backstage is the toilets.'

He nods and I continue on over towards Denise. Then she steps to the left, and out from behind Coo … Coov … the baby in the sling, appears a blonde bombshell and she's hanging off John's arm, looking up at him like she's ready to eat him. I actually gasp because she looks just like one of those GAA wags I've seen in magazines. Although she's even browner, and blonder, and more glamorous, if that's possible. And that's when I realise I can't go over there. I thought I was ready, I thought I'd moved on, but I cannot meet John's new girlfriend.

The only place to go is down, so I hit the floor and crawl under a row of seats – very neat: I must remember to compliment Titch on his symmetry – and scurry to the opposite side of the room, a safe distance away. I'm about to sneak out when a pair of millennial pink suede mules appear in front of me. I'd know those perfectly pedicured toes anywhere.

'Sadhbh,' I hiss. 'Down here.'

Her upside-down face appears in front of me, her expression understandably confused. I wait for her mop of grey hair to fall downwards but there's … nothing.

'Ais, what the hell are you doing down there?' she says, simultaneously laughing and reaching down to pull me out from under the chair.

'It's John,' I whisper, struggling to my feet. 'He's over there with his swanky new girlfriend. I couldn't face him. I thought I could, but I couldn't.'

She's nodding along sympathetically but I can't take my eyes off her head – it's bald as a badger's arse. What has she done to her hair? Her lovely hair! It was so well conditioned and shiny and swingy.

'Do you really care, Ais? Like, *really*?'

I think for a second. 'No, I suppose I don't. I just wasn't ready to see him with another woman,' I say to her scalp. 'Sadhbh, your … hair, where is it gone?'

'Couldn't get rid of the nits so I just thought, fuck it,' she says.

'Well, you look great!' I say, and I do mean it. Her skull is the perfect shape. 'You didn't bring Don with you?'

'He's in London for the Brits tonight,' she says, 'but he told me to stick a few quid in a bucket on his behalf. Mad Tom caught me with one on the way in.'

'Ah, well tell him thanks a million from us – we really appreciate it. Are The Peigs nominated or what?'

'Best Newcomer,' Sadhbh says proudly, fishing out her phone. 'Here, look, he just sent me a pic. They're all wearing suits. It's gas.'

But when she holds up the phone, the picture on the screen looks nothing like The Peigs. It takes me a minute to register why.

'Jesus, they're all bald too!' I scream. Bloody Mairead has a lot to answer for. 'So I take it you fessed up?'

'Yeah, I told Don last week. He was grand about it. He had just bumped into Beyoncé at a recording studio, though, so cross your fingers she doesn't have them now too.'

'Ah, she's another one who'd look good with a shaved head, to be fair,' I say. 'Although if Mairead can trace herself back as the one who gave Beyoncé nits, we'll never hear the end of it.'

'It's weird – since I arrived at the hotel, three people have offered me their seats,' Sadhbh goes, looking perplexed. 'No idea what's going on.'

'I think I do,' I say. 'They probably think you have cancer. We don't get a lot of baldies around here.'

She pales ever so slightly. 'Oh my God, now it makes sense. Some auld lad in the car park said he'd light a candle for me!'

'Maybe it will keep the nits away,' I say hopefully. 'Now listen, I have to run. I'm up to my eyes here.'

'I can't believe you pulled this off, Aisling. The place is chockers. Where's Majella and the fam?'

I consult my clipboard. 'The Morans will come in when everyone's seated and the lights go down. Father Fenlon is going to say a few words, possibly a prayer. And then we'll get started.'

'Why is a … priest–?'

'Just because, Sadhbh. You're not in Dublin now.'

'Right, where do you want me?'

I direct her to the second last row (you snooze, you lose) and head backstage to see how hair and make-up is getting on. The smell of fake tan nearly knocks me out when I open the door, and I notice the toilets are doubling as perfect make-up chairs. Very handy.

Suddenly, Sharon appears in front of me. 'Sorry, hun,' she goes, her voice a bit shaky. Her phone is in her hand. 'I just got a call off PhoneWatch to say the alarm in the salon is going off. One of the windows is open.'

'Jesus, get one of the lads to go with you if you're going over there,' I say anxiously. I'm extra security conscious after what happened the café. Not that I was in anyway lax about it beforehand.'

'Can you spare one? Is their segment not on before the interval?'

'It is, but you'll be back by then. I'm sure Cyclops would be delighted to go with you. He's around here somewhere.'

She gives me a quick hug and then teeters off to find him. I can't believe the progress she's made with the Gaels. They're all looking in the mirror, mooning over themselves. Gillian Browne suddenly has cheekbones sharper than a

Penali pen, and Avril O'Leary looks like she's had lip implants since I last saw her an hour ago. Sharon is some make-up artist, and this show couldn't be a better advertisement for the salon.

'Girls, you're all looking faboo,' I shout over the din, and they all quieten down. 'Geraldine will be in shortly to give you your outfits. Remember, loads of smiling on the catwalk. The Morans have been through enough.'

It's twenty minutes to showtime, so I decide to sneak out to the bar for a quick drink to steady my nerves. I might seem calm as anything on the outside, but I'm fairly shitting it in case something goes wrong. It's like that sign Mammy used to have hanging up in the kitchen – something about nurses being like icebergs because you can only see a tiny bit of what they're doing. I can't remember the exact wording but I got the gist.

My arm is nearly waved off me walking through the function room – it's like everyone I've ever met is out – so I'm delighted to be the only one in the bar.

'A West Coast Cooler and a glass of ice, please, Jocksey.' He nearly has it in my hand before I've finished saying it, and I pay and sneak off into the snug to take the weight off my feet. I really wish I'd just worn my Crocs instead of my good Clark's boots – is this what it's like to be a fashion victim, I wonder.

'Long time no see, Ais.'

It's John. He's sitting on the leather couch behind the door. I should have known he'd be in here; this used to be our secret little spot when we first started going out and wanted to talk without being interrupted. All that talking and now look at us – we don't know each other at all.

'Eh, hiya. What has you hiding in here?' I don't know what to say. Seeing him again makes me feel so sad. He's wearing clothes that I don't recognise. Did his girlfriend pick out that waistcoat? Did she buy him that new aftershave for his birthday? He never let me buy him aftershave, said it was a waste of money. Now he smells like the inside of Brown Thomas's and he has no socks on.

'Ah, I just wanted a bit of peace and quiet. Everyone keeps asking me about the county team. I'm worn out talking about it.'

'You must be enjoying it, though, are you?'

'It's good craic alright. Hard going, though, when I'm working full-time. Mammy is going mad that I'm not home enough.'

Fran. The last time I saw her I was leaving the hospital with Piotr and I've somehow managed to avoid seeing her since. I'm still not recovered from the look she threw me.

'How is Fran?' I dutifully ask. 'And Mel?'

'Grand, grand,' he says, toeing at a broken tile with his shoe. I notice he's still wearing those brown pisscatchers and smile. Socks or no socks, some things will never change.

I'm about to bite the bullet and ask him where the girlfriend is when I hear Sadhbh calling my name out in the corridor and look at my watch. Jesus, it's less than five minutes till showtime! I have to get out there and make sure Geraldine has put the right shoes with the right outfits. She had a mad idea about 'clashing colours' earlier, and I had to put my foot down. Next thing she'll be putting blue with green, and God knows they should never be seen.

'Bye, John,' I say, standing up and taking a few gulps of the Cooler. 'It was really nice to see you.' And I mean it.

****

The fashion show went off without a hitch. Well, with minimal hitches. Sharon and Cyclops arrived back just as Shem was taking to the stage to thank everyone for coming. She said she was full sure she'd closed all the windows, but I had to remind her she'd had a busy day. It's no mean feat looking at twelve camogie players in their knickers for hours on end. She also forgot to bring enough fake eyelashes for everyone, which really wasn't like her.

The Gaels played a blinder in the first half, apart from Áine Farrell who thought she was Kate Moss, blowing kisses and winking at people with her tongue out. There were two anonymous complaints for vulgarity lodged at reception. And the lads had apparently sneaked a bottle of whiskey into the toilets for Dutch courage, so they were fairly rowdy during their segment. Geraldine was no help, patting them down with baby oil backstage and loving every second of it too. You can imagine the moves when they got out on the catwalk. Even James Matthews had a spring in his step when he weaved up and down. John's arrival nearly lifted the roof off the place, and an ambulance had to be called for Mad Tom, who thought it would be a good idea to stage dive; there's another stamp on his A & E loyalty card. Still, all in all, I'd call it a success, and between the tickets, raffle and pig-on-a-spit, we raised €6,284 for the Morans. I wanted to get one of those big novelty cheques to present to them, but Liz said it was probably a waste of funds. Good craic in a picture, though.

After the show, The Truck fires up his legendary mobile disco and the place really starts hopping, while a few of us try to tidy up. I asked Sadhbh to stack chairs but she got cornered by Geraldine, who insists on demonstrating the various ways she could wrap a floaty scarf around her head. There's not much of the pig left, but Carol is making some noises about bones and trotters and stock for soup for the café. It sounds manky, but she knows what she's talking about so I leave her off.

When Sharon appears out of the toilets with her make-up kit, I finally realise how she managed to transform the Gaels. She has suitcases of it. Actual suitcases of make-up! How many trios of eyeshadow and lipsticks does one person need?

'Hun, I'm going to do a run out with this stuff,' she says, grabbing the handle of a case, 'and then I'll swing the car in closer to the door. Be easier.'

She'll be in and out all night if someone doesn't give her a hand, so I scoop up two of the smaller bags and head after her. But even though she's in the heels, there's no catching her. When I get to the side door of the Mountrath I scan the pitch-dark car park – no sign. Then I hear the scream.

CHAPTER 39

'Sharon? Sharon? *Sharon?*' Jesus Christ what's going on? '*Sharon?*'

I rush in the direction of where I saw her Beetle earlier, weaving in between parked cars. The car park is eerily quiet and dark save for a solitary floodlight. Before I can find her I trip over something. Sharon's stuff. Part of her make-up kit. Where is she? My heart is pounding in my ears and I fumble in my pocket for my phone. It's not there. I've left it inside. I can hear muffled laughter and chat from inside the hotel, and I turn to run back in for help when I hear her scream again, coming from my right. I turn in the direction of the noise and begin walking, and then running. There's a silver car, parked right at the edge of the car park, and the interior light is on. As I get closer I can see movement inside. I can see the orange of Sharon's dress in the weak illumination, and I can see the driver – a man with dark hair – has one hand over her mouth and another around her throat.

'Jesus Christ. *Help. Helllp!*' I race towards the car, and as I reach the passenger door and uselessly flip the handle, I can see Sharon clawing desperately at his face. She's kicking her legs against the dashboard and the door as I pound from the other side. He lets go of her for a second to start the car, and

I look around for something to smash the window. Plenty of empty cans under the hedge. Sure, you'd be sober as a judge in the queue for the Vortex without a can of something to keep you going. There's nothing substantial enough to break glass under there, though.

The man grabs Sharon by the hair again and, with the other hand, awkwardly tries to manoeuvre the car out of the space, reversing around and back towards the exit. The place is packed and there isn't enough space for him to turn. I look around desperately for a rock or something, anything. The lights of a car flash into my face as a jeep pulls in off the road at the other end of the car park. I frantically wave my hands in the air, screaming for help, but all I get in return is a friendly salute and a 'There you are now, good girl.' It's Jocksey Cullen's elderly father. Deaf as a post and wouldn't see the Pope himself standing in front of him, he's that blind.

'*Helllppp!*' I scream again. But he shuffles inside with a cheery, 'Lovely night for it.'

I frantically try the handles on other cars around me, and the second one I try gives way. God bless the parish and its trusting nature. As the silver car slowly moves away from me, Sharon still fighting and screaming, my hand closes around the long handle of a hurl. Perfect. Pulling it from the back seat, I sweep around to where the silver car has once again stalled. Running to the passenger window I scream at Sharon to '*Get down,*' line the metal band up with the window and swing. It smashes first time, covering Sharon's hair and clothes in shattered glass. I reach inside the car and pull the lever on the passenger door, which opens, and I grab her arm and drag her out. The driver's attentions turn to escape, and she's barely clear of the car when he puts his foot to the floor, reversing at speed all the way back towards the entrance. Sharon is shaking and keening, a kind of a high-pitched moan, and I help her to her feet.

'You're alright. You're alright. I have you.' I look desperately towards the main entrance for any sign of life, when a familiar shape appears in the doorway.

'Aisling,' he calls. 'Aisling, are you out here?' I've never been happier to see him.

'James! James, c'mere I need your help.' He turns at the sound of my voice and sees me struggling with Sharon. He starts running.

'Jesus Christ,' he pants, reaching us, his accent stronger than ever. 'What happened?'

'He attacked her. There! That fella!' I point at the silver car, now successfully reversed the width of the car park and doing a screeching turn out the main entrance. 'Get the number plate!'

'What the hell?' James whips out his phone to call 999, and between us we help Sharon back towards the hotel.

'Please, I don't want anyone to see me,' she begs, straightening up and pulling at her dress. I steer her towards the disabled toilet off the lobby, away from the hustle of the function room.

'Sharon, do you know him? Was it … was it your ex?' I ask.

'Yes,' she sobs. 'Frank Bolger. Frankie Bolger.' And she rattles off an address in Waterford and gives a rueful smile. 'My old address.'

James nods and strides down the hallway, barking details into the phone.

Once inside the toilet, I lock the door and lower the seat. 'Go on. Sit down. You're okay now. Shh, you're okay.'

She sits and shudders, looking at her hands. At least three of her glamorous nails are gone. Ripped off in the fight. And her knees are grazed from where she tumbled out of the car.

'Your good nails!' I exclaim, unable to stop myself. She laughs, a tiny, brief laugh.

'Sharon. Do we … should I call an ambulance or something? Should we bring you to hospital? Did he–?'

'No!' she whispers, absentmindedly pulling cubes of safety glass out of her hair. I place my hand over hers, mostly to stop her from reefing the fingers off herself, but also to give it a squeeze.

'No,' she says, more softly. 'He didn't. Not this time.'

The guards, fair dues to them, had Frankie Bolger caught before he even made it to the motorway. James met the two gardaí that came to the hotel to follow up, leading the female guard to where we're sitting disabled toilet and knocking gently.

'Sharon,' she says firmly but gently. 'Can I come in?'

'Should I go?' I stutter as Sharon nods and the guard, Hannah she said her name was, comes in. All a guard has to do is look at me and I'm ready to confess to all my crimes: twice forgetting to renew my tax on time and one mad and speedy dash to Kildare Village for a sale on Orla Kiely homewares. I wanted the bread bin badly. It was 30 per cent off!

Hannah motions for me to stay and kneels down beside Sharon. 'First of all, are you injured at all? Does anything hurt?'

Sharon shakes her head. 'Not really. My knees but they're grand.'

'And Sharon, I just want to explain to you that we can transport you to the Sexual Assault Treatment Unit in–'

'I don't need to go. He didn't. He didn't sexually assault me.'

'But he has before.'

Sharon nods.

'I had his records emailed to me,' Hannah says evenly. 'I know it has been a traumatic time for you. I'm sorry this happened to you, Sharon.'

'Not sorry enough to put him in prison,' Sharon snarls.

The guard is silent for a moment. 'I'm sorry Sharon,' she repeats again.

The guards leave and ask me to make sure Sharon comes in tomorrow morning to give a statement. They leave a card. Hannah shakes her head solemnly as she walks away.

'Will you get Majella?' I ask James. And then add, 'And Carol.' By now everyone knows something is up. James has given the minimal information and tried to keep the looky-loos at bay. Majella arrives and is quickly dispatched again to bring a coat for Sharon and my handbag. Sadhbh passes a message that she'll see me back at home. Carol, a little surprised to be summoned, immediately takes on a role of carer, smoothing Sharon's hair and making small talk about what the dickens balayage is and whether highlights would do anything for her. Then we bundle Sharon out to my car to take her back to her little flat above the salon. We pass John pacing up and down outside. He sees me and reaches out to grab my arm.

'Ais, are you okay?'

I stiffen and then see the worry in his face and smile and say, 'I'm fine.'

The blonde bombshell – although on closer inspection she's just a normal girl with a load of teeth and a load of tan – arrives at his side and takes his arm. I smile at her too and repeat, 'I'm fine. We're fine.'

****

Sharon's ex had assaulted her many times and raped her twice. When he did it the second time she went to the guards five days later. They questioned him. He said she was lying, that he'd dumped her and she wanted revenge. There was insufficient evidence, they said. She left him shortly afterwards, packing up her things while he was at the pub. She hoped and prayed he'd never find her.

'When we first got together he wanted to be with me all the time,' she explains, curled up on the couch. 'I was only twenty-two – I thought it was romantic. He always wanted to know where I was and who I was with.'

'How long was it before he got violent?' Carol asks gently.

'Only a matter of months.' Sharon sniffs, and I gasp. 'He followed me on a night out with my friends. Said he'd seen me dancing with some fella. Accused me of cheating on him. That was the first time he hit me. I felt so guilty, I couldn't tell anyone. It was my own fault. He had me convinced.'

'Sharon, it wasn't your fault at all!' I interject. 'You're entitled to go out with your friends and dance with who you like.'

'I know that now,' she says. 'But it wasn't so clear back then. It was like he had me brainwashed.' She turns to me. 'How did you know it was him, Aisling? I never told you.'

'I just had a feeling. Your whole face went dark when you mentioned him ages ago. I knew there must have been something. And you were so worried when the café was attacked.'

She looks down at her hands.

'How did he find you?' I continue. 'Does he know you have family around here?'

'I don't know,' she says. 'I just don't know.'

And then I remember something. I tagged her in an Instagram picture at the soft opening of BallyGoBrunch. It was a shot of Carol's smashed avocado on toast. Very arty. I noticed she'd removed the tag the next day, and I was a bit put out that she didn't want to be linked to the café, although I never said anything. 'Could it have been Instagram?' I ask the room, not quite able to meet her eye.

Sharon looks up at me and nods. 'I think it might have been,' she says. 'And I think that might have been why your café got smashed up, Ais. I'm sorry. I should have said something. Frankie Bolger is dangerous. He did something similar to my salon in Waterford. I just didn't want to believe he was after me – that's why I never said anything. I feel so guilty.'

'Don't you dare say sorry,' I quickly admonish her. 'I'm the one who should be saying sorry. I was so busy trying to go viral that I put you in danger. I'm a right gom.' Then I pull her in for a hug.

'The main thing is you're safe now, Sharon,' Carol says, tucking a blanket around her legs. 'The man I was engaged to before Marty hit me too,' she adds, looking down at her hands. 'When I met Marty I thought he had saved me from him. But the truth is that he could see I was vulnerable.'

'They know, don't they, somehow?' Sharon says with a rueful smile, and Carol looks up at her. 'They do,' she agrees. 'And they pounce.'

I'm not much use but I do have a share bag of Maltesers in my handbag – I always mean to just have a handful (9 Points) but somehow the whole lot always goes down the hatch. Anyway, the girls are lucky that this is a new packet.

'What was it like with Marty?' Sharon asks.

'He never hit me. It was more … emotional. He has plenty of money, but he used to only give me the bare minimum for my housekeeping every week. He said he'd up it when the children came, but of course that didn't happen. It wasn't my fault – it just wasn't to be. He told me that I was useless, a waste of space, only a housewife. He said I'd never have the gumption to leave him.'

'Well, he was wrong about that, wasn't he?' I say. What these women have been through – the things that happen behind closed doors. My heart breaks for them.

Carol smiles. 'He was,' she says. 'I'm tougher than I look.'

'I knew Frankie was around as soon as PhoneWatch called earlier to say the alarm was going off. He's an electrician – he knows what wires to cut and which ones to leave. I knew he was trying to lure me over. I should have just called the guards then.'

'Ah, Sharon, you know yourself that there's nothing they could have done,' I say, throwing an arm around her shoulders. 'They weren't going to hunt down a lad for opening a window. You did everything right.'

At 1 a.m., Sharon is exhausted. Carol offers to stay on the couch so that I can go back to Sadhbh and Mammy and

Majella can put Pablo's mind at ease. 'You'll be okay,' I hear Carol say as she tucks Sharon in. 'You're made of strong stuff, missy. Strong stuff.'

'Sharon!' I poke my head back around the door. 'That's what you should call the salon. Strong Stuff. The Strong Stuff Salon! You might get a few head-the-balls thinking it's an off-licence but … what do you think?'

Sharon smiles sleepily. 'It's perfect.'

CHAPTER 40

'**A**re you settling in alright?'

Carol has the place lovely. She's already found places for all of her bits that she liberated from the home she shared with Marty Boland, and James Matthews put up a magnetic knife holder especially for her in the kitchen.

'It's lovely. I love it. I don't know myself.'

'And you'll never have an excuse for being late for work.'

She's taken one of the new apartments above the café. I gave her a loan to help her with the deposit, and she and Sharon went and packed up her things and moved her out of her home for the last twenty years. Sharon said she didn't even look back once. They're great pals now.

'Any word from Marty since you left?'

'Not a peep. Did I tell you he had locked the door to the workshop?'

'The louser! Those sausages are yours! Your creation, your hard work – you should have the glory.'

'I'm going to carry on making them in the café. He can't stop me. And the recipe is in my head. He can try all he likes but he'll never get it just right. And anyway, I know they're my sausages. And that's enough for me.'

'Well, BallyGoBrunch will be stocking Carol Boland Sausages, not Marty Boland Sausages, and Mammy will be selling yours up at the eco-farm too. I'll make sure of it.'

'You're a great girl, Aisling. Your father would be very proud of you. Not that he wasn't anyway. He used to be in the butcher's telling anyone who'd listen about you running the show at a big pensions place in Dublin.'

I've never heard this titbit before. What else was he saying about me, I wonder?

'Well, running the show is a bit of a stretch.' I can't take all the credit for PensionsPlus, although if it wasn't for me the kitchen would have been shut down by the Health and Safety Authority and nobody would have ever had a pen or Post-its.

Carol raises her eyebrows and smiles. 'Well, you're running the show here now, so you must have been doing something right. Go on down, I'll be after you shortly.'

Sadhbh and Elaine went on another scout of charity shops around Dublin for me and dug up a fresh range of ancient lampshades and mad old pictures of couples who look like they're about to brain each other. I'd rather a nice bit of inspirational calligraphy, but if anyone knows shabby chic brunch décor it's Sadhbh and Elaine. They dropped them down to me yesterday – what would I do without them? And now James Matthews is going to help me hang them – what would I do without him? He's more or less finished on this project, but he's been there at every turn to help out. He was lugging the Morans' stuff in out of the jeep earlier. They're going to be Carol's neighbours upstairs for the time being. It's not ideal to have them squashed into a two-bed apartment, but at least it will be their own.

Shem and Pablo have really bonded since the fire – over Willy, strangely enough. It turns out Pablo had got fond of the little fecker and had even stopped sleeping with a washing basket over his head to prevent Willy from humping his ear during the night. Poor Willy. May he rest in peace. They're still waiting for the insurance money to come through, but it shouldn't take much longer now that the cause of the fire has been established. For half a second I had it pinned on Frankie Bolger but it was actually lint in the dryer drawer. It shook me to my core – what was Liz Moran doing with the dryer on in June? And why hadn't she cleaned out the lint drawer? They kept it to themselves until rumours of insurance fraud started to trickle through the village, but to be quite honest, I'd rather be suspected of burning down my house than having the dryer on in summer.

The money raised from the fashion show gave them a big boost, and Majella's job means they can keep their heads above water. Mammy's made noises about giving Shem some work as she and Constance start getting their eco-farm in gear. They're off meeting a yurt consultant today. I warned Mammy to bring a can of hairspray in her bag in case they need to make a quick getaway. 'Yurt consultant' just doesn't seem like a real profession, so I want them to be prepared in case it's someone trying to sex traffic them or something.

'Ah, there you are – I was just getting worried,' James Matthews jokes as I drag the last of the lampshades with me through the kitchen from the store room into the café. He has all the gear with him and has already started marking places to hang the new pictures. Most of my wall decorations were destroyed by Frankie Bolger – we know it was him now.

The one fingerprint he left was a match. I have even more stuff for the walls now though, and James has his work cut out for him with screws and rawl plugs and what have you. My DIY vocabulary has come on no end over the past couple of months. His T-shirt is a teeny bit too short for his torso, and every time he reaches up to mark a spot on the wall I catch a glimpse of his knickers and his smooth skin. He has so many important pockets in his trousers too. I used to think that men were just being dramatic having that many pockets, but I've seen the various things he pulls out of them and I'm considering a pair myself now, to be honest. I had a pair of combats when I was seventeen but the pockets were sewn up, and Majella warned me against cutting them open or else I'd 'ruin the line'. She'd read it in a magazine, but it was the same one that told her that putting mouthwash on her spots was a good idea, so I'm not sure it was the lifestyle bible she made it out to be. The skin was burnt off her.

James is stretching and marking and occasionally putting his hands on his hips to consider his work. The T-shirt is in bits but I bet it smells–

'Aisling.'

Jesus, he's talking to me. 'Sorry! What?'

'Will you hold the other end of this spirit level for me? The darned thing keeps slipping.' His English accent is like butter. Now, I've nothing against English people at all, but there'd be people around BGB who'd be muttering about spuds and 800 years any time James might cross their paths.

I stand in beside him, close to the wall, and take one end. He gestures with his head towards the other end of the level. 'And that end. I need both hands.' I slide in in front of him and place my other hand on the far edge of the spirit level, holding it against the wall. Mother of Divine, he's very close to me. His front is almost touching my back. But I know for a fact my hair smells nice. Thank you, Herbal Essences Anti-Frizz with Jojoba. You never let me down. James reaches down and picks up his drill and then stretches up and places his arms over my head, one each side.

'Hold still.' He leans in and *bzzzrrr*: the drill crunches into the wall, sending a tiny cloud of dust into my face and me backwards into him with a loud '*Hey!*' He puts his hands on my shoulders and we laugh. He twists me around and sets about brushing the dust from my forehead and nose. His eyes are very brown. I wonder can he see the yellow flecks in mine. I got my make-up done for a wedding once and it was a big mistake. She had me convinced to try golden eyeshadow, saying it would bring out the bits of yellow in my blue eyes, and I believed her, like a clown. I can't pull off gold eyeshadow. I have examined my eyes for the yellow bits, though, and she's right. They're there. James is staring hard enough at them anyway. One hand still on my shoulder. The other pulling gently at the front of my hair. One dimple just about showing in his cheek. He's close enough that I can hear his breathing, and it's a little bit fast. And is he … getting closer?

'Hello?' The door opens. I know that voice.

Peering out around James's torso, I see John standing at the café entrance, looking awkward.

'Ais, hiya. I didn't see you there. If you're busy …'

'No, no!' I jump out in front of James and, in a moment of panic, blather, 'You know James, don't you? James, this is

Aisling – I mean John,' swinging my arm from one man to the other. John reaches his hand out to James to shake. 'We've met a couple of times. Howiya, lad.'

'If it's a breakfast sandwich you're after, you'll have to wait another few days I'm afraid.' What in the name of all that is holy is he doing here?

'No, no. I just had, well, a bit of a favour to ask you.'

James pipes up. 'I'll leave you to it for a minute. Have a few things to sort out in the jeep.'

Left alone in BallyGoBrunch, John and I look at each other awkwardly.

'I could probably scare up some tea.' I gesture towards the kitchen.

He waves me away. 'Ais, we're having a bit of trouble with sponsorship. For the jerseys.'

'For Rangers?'

The Knock jerseys have had 'Oifig an Chips' emblazoned across their fronts for as long as I can remember. It's the town's foremost chipper and a proud GAA supporter.

'No, for the county jerseys.'

'And?' Where is he going with this?

'I was wondering if you might be interested in BallyGoBrunch sponsoring them?'

'What happened to Mulcahy Feeds?'

'They've pulled out. Johnnie Mulcahy's son isn't going to make the team and he's thrown a fit. And I'm being blamed because I didn't pick him. He's like the Honey Monster trying to hold a hurl, though, Ais. I couldn't put him in, in all good conscience.'

'John, you're cracked. This is a tiny café. County jerseys have car brands and insurance companies and grain providers on the front of them. Not BallyGoBrunch.'

'Well, look, I heard about your money. And you'd get a great deal. And the team is so good this year, Aisling. I swear.'

He looks so earnest. And the idea of fifteen strapping players with my logo across their chests is very enticing. 'I'll think about it.' A smile spreads across his face. 'I said I'll *think* about it.' But he knows me well enough to know I mean yes. 'So you're doing well for yourself, anyway, with the coaching and the big leagues?'

'Ah, sure I am. It's great. A dream role.'

'And you're managing work alright too?'

'Just about, just about.'

I can't leave it unsaid. 'What's all this about you diva-ing around the place, looking for your own stool in Maguire's and velvet ropes at the Vortex and being too big for your boots to train with Rangers?' I pause and then add, 'And showing off your VIP girlfriend.'

John's cheeks flush and his deep scowl appears. 'Jesus, Ais, not you too? All that stuff is bullshit. I've never asked for special treatment in my life. It's all big talk by lads who have nothing better to do than be jealous. I'm too busy to be training – there are only so many hours in the day. And Megan's not a VIP. She's a teacher.' I thought she had a St Pat's look off her alright, underneath the tan.

'Well, is it true you let the school down on medal day?'

'I was at work! I never said I could make it – people just assume I have all this free time but I have a paid job too.'

'Alright, alright.' I laugh and the tension breaks.

John turns to look out the window. He nods towards James, who's studiously examining the contents of the back of his jeep. 'He seems nice. Yer man. Yer fella.' He looks back for my reaction. My cheeks are immediately aflame. I grab a brush that's leaning against the wall and try to sweep up James's drill.

'He's a lovely fella. Great to work with. Lovely lad.' I'm sweeping. I'm sweeping. I'm sweeping.

'Are you sure that's all?' John teases gently. Jesus, this feels weird. Him slagging me about another man.

'Yes, I'm sure.'

As I look up I see a car pulling into the car park, driving up alongside James's jeep. I'd know that blonde head anywhere. Natasia leaps out and straight into James's arms.

'Sure look,' I say, trying to keep the flatness out of my voice. 'There's his girlfriend.'

CHAPTER 41

'And this is where we'll have the tasting station, sampling all the local produce for people to try before they buy. That was Constance's idea.' Mammy and Constance are going full steam ahead on plans for the eco-farm. One of the big sheds has already been earmarked for the farm shop, and they have Shem Moran and William Foley levelling the ground for yurts. I've gone in with them on the yurts. They'll be flat out with hen parties. I'm convinced of it. William will be picking willy straws out of the hedgerows.

I've invited Majella, Sharon and Carol out for a look. Mammy has agreed to exclusively stock Carol's sausages when they're up and running. Carol is going to be doing her own branding and everything. I'm going in with her on that too, with Sharon's cajoling. She's got such a head for business, Sharon. Now, I don't know how she even lifts her head with the weight of all the extensions and eyelashes, but a bit of glam never hurt anyone. At least that's what she told me when she insisted on giving me an eyebrow shape and a bikini wax this morning, in preparation for the big café reopening. I tried to insist that nobody was going to be seeing my goother, but she said it would make me feel 'strong and sexy and empowered'. I don't know what she was on about, but before I knew it she had me bald as a coot. I swear I can feel a breeze. Thank God nobody's going to see it.

'And this is going to be the petting z–'

Constance is interrupted by a screeching of tyres in the front driveway.

'Who's that now, flying in the gate?' Mammy marches out towards the front of the house and we all follow.

I see the red van, Marty Boland's van. Then I hear him.

'Where is she?'

And as I turn the side of the house I see him standing there, big beetroot face on him and veins about to explode out the side of his neck.

Mammy is calm as can be. 'Who's "she", Marty? The cat's mother?'

Carol steps out from the back of the group of women. 'Is it me you're after?' Her voice is slow and steady.

'You have some neck.' He has some neck, if you ask me. He literally looks like he's about to take off. 'Carol Boland Sausages? You have *some neck*!' he bellows.

Constance Swinford lets out the poshest gasp I've ever heard and rears up to him. 'Sorry, whom exactly do you think you're talking to? How can we help you?' she says in her snootiest voice.

'I want you to tell that bitch that she's not destroying my business. Those are my sausages. My name was on them first. I own them.'

Silence for a moment. The 'bitch' hangs in the air.

Sharon speaks first. 'Look, you, you fuckin' bully. You built a business exploiting your wife and taking all the glory.

And now she's gone and you've nothing to use as a doormat. Serves you right.'

Marty looks like he's going to combust. 'How dare you! I knew you were trouble the minute you arrived with your short skirts and your hair, tarting women up. Strutting around the place, asking for it. *Asking for it!*'

Mammy gasps and tuts and pushes Marty's arm. 'Get off my land now. Making a holy show of yourself. Get off right now before I call the guards.' Marty shoves her away, enough to make her stumble back, and before I know it I'm going for him.

'You pig! You miserable pig.' I get two good shoves in before Majella pulls me off him.

'He's not worth it, bird. You're not worth it.' She practically spits on Marty's feet.

'No.' Carol speaks quietly. 'No, he's not worth it.'

She steps forward. Right up in front of him, all five feet nothing of her. Apron still on. She hardly ever takes it off. 'I feel sorry for you, Marty. I really do. But I will not listen to your abuse and your temper for one more second. I gave you that business, and now I'm taking it away. You don't deserve it. You don't deserve it, and I do. You'll have to find someone else to walk all over.'

She turns her back on him and goes back towards the shed. Sharon sticks her neck out at him, snarling, 'Shove your sausages up your hole,' and runs after Carol.

Constance is the first to regain her composure and address Marty matter-of-factly. 'You best be off now, Mr Boland. I heard you lost the Ard Rí contract. My condolences. But that's business, isn't it?'

Mammy adds, 'If Seamus had seen this display in his own driveway today he would have been disgusted. Shame on you, Marty Boland. Come on, ladies.'

And we all turn and walk away, like something out of the *A-Team*. If the A-Team had bald goothers and wide-brimmed brown hats and eyelashes like sweeping brushes.

'Are you alright, Carol?' When we reach them, she and Sharon are sitting on two upturned crates, lifting their faces up to the sun.

'I'm grand, Aisling. Just grand. Right, let's get back. Work to do.'

Carol, Sharon and Majella all bundle into my Micra, and I'm just saying my 'bye, bye, bye, bye, byes' to Mammy and Constance when there's a call from across the road.

'Aisling! Aisling!'

It's Niamh from Across the Road. Calling at me from across the road – probably to give out to me that the café isn't vegan and gluten free. She's not alone.

'Hello, Niamh. Hiya, Natasia.'

'Massive congrats, Aisling!' Niamh exclaims. 'Mum has told me all about your little café. Good for you!'

'Yes, that's excellent, Aisling. How proud I am.' Natasia is so nice. I feel bad for hating her, but I can't help it.

'Lovely to see you, Natasia. You're around a good bit these days, though, aren't you?' I can't stop now that I've started. It's like picking at a Shellac manicure that Sharon warned you not to pick at. 'Mammy saw you at the Mountrath and I'm sure I saw you the other day out the road at the café – you were gone again before I had the chance to say hello.' In truth, I said goodbye to John and went and hid in the kitchen. James stuck his head into the café to tell me he was heading off for an hour or so but I didn't respond.

'Oh yes,' Niamh butts in, 'of course, you came to see James.'

'James Matthews?' Majella's head comes out the back window of the car. I've confided in her a little bit about my crush on him. It may have been a mistake. She has us married off in his castle on a lough in Scotland already. I've tried to explain to her that I don't think there's a castle or a lough, but she's got romance fever too bad.

Natasia smiles. 'Yes, James. It's such a coincidence that he's working down here too. I hadn't seen him in so long, not since Harry's birthday party last year.'

'Come again?' Majella is half out the window at this stage. Sharon is holding onto her legs in the back seat.

'My boyfriend, Harry. James's brother.'

Majella eyes swivel around to me so fast I think they might come out of their sockets. She grunts as the car window digs into her midsection but manages to get out, 'So James is single?'

'I know, can you believe it?' Natasia laughs. 'But I feel like he's … what's that expression … got his eyes on someone?'

There's that breeze again. At least, I think it was a breeze.

CHAPTER 42

'Does that feel nice?'

By God it does. I haven't been touched like this since – Jesus, I can barely even think about it without screwing my feet up into balls – since Antony in Vegas.

'How about that?'

The rubbing gets more intense, over my shoulders and down between my shoulder blades. It's a completely new sensation with someone I've only known for such a short time. But it feels right. So right.

'Okay, lie back down there and I'll wash that treatment out.'

Sharon offered to do my hair and make-up for the re-opening party, and I couldn't exactly say no, although I'm terrified of what's she's capable of after she stripped me bald. My eyebrows look great, though, I must say. Strong Stuff is looking great too, fair dues to her. She finally has it exactly how she wants it. In the front, she has three cutting stations with nice, big mirrors. In one corner there's a manicure station and one of those big electronic pedicure chairs that beat your back black and blue under the pretence of giving it a massage. Along the back wall are the sinks for hair washing, and to the side is a door out to a corridor with a treatment room for waxing and then the new sunbed room.

I must say, I'm impressed with the swanky décor and up-to-date magazines, and the tinkly music is very relaxing. Most importantly, the place is absolutely spotless.

'So what are you thinking, hun?' Sharon says to my reflection in the mirror. 'Let me guess, nothing too mad?'

'You have me there,' I admit. 'I just want to … look my best. But still, you know, like myself just a bit better.'

'Gotcha, hun,' she says, cranking up my chair with her pointy red stiletto. 'How about some nice, simple make-up – just a bit of definition, nothing wild? And a curly blow-dry?'

'That sounds perfect, Sharon. Thanks.'

I know the soft opening for BallyGoBrunch was grand at the time, but after everything that's happened I decided that the reopening deserves a bit of fanfare. Feck the cost. Nothing too exciting, mind, but definitely some free wine and balloons and the finest cocktail sausages anyone has ever tasted – Carol's exclusive new recipe in an exclusive new size, just for tonight. It's the least I can do to thank everyone for pitching in these past couple of weeks, and I'm hoping to get a bit of a buzz going online.

I decided to splash out on caterers for the evening so myself and Carol can actually relax and let our hair down. We were up late last night drawing up the contract so I can officially become a 49 per cent stakeholder in Carol Boland Sausages Ltd. We even lodged the name as a trademark – it's mad what you can do online now – and there's a patent pending on her secret recipe. I told her to put it all down on paper in case she pops her clogs, and she's going to have the location written into her will. You can't take any chances when you're sitting on a potential goldmine.

I've seen enough *Dragons' Den* to know that branding is just as important as how a product tastes – no problems there, anyway – so Elaine is hooking us up with a swanky designer to make the packaging look fancy. Carol's greatest ambition is to get them stocked in SuperValu, but I said to her, why stop there? I'll get them into Avoca if it kills me. Maybe even Fallon & Byrne. She'd never heard of Fallon & Byrne herself, and I had to confess I only know about it from the one time Sadhbh dragged me in there for some of that mouldy cheese she loves and we saw Louis Walsh doing his Big Shop. Even she was a bit starstruck. Well for some paying €9 for imported breakfast cereal.

I'm sitting at one of the front tables in the café blaring Destiny's Child over my new fancy sound system and folding napkins when I spot Pablo's little banger pulling in to the car park. I'm not expecting him, or anyone, for hours yet. He gets out and immediately runs around to open the passenger door for Majella, and the two of them walk towards the front door arm in arm. Maj is carrying a big bunch of sunflowers and laughing her head off and it makes me smile to see her so happy. She's another one who's made of strong stuff. We all are, I've discovered.

I'm so distracted by the flowers I don't even look at Pablo until they're inside the café and only a few feet from me.

'Tell him they suit him, Ais,' Majella goes. 'He's very self-conscious but I think they make him look sexy.'

Pablo is wearing glasses. Not the glasses he was so morto about in Mammy's kitchen – they're a lovely stylish brown pair. Turtleshell, or whatever it's called. And they suit him down to the ground.

'Pablo, you look mighty,' I say, and he smiles coyly at Majella. 'Very distinguished.'

'I explain everything, and Majella, *mi amor*, is so understanding,' he says, gazing down at her.

'I couldn't give a shite about your vision,' Maj says, staring up into his eyes. 'The only problem was the glasses he had were minging. I went into Susie Ó Súilleabháin's with him and we picked this pair together. Much better.'

'Ah, how's Susie?' I ask with a smirk.

'Still charging too much for contacts, but I'm over it,' Majella replies. 'She was very good to Pab, and since we found out laser surgery won't help him, she gave us her family discount on these frames. They're designer, you know.'

'They look it and all,' I say, nodding furiously. Designer my eye but, sure, look, if it keeps them happy, what harm.

'Pablo has something he wants to say to you, don't you, Pab?'

He nods and takes a deep breath. 'I'm sorry I ask you to lie to Majella, Aisling. I know is wrong. She believes ...' and he turns to Majella and cocks his head, 'sister before mister.'

Majella nods approvingly and looks at me. 'Will you still be my chief bridesmaid, Ais? I don't want anyone else up there with me.'

I feel like crying. Me and Majella have had this pact since we were kids and used to walk around with pillowcases on our heads pretending to be brides. Someday I hope she'll do the same for me. 'I'd be honoured,' I say and let out an involuntary squeal, throwing my arms around her. Visions of the hen party are already running through my head. I'll have to give Maj the send-off of all send-offs. Is it too Celtic Tigery to think about going abroad? I have half a notion to head back to Vegas, although I'm not sure we'd get out alive this time. I must see if the Thunder from Down Under are doing any European tours.

'Speaking of which,' I say. 'Hang on there a second.' I leg it into my little office and grab the crisp white envelope I collected last night. Breathlessly, I hand it to her. 'This is my engagement present to you,' I say. 'I want it to be the happiest day of your life.'

Majella takes the fancy gift voucher wallet out of the envelope, and the Ard Rí wedding brochure falls out on to the floor. Pablo picks it up, looking confused.

'I've paid for your wedding,' I explain. 'The Ard Rí Effortless Elegance Package. The voucher is valid for any Saturday in the next twenty-four months, but I'd advise you to book fast because you know yourself how–'

Majella bursts into tears and her hands fly up to her face. Pablo immediately throws his arm over her shoulder and starts rubbing her hair.

'Ais, I can't,' she stammers. 'It's too much. We were going to just have a few drinks in the back of Maguire's ...'

'Majella! What way is that to celebrate the best day of your life?! You could have a drink in Maguire's any night of the week. I know you've always wanted an Ard Rí wedding, and an Ard Rí wedding is what you're having.'

'It's too much!'

'Not at *all*,' I say firmly. 'It'll take some of the pressure off you, anyway. Now, can you both feck off so I can finish what I'm doing here and start getting ready for tonight?'

****

'Aisling, you look gorgeous! Your hair!' Sadhbh and Don – who are the best-looking baldy couple I've ever seen – are among the first to arrive. She's drawn little dots in the corners of her eyes, and instead of looking like a madwoman she looks stunning, and her three-quarter-length purple culottes don't look a bit confirmationy, despite how they sounded when she described them on the phone.

'Hiya, Sadhbhy, hiya, Don.' It still makes me shy to be in Don Shields's presence, although at this very moment my most pressing concern is my own hair – the sheer amount of it. Now, I love a good curly blow-dry as much as the next girl, but I really think Sharon took liberties.

'The curls will drop,' she reassured me as she gently pushed me out of the salon. 'Go on, I'll see you later.'

I caught sight of Marty Boland behind the butcher's counter as I headed to the car and felt a twinge of pity for him. It soon passed, though. Carol is doing so much better, no thanks to that oaf.

Sadhbh touches my hair softly. 'It's fabulous, Aisling, so much volume. You look so sultry.' Sharon had drawn around my eyes in black eyeliner and did some flicks. I wouldn't be out of place in the Presentation's transition year production of *Grease*, but Sadhbh seems very taken with it. Even Don is nodding approvingly.

Mammy, Majella, Pablo and Carol are over by the buffet, Carol casting a critical eye over everything. There's a minibus due shortly with all the girls on it: Deirdre Ruane, Maeve Hennessey, the whole gang. The Tidy Towns committee are en route too, and Father Fenlon said he'll pop in and bless the place. It can't hurt, I suppose. After everything that's happened. Even John and Megan are here with some of the Rangers crew and when I see them together I feel … grand. Genuinely grand. Happy for them, even. I'm watching the door like a hawk. My nerves are at me and I'm as close to a dose of the skitters as I've ever been.

'Nervous about the special guest?' Sadhbh, Don and Elaine sidle up beside me as I chew on a Carol Boland Cocktail Sausage and hover.

'What? Oh, he probably won't even come.'

'You mean *she*?' Sadhbh looks amused. 'And she's definitely coming. Just a few minutes away.'

What is she on about? Ruby interrupts us. She's marvelling at my lampshades and taking about a million photos. 'These are going straight on the 'Gram.'

'Don't forget to plug your phone in!' I'll have everyone's phones charged to 100 per cent if it kills me.

Sharon arrives in a flurry of glamour and sequins and is over to Don like a hot snot, twisting him into all sorts of selfies. The BGB girls and the Tidy Towns crowd arrive all at once, and soon they're all crowding around Don too, and Sadhbh looks on and laughs. I'm in the process of trying to extricate Martina Cloghessy from lying on the floor between his legs when there's a tap on my shoulder.

'Aisling.' That voice. That buttery voice.

I swing around and it's James Matthews, his face almost obscured by a huge bunch of roses. 'You look lovely. These are for you.' He looks unusually shy. His pale-blue shirt and navy jacket make him the most dressed up I've ever seen him. He looks like he was born to wear it.

'Eh – ah. Hiya, James. The sausages are over there.' It's all a bit too much for me all of a sudden. I scuttle away, spotted by Majella, who frees herself from Pablo and clip-clops after me into the kitchen, where the caterers are working away.

'What are you at? You've been waiting for him all evening, and now here he is.'

'I know. I just – I fancy him too much, Majella. I can't cope.'

'He fancies you too! Any dope can see that.'

'He does not. I'm not … I'm grand. I'm an independent woman. Throw your hands up at me.'

'You can be an independent woman and still fancy the arse off him. I fancy him!' She quickly follows it up with, 'Don't tell Pablo.'

'I suppose–'

We're interrupted by Sadhbh, poking her head into the kitchen. 'Guest of honour is here, Aisling.'

'Who's this now?' Majella is all ears. 'Guest of honour? This is news to me.' And me too. What is Sadhbh up to? Maj heads out of the kitchen first and nearly skids on an errant sausage at the sight before her.

It's Colette Green – and her glamorous entourage! Ireland's premier fashion and beauty blogger. Colette is kissing Elaine warmly on the cheek and greeting Sadhbh and Don with delight, saying she didn't know shaving your head was all the rage. Don and Colette go way back, it turns out, and with both Elaine and Don harping on about this great new café, she couldn't turn down the offer of an invite. Colette is wearing her own jeans, of course, with the elaborate C embroidered into the pocket. So elegant, and even though paying €110 for a pair of jeans would nearly choke me, you have to admit she looks very swish. Majella has two pairs. I'd say she's raging she's not wearing them tonight.

Sharon pushes through the throng and places a bottle in my hands. I notice Cyclops is never more than a foot from her, and she finally looks relaxed about it. 'Time for a toast, I think.' It's the fancy Champagne, the bottle James gave me all those months ago – I still have the bag. I look up and catch his eye and lift the Champagne in a nod of thanks. He gives me a 'don't mention it' smile. After a bit of cajoling of the cork and a sizeable amount of conflicting advice from the crowd: 'Squeeze it out, Ais,' 'Turn the bottle clockwise,' 'Put your back into it, girl,' we have a *pop* and a cheer. I turn down the calls for a speech, and they make do with three cheers and a round of 'For She's a Jolly Good Fellow'.

The Champagne is the catalyst for the wine to really start flowing, and soon Majella's iPhone is connected to a speaker and multiple shapes are being thrown to Take That's greatest hits, with a few The Peigs classics for good measure, much to Don's embarrassment.

Colette is Snapchatting and Instagramming up a storm and has said she'll get BallyGoBrunch trending if it kills her. She's been raving about Carol's sausages too, although she's such a rake I don't know how she eats anything more than leaves. A few more sausages would do her no harm. I'm flat out getting in the caterers' way, refilling glasses, chatting to people and generally avoiding James. Like I told Majella, I fancy him too much. I'm not able.

As the night draws in and the glass windows of BallyGoBrunch are nearly shaking with the dancing and good cheer, I slip off to the office for a few minutes' peace.

Mammy and Constance have just headed home, squiffy on white wine and locking Colette Green in for a visit to the yurts. I've just slipped off my court shoes when there's a teeny knock on the door behind me.

'Hello.' Oh, Christ. The door is ajar and he pushes it open.

'Hiya,' is all I can manage, my cheeks like two big tomatoes. I rest my arse on the desk in an attempt to stop my shaking legs.

'I was thinking of heading …' James trails off, looking at me for encouragement.

'Oh, you don't have to,' I stammer. I can simultaneously imagine nothing worse and nothing better.

'Okay. Then I'll stay.' He stands where he is and surveys me for a moment, before taking a deep breath. 'And I'll do this.'

He closes the space between us in one stride, landing his lips on mine and just going for it. Hands in my mad hair, pressing me against the desk, pressing himself into me. It goes on for minutes, soundtracked by the caterers clattering and the mass singsong out on the floor.

'Yeah, you and me, we can ride on a star,

If you stay with me, girl,

We can rule the world.'

'AAAisssling,' Majella calls loudly and deliberately as she approaches, and we break apart and turn to face the door like bold children.

'Sorry to interrupt,' she says, smirking, 'but Colette and the girls are heading off.'

'Oh right, eh, I'll be right out.'

'Give your face a wipe,' she says conspiratorially as she turns to leave. 'You too.' She winks at James. We look at each other and burst out laughing. My lipstick is smeared across both of our faces.

Two minutes of scrubbing and giggling later and we're out, sheepishly waving Colette's gang off and thanking Don, who's giving them a lift back up to Dublin. 'You're staying, though, Sadhbhy?' I check. 'Of course I am! I wouldn't miss Marian's spare-room cushions for anything.' Mammy is fond of a decorative cushion, I'll give her that.

As Don and the girls fall out the door, they're passed by Shem Moran, who's holding something in his hands – or trying to. Whatever it is, it's wiggling and writhing like a mad yoke.

'What have you got there, Shem?' I call, peering out into the dark. I'm hoping he's not going to try and sell me a live animal. I think we've cut our ties with a certain butcher, and I'm not about to slaughter a lamb or pluck a turkey myself.

'Lads, you'll never believe it.' He's absolutely creasing himself laughing.

Between the Champagne and the wine and the pitch dark, I really haven't a notion what's going on. Then there's an unmistakable howl and the penny drops. I know exactly what it is. Or *who* it is.

'*Willy!*' Majella shrieks. 'Daddy, where did you find him?'

'Billy Foran rang me this evening to say he caught him in the feed shed,' Shem bellows. 'His own Lassie was in heat and they had every hound in the county sniffing after her.'

It's a miracle. A modern-day miracle.

'He's looking a bit skinny, and the hair on his tail is singed off, but apart from that he's perfect – aren't ya, fella?' Shem continues, rubbing Willy's belly. The dog is loving the attention, it has to be said.

There's another shriek. Pablo, feeling a little worse for wear and half-collapsed in a chair, has spotted Willy out the window.

'*Dios mío!* My little friend. My tiny humping man. You come back to me!' I think he's in tears.

'Daddy, will you take Pablo upstairs? I think he's had enough.' Majella helps Pablo to the door and he disappears with Shem, crying Willy's name over and over again.

Beside me, James clears his throat. 'I, eh, might head on too,' he says into my ear. 'Leave you girls to it.' He surveys the remaining crowd. Sinéad, Deirdre and Maeve. Sharon and Carol. Sadhbh and Elaine. And Ruby the techno fan screaming at Majella to 'Keep it post-Robbie.'

He sees my crestfallen look and whispers in my ear. 'Room forty-three at the Mountrath. I'll see you later.' He kisses my cheek and he's gone. My God. And me bald as a coot.

I look around at the eclectic bunch of women in my café, roaring along with the music, fists of pure emotion rising and falling. It doesn't seem too long ago that I was worried about living in Ballygobbard full-time and panicking about missing my swanky Dublin life. But if the last few weeks have taught me anything, it's that location doesn't matter – home is what you make of it. It's the people you surround yourself with. Pablo is living proof of that. Then Sharon grabs me in a headlock and pulls me into the centre of the group and we all sway to the music, our arms linked together, the bright lights of BallyGoBrunch shining out into the darkness.

'Yeah, you and me, we can ride on a star,

If you stay with me, girl,

We can rule the world.'